A BABY TO SAVE
THEIR MARRIAGE

BY
SCARLET WILSON

This book is sold subject to the condition that it shall not, by way of trade or otherwise, be lent, resold, hired out or otherwise circulated without the prior consent of the publisher in any form of binding or cover other than that in which it is published and without a similar condition including this condition being imposed on the subsequent purchaser.

All the characters in this book have no existence outside the imagination of the author, and have no relation whatsoever to anyone bearing the same name or names. They are not even distantly inspired by any individual known or unknown to the author, and all the incidents are pure invention.

All Rights Reserved including the right of reproduction in whole or in part in any form. This edition is published by arrangement with Harlequin Books S.A.

The text of this publication or any part thereof may not be reproduced or transmitted in any form or by any means, electronic or mechanical, including photocopying, recording, storage in an information retrieval system, or otherwise, without the written permission of the publisher.

First published in Great Britain 2016
By Mills & Boon, an imprint of HarperCollins Publishers
1 London Bridge Street, London, SE1 9GF

© 2016 Scarlet Wilson

First Published in Great Britain 2016
By Mills & Boon, an imprint of HarperCollins*Publishers*
1 London Bridge Street, London, SE1 9GF

© 2016 Scarlet Wilson

ISBN: 978-0-263-91991-2

23-0616

Our policy is to use papers that are natural, renewable and recyclable products and made from wood grown in sustainable forests. The logging and manufacturing processes conform to the legal environmental regulations of the country of origin.

In this exciting new duet by

Scarlet Wilson

discover these

Tycoons in a Million

Romance in a rich man's world...

Friends Reuben Tyler and Caleb Connor
have chosen very different paths in life.
Caleb married his sweetheart while Reuben
played the field, but they both climbed
to the dizzying heights of success!

Now, with the world at their fingertips, these
millionaires can have anything they want.

But when it comes to love, Reuben and Caleb
realize there are some things money can't buy...

The Connors' nanny, Lara Callaway, is a breath
of fresh air for rebellious Reuben in

Holiday with the Millionaire

And can the Connors save their seemingly
perfect marriage?

Find out in Caleb and Addison's story...

A Baby to Save Their Marriage

Available now!

Scarlet Wilson writes for both Mills & Boon Cherish and Mills & Boon Medical Romance. She lives on the west coast of Scotland with her fiancé and their two sons. She loves to hear from readers and can be reached via her website, www.scarlet-wilson.com.

This book is dedicated to my two honorary
"crazy" nieces, Sarah Mason and Jakki Lee.
Just remember in later life I'll blackmail
you with all the stories!

CHAPTER ONE

ADDISON WAS PACING. She couldn't help it. It was three o'clock and Caleb still wasn't home. They had to leave for the airport in an hour and he hadn't even packed.

The doorbell rang and she hurried to answer. Lara, her son Tristan's nanny, stood on the doorstep, rain dripping from her hair and nose.

'Lara? What on earth? Come in, come in.'

Lara stumbled over the doorstep, dragging a large suitcase behind her. 'I'm so sorry, Addison. I know you're just about to leave for your holiday. But I had nowhere else to go.'

'What's wrong?' Addison was trying not to panic. Lara was the perfect nanny. Her son Tristan adored her. It didn't matter they were about to go on a month-long holiday, she wanted to be sure Lara wasn't in any kind of trouble.

Lara sniffed. 'I had a *Sliding* Doors moment. I got the earlier Tube home and Josh...' her voice wobbled '...he was in bed with the next-door neighbour.' Her shoulders started to shake.

'What? He what?' Addison was enraged. 'That lazy, good-for-nothing ratbag. You've paid the rent for how long? He doesn't even contribute and he treats you like that?' She'd never liked Lara's boyfriend and now she knew exactly why.

She put her arm around Lara's shoulders and guided her into the kitchen, pressing a few buttons on her coffee machine.

'Here, let me get you something.' The machine only took a few minutes, then she sat down across from Lara. 'What are you going to do?'

Lara bit her lip. 'I'm sorry, I panicked. I just stuffed a case and left. I know this is the last thing you need right now.'

Addison silently sucked in a breath. Lara was perceptive. Addison had never said a word to her but she'd obviously picked up on the stress in the household.

'What do you need?'

Lara seemed nervous. 'I was wondering…I'll need to find somewhere else to stay. Is there any chance I could stay here while you're away?'

Something simple. 'Absolutely. No problem at all.' She stood up. 'And, Lara? Don't give up your holiday. You saved long and hard for that. Don't let him spoil it for you. Go, and enjoy every second without him.' She reached over and gave Lara's shoulder a squeeze. 'Now, will you be okay? Caleb and I will be out of your hair within the hour. I need to finish packing.'

Lara gave a nod and a grateful smile. 'Thanks, Addison. I owe you, big time.'

Addison met her gaze. 'You deserve someone who loves and respects you, just remember that.'

She walked out of the kitchen and into the large hallway just as the door opened again. Caleb. Also soaked to the skin and still on his phone.

She felt herself prickle. 'Caleb? Do you know—?'

He gestured to her to stop talking as he continued his conversation. 'Frank, I know exactly how important this is. I will deal with it. I promise you. The price of the stock won't fall. I've been working on these negotiations for months. I'm not about to let anything get in the way.'

He looked tired. His shirt and trousers were wrinkled and she knew that he'd worked through the night. He was doing that more and more now as the business had just exploded.

With Caleb, she would never need to worry about another woman. He didn't have enough hours in the day for her and Tristan, let alone another woman. For the last three years his work had been everything. They'd drifted further and further apart. The man she used to love cuddling up to barely came to bed any more. If he wasn't working at his office in the city, he was working in his office in the house.

Her work had exploded too. She'd started as a naïve young student who'd lost her sister to ovarian cancer, setting up a website and trying to get information out to others. Then, a famous celebrity had been diagnosed with the same cancer—and credited the information she'd read on Addison's site as being the catalyst for her challenging her doctor's diagnosis. After that, things had just gone crazy.

The last ten years had been a whirlwind. She'd met Caleb at a charity auction and fallen head over heels in love. They'd got married, had Tristan and life had seemed perfect. She'd hired some people to help her with the charity and Caleb's business had started to take off.

To the outside world they were the perfect couple— the perfect family. She couldn't deny her husband was handsome; even with the deep furrows in his brow and tired lines around his eyes he could still make her heart flutter. Tristan, their son, was like a mini-me version of his father. They lived in one of the best areas in London.

But a few weeks ago she'd got a wake-up call. Something she hadn't even had a chance to sit down and talk to her husband about.

That was when she'd realised just how far they'd slipped from one another. That was when she'd booked this holiday and told Caleb to arrange the time off. She had some major decisions to make. And they desperately needed some time away together as a family. She needed to be able to talk to her husband without fear of a phone ringing or an email pinging into his inbox to distract him.

He was still talking into his mobile. He'd barely even acknowledged her. Her stomach gave a little twist. She couldn't keep living like this. This wasn't living. It was existing.

This was the man who'd made her laugh, cry and scream with excitement when they'd first met. This was the man who'd spent every single night taking her in his arms and talking until the early hours of the morning. Then, he'd get up early and bring her breakfast in bed. When they'd got married he'd surprised her by flying in her friends from all over the world—all expenses covered. When she'd shown him the pregnancy test one morning he'd whooped with joy and by the time she'd got home after work the house had been filled with pink and blue helium balloons.

A million special memories of a relationship that seemed to have died.

A few weeks ago she'd tried to arrange something special. Lara had watched Tristan and she'd spent hours preparing Caleb's favourite meal, setting the table and lighting candles on their rarely used dining table. She'd changed into a dark pink dress that he'd bought her a few years earlier and sat and waited for him to appear. And waited…and waited…and waited.

The silver dome covering the second pregnancy test had never been lifted.

The candles had finally burned down and gone out. The dinner had been ruined and her dress tossed back into the wardrobe. He hadn't got in until just after two a.m.—that was when she'd finally felt the sag of the bed as he'd sat down.

She'd never mentioned a thing to him. A tiny little part of her was worried. They'd disagreed a year earlier about expanding their family. She'd been keen—but Caleb hadn't.

She'd been hoping and praying that he'd be delighted they were unexpectedly pregnant—just as he'd been the last time. And that tiny little seed of doubt had allowed itself to take root and grow over the last few weeks because it just felt as if he was slipping further and further away from her.

The phone rang and she picked it up. Caleb was still talking on his mobile—still not even looking at her.

'Hello, can I speak to Addison Connor please?'

She vaguely recognised the voice. 'This is Mrs Connor.'

'Ah, Addison. It's Dr Mackay.'

It was like a cool breeze dancing over her skin. Her obstetrician. She'd seen him last week to have her pregnancy confirmed and her first scan and tests.

Her eyes went automatically to Caleb. She was conscious he would be able to hear her words but he was far too engrossed in his own phone call to notice her.

'What can I do for you?'

The doctor hesitated. 'I wonder if you would be able to come along to the clinic later today, or tomorrow.'

The cool breeze turned into an arctic chill. 'Why?'

'We need to have a chat.'

'I'm leaving in an hour's time. I'll be out of the country for a month. I can't come to the clinic. If you need to discuss something with me then do it now.'

She was being curt. But she couldn't help it. This didn't sound like good news. Everything had seemed fine the other day. Her ultrasound had appeared fine and her pregnancy had seemed to be progressing as normal.

She heard him draw in a deep breath. 'This isn't ideal. I'd prefer to do this face to face.'

'I'm sorry, that just isn't possible. What do you need to tell me?'

He gave a sigh. 'We need to talk about your test results from your NT test.'

She straightened up. 'The measurement at the back of neck? I saw that being done. The...' She glanced towards Caleb. She'd almost said sonographer. But he'd turned his back and was facing into their front room. 'The technician never said there was a problem.' She paid attention. She could remember the sonographer taking a few minutes to take the tiny measurement needed.

'I realise that. But you'll know that we calculate risk based on a number of things. We use the nuchal translucency measurement, along with the blood test and mother's age, to calculate risk. Our tests at this stage show you could be at higher risk of having a baby affected by Down's syndrome.'

Her heart skipped a beat. 'How high?'

All other noise just faded into the background. The only thing she could focus on right now was what the doctor was saying.

He spoke clearly. 'The screening test gives us a range. We would normally expect the measurement of a nuchal translucency test to be under three point five millimetres. Yours was slightly above that at three point seven.

A woman of thirty would normally have a risk of around one in a thousand. Along with your age and your blood test results it means that your risk of having a baby affected by Down's syndrome is around one in one hundred and forty.'

There was a roaring sound in her ears. This wasn't happening. This couldn't be happening. Everything had looked fine. She'd had this test before when she was pregnant with Tristan. No one had phoned her then. She'd just received a letter in the post a week later saying she was low risk.

'Mrs Connor?'

'I thought you were more at risk if you were in your forties. I've just turned thirty.' Her brain was trying to make sense of what she'd just been told.

'Age can be a factor, but that's not always the case. If you'd like we can consider some other tests. You've just passed the first trimester of pregnancy so we're too late for a CVS test.'

She had no idea what he was talking about.

'But we could arrange an amniocentesis at fifteen weeks. Along with other detailed scans.'

'That has risks, doesn't it?'

'There is a small risk of miscarriage associated with amniocentesis.'

'Then, no. In fact, no to other tests. I don't want any. It won't change my mind about anything.'

There was a few seconds' silence. From the other side of the room Caleb caught her eye momentarily. A few years ago he'd been her rock—her everything. But as she was hearing this news today she'd never felt so alone.

'Mrs Connor, I'll support you in any decision. You would be offered a detailed scan routinely at twenty weeks. I'd really like you to still attend. If your child is affected by Down's syndrome there is a chance of cardiac defects. It's something we could pick up on the scan and plan for prior to your delivery. It's really in the best interests of your child.'

She tried to be rational. She took a deep breath and paused a few seconds to think. She could remember having the detailed scan with Tristan. That was when they'd found out they were having a little boy. They'd been so excited as soon as they'd left the scan room they'd headed to the nearest baby shop to look for baby-boy clothes.

She squeezed her eyes closed for a few seconds. Now, she felt as if she couldn't even rely on Caleb to make time in his diary for their baby scan. In her head she could already see herself attending alone.

The background noise that had muted before became crystal clear.

Caleb was still on the phone. 'I can do that tonight. No problem. Just give me a bit of time.' He glanced over towards Addison and jerked when he saw her watching him. 'There's something I need to sort out at home.'

Anger sparked through her. Was he talking about her? Had he forgotten they were supposed to be leaving for the airport in less than an hour?

Her stomach turned over. Oh, no. He wouldn't dare? Would he?

She turned her attention back to the phone. 'Of course I'll attend. I leave today and will be gone for a month. Can I make an appointment to see you when I come back?'

'Of course, Mrs Connor. My secretary will arrange that and get both appointments to you shortly. In the meantime, if you need to contact me, please feel free.'

Addison put down the phone and turned to face Caleb. He took a step towards her. 'Addison—honey…'

When was the last time he'd called her that? Was it

when he'd missed Tristan singing Christmas carols at nursery? Or was it when he'd promised to bath Tristan and put him to bed but got delayed at work once again? Tristan had finally fallen asleep clutching the book he'd wanted Caleb to read to him.

She held up her hand. 'Get packed, Caleb. Taxi will be here in forty minutes.'

He held up his phone. 'Things have gone crazy at work. This merger is just huge. It's taking up every hour of every day. Timing is crucial. I just can't go away right now. As for four weeks? It's just far too long. There's no way I can make that work. I have to be here.'

All the pent-up rage, frustration and disappointment that had been bubbling under the surface for the last three years erupted to the surface.

'Everything takes up every hour of the day for you, Caleb—or haven't you noticed? You don't even seem to realise you have a family any more. You're never here and when you are here, you might as well not be.'

He flinched. But she wasn't sorry. She'd had too many let-downs over the last year and too many dinners for one to care any more.

He shook his head. 'That's not fair, Addison.'

'That's not fair? That's not fair?' She couldn't help it. She was shouting now. 'Let me tell you what's not fair. Your son, spending the whole time at nursery with his eyes fixed on the door when he was singing his Christmas carols and waiting for you to appear. I know you said there was an emergency at work—something that couldn't wait—but try explaining that to a four-year-old.' She pointed to herself. 'It's not you that has to see his face, Caleb. It's me.'

She could see the pure frustration on his face. He dropped his case and ran his fingers through his still-damp hair. He could barely meet her gaze. And that just made her worse.

'Please stop.'

She was shaking now. This had been building for a while. They'd needed to sit down and talk for a long time. But they just hadn't got around to it—probably because Caleb was never there.

It was a miracle she was pregnant at all. But twelve weeks ago had been the last time they'd made love after Caleb had fallen into bed late one night. She'd had the faintest glimmer of hope that maybe he'd start noticing her again, maybe he'd start talking. It had been their anniversary and she'd thought that he'd forgotten. For their first few anniversaries they'd always made a fuss of each other and gone away to a hotel overnight. He'd finally come home clutching a beautiful bunch of flowers, a hastily written card and a thin gold bracelet that came from a jeweller's based inside a popular London hotel—it was probably the only place that was open late at night. The effort had brought tears to her eyes and ignited a spark of passion that had been missing between them for a while. She'd hoped that it would be a turning point for them both. But the next day had been no different from all the others.

'This deal is crucial. I've been working on it for months. The next couple of weeks will be the most vital. I *need* to be here.'

'You *need* to be with your family.'

He held up his hands. 'Maybe I could come out in a few weeks, once things have quietened down, and spend some time with you and Tristan then?'

'But things never quieten down. You and I both know that, Caleb.' She straightened her shoulders. She'd had enough. She'd been pushed as far as she could go and tolerated as much as she could.

This was the point of no return.

'In thirty minutes' time, Tristan and I are leaving for the airport. If you're not on that plane with us, when we come back in a month, we won't be coming back here.'

'What?' His eyes widened.

'I'm done, Caleb. I'm done with Tristan and I playing second best to everything else in your life. Let me make this easy for you. Make a decision. You have thirty minutes.'

Caleb Connor's life seemed to be falling apart around him. He'd never seen his beautiful wife look so angry. But there was more than that: she looked cold—something he'd never associated with Addison.

He'd come home, hoping to placate her and send her and Tristan on the holiday she'd insisted on booking. She'd seemed so unhappy recently and he knew it was partly his fault.

She was right. He was never here. Work just seemed to have taken over his whole life. He'd won an award a few years ago as Business Person of the Year and since then everything had skyrocketed.

And things just kept slipping. The nursery carol service, putting Tristan to bed, and he was sure he'd missed a few things he was supposed to be doing with Addison. But she'd never said anything. He'd just got the frosty reception when he'd come home at night. Most times he hadn't even noticed the frosty reception because he'd been so late Addison had already been sleeping.

It was a mistake. And he knew it. But right now was a vital time. He, and his partner, were building their business. Making sure they had a good foundation and reputation on which to base other business. This was a temporary situation. He'd never expected Addison to react like this. He'd never seen her act like this before.

But that wasn't all. She looked pale. She looked worried. And that was before she told him she and Tristan might not come back.

'Addison, be reasonable.'

Her voice chilled him. 'I've spent the last three years being reasonable and making excuses for you never being around. I'm done. I'm done doing that. I manage to get a work-life balance and so should you. If your family isn't your priority, then you don't deserve a family.'

The words stung. But the truth was he couldn't be completely surprised. Things had been strained for so long. What had happened to the relaxed, happy people they both used to be? Last year they'd finally employed a nanny when Addison had felt her work commitments had increased. Lara had been a blessing. But Addison still made time for Tristan. She never missed any of his doctor's appointments or nursery performances.

Not like him.

A wave of guilt washed over him.

'Maybe we could wait, maybe we could go somewhere later in the year?'

Addison picked up the notepad she'd been writing on next to the phone.

She sighed. 'Then it will be another deal, another business. I'm tired of this. Decide what your priorities are. Because I've had enough.'

'You're giving me an ultimatum?'

He couldn't believe it. It felt like a bolt out of the blue. And he couldn't believe Addison was actually behaving like this.

She walked over to him and looked up at him with her clear green eyes. He'd never seen them look so sincere.

There was no hesitation. None at all. 'Yes, I am.' She turned and walked up the stairs.

He sagged against the wall as his phone rang again. He pulled it out of his pocket. Harry. His partner. He'd need to talk to him later.

He shrugged off his damp coat. What on earth was he going to do? He had a million different things still to sort out for this deal. He'd assumed he would come home, placate Addison, give both her and Tristan a kiss, send them on their way and get back to work.

'Daddy!' Tristan ran down the stairs towards him. 'Come and see what I've packed.'

His heart melted as he scooped the little guy up into his arms. Tristan kept talking. 'We're going on a big plane. And then on a little plane. Can you buy a plane, Daddy?'

He walked up the stairs towards Tristan's room. 'Daddy, you're all wet. What have you been doing?'

He smiled. 'I've been out in the rain.'

He set Tristan down at the entrance to his room and Tristan dive-bombed on top of his neatly packed case. 'Whee! Look, Daddy, I've sneaked in some extra toys.' He peered over his shoulder. 'Shh…don't tell Mummy.'

Caleb sat down on the bed and glanced in the case. Sure enough, tucked in between socks and suncream were a whole array of wrestlers and a tiny army of cars. He let out a laugh. Tristan always did this. Addison would tell him he was allowed to bring two wrestlers, or two cars, depending on where they were going, and Tristan would find a way to sneak another few into his pockets, Addison's bag or, on occasion, Caleb's briefcase.

He felt a little pang. When was the last time Tristan had done that?

And more importantly, why would it be his briefcase?

It felt as if it were permanently attached to his hand—and that must be the way it seemed to his son.

He leaned forward as he watched Tristan play. A full-blown wrestling match had started above the clothes. When was the last time he'd watched Tristan play?

Everything Addison had just said to him was firing off sparks in his brain. In most instances, he was searching desperately for memories of the last time he'd done something with his wife and son. And the more he searched, the guiltier he felt.

She'd meant it. She'd looked into his eyes and meant it when she'd said they wouldn't come home.

He'd thought Addison and he would be together for ever. At least, that was what it used to feel like. He'd already decided a few days ago that there was no way he could go on this holiday. He just actually hadn't taken the time to sit down and talk to his wife about it.

More fool him.

Something was wrong. Something was very wrong and he hadn't paid attention until around ten minutes ago.

He knew exactly what had happened to Addison.

He had.

He pulled his phone out of his pocket as he watched Tristan. He was still in charge of the wrestling match. He was so happy and good-natured. He couldn't ask for a better son.

Tristan glanced at him and thrust a wrestler towards him. 'Here, Daddy, you can have this one. He's getting old, like you.'

There was such an innocence in his words. Tristan thought he was old? But of course he did. He'd spent the last three years looking tired and that would be all the memories that Tristan had of him.

He looked around the room. It was still decorated in

baby blues. Underneath the bed was a pile of fresh wall-paper, bedding and stickers all covered in pictures of planets. He'd promised to decorate around eight months ago. The pile had been there ever since.

But there was more. Addison had brought up the subject of having another baby around a year ago.

He'd always imagined they'd have a big family. He'd always wanted to have a big family.

But her words had gripped him in a way he hadn't expected.

They'd never really sat down and discussed it. But Addison had paled into a shadow of herself in the months after giving birth to Tristan. He'd helped as much as he could. He'd frequently got up and done the night feeds. He'd made excuses for not being at work. He'd stayed around as frequently as he could, at first, to try and give her a break, and then to try and get them to spend time together as a family. For the first few months her face had been almost blank when she'd looked at Tristan. It had felt as if she were slipping away a little more each day.

He'd spoken to the GP. He'd spoken to the health visitor—asking what else he could do. They'd reassured him he was doing everything he could and just to be patient. Finally, he'd seen little glimpses of his wife again. A smile when she saw Tristan smile. A willingness to take part. The dark circles had eventually dimmed beneath her eyes and the spark of life that always surrounded her had finally emerged again.

He couldn't let that happen to her again. *He* wouldn't do that to his wife again.

As he stared around Tristan's room it was as if everything came crashing down on him all at once.

He'd thought he might lose his family once before.

There was no way he could let this happen. There was

no way he was letting his family slip through his fingers. The thought of coming home at night to an empty house filled him with horror.

He had to sort this. He had to. He didn't want to imagine his world without them in it.

He pressed the redial button on his phone. 'Harry, there's been a change of plan.'

His phone buzzed as he kept talking. He walked through to the bedroom. Addison wasn't there. A large suitcase was sitting open on the bed, completely empty. It must be for him.

As Harry kept talking Caleb reached into his large wardrobe and picked up a whole stack of T-shirts, dropping them into the suitcase exactly the way they were. He had to lean further back to find a pile of shorts. He sent a silent prayer above that they might actually still fit as he threw them and some swimming shorts into the case. Underwear was easy. He pulled out one entire drawer and tipped it up into the case.

Feet. What would he wear on his feet?

He looked down. His feet were damp from his earlier walk through the soaked London streets. He kicked off his shoes and dropped his trousers to the floor. His shirt was pulled over his head and abandoned with the rest of his things on the floor.

What to travel in? He grabbed a pair of three-quarter-length trousers and a polo shirt, sticking his feet into a pair of baseball boots and throwing some others in the case.

Tristan appeared at the door and smiled at his father's packing efforts. He tucked a few wrestlers into the case along with a London bus, New York taxi cab and space shuttle. 'I had a few spares. I'll give you a little loan.'

Caleb laughed. By the time Tristan was finished the

entire contents of his room would be hidden between the three cases.

Caleb looked around. Was he done? His briefcase sat in the corner of the room. The charging cables for his phone and laptop were in there. He'd be able to work wherever they were. Internet was everywhere these days and as for international calls? He'd just need to swallow the costs.

A quick check of the en suite gave him some deodorant, his toothbrush and his shaving gear. At the last second he reached over to grab some aftershave and then stopped, put it back, and grabbed another one from under the sink. Harry had finally finished talking.

'I'll be at the airport in an hour. I'll send you that report from the lounge.' He rang off. The buzz had been a text message.

His best friend, Reuben Tyler. He was on his way back from LA. Reuben's roof had been undergoing repairs and the roofers had discovered asbestos. He couldn't stay there. He knew Caleb was going on holiday, could he stay at his?

Caleb dashed off a reply telling him where the key was and how to turn off the alarm. Best not mention it to Addison. Reuben wasn't exactly her favourite of Caleb's friends.

He glanced at the case. Done. What else could he need? Why did some people spend days packing?

He zipped it up and picked it off the bed.

As he walked down the stairs he heard the taxi beep outside.

'Come on, Tristan!' shouted Addison. 'It's time to go.'

She hadn't noticed him yet. Was she really just going to walk out of the front door without talking to him again?

The taxi driver appeared at the door and picked up the two waiting cases.

Tristan bolted down the stairs ahead of him carrying two wrestlers. Addison smiled and shook her head. 'No way, you've already got ten in your backpack. That's the limit.' She held out his small red baseball jacket and waited for him to slide his arms inside.

She'd changed. She was wearing cream casual trousers and a pink top.

Caleb cleared his throat.

Addison did a double take. She was shocked. She was stunned that he'd actually packed and changed. Did she really think that little of him? Did she really think that he'd just let his wife and child leave without a fight?

'You've packed.'

He stepped forward and sat his case down. 'I've packed.' He looked her straight in the eye.

She blinked and picked up the passport she'd left sitting on the side table and slid it into her bag.

The taxi driver stuck his head inside and picked up the case. 'Last one?'

Caleb nodded.

'And where we headed?'

'Heathrow.'

Caleb cringed inwardly. He couldn't even remember where they were going. He knew it was hot. It might be the Caribbean, or the Seychelles—somewhere like that. He remembered her mentioning it was a long flight, first stop LA and after that…

Nope. He just couldn't remember. It hadn't registered in his brain.

Like so many other things.

He turned back to pick up his briefcase. Addison frowned and he tried not to be annoyed.

He was coming on holiday. He would be spending time

with them. But he also needed to do some work. Surely she could understand that?

She took Tristan's hand firmly in hers. 'Let's go, honey, we need to get on the big plane.'

'Come on, Daddy!' yelled Tristan over his shoulder.

Caleb glanced at the abandoned wrestlers on the side table. He picked them up and tucked them in his brief-case. Anything to keep the little guy happy.

Addison was strapping Tristan into the back of the cab.

She straightened up and stretched her back. 'Okay?' he asked as he walked up behind her.

She didn't even answer the question. Her mind seemed to be away in a world of its own.

He paused before he climbed in the cab. 'Addison, everything will be fine.'

He didn't want to acknowledge what had just happened between them. He didn't want to acknowledge the fact his wife had just issued him with an ultimatum. He didn't want to give brain space to the fact she'd just threatened to leave.

Her clear green eyes met his. 'Will it?' she asked before she climbed in the cab and slammed the door, staring straight ahead.

Caleb swallowed. Addison seemed anything but fine. Where did they go from here?

CHAPTER TWO

THREE HOURS LATER they were finally on their flight. Addison had felt herself silently fume as Caleb had spent most of his time on his computer or on his phone in the business lounge while she kept Tristan entertained.

Her head was in turmoil. She wanted to snatch the computer from his hands and search for everything she could find on nuchal screening and being labelled high risk.

But that wouldn't help her. Nothing would help her right now. Her heart had flip-flopped when Dr Mackay had told her children with Down's syndrome could have heart problems. Somewhere in the back of her mind she'd heard that before. Weren't there other associated conditions? She just didn't know enough about these things. She had no background knowledge in anything medical related.

At some point she would need to tell Caleb about the pregnancy. Then, she'd need to tell him about the phone call.

She wasn't sure how he would react to any of it.

She was still shocked that he'd actually come.

It was weird. Even though things had been awkward between them, if you'd asked her a few days ago, she would never have thought that Caleb would try and back out of the holiday.

Even though she'd reminded him on a few occasions to pack his case—and he hadn't got around to it—she'd still hoped he'd remember.

But when he'd been late back today and been so busy on his phone her heart had sunk like a stone. And when he'd actually started to say that he was too busy and the timing didn't suit she'd wanted to throw something at him.

That had been it. That had been the point that the mist had come down and she'd been at the point of no return. The phone call hadn't helped. But it hadn't been the catalyst. Caleb and his complete disregard of her and Tristan had been the catalyst.

When she'd given him the ultimatum she'd actually thought he wouldn't come. She'd actually thought she'd just called time on their marriage.

She'd had to disappear into one of the empty bathrooms upstairs to allow herself some silent sobs.

All she could think about right now was how she would cope on her own with two children. Tristan was just a ball of energy. He would be over the moon to find out he was going to have a little brother or sister. But Tristan had been a poor sleeper. He'd suffered from colic and no amount of remedies or different kinds of bottles had helped. Sometimes at night he'd screamed for hours. She'd only managed to cope because she'd had Caleb right by her side.

He'd always known when to send her back to bed and disappear with the screaming Tristan downstairs. A few hours later she'd find him slumped on the sofa with a peaceful Tristan sleeping on his chest.

How would she manage if this baby was the same and there was no Caleb to help?

She sucked in a deep breath. She'd never felt so unsettled. She'd never felt so restless. She'd never felt so alone.

She was scared. The next few weeks would tell her

everything she needed to know. Whether she was in this alone, or whether her husband would be at her side.

They couldn't keep going the way they were. Somewhere along the line they'd lost each other.

'Flight 234 to LAX is now boarding at Gate Twelve.'

She sat upright. 'Come on, Tristan, that's us. It's time to go.'

He scrambled to his feet, anxious to get on board the plane. Caleb was still typing away on his computer.

Addison couldn't help a silent smirk. When he reached their destination he'd get a huge wake-up call when he realised there was no phone line and no Internet. Did he honestly think it was acceptable to come on holiday with his family and spend his time working?

Sometimes Caleb had rocks in his head.

She boarded the plane with Tristan and helped him set up his television for a kids' show. She didn't say a word when Caleb finally sat down next to them.

The stewardess appeared. 'Champagne?'

'Apple juice, please.'

Caleb looked surprised but didn't comment. He accepted the glass of champagne and started sipping.

The ten-hour flight took them well into the middle of the night and Tristan spent a good part of it fast asleep. When they had to change planes at LAX for Tahiti, Caleb carried him through the airport and settled him back into his seat on the next plane.

Eight hours later they switched onto their final fifty-minute flight to the Bora Boras.

As they'd landed in Tahiti his phone had beeped. He'd pulled it out of his pocket, glanced at it and pushed it away again.

She felt a little twinge. Maybe she should warn him that after the next flight he wouldn't get a signal? But part of her was afraid he might refuse to get on the next plane. And she was just too exhausted to have another fight.

She hadn't been able to relax on any of the flights so far. She was too keyed up. Her mind was constantly spinning. By the time she reached the Bora Boras she would be fit only to fall into bed.

The small white plane had only fifty passengers. Even though she was absolutely exhausted, the view from the plane was spectacular. The travel agent had told her that writers and artists called the Bora Boras the most beautiful islands in the world. They weren't wrong.

For this part of the journey, she was glad she was still awake.

The aerial view of the green, jagged volcanic peak of towering Mount Otemanu appeared on the horizon. It was surrounded by a captivating, vivid blue lagoon. As they descended she was amazed by the many blues of the Bora Bora lagoon. It wasn't one island, instead it was a collection. The airport was on its own islet, one of a number of small barrier islands forming a ring around the lagoon. There were a variety of resorts set on the beautiful sandy beaches. Some extended out over the lagoon with their wooden walkways connecting to thatched-roof over-water bungalows. Others had lodges perched on the steep hillside and some had hideaway villas set right on the water's edge. Each resort seemed more beautiful than the one before.

Fifty minutes later they had arrived in paradise.

'Welcome to the Bora Boras,' shouted the pilot as they landed.

The airport was small. A smart dark-skinned man was waiting with a sign saying Connor.

He gave them a polite nod and took their luggage, guiding them over to a glistening white boat on a wooden pier.

Caleb stopped and looked around. The view of the blue lagoon was dazzling, bright turquoise next to white sandy beaches. And even though the lagoon was a hive of activity, it also had an air of tranquillity about it.

'Wow,' he said quietly.

Addison pressed her lips together. This was entirely what she'd wanted to capture. A bit of peace. A bit of luxury. And a bit of togetherness. Would they really be able to capture all three?

'We get to go on a boat!' shouted Tristan. She'd no idea where he got his energy from. After twenty hours of travel she'd expected him to be as exhausted as she was. But he'd slept part way on both flights while, no matter how hard she tried, she just couldn't sleep sitting up.

They climbed on board the sleek white boat. Tristan ran up to the front where he could watch the boat being steered. It didn't take long to cross the beautiful lagoon and drop them at their resort where they were met with staff greeting them with fresh leis, who picked up their bags and checked them in. Their bungalow sat on the white sandy beach. It had a large sitting room and kitchen, with two bedrooms and a master suite that opened out onto the beach. The rooms were luxurious while still paying homage to the Polynesian style. They also had a small over-water bungalow with thatched roof and walkway and its own hot tub. Tristan couldn't hide his excitement when he saw the glass panel in the floor with fish swimming underneath in the tropical waters. 'Look, Mummy, look!'

It couldn't be more perfect. She'd been nervous about them staying in the bungalows over water since Tristan was coming with them. But this had been a compromise. This way she had the safety of a beach house with the magic of the water bungalow too.

She unpacked their clothes as Caleb looked around.

The first thing he unpacked was his computer. Apart from when stepping off the plane, he hadn't really taken in the beauty around them.

She tried to hide her frustration but twenty hours of travel would wear anyone's patience thin.

She dug out Tristan's beach wear and covered him in suncream. It took him less than a minute to run across the sand and start digging with his spade and splashing in the water. She changed into her swimming costume and arranged herself under the nearby parasol and sun lounger where she could watch him.

Her peace lasted less than five minutes.

'How do I connect to the Internet?' Caleb asked from the doorway of the bungalow.

'You don't.'

He frowned. 'What do you mean?'

She shook her head. 'There is no Internet.'

The furrows on his brow deepened. He hadn't changed his clothes or stopped to appreciate their surroundings. 'There has to be. Where is the phone line?'

She shrugged. 'I don't think there is one. There's an intercom that links to Reception if we need anything. I think we just use that.'

She was doing her absolute best to appear casual. It was pretty ironic really since she was staring over at the volcanic peak of Mount Otemanu. She absolutely knew that when he realised there was definitely no phone or Internet he'd go off with more explosions than Mount Otemanu ever had.

The doors to the house were wide open so she could hear him moving around inside. Part of her felt a little sad. They'd just landed in paradise and he hadn't come out to play with his son in the sand, or to sit next to her on the sun lounger. It made her absolutely determined that she'd made the right decision. She needed a chance to see her husband again. She needed a chance to see how he was without any of the trappings of work attached to him. *They* needed a chance to be stripped bare. And this was the only place to do it. There was no room for distractions here. It was just them, and Tristan.

And the secret baby package.

She looked back at the bungalow and watched as he paced around inside, stressing and searching the room for any hidden phone lines or Wi-Fi connections.

The Caleb Connor that she'd met ten years ago would never have stressed about being constantly connected to the world. He would never have spent time on holiday virtually ignoring his wife and child.

This was the life she led now. And this was the reason she knew she had to take a step to see if this marriage could be saved. She would never introduce another child into this way of life.

Oh, no matter what the outcome of this holiday, she would always have this baby. But she wanted to be prepared. She wanted to have time to plan, to know whether she would be doing this alone or not—particularly if she and her baby needed additional support.

One in one hundred and forty. Most people would think the odds were in their favour.

In one hundred and thirty-nine chances the baby wouldn't be affected.

But in one of those chances it would.

She'd thought about this before. When she'd had Tristan she'd been told she was low risk. But her midwife had carefully explained that low risk didn't equal *no* risk. There was always that possibility. And she'd understood that then, just as she did now.

It was amazing how much this had caused her to focus.

The holiday had been booked. Since she'd found out she was pregnant she knew she needed to deal with the elephant in the room. In fact, she was pretty sure an elephant could have been sitting in their front room and Caleb wouldn't have noticed. That was how distant he'd been.

The distance made her uncomfortable. It reminded her of a time before—a time that seemed a little hazy for her—a time where the distance between them had been her fault. She squeezed her eyes closed for a second. She didn't like to remember anything about that.

She heard a loud beep. It was Caleb on the intercom. 'How do I connect to the Internet?'

The bright sing-song voice answered straight away. 'No Internet here. Sorry.'

'What do you mean there's no Internet? Everywhere has Internet. There must be somewhere I can get a connection?' She could hear the anger in his voice. It drifted out of the doors towards them and Tristan, who had come back to play next to her, looked up from digging in the sand. She shook her head and he put his head back down and kept building his castle.

'No connection on the Bora Boras, sir.'

'What about a phone? Can I have access to a phone?'

'Only radio contact with the mainland, sir. That's the beauty of our resort. Most people come here specially.'

She heard the click again then the thudding footsteps. A few seconds later the small amount of sun sneaking under the parasol was blocked out.

He had his hands on his hips. His lips were pressed tightly together and there was a tic in his jaw. 'Tell you know where the Wi-Fi is.' There was a tad of desperation in his voice.

She pushed her sunglasses up on her head and pressed her hand against her chest in mock horror. 'There's no Wi-

Fi?' She sagged back against the sun lounger. 'Tragedy.' She shot him a little smile. 'Your computer and phone will probably spontaneously combust now. Just as well there's a perfect ocean to throw them in.'

He sighed and sat down, running his fingers through his hair. 'Oh, Addison. I'm in the middle of a deal right now. This could make or break our company. The only reason I came was because I knew I could still work remotely.'

'And that's why I didn't tell you.'

She put her hand on Tristan's shoulder. 'Why don't you go inside and have a little lie down for a while? I'll come inside and put a DVD on for you.' He disappeared quickly into the bungalow.

Addison swung her legs around and stood up, the warm sand beneath her feet.

'You're absolutely right. I deliberately picked a place with no phone and no Internet. Ask yourself why. You've forgotten we even exist. You treat us as if we're not important. This deal could make or break your company?' She waved her hand. 'I've heard that for the last three years. Maybe the first time I believed it. But every time after that? I don't think so.'

She stepped closer to him. Close enough that she could see the exhaustion in his face and the fine lines that had appeared all around his eyes. 'What I do believe is that the only reason you came is because you thought you could work here remotely.' She shook her head. 'Think about that for a minute, Caleb. Just think about it. Do you think that's normal for a family holiday? Do you think that's what most husbands and fathers do on holiday?'

He at least had the good sense to look embarrassed. 'You know how important this is.'

'No, Caleb. I know how important you *think* it is.

There's a difference. I think you'll find that in the scale of life it's not that important at all.'

Now he looked annoyed again. 'Well, in order to pay the mortgage and the bills I think you'll find work is important.'

'More important than your family?'

He waved his hand. 'Now you're just being ridiculous.'

'No. No, I'm not. And don't worry about your business. Harry will deal with everything. He's more than capable.'

'And how do you know that?'

She sighed. 'Because I spoke to him before we left. He knew that once you got here you'd have no phone, no Internet.'

Caleb looked stunned. 'What? Harry knew?'

She started to walk away. She'd had enough of this. 'Of course he knew. Seems like he didn't think it was such a bad idea. And you can stop checking your phone for emails or messages. There are no signal towers out here. I'm actually surprised Harry messaged you at all.'

Caleb shook his head. 'Earlier? In Tahiti? It wasn't Harry. It was Reuben.'

She couldn't help it. She raised her eyebrows. She always did that when she heard this name. 'Reuben Tyler? What did he want?'

Caleb shrugged. 'He needed somewhere to stay. His flat's got asbestos in the roof. I told him he could stay at ours.'

Her mouth fell open. 'You did what?'

He seemed surprised. 'What's the big deal? We're not there. The house is empty.'

'Oh, no.' Now she started pacing. 'The house isn't empty. Lara. Lara's in the house.'

Now Caleb looked confused. 'Why would Lara be in the house? I never saw her.'

Addison spun around. 'She appeared just before you did. Seems she went home and found her boyfriend in bed with the neighbour.' She threw up her hands. 'This is what I'm talking about, Caleb. She was right there. Right there sitting in our kitchen. You didn't even notice.'

He frowned. 'Reuben will be expecting the place to be empty. That's what I told him.'

'And Lara will be expecting to have the house to herself. She needs a bit of time to sort herself out. The last thing she needs right now is Reuben Tyler. She won't even know who he is.'

Caleb shook his head. 'Well, it's too late now. They'll both be in the house and according to you we have no way to get in touch.'

Addison cringed. He was right. There was no way to get in touch. The world seemed to love Reuben Tyler but she didn't. Probably because she'd walked in one night just as he'd taken a swing at her husband. Caleb had said it was nothing. But it wasn't nothing to her.

'There's really no Internet?'

'We're back to that again?'

He nodded. She could see the stress on his face. It was practically emanating from his pores. Part of her felt a tiny bit sorry for him. It was like going cold turkey. But there was nothing he could do.

She folded her arms across her chest. 'There is no Internet, Caleb. It's four weeks. Live with it.'

He took a deep breath and turned towards her. His brown eyes fixed on hers. It was the first time in for ever that he'd really looked at her. *Really* looked at her.

'What's going on with you, Addison?'

She blinked. 'What's going on with me? Are you serious?'

Why did every conversation feel as if it ended up as a fight?

'Yeah, I'm serious. I can't believe what you said to me back home.'

'And I can't believe you came home from work an hour before we were due to leave and thought you would tell me you weren't coming on holiday. At what point in your life did that seem okay to you?'

'Everything is a fight with you these days.'

He'd just echoed her thoughts. She thought this was all him. Was he trying to imply it was her too?

It lit a fuse in her. How dared he? Didn't he know what she'd just been told? Didn't he understand how worried she was?

Of course he didn't. She hadn't told him yet.

And at some point she'd need to.

Just not yet. Not until she knew.

She didn't want to tell him about the pregnancy. She didn't want to tell him about the scary news. She didn't need her husband to feel sorry for her. She needed him to love her. To love her enough to feel as if he could be there and support her.

Telling him about the pregnancy right now could make him tell her everything would be fine. And knowing Caleb, he'd probably think it would be. Then he'd go right home and start working hundred-hour weeks again.

She needed more than that. She needed more for this marriage.

'How can everything be a fight when you're never there?'

He sighed. 'You work too. There's been nights when you've been busy too. There have been events you've had to go to—people you've had to meet.'

She nodded her head. 'You're absolutely right. But the

difference between you and me is that, when I know I'm going to be out at night, I make sure I've spent time with Tristan during the day.'

'That's easy for you to do.'

'Actually, it isn't. But I make the time.'

She bit her lip. Everything was a fight between them right now. And she hated that.

'Always fault-finding, always criticising. Can I ever do anything right in your eyes these days?'

And it looked as if this was going to become a fight too.

Trouble was, she was just too tired for this. She wasn't sure if it was the travel that had exhausted her, or the pregnancy. She could remember at this stage in her pregnancy with Tristan she'd come home from work and go straight to bed. In those days, Caleb would just come to bed with her.

She turned away. She just wanted to sleep now. She couldn't even be bothered changing out of her swimsuit.

'You gave me an ultimatum.' His voice was quiet, almost whispered. It was as if he was still getting over the shock. 'Why would you do that? It was just straight out of the blue.'

She stopped walking. Her hand was on the door. From here she could see that Tristan was already sleeping. She hadn't even got around to putting the DVD on. That was fine. She would just climb in next to him.

She kept her voice low too. 'It wasn't out of the blue, Caleb. This has been building for the last few years. We've slipped away from each other—we've lost each other...' her voice started to break '...and I've had enough. I can't live like this any more because I don't feel as if I'm living.'

She glanced over her shoulder. 'This is it for us, Caleb. I chose this place deliberately because I didn't want Tristan and I to compete with your work any more. Some people think this place is paradise. You? I think you've barely noticed. We came here because I wanted to see if we had anything left worth saving. Because right now—I just don't know.'

She took one final look. He looked as if she'd just punched him in the guts.

So she turned, and went to bed.

CHAPTER THREE

CALEB COULDN'T SLEEP. He should be sleeping after twenty hours' travel and staying up since they'd arrived but after the conversation with Addison, sleep was nowhere near him.

It felt as if she'd stuck a knife into his chest and twisted it.

But more importantly it was obvious that she didn't think this marriage could be saved. How on earth had he reached this point? Had he been sleepwalking through life not to have noticed how his wife felt?

Tristan and Addison were sleeping in one of the double beds together. He'd tried to sleep in the other with no success. Then, he'd tried the bed in the water bungalow. But the gentle lap, lap of the water underneath had only kept his mind buzzing. In the end, he'd ended up on the beach.

They'd probably spent a fortune on this holiday and he was sleeping like a beach bum. But the air seemed stiller out here. And although there was still a background noise from the lapping waves, it didn't seem as amplified out here.

He couldn't sleep because he was gripped with panic. Panic that life as he knew it was just about to slip through his fingers.

Work was still preying on his mind. At one point in

the middle of the night he'd actually opened his computer and started working on something. But after half an hour he'd realised the futility of his actions. By the time he'd got home Harry would have worked on another version of this. It made no sense for him to do the same thing. But that didn't stop his fingers drumming on the table in irritation.

He couldn't help it. Working had almost become a compulsion—an addiction. How sad was that?

He wasn't sure he even knew how to relax any more. Just sitting annoyed him. His brain constantly revolving, thinking about the work-related things he could be doing.

Part of him was angry at Addison for forcing this on him.

Part of him understood the point she was trying to make. If he had an Internet connection he probably wouldn't have seen the sun set or rise again. He probably wouldn't have watched the fishes swimming underneath the glass panel under the coffee table.

He probably wouldn't have had time to wonder what he could say to his wife to make her change her mind.

She seemed different. Distant. As if she had a hundred other things that she wasn't saying to him. And to be honest, what she'd already said felt like enough. He didn't know how he'd cope if she said any more.

A waiter appeared at the beach bungalow carrying a large tray. Breakfast. Was it that time already?

Caleb nodded as the man set the loaded tray down in the kitchen and left again. Eggs, bacon, croissants and breakfast cereal for Tristan. Addison must have pre-ordered all this. He glanced into the bedroom. They were still sleeping.

He jumped in the shower and quickly changed. He wasn't sure quite what Addison expected today. He hadn't paid enough attention; he didn't even know what there was to do around here.

He stood at the bedroom door for a minute. Even sleeping, she looked stressed. The bedclothes were all messed up and it was obvious she'd tossed and turned all night. That wasn't like her. Addison used to sleep like the dead. He used to joke that a marching band could come through their house in the middle of the night and she wouldn't hear it.

Tristan was lying halfway across his mother's chest in his superhero pyjamas. Caleb's heart gave a squeeze. When was the last time he'd had a chance to see them like this?

It had been too long. She was right about the Christmas carol stuff. He'd had every intention of being there. But just as he'd been about to leave he'd received an emergency call from Singapore. One of their investors had taken unwell and he'd been asked to contact the family urgently. It had taken fourteen phone calls to track down his son and by the time he'd finally left the office Tristan's concert was already finished. He'd sat in the car park outside, looking at the darkened building and cursing himself that he hadn't got there on time.

He walked over to the bed and gave Tristan a little shake. 'Hey, superhero. Wake up. It's breakfast time and we've got a beach to play on.'

Bing. Just like that he was wide awake. He jumped down from the bed and ran through to the bathroom. Addison's eyes flickered open. Just for a second she looked fine. Then, whatever it was that was on her mind seemed to come flooding in again. He could almost see the shutters coming down.

'Breakfast is here,' he said. 'I'll take Tristan through.' She gave a nod and turned away, climbing out of the bed and slipping on her dressing gown. This wasn't how they used to wake up. Before Tristan, some days they hadn't got up at all. When Tristan was a baby they used to bring him in beside them in the morning. He'd coo and smile quite happily, with not a single bit of guilt that he'd kept them up most of the night.

But those days were long gone. Caleb got up at five these days and was in the office for six. He didn't even recognise the breakfast cereal sitting on the kitchen table. He picked it up and stared at it.

'My favourite!' shouted Tristan, pulling himself up onto one of the chairs. 'What's the toy?'

'Let's see,' said Caleb, sitting down next to him and opening the pack. A horrible plastic spider dropped out onto the table. Tristan let out a shriek and jumped up laughing. Caleb started laughing too. Within a few minutes the breakfast cereal was scattered everywhere and the bowls upturned as they played 'catch the spider'.

By the time he looked up Addison was standing in the doorway, watching Tristan and smiling. 'What's all this noise?'

Tristan lifted his prize. 'It was a spider this time, Mum!'

'Oh, no! Not a spider.' She came over to the table and sat around the other side. 'Well, I'm not sitting next to a spider.'

She stared at the covered plates for a second. It was almost as if the silver domes lost her in thought. But she blinked and removed them. The smell of bacon and eggs filled the room.

Caleb lifted up the cups and coffee pot and started pouring.

'Oh, no. I'm going to have lemon tea instead.'

He raised his eyebrows. 'But you love coffee.'

She shrugged. 'I'm on a health kick.'

He sat down opposite her and picked up his knife and fork. 'Skinny latte with sugar-free caramel, skinny extra shot macchiato.'

The edges of her lips started to turn upwards.

'Skinny cortado, skinny mocha cortado. Shall I keep going?'

She rolled her eyes as she poured boiling water into her cup and added a slice of freshly cut lemon.

'You know what they say—too much caffeine makes a girl cranky.'

He couldn't help but smile. There was definitely an atmosphere between them. How could there be anything else after what had happened? But things didn't seem quite so antagonistic this morning.

'This from a woman who had a state-of-the-art coffee machine installed in our kitchen because...' he leaned across the table towards her '...and I quote, "it's got to be cheaper than the ten cups I buy a day from the coffee shops".' He pointed to her cup. 'And now you're drinking tea?'

'A girl's entitled to change her mind.' The words came out like lightning—just the way Addison usually was. But as soon as she'd said them her face fell. Almost as if she realised how they could be interpreted.

Had Addison changed her mind about him?

Tristan chose that second to ping his plastic spider across the table and straight into Addison's cup.

'Yow!' She stood up as water splashed all over her. It was the first time he'd noticed she'd barely touched her breakfast.

She held her hand out towards Tristan. 'Let's go and get ready.' She looked up at Caleb. 'There's a kids' club every morning for a few hours. Playing with other kids will be good for him. He'll be back with us every after-noon.'

Work. It was the first thought that shot across his mind.

Addison walked away holding Tristan's hand, her out-line silhouetted by the sun streaming through one of the windows. Her hair might be tied up in a funny knot on top of her head, and she didn't have a scrap of make-up on, but his wife was still a stunner.

So, why was it, when he knew Tristan would be gone every morning, his first thought had been he could work?

He leaned forward and put his head in his hands. Five years ago that absolutely wouldn't have been the first thought on his mind. His mind would probably have gone in a whole other direction.

He was embarrassed to admit that thought—even to himself.

He stood up and walked through to the bedroom. 'I'll take him.'

'What?' Addison looked surprised; she was pulling some clothes for Tristan out of the drawers.

'If you point me in the right direction, I'll take him to the kids' club. You can stay and get showered and dressed.'

'No.' It was out before he'd barely finished speaking. 'I mean… I haven't seen the kids' club yet. I want to check it out. To make sure I'm happy to leave him there.'

His annoyance flared. It was almost as if she didn't trust him to be able to do that. To take Tristan to the kids' club and make sure it was okay. But he tempered it down. The last thing he needed to do today was have an-other argument. He picked up the clothes she'd looked out. 'In that case, we'll do it together. I'll get Tristan dressed while you shower.'

She hesitated for second, then nodded. 'Okay, I'll be ready in ten minutes.'

She grabbed a dress and some underwear and headed into the bathroom, closing the door behind her.

It was the little things. The little things he was starting to notice. She didn't used to close the door when she showered. On past occasions he'd joined her.

But today, it felt like just another sign that Addison was shutting him out.

He sighed and dressed Tristan, taking him out to the beach when he was ready. But Tristan pointed to the clear blue sea. 'Can we see the fishes?'

'Sure.' Caleb took his hand and led him along the walkway and into the over-water bungalow. They pushed the coffee table away and lay down next to the glass panel. There was a small piece of coral underneath and it was alive with activity.

'What's that one, Dad? The red and white one? And what's the blue one? It looks like Dory. Do you think we'll see Nemo too?'

Caleb shook his head and stared down at the gorgeous brightly coloured fish. He didn't have a single clue what any of them were. A large one swam past right underneath their noses. It was turquoise blue with pink stripes and little dashes of yellow. It looked like a painting Tristan would do at nursery. It was followed by a few much smaller, zebra-striped fish.

'I like that one,' said Tristan. 'Can we give it a name?'

Caleb smiled. 'Sure we can. What will we call it?'

'Tristan,' he suggested.

Caleb tried not to laugh. 'We'll have to see if we can buy a book somewhere to tell us what all the fishes are.' He looked around. 'And there are lots of boats. Maybe one day we can swim along the coral reef and go snorkelling.'

'What's snokling?'

Caleb laughed. 'It's where you go under the water and breathe through a little tube. You have a pair of goggles on so you can see all the fishes.'

'We can go and swim with the fishes?' Tristan looked mesmerised.

'Sure we can. Daddy will find out how today.'

Tristan's innocent gaze narrowed. 'You won't forget?'

Something twisted inside him. That was what his four-year-old associated with him—Daddy always forgetting his promises?

'I won't forget,' he said quickly. It felt like a kick somewhere painful. There was something horrible and uncomfortable about his little boy asking him that question. It was one thing for Addison to call him on his misdeeds, it was quite another for his four-year-old.

But there was something else. His brain was still spinning. Review a contract, phone that client, check the small print on another contract, speak to their lawyer about an impending business deal. He moved uncomfortably and glanced around. His shoulders were tense. His little boy was playing around him and his mind was still full of work things. Work things he could do nothing about.

So why were they still there? Why were they still running through his brain? Why couldn't he just relax and spend time with his son? Was it possible he'd forgotten how to relax?

There was a movement out of the corner of his eye. Addison was standing in the doorway, carrying Tristan's backpack in one hand. She was wearing a short red sundress and had a pair of sunglasses on her head.

She knelt down next to them and pulled some suncream out of the backpack, slathering it over Tristan's skin as he squirmed. When she finished she pulled a baseball cap from the backpack and stuck it on his head. 'Right. Let's go and see the kids' club.'

It was odd—walking away from a place and not locking all the doors behind you.

They strolled up the path towards the main resort. There was a variety of palm trees and green bushes with the occasional burst of bright red and orange flowers. The whole resort seemed to have been planned to perfection.

The kids' club was through the main reception and next to a small kids' pool. It was shaded, with a variety of toys, ranging from chalk boards, to racing cars, a complete tiny wooden house and a table for arts and crafts. There were four other kids all playing already with two play leaders. One of the play leaders came over straight away. 'Hi, I'm Kohia. Is this Tristan?'

Tristan nodded. 'How did she know my name, Mummy?'

Kohia knelt down. 'I know all the special boys and girls that are coming to play here.' She handed a clipboard to Addison. 'We need you to answer a few questions about Tristan's medical history, any allergies and likes and dislikes. After that we're good to go.'

Caleb looked around. Everything seemed fine. The area was clean and tidy, the kids looked happy and the play leaders seemed to know what they were doing. Addison handed back the clipboard and waited a few minutes to make sure Tristan was settled. He was instantly distracted by a painting session at a nearby table. Kohia gave them a wave. 'Come back around one o'clock.'

Caleb glanced at his watch. Three and a half hours. What on earth would they do?

This morning had been strange. Caleb seemed in a better mood. He'd finally accepted there was no Internet or phone line and she hadn't seen him touch his computer at all. It felt like a miracle.

He was still on edge. They both were. But the tenseness in his muscles seemed to have dissipated a little. His shoulders weren't quite as tense but the furrows in his brow were still there. She could only imagine hers were the same.

Kohia shouted to them as they walked down the path. 'If you haven't tried the patisserie inside yet, you should definitely give it a go. The coconut cake is the best *ever*!'

Caleb turned towards her. 'Well, there's a recommendation. Why don't we give it a try when we've looked around?'

She gave a nod. She could sense his nerves jangling again. Was he worried he might actually need to talk to her—spend time with her?

Her stomach gave a little lurch. She'd thought the other night that she might have fallen out of love with her husband. And that made her feel horrible. But it hadn't occurred to her that the same might have happened for him.

They walked in silence for a while, strolling through the tropical gardens. She'd never seen so many shades of green dotted with bright splashes of colour. Every now and then the foliage parted to give perfect views of the blue ocean and rolling sands. The resort complex was huge. There were five other beach bungalows like theirs, each with their own smaller over-water bungalow. Around the other side of the complex were twenty larger over-water bungalows with thatched roofs and a variety of walkways. The central hotel had four restaurants, three bars, a gym, training classes, a few shops, a spa and the huge, welcoming patisserie. The smell of coffee almost came to meet them.

She felt herself twitch. She craved it. She craved it so

badly. She hadn't actually realised how much she loved it, or how much she drank. But as soon as she'd realised she was pregnant she'd switched to caffeine-free tea. She didn't want to take any chances with this baby. Not when the odds were apparently stacked against her anyway.

Caleb automatically walked in the direction of the patisserie, his eyes drawn to a huge glass cabinet packed with a variety of cakes.

'Skinny caramel latte?' She shook her head again.

'I'll have green tea.' She drifted along the edge of the glass cabinet just as her stomach gave a telltale rumble.

Caleb pointed to the cakes. 'Which one do you want?' He turned towards her, a quizzical look on his face. 'You didn't eat much this morning at all. You must be starving.'

She was. She'd been unsettled at breakfast and she didn't think it was anything to do with her pregnancy. Morning sickness had never been a problem before. It was most likely just the state of her life and the decisions she'd need to make.

She licked her lips as she looked at the labels on the cakes. She pointed to the coconut cake. Four layers of sponge with jam and coconut cream frosting. She didn't even want to think about the calories. Since she'd hardly had any breakfast—or eaten much on the flights yesterday—she figured it would all work out. 'I'll have a piece of that. What about you?'

Caleb had never been a cake kind of guy. But he pointed towards another cabinet. 'I'll have a piece of peach pie. And a cappuccino.' He placed the orders and carried the tray outside to a terrace with a thatched roof and comfortable chairs.

Addison sat down. The view over the ocean was picture perfect and stretched on for miles and miles. There wasn't a single thing on the water in front of them. Although the temperature was warm, a gentle breeze blew off the ocean.

As he set the tray down and unloaded the food and drinks, again she got a little whiff of coffee. She could kill for a coffee right now. And poor Caleb would be right in the firing line.

Maybe now was the time to tell him about the pregnancy? It wouldn't take him long to notice that she wasn't drinking alcohol either. But would he join up the dots?

Something was stopping her. As soon as she told him he would immediately talk about plans for the future. She didn't want to do that. Not until she knew what she was doing. Not until she knew if she would be with him, or without him.

There were three other women sitting at a table behind them. She could see the admiring glances they were throwing in Caleb's direction. She was used to them. Caleb always got a second glance. With his deep brown eyes, dark hair and muscular build he was handsome. He filled out his clothes well. In around two days he'd have a killer tan too. But it wasn't a tan she worried about. It was the lines that had appeared on his forehead and around his eyes these last few years. It was the fact he permanently looked tired and as if he were thinking about three different things at once. It was the fact she didn't even feel, when she talked to him, that she was the actual focus of his attention.

That had to change. It had to. Or this relationship would just come to a sad end. Did she really want that to happen?

Caleb sat down and started sipping his coffee. He gave her a careful smile. 'If I know you, any minute now you'll start to have coffee withdrawals and you'll leap across the table like a snarling wolf and grab my coffee.'

He hadn't noticed she'd been off it for weeks now, but then, he was never around.

She gave a nod. 'I could do. So beware. You never know when I'll pounce.' She lifted her fork. 'But in the meantime I'm going to focus on having some sinful calories.' She dug her fork into the four layers of cake. One forkful told her all she needed to know. 'Hmm, gorgeous.'

'Thank you,' came the cheeky reply. 'You're not so bad yourself.'

She couldn't help but smile. This was the Caleb she used to know. The one who found it easy to make quick quips.

She leaned over and speared a bit of his peach pie.

'Hoy!' His hand had been hovering just above the plate.

'You're too slow,' she joked. 'If you're not fast, you're last.'

As she put the pie into her mouth a bit of the syrup on the peaches dripped down her chin.

Caleb laughed and leaned forward. 'Can't take you anywhere.' He had a paper napkin in his hand and he caught the drip before it landed on her dress. But as he pulled his hand away his fingers caught the underside of her chin.

She froze. When was the last time he'd actually touched her face like that? She couldn't even remember. She swallowed the pie quickly and picked up her plate. 'Here, you try mine.'

But Caleb had caught the moment too. He was looking at her and it took him a few seconds to move. He picked up his fork. 'If it isn't as good as she said, can we demand a refund?' He took a piece of the cake. 'I take it back. It's delicious.'

He leaned back in his chair and looked out over the ocean, sipping his coffee. 'Why did you pick here?'

It was the first time he'd asked that. She didn't think he'd paid much attention at all when she'd told him about the holiday.

She sighed. 'It's been three years since we've had a holiday. I don't actually think we've had a week off together in all that time—just a few days here and there.' She glanced out over the ocean too. 'I told the travel agent I wanted somewhere warm, quiet and luxurious that catered for kids. She'd been here on her honeymoon, so she recommended it.'

He nodded. 'Well, they've got the luxury part right. But it's not too stuffy either. It's quite relaxed.'

She raised her eyebrows. 'Relaxed. There's a word you don't recognise.'

He gave her the look. The one that told her he wasn't going to say out loud what was in his head right now.

'How are things at your work?'

She briefly pressed her lips together as she played with her cup. 'Things are good. It's busy. The conference for next year is booked. The advertising campaign is sorted. We've got about twenty interviews lined up with the national newspapers. And I'm meeting the medical director from St Peter's hospital in a few weeks.'

'Why's that?' He looked curious.

'Because one of the consultant gynaecologists there said we weren't allowed to display our posters about ovarian cancer. It would frighten the patients.'

She could see Caleb trying to choke back his indignation.

She nodded. 'Right there with you. That's why I've bypassed him completely and arranged to meet the medical director.' She took another breath. 'In fact, I've been so busy, that I've been thinking about hiring someone else.'

Caleb had started eating his pie again and looked up. 'Another admin assistant?'

She tried to pick her words. She wasn't ready to tell

him everything so that made this kind of awkward. 'No. Another me.'

He put down his fork. 'What do you mean another you?'

She picked at her cake. Anything was better than looking at him right now. Caleb's gaze could be intense. Particularly if he thought you were hiding something—and it had been a long time since she'd done that.

She tried to keep things light. 'I'd be looking for someone who could job share with me. Lara is great and I definitely want to keep her, but Tristan only has another year before school. He's already at nursery. I want to spend as much time with him as I can.'

And with our new baby, she thought silently to herself.

She finally met his gaze. 'I feel a bit guilty. I had Tristan just as the whole charity thing exploded. I probably should have done this right from the start. But it's difficult then—when everything is new—and you don't really realise how much work it will entail. I feel like I've missed out.' She bit her lip. 'Like we've both missed out.'

He shifted in his chair.

'It's time for me to re-evaluate. And this is part of what I think I should do. When we get home I'm going to put the advert out. It's hard to let things go—I get that and I don't really want to do it. But, at the end of the day, it doesn't need to be me that does everything.' She waved her hand. 'If I get hit by a bus in London, or hit by a speedboat here, someone else will step in. The charity won't disappear. Someone else will do what needs to be done.'

It hadn't been as hard to say out loud as she thought. And while she might have been talking about her own business, she knew that everything she'd just said could be reflected in Caleb and his business for the last three years too. And it was clear he knew that. He had that frown again and she could see the tension across his neck and shoulders.

'Sounds like you re-evaluated a whole lot more than your business in these thoughts.'

She bristled. She hadn't said anything about them. But she could hardly deny it. They had actually been much more of a focus than the business.

'At any point did you think to talk to me?' His tone was accusing.

One of the women at the nearby table looked around.

Addison leaned forward and kept her voice low. 'How can I talk to you when you're never there?'

Frustration was building inside her. For a few moments this morning she'd wondered if they could start to mend bridges. Now it seemed they were right back to where they'd started.

Could she really do this for the next four weeks? Maybe she should just tell him everything and see if they could survive the next four weeks.

Caleb sighed and sat back in his chair. She didn't want to fight. She didn't have the energy to fight.

After a few moments he spoke again. 'Tristan loved the fish. I want a chance to get him in the water and maybe see some. I think that part of the lagoon looks quite shallow. I'm going to ask at Reception if there are any scuba-diving trips that are family friendly. What do you think?'

They were back to safer waters. Maybe he didn't want to fight either. And at least he was making an effort for them to do something together as a family. She nodded. 'I think he'll love that. There's also a boat trip around the island we could do and a place we can hire bikes for the day.'

'You on a bike, really? I've never seen you on a bike.'

'And I've never seen you on one either. But no wonder.

It's a death wish with the traffic in London. Here—there's hardly any cars. It might be fun.'

Fun. There was a word she hadn't heard in a while. That was what she wanted for Tristan. Fun.

One of the hotel staff walked past and handed them a leaflet. 'Just in case you didn't see our sign in Reception. We screen movies on our private beach. Tonight's movie is *Sliding Doors*. Come along and enjoy—the staff will be there to serve cocktails.'

Addison picked up the flyer and wrinkled her nose. '*Sliding Doors*? Lara mentioned that to me.'

'When?'

'When she turned up at the door crying. She said she'd had a *Sliding Doors* moment. I didn't know what she meant.'

He leaned a bit closer. 'You've never seen the movie?'

She shook her head.

'I can't believe that. You'd love it. We'll need to see if we can get Tristan settled in bed tonight. If we do, we can watch the film.'

Addison nodded. She couldn't remember the last time she'd watched a grown-up film. Her last cinema visits had all been with Tristan to see some kind of kids' cartoon-style film. Some of them had been good and some of them had almost sent her to sleep.

Caleb gave a little smile. 'I wonder how Lara and Reuben are getting on.'

Addison shuddered. 'I can't imagine. I can't believe you never told me you'd agreed to let him stay. At least I could have warned her.'

'There's no need to warn her about Reuben. He's a good guy. He'll look after her.'

'Reuben Tyler? A good guy? That'll explain why I walked in on him punching you.'

Caleb shook his head. 'That was nothing. It was guy stuff. And I was partly to blame.'

'How?'

'Reuben doesn't really believe in happy ever afters. He doesn't really believe that love exists. And I called him on it that night. His parents' relationship isn't exactly ideal. When that's the example you've seen all your life it can have a real effect.'

'So he punched you?'

'What's a punch between friends? You didn't hang around to see the rest. He was sorry. He was instantly sorry. But you've never really given him a chance—you can't see past the punch.'

She shifted in her chair. It might be a little true. 'When you see someone punching the man you love it kind of puts you off them for life.' She looked up at him. 'Why have you never told me this about him before?'

He looked a bit uncomfortable. 'Reuben's a private kind of guy. He doesn't like his life being reviewed.'

'But we've never kept secrets from each other.'

He met her gaze. 'It wasn't my secret—it was his. Look, Reuben has good points. You just haven't had a chance to see them. We've been friends since school and I trust him—I'll always trust him. Lara is in safe hands. Don't doubt it. Ask her when we get back.'

'I'm just praying I don't get back and find a note with her written notice because she's not been able to stand sharing a house with Reuben.'

'No way. I'd take bets on it. Reuben can be a real charmer.'

'And that's supposed to reassure me? I think that actually makes me feel worse.'

He rolled his eyes. 'I promise you, they'll be fine.'

'Well, she has no way to get in touch. I'll just need to wait and see.'

One of the hotel staff passed by and picked up their dishes.

It was odd. He felt nervous. Tristan had gone to bed like a dream. The hotel staff had given them a monitor so they would hear if he wakened, leaving them free to sit outside on the beach and watch the film.

The screen had been set up just a little way down the beach from their bungalow. A number of other guests had arrived and had already staked out their space on the sand. Waiters came back with brightly coloured cocktails as the sun set in the sky and the purples turned to dark blue.

Caleb paced about the kitchen. It almost felt like going on a first date. Which was ridiculous. They'd known each other for ten years.

He would always remember his first sight of her. Nervously laughing at a charity event, wearing a bright pink dress, glittery sandals and a sash that said *Ask me about ovarian cancer*.

So he had. Her blonde hair had been curly then, sitting in ringlets around her face and bouncing on her shoulders. He'd been struck by the sincerity in her clear green eyes as she'd told him about her sister and ovarian cancer and what she was doing to try and raise the profile of the disease.

And when she'd stood on her tiptoes and asked him in a whisper if she was doing okay he'd fallen in love instantly. And that had been that.

He hadn't been able to contain himself. He'd wanted to see her every day. His family had loved her almost as instantly as he had and they'd all helped over the years supporting the work of her charity.

They'd waited a few years to get married. His business had been doing really well at that point and when he'd handed her the keys to their new house in Belgravia she'd almost choked.

When she'd walked down the aisle on their wedding day in her slim, cream fitted gown her eyes had widened in shock at the amount of good friends he'd managed to fly in from around the world. It had been a logistical nightmare but her mum and dad had helped a lot. Friends from the US, Australia, France and Denmark had all attended the wedding and she'd been delighted. The expense and effort had been worth it for the expression on her face alone.

It seemed such a long time ago.

Addison came out of the bedroom. She had a full-length blue patterned dress on and a pair of flat sandals.

'Have you got the monitor?'

He nodded and held up his hand.

'Should we take something to sit on for the beach?'

'I've had a look. They've got big blankets on the beach already. We just need to find one to sit on.'

She gave a nod and had a final check on Tristan, planting a kiss on his forehead before she finally came back out. She took a deep breath. 'Okay, let's go.'

They walked along the beach. It was cooler than during the day, but still warm, even though the sun had set. They settled on a blanket near the screen and a waiter appeared instantly to take their order.

Caleb didn't even need to ask. Addison loved cocktails. Even if she hadn't wanted to see the film, he'd bet she would have come along for the cocktails.

'A strawberry daiquiri for my wife and I'll have whatever the local speciality is.'

Addison gave a weird kind of smile and jumped up

as the waiter walked away, catching his arm and saying something in a low voice to him. The waiter looked at her with a smile and left.

'What's wrong?'

She shook her head. 'Nothing. It's just that some places put mint leaves in the strawberry daiquiri and I don't like them. I was asking him to leave them out.'

He wrinkled his nose. 'Do they? I don't remember that.'

She gave him a nudge. 'That's because you don't drink enough of them.'

There was something about the way she did it. The way she said it.

One thing that Addison had never been was a fake. And all of a sudden he got the strangest sensation. She wasn't being entirely truthful. Was it the nudge, the joke?

He settled back on the blanket and tried to put it out of his mind. Addison sat next to him without touching. She pulled her knees up to her chin and wrapped her arms around them as the film started.

He couldn't believe how uncomfortable he felt. Any time in the past he'd been this close to Addison he'd been touching her. His arm was literally itching right now to move around her shoulders and pull her closer. But since her ultimatum he hadn't felt sure about anything.

He glanced around at all the other couples spread out across the beach. Some were lying completely flat on their blankets, staring at the giant screen. Others were side by side. But all were touching. All looked like they were couples. Him and Addison?

He moved. He shifted over on the blanket so his legs were touching hers. She didn't flinch. She didn't jump away. He waited a few seconds then put his arm around her shoulders. A few seconds later he pulled her closer.

She shifted into a more comfortable position, putting

her head against his shoulder, and he finally let out the breath he'd been holding.

'I can't believe you haven't seen this film,' he whispered. 'It's a chick flick.'

'Oh, well, if it's a chick flick I must have seen it.'

'Well, it's right up there with *Dirty Dancing* and *Pretty Woman*, except, of course, it's British. Actually, it's really quite good. You'll like it.'

The waiter appeared back with their drinks. 'The strawberry daiquiri for the lady, and a Bora Bora Delight for the gentleman. Enjoy. Give me a wave if you want a refill.'

Caleb took a drink of the yellow and orange concoction. The rum hit the back of his throat straight away, quickly followed by a burst of orange liqueur and a hint of coconut.

'Wow, take a sip of this.'

For a second she looked as though she might actually say no, then she gave a little nod and took the glass and straw in her hand, taking a sip. 'Lovely,' she said.

'Hits you right in the back of the throat, doesn't it?' She gave a smile and handed it back.

'I'll stick with my strawberry daiquiri,' she said quickly. 'I'd be drunk in five minutes if I took one of those.' She settled her head back on his shoulder.

And, for the first time since the holiday had begun, Caleb finally started to relax.

This was getting awkward. Things would be so much simpler if she could just tell him the truth.

Trouble was, apart from all the emotional stuff, there was the practical stuff too. Caleb would immediately want to get online and find out everything possible about the NT test and the type of results you could get.

She'd done a quick five-minute search at the airport. That was enough. She'd closed her phone down. She didn't need to be bamboozled by everything else. What Dr Mackay had told her was enough. She'd been given a set of odds.

Odds that she had to accept because she was having this baby.

She shifted a little on the beach rug. Caleb's arm was draped around her shoulders. It felt good there. It felt comforting, even though he had no idea what he was comforting her about.

She was quite sure he hadn't noticed anything yet. Her pregnancy wasn't obvious. Her breasts were bigger and her waist had thickened. All things that could be easily hidden in beach dresses and palazzo pants. In her bikini it might not be so easy to hide. Thank goodness she'd packed some swimsuits and a variety of sarongs.

She hadn't known quite what excuse to make when Caleb had ordered her a cocktail. The waiter had given a pleasant nod when she'd asked him to leave the daiquiri out of the strawberry daiquiri. She'd just need to make sure they used the same waiter again.

The film was getting interesting. A time split. In one version she missed the Tube. In the second she caught it and got home to find her boyfriend in bed with another woman. Now she understood what Lara had meant when she'd said she'd had a *Sliding Doors* moment. Now it made perfect sense.

She could feel the heat emanating from Caleb's body. His arm moved slightly, his fingers at the back of her neck. She gave a little groan. She loved that. She loved that light, tickling feeling at the back of her neck. It totally and utterly relaxed her. She could let him do this for hours—and he knew that.

As the film progressed her mind started to spin. Two different versions of the same life. What if that was her?

If someone could give her a flash forward into the future, one with Caleb and one without, which would she pick? Which one would be best for her? Best for Tristan and best for the baby?

She took another sip of her cocktail. Cocktails weren't quite so good without the alcohol. But it would be around another year before she could get the real thing again. This would have to do.

Caleb leaned a bit closer. 'You enjoying this? I told you it was a good film.'

She smiled as a sea breeze blew past, carrying the scent of Caleb's aftershave with it. It was different. It was different from the one he normally wore to work every day. And yet it was familiar. She'd bought it for him on honeymoon years before.

Something stirred inside her. He'd bought another one of these? When had he done that? Surely that must mean something?

She kept watching the film. All the way through hoping the heroine would have one life, then, after the twist at the end, realising she had to live the other. Nothing was simple. Life was completely complicated.

A tear slid down her cheek.

'Hey,' said Caleb. 'It's meant to be a happy ending. Just a little—different.'

She wiped the tear away as they stood up. He kept his arm around her as they walked back down the beach to the bungalow.

'That was good, wasn't it? We'll see what they have in store for tomorrow night.'

'Sure.' Her stomach was starting to churn a little as

they walked through the doors of the bungalow. She wasn't quite sure what came next.

But Caleb just dropped a kiss on her head and walked off to the bedroom.

She felt a little wave of relief. And then a little pang of regret.

Shouldn't her husband be trying to persuade her to join him?

The relaxation of the night felt ruined. She snuck in next to Tristan and tossed and turned all night.

CHAPTER FOUR

FOR A TIME last night, Caleb had felt as if things were almost normal.

Or they would be if there weren't this strange vibe between them.

It felt as if his wife was hiding something from him. He'd never felt like this before. Or maybe he just hadn't noticed how things were with Addison? And that made him feel even guiltier.

Since she'd issued him with the ultimatum he'd noticed *everything*.

Every passing expression on her face. The times she looked as if she might say something but then just pressed her lips together.

The physical stuff too. If she gave the tiniest flinch or shudder. The way she wore her hair, or her clothes. Her attentiveness to Tristan. The far-off look in her eyes sometimes.

But the thing that he noticed most was the aura of sadness around her.

Even when she laughed and smiled it was still there.

And that was like a tight fist squeezing around the muscles of his heart.

Was it him? Had he done this to her?

Please no.

His mind was starting to play tricks on him. Addison had always spoken her mind. But, the ultimatum, must have been building inside her for some time. Which meant she hadn't been speaking her mind to Caleb.

He could remember lots of conversations—or parts of conversations—when she'd mentioned things he'd forgotten—or things he should remember. The irony almost killed him.

Maybe he was naïve, but he couldn't think of a single thing that Addison couldn't tell him. And that was when his mind started playing tricks on him.

Had she met someone else? Was that what all this was about? Had she developed feelings for someone else and she was trying this holiday to see how she still felt about this marriage?

That lit a fire inside him, a burning rage. He couldn't bear the thought of Addison with someone else. But she'd never been that type of person, so why would she do that now?

But what else could it be? She couldn't possibly have murdered someone. She wouldn't have done anything illegal. Could it be business related? The charity could be in trouble. But she'd told him she was going to hire someone else—that just wouldn't fit.

Was there any chance that Addison could have money worries? Maybe she was one of those secret spenders that ran up credit cards without telling anyone and couldn't pay them off? Ridiculous. Their bank account was more than healthy.

Bottom line was he couldn't think of a single reason for his wife to be so down. To be so upset. To be so frustrated.

For the first time in the last few years he didn't want to think about work. He didn't want to think about business. He wanted to think about his family. He wanted to think about his wife.

It was the second morning he'd seen the sunrise. Lots of red, oranges and peaches lighting up the sky. Bora Bora was definitely one of the most beautiful places on Earth.

He glanced at his watch. Reception would be opened by now. He could do what he needed to.

By the time he came back the waiter had just arrived with breakfast. He went through to wake up Tristan and Addison.

'Come on, guys, breakfast time. We have some plans today.'

'We do?' Addison sat up in bed and rubbed her sleepy eyes.

'I've booked us on a circle boat tour of the island. We get to meet some rays and sharks. And I've changed Tristan to an afternoon slot for the kids' club.'

Addison looked surprised. 'Oh, okay. I guess we better get up, then.'

They washed their faces and hands and came through for breakfast. At least she ate something this morning. A croissant with butter and jam and another cup of lemon tea.

It didn't take them long to get ready. While Addison showered and changed he plastered Tristan in suncream and looked out the strange all-in-one swimsuit she had for him, and the baseball cap with the flappy bit at the back of the neck.

She came out of the bathroom with a long pink dress on, her swimming costume straps visible underneath. She was carrying a floppy hat and some sunglasses. 'Oh, great, I was just about to do that.'

She gave him a wary glance. 'I'm not sure how I feel about swimming with sharks or rays.' Then she shook her head. 'Actually, that's not true. I'm entirely sure how I feel about swimming with sharks and rays.'

He laughed. 'Don't worry. I'm sure it's perfectly safe or they wouldn't do it. Let's just wait until we're there and see how you feel then.'

'I get to swim with a shark?' Tristan was astounded.

Caleb laughed and swung him up onto his shoulders. 'Maybe. We'll see what we think.' He bent down and grabbed the bucket and spade. 'Let's take these too. I'm sure we'll stop at a beach somewhere and we'll get to build a castle.'

It didn't take them long to reach the boat. It was even better than he'd hoped for—a traditional Tahitian outrigger canoe made of polished wood for ten people with a motor attached.

Addison looked a little wary. 'That's what we're going in?' she whispered. He nodded and handed her and Tristan the life jackets that everyone was required to wear.

'I thought it might be fun to see the island the traditional way. We don't need to paddle. They have a motor, but I think the guides might do a bit of paddling.'

One of the guides came over to meet them and check their life jackets. He stood in the shallow waters and helped them into the boat. Although it looked small it was actually quite comfortable and there was nothing like being on the perfect crystal-blue lagoon waters. Another few tourists joined them and they set off. From the lagoon they could admire the towering, rocky, green summit of Mount Otemanu.

Addison was sitting directly in front of him with her camera in her hand. He leaned forward. 'The colours here seem unreal, don't they?'

She gave a nod and leaned back a little towards him. The dazzling blue of the lagoon was enhanced by the green of the palm trees and white sandy beaches. Every turn of the head gave a different view. And every single view was like a perfect painting.

As they crossed the lagoon they could see a variety of tropical fish swimming beneath them. After a while the boat pulled up on one of the private beaches of a *motus* and the guides picked fresh fruit from the trees for them.

They stayed there for an hour, eating the fruit and some freshly prepared fish. Caleb used the extra time to build sandcastles with Tristan. For a four-year-old he was serious. He knew exactly what he wanted his creation to look like and wasted no time in telling his father exactly what to do.

Addison was sitting on the beach with her legs curled under her, watching them. After a while she called Tristan over and whispered in his ear.

Tristan shot Caleb a mischievous look. 'That sounds like a good idea.'

Caleb knew when he was being set up. 'What's going on?'

Addison smiled as she stood. 'Oh, nothing. I was just telling Tristan that my favourite memory of being on a beach as a child was when me and my sister buried my dad up to his neck in the sand.'

Tristan didn't need to be told twice. He'd already started digging in the sand with his plastic spade with an enthusiasm that made Caleb laugh. The guides and fellow tourists all laughed and joined in too. Caleb walked over and slung his arm around Addison's shoulders. 'There's no getting out of this, is there?'

She gave him a wide smile. 'Not a chance.'

It was the first time he felt she'd genuinely smiled since they'd got there. She seemed more relaxed today, more at ease. And if getting buried up to his neck in the sand could make her laugh, he would do it—every day for the rest of his life.

It was amazing what a bit of teamwork could do. It wasn't long before Tristan jumped up and down and shouted him over. Caleb looked at the hole. It wasn't quite deep enough, but if he went on his knees he could be buried up to his neck.

Addison was trying to hide her laughter. But she wasn't doing a good job. He jumped straight in the hole. 'Come on, guys, do your worst.'

The sand quickly filled up around him. It wasn't too tight and wasn't too heavy. Tristan pushed as much sand in as he could. He couldn't contain his excitement and it was probably the cutest thing Caleb had ever seen. As the sand came around his neck Addison came over with her camera in hand.

'Come on, Tristan, let's get a picture of you next to this big head in the sand.'

'Who are you saying has a big head?'

'Oh, that would always be you,' she quipped back as she snapped away.

The others snapped away too. 'Come on,' shouted one of the tour guides with a wink. 'Let's all get back on the boat.'

Addison held out her hand to Tristan. 'Let's go, honey. We need to see if there are more fish.'

Tristan's head flicked between Caleb, trapped in the sand, and the boat, which everyone else was climbing on. He dragged behind his mother walking slowly.

Caleb started shouting. 'You can't leave me here. What if a crocodile comes out of the water and eats me?'

Tristan's eyes widened. 'There are crocodiles?'

The guide shook his head. 'No. There aren't any crocodiles.' He leaned down and whispered not so quietly in

Tristan's ear, 'But there are giant octopi that can crawl out the sea and swallow someone whole.'

Tristan's mouth fell open. 'But what about Daddy?' he asked.

The guide turned to the people on the boat. 'Should we let him back out?'

One of the other tourists shrugged. 'We might need him. If the motor breaks we might need help rowing home.'

Addison was watching the whole thing with a smile on her face.

The guide gave a little nod then. He waved his arm. 'Okay, then, folks. Everybody back out. The octopi aren't getting fed today.'

Caleb waited patiently for them to dig him back out. Being buried in the sand was surprisingly cool. But his head was warm. And sand had got into places that sand shouldn't get into.

Digging out took longer than digging in. But after ten minutes he was out, shaking sand off his clothes and picking up his baseball boots. Tristan ran over and gave him a bear hug and his heart gave a little surge.

When was the last time he'd been his son's hero?

That made him uncomfortable. Every father should be their son's hero. He'd just let other things get in the way. He swung Tristan up into his arms and made his way back over to the outrigger canoe.

As they waited to climb back on board he took a deep breath and looked around. This really was like a little piece of paradise. He couldn't, for one second, think of any other people he'd want to be here with.

Tristan and Addison were his whole world.

He'd forgotten about the feel of his little boy's arms around his neck. Tristan was brushing some sand out of

Caleb's hair and laughing. Then, he immediately started talking about his favourite wrestlers. Caleb smiled. He'd heard these stories time and time again. But when was the last time he'd actually listened?

He gave Tristan a tickle. 'You honestly think Cena could take The Rock? Not a chance. Not ever.'

He spun around. Addison was leaning against a palm tree watching them and waiting for her turn to board.

There was something about her expression on her face. She didn't look happy or sad, just thoughtful—the way she'd looked a lot in the last few days.

She blinked and realised he was staring at her. She gave a little shake, then gave them a wave and walked back over. She tapped her camera. 'I think I have all the blackmail material that I'll need.'

Caleb groaned. 'How much is this going to cost me?'

She shrugged. 'Maybe another piece of cake. There was a chocolate one I've got my eye on.'

One of the tourist guides held out his hand to help Addison on the boat. She picked up the skirts of her dress, giving him a little flash of her legs.

He smiled. He hadn't pursued her last night—even though he'd wanted to. They were at a strange kind of impasse. She hadn't seemed so angry, or so reserved. But he hadn't wanted to cross any lines.

He hadn't banked on having to win back his wife. Especially when he hadn't realised he'd almost lost her.

He'd been angry at her at first, taking him away from the business he loved. The fact he had no Internet or phone access literally made him twitch.

But he was beginning to get a little perspective. How many hours a week had he actually been working? When was the last time he'd sat on the sofa with Tristan and watched some cartoons? And when was the last time he'd spent an evening solely with his wife?

The tour guide waved them over and he and Tristan climbed back on board. Tristan couldn't contain himself. He kept hanging over the side.

'What are you doing, little guy?'

Tristan grinned. 'I'm looking for crocodiles and octopuses.'

Caleb nodded. 'And can you see any?'

'Not yet. But I'm going to keep looking.'

The canoe moved off. There was no one else around; they had this whole piece of the ocean to themselves. The crystal-blue waters stretched out as far as the eye could see, merging with the pale blue sky and white clouds. As they ventured further around the island a little speck of red appeared on the horizon—a windsurfer. It was like a scene from a postcard or a travel brochure.

The tour guide started talking. 'We're coming up on the shallow waters where we'll go swimming with sharks and rays. I'll give you all some instructions before you go in the water.' He gave them all a wink. 'And don't worry, I haven't lost a tourist yet.'

Addison leaned forward and whispered in his ear. 'Not a chance. Not a blooming chance.'

He leaned his head back. 'Addison Connor, are you scared?'

He was baiting her. He knew he was. But it always worked with Addison.

She hit his shoulder. 'Don't you start on me, sand boy.'

She sat back again. Her hands were gripping her bag just a little too tightly. He leaned back and put his hand on her leg. 'Hey, I'm happy to take one for the Connor team. You and Tristan can take pictures if you want.'

Her head gave the slightest nod.

'Look, Daddy!' Tristan's voice was full of wonder and the tourist guide started to laugh.

'Well, as our young friend has already noticed, this is where the wildlife come to meet us.' He waved his hand. 'Look around you.'

He pointed across the clear waters. 'Blacktip reef sharks, stingrays and sergeant major fish.'

It was like something from a film. The first blacktip reef sharks appeared before the boat had even come to a complete stop.

As the guide worked to tie them off to an anchored buoy, a half-dozen or so of the five-foot-long sharks swam in slow circles nearby, along with several stingrays and a school of yellow-and-black-striped sergeant major fish. Caleb felt as if he were in the middle of a giant aquarium.

The sharks weren't shy. They came up and nudged the canoe.

The guide laughed and jumped in the water. 'We come here every day. Blacktip sharks normally stay around coral reefs and shallow waters. They are generally quite timid, but they've got used to us. They eat other small fishes.'

Addison's eyes were following the stingrays. 'What about them?'

'They're docile too. They just don't like to be stood on. But I'll make sure there are none on the ocean floor before you all get in.'

Several of the others tourists were already stripping off their clothes. Caleb did the same. He shed his T-shirt and shorts quickly until he was down to just his swimming shorts.

'Wait,' said Addison as she rummaged through her bag. She pulled out a bottle of sunscreen. 'Turn around until I spray some of this on your back. You don't want to get burned.'

He turned around and winced as the spray hit his back. How come these sprays were always cold?

Next minute he felt the warmth of Addison's palm on his back. Both palms. He sucked in a breath.

She'd been so distant. And what she was doing right now was an everyday thing. But having Addison's palms massaging his back didn't feel like an everyday thing. It felt a whole lot more than that.

Her movements weren't sensual, they were brisk, perfunctory. Rubbing in suncream was second nature to Addison.

She finished with a little slap on his back. 'All done.'

He smiled and jumped overboard into the waist-high water. The water was warm and inviting. Tristan leaned over and stuck his hands in just as the shoal of yellow-and-black-striped sergeant major fish swam past.

'Woo-hoo! Look, Mummy, look at the fish.'

Caleb held his hands out towards him. 'Want to jump in next to Dad? I'll hold you.'

Tristan jumped up and down, rocking the canoe. He could see a flash of mad panic in Addison's eyes. 'You want to take him in with sharks and stingrays?'

He nodded. 'You heard the guides. They haven't lost a tourist yet. It's safe. Let's give him a chance to see them. He'll probably never get this chance again. It's only for a few minutes.'

He could see Addison suck in a deep breath. The rest of the tourists were in the water, touching the sharks and stingrays around them. The guides were showing them what to do.

He kept Tristan in his arms, with his little legs wrapped around his waist. The guides were fantastic. The sharks and rays seemed comfortable around the people. They swam around, occasionally bumping against them. But never in a way that made him concerned.

Addison finally relaxed a little, taking out her camera and snapping pics of them both. They ended up being in the water for much longer than he'd planned. It was so tranquil. The experience of being this close to the creatures was just too good an opportunity. The whole time that the tourists were in the water the guides gave them a rundown of the different species and how they lived. They emphasised the importance of the coral reefs and natural habitats for the creatures and things that could threaten their existence. Caleb had never really experienced anything like this before.

And it was so much better because of the people he was with.

Addison finally plucked up the courage to stick her toes in the water but that was it. She snapped away taking pictures of Tristan and Caleb together in the water.

After a while he grabbed the camera back and snapped a few pictures of her sitting on the canoe. He took a quick glance before he handed it back. Addison was as beautiful as ever, the floppy hat on her head and in her long pink sundress. She didn't have her glasses on and—it couldn't be hidden—there was still something in her eyes. An inherent sadness that he just couldn't get to the bottom of. They had to talk. They had to sit down and actually *talk*.

A little wash of guilt swept over him. Could they talk? Could he actually tell her that he already had a pile of CVs in his drawer of potential employees?

Could he tell her he'd deliberately been putting things off because—in a way—his work was his escape?

If he was at work, he didn't need to tell his wife why he wasn't keen to have another child. A child that he actually longed for.

Right now the irony killed him. He'd spent time avoiding Addison because he couldn't tell her what he feared—that if they had another child she might slip away from him again. It turned out his wife had been slipping away from him the whole time anyway.

The conversation from a year ago had never left him. The disappointment on her face about not considering another child. He'd avoided every opportunity to discuss it—and that hadn't exactly helped the atmosphere at home. The one and only time he'd tried to talk to her about how she'd felt after having Tristan—she'd brushed him off. She'd made light of how down she'd been. It was almost as if her head wouldn't let her acknowledge that again. It made him think she might be just as afraid as he was. Which was why he'd left things and the tension had built.

But today had felt different. Today had felt good. He'd actually been relaxed—really relaxed. He hadn't let work thoughts plague his mind at all. He couldn't remember the last time that had happened.

The heat of the day started to build as the canoe made its way back over the lagoon towards their resort. It was a relief to get back into the main building and the air conditioning.

Tristan bounded off to join the rest of the children at the kids' club. His energy was incredible.

Caleb turned to Addison. 'Chocolate cake?'

She shook her head. 'Not yet, maybe later. Let's take a walk. I'd like to see a little of Bora Bora outside of the resort.'

He nodded. 'Sure. Give me five minutes to change. I've got sand in difficult places.'

She laughed and nodded. 'Okay, I'll get us something cool to drink.'

* * *

Addison watched as Caleb crossed the reception area of the resort. He always managed to cut an impressive stride and today was no different. Her palms tingled as she remembered the feel of his skin under them.

She hated being distant from Caleb. She hated this huge abyss that had appeared between them—one she didn't know if they'd be able to cross.

Today had felt a little different. Today, he'd taken all the time in the world for them.

When she'd watched him today getting buried in the sand and swimming with the sharks with Tristan it had made her heart melt a little. This was the guy she remembered. He'd been totally focused on making their son happy.

And Tristan had loved being the focus of his father's attention.

Caleb was being easy around her, he was being familiar. He was reminding her of what they used to have. In some ways it was comforting, and in others it hurt because it reminded her of how much they'd lost.

If she ended up on her own this was what she'd miss. This was what her son would miss out on. The real sharing and connection to his father. This was what the new baby would miss too.

By the time she'd paid for the frozen lemonades, Caleb was back, wearing a pair of khaki shorts and a blue polo shirt.

'Better?'

'Much.' He took the lemonade. 'Thanks. Right, where are we headed?'

She pointed to the path reaching out of the resort. 'I thought we could just take a wander along here and see what there is.'

'Fine by me.'

They walked down the long path shaded with palm trees and tropical flowers. As they left the entrance to the resort they passed a few people on bikes. Cars weren't widely used on Bora Bora, and the roads weren't particularly good. There were only a few taxis for the whole island.

They walked towards the main dock of Vaitape. There were a number of shops and cafés dotted along the way. Addison wandered into the first shop they came to.

Across the shelves was a whole variety of wooden carved ornaments of every kind of animal imaginable—plus a few she didn't even recognise.

Hanging from the walls were the colourful *pareo* fabrics worn by the islanders. Every bright colour was there: red, yellow, blue, green and orange. Clothes were nearby with some of the dresses hand-painted with beautiful Tahitian flowers.

Addison picked up a white dress, strapless with a gathered bodice, trimmed with deep pink at the top and around the bottom hem. The skirt of the dress was hand-painted with intricate pale pink flowers and large pale green leaves. Caleb walked up behind her. 'What have you found?'

She held up the dress. 'This. Isn't it gorgeous?'

He held out the skirt. 'Someone painted this? Really?' His eyes skimmed up and down her body. Unconsciously she found herself sucking in her stomach.

It was ridiculous. She was wearing a long pink jersey beach dress. Nothing was obvious in this. She had no reason to be self-conscious.

'It would suit you—you'd look good in it,' said Caleb decisively. 'Buy it.' He wandered off and picked up some stuffed sharks and stingrays. 'What about these for Tristan?'

She gave a little nod as she still admired the dress. It was madness to buy something like this. She'd never get to wear it back in London—they just wouldn't get the weather. But she really liked it, and the thought of supporting the people on Bora Bora by buying local goods was definitely something she wanted to do.

It only took a few moments to make their purchases and then Addison moved on to the next shop. There she found more jewellery, pendants she could buy for the women who worked with her at the charity. Something simple and easy to carry home.

In the next shop she found black pearl earrings. 'What about these for your secretary?' she asked Caleb.

He raised his eyebrows. 'The secretary that I just deserted for a month without giving her warning?'

Addison tried to think on her toes but she could feel her cheeks start to flush.

He stepped closer. 'What, you told her too? You told Harry and you told Libby, but you didn't tell me?'

She held up her finger. 'I did tell you. I told you weeks before we were going on holiday for a month. *You* chose not to tell me you weren't going to come.'

He could have got angry. He could have got defensive.

Instead, the edges of his lips turned upwards. 'You're just trying to make me look bad,' he quipped.

She walked over to pay for the earrings. 'If the cap fits,' she shot over her shoulder.

He was behind her in an instant, his hands on either side of her hips as she paid. She could feel the whole of his body gently pressed up behind her.

The shop assistant looked up and smiled. 'Honeymoon?' she asked.

'Oh, no.' Addison shook her head and turned to catch the look on Caleb's face. 'That was a long time ago.'

His gaze met hers. And held it.

It seemed like the longest time. It seemed like for ever. The little hairs on her arms stood on end as if a cool breeze had just danced across her skin.

His voice was low. 'Too long,' he whispered.

He threaded his fingers through hers and reached over to take the bag from the shop assistant.

This time as they left Caleb led the way. And he wasn't walking slowly. He was walking quickly and heading straight back to their resort. She almost had to run to keep up. Her heart was racing.

If he undressed her right now, in the bright sunlight, would he notice anything different about her? Of course he would. And it would bring on a whole conversation she didn't know if she was ready for.

Connections had been tenuous these last few days. But at least they were there. And she didn't want to harm that. She wanted to build on them to see if they could recapture some of what had been lost.

As they approached the resort Caleb took a different route. He must have thought it would take them quicker to their bungalow. Instead, it took them on a winding route to a beautiful bandstand covered in pink and red flowers.

'Wow!' Addison's hand shot up to her mouth.

Caleb looked from side to side, obviously confused about where they had ended up. 'Where on earth are we?'

She smiled and walked slowly up the steps, setting down her bags. 'It looks like a bandstand. I've no idea why it's at the bottom of the path.' Her hand reached up and touched the dark green foliage. The aroma from the flowers and surrounding plants was intoxicating.

'I can't believe this is here. It's the kind of thing every

teenage girl would dream about having in their garden.'
She stepped inside. The foliage covered the top of the
structure, making it like an enchanted hideaway.

Caleb touched her shoulder. 'I'm almost scared to ask,
but what else do teenage girls dream about?' His voice
was low and husky.

She sucked in a breath as she turned back towards him.
In the shaded bandstand all she could focus on were his
brown eyes.

She could feel her heart thudding against her chest and
her breath stall somewhere in her throat.

'Addison.' He reached up and tangled his fingers
through her hair. She let out a little groan.

He leaned forward a little, blocking out her surrounding view of the tropical flowers. All she could see was
Caleb.

But something was different. Something she hadn't
seen in such a long time. He had that little twinkle in his
eye again. The one that made her think there was no one
on this planet like her husband.

His voice was low. 'It seems wrong not to take advan-
tage of such a beautiful setting.'

He bent to kiss her. He tasted of lemonade. His firm
lips pressing against hers and gently nudging hers open.
One hand stayed in her hair and the other traced light
patterns on her back. Everything that he knew she liked.

She couldn't help herself. Her arms lifted automatically and wound around his neck.

Last time they'd been this up close and personal they'd
been almost naked. Last time they'd been this close they'd
made another baby.

Her body gave an involuntary shudder. Caleb pulled his
lips from hers and concentrated on her neck. She could
get lost in this. She could get lost in this so easily.

Memories came flooding back. In the first few years all Caleb had done was kiss her. It hadn't mattered where they had been, or what they'd been doing. He'd pulled her into doorways when shopping, and behind trees when they'd been out walking. His hand had permanently been in hers—or his arm had been around her shoulders.

When she'd become pregnant he'd been the most attentive husband on the planet. He'd bought cookery books and tried to master all her favourite recipes. He'd become an expert at running warm bubble baths surrounded by cotton-fresh candles. He'd come with her to every appointment, every scan. He'd huffed and puffed with her through every part of the labour and when Tristan had been born he'd been the proudest father in the world.

He'd spend hours at night sitting looking at their son. Then he'd spend even more time in the small hours of the morning when Tristan had screamed with colic. He'd paced the floor for hours after hours. Addison hadn't been able to bear it. She'd always ended up in tears herself and Caleb had always herded her back to bed.

Even then, even when she'd been tired and exhausted, a kiss from her husband had made everything seem okay.

Why couldn't it do the same now?

Kissing Caleb now was different. It was terrifying. It reminded her of what she could lose. What she would miss.

His kisses moved back up from her neck and around her ear to her lips again. She took a few steps back to the evergreen wall of the bandstand, praying that no one else would choose to walk along this path.

Her hands moved from around his neck, across his back and under his polo shirt. His warm, firm flesh was under her palms again.

His hand came up and brushed against her breast. She

froze. Would he notice? Would he notice her breasts had mysteriously got bigger?

He pulled back for a second. 'Addison?'

Her heart was racing.

'Are you going to tell me what's going on?'

For a second she couldn't breathe. Couldn't move.

It was like a trick question. She wanted to tell him. She wanted to share with him.

But *this* was the Caleb she wanted. Not the one she had back home. The one who had time for her, who had time for Tristan, and would have time for this new baby.

Maybe she was being unrealistic? Maybe she wanted too much? But she'd had it before—and she knew how good they could be together. How good they could be as a family.

She wasn't stupid. Of course life got in the way. Everyone had busy times at work. Other pressures cropped up. She could deal with that. She had dealt with that. The likelihood was that, in seven or eight years' time, they would be permanent chauffeurs for their kids, taking them to football, dance lessons, swimming lessons, music lessons or whatever else they wanted to attend. They'd end up being like ships passing in the night. And she'd cope with that. She would.

But what she needed right now from her husband was that their family had priority. Their family came first. And back home in London? It just wasn't like that. She wanted Caleb back. She wanted her husband back.

'I've missed you,' she whispered.

His brow furrowed. 'But I've been right here.'

She felt tears spring to her eyes. 'But you haven't been. Tristan and I are like parts of your life that don't count any more. I keep thinking it will stop. Work will slow down. But you just take on more and more. Three years, Caleb.

That's how long it's been. We never see each other any more, we never spend time together.' She slid her hand out from under his polo shirt.

'I don't want an appointment in your diary. I don't want to speak to your secretary—as much as I love her.'

He waved his hand as he looked at her. 'I'll look at things when I go home. I'll try and pass some things on to Harry. I'll make sure I'm about more.'

Her stomach gave a horrible little twist. He meant it. She knew he meant it.

But he wasn't really getting it. The casual wave of his hand proved that. She wanted to know that she and Tristan were enough for him—were important enough to him to re-evaluate what he was doing.

But her face must have betrayed her. 'What?' he asked. 'What is it? What else is making you so crazy?'

She shook her head and bit her lip.

Caleb dropped his hands and stepped back. 'Tell me, Addison. This is ridiculous. Tell me what else is going on. Because it has to be something. You're making me feel like I'm on trial here—and for what?'

A tear slid down her cheek and she shook her head again. 'I just want to know that you value us. That we're enough to make you stop and think about how you're living your life.'

Now, he was getting frustrated. 'What is this? You gave me an ultimatum and I'm here. I came.'

'You came because you thought you'd still have access to the phone and the Internet. You thought you could still work. Would you have come if you'd known the truth?'

He hesitated. Just for a second. But it was enough.

She threw up her hands. 'See? I'm trying to decide what's best for me, best for Tristan. What use is a husband and father who is never there? Who never connects with his wife or his child? Who forgets about the things that should be important?'

'What's important? What have I forgot?' Their voices were raised now, ruining the tranquillity of the beautiful gardens.

'You forget everything! I can't rely on you for Tristan.'

'That's not true. I'm Tristan's father. Of course I can be relied upon. And isn't this why we got some extra help?'

She kept her voice steady. 'Lara's not Tristan's parent. Lara is someone we employ. Tell me, Caleb, if I got knocked down by a bus tomorrow is that what you'd do with our son? Have him looked after on a permanent basis while you continued to work ridiculous hours?'

'What a stupid question. Why would you even ask something like that?'

She stared down at her ring. 'Because getting married meant something to me—'

'It meant something to me too!'

She held up her hand and cut him dead. 'This wasn't what I expected. I feel as if I'm a single parent and a single woman. We never see you—you're never around. And even when you do appear you're not with us. Your mind is always on the next business deal.' She took a deep breath. She was exhausted. Emotionally and physically. Being out in the sun all morning, then walking along to the shops, had taken more out of her than she'd thought. Or maybe it was just this—the constant tension in the air between them.

One thing she knew for sure. She didn't want to go back home and for things to continue the way they were.

'You're being ridiculous now. Okay, so I might have been working too much—but that won't be for ever.' Something flickered across his face—as if he'd just realised what she'd said. 'Is that what you want—to be a single woman? Have you met someone else?'

'What? No.' She was horrified he might even suggest that. She'd neither the time nor the inclination to meet anyone else. That was the absolute last thing on her mind. 'All I'm saying is that I can't live the next twenty years like this. In fact, I can't live the next year like this.'

As she said the words something happened. The green around her started to spin.

She heard the shout. 'Addison?' and saw the flash of movement but for a few seconds it was as if she almost weren't there.

She couldn't really focus on anything. She was conscious of being lowered to the floor. It was cool there. It felt fine.

The very next second someone was pinching her hand. 'Addison?'

She blinked but couldn't see him. That was odd.

The face came around from behind her. He was on the floor next to her and she was leaning against his chest.

His hand rubbed up and down her arm, almost as if he was trying to heat her up, but that didn't make sense—because she wasn't cold.

'Addison,' he said again. 'Are you with me?'

She tried to straighten up a little as she looked around. She was on the floor of the bandstand. How on earth did she get there?

His strong arms wrapped around her. 'What happened?'

'You tell me. Do you want me to go and get you a doctor?'

She shook her head quickly. 'No. No doctor. I just felt a bit woozy. We must have been out in the sun too long. Give me a second. I'll be fine.' She pushed herself up onto her knees and sucked in a deep breath to try and clear her head.

She'd been fighting. She'd been fighting with Caleb.

'Are you sick? Are you ill?'

She shook her head again. 'I told you, too much sun.' She stood up and held her hand out to catch hold of the foliage wall. But Caleb was too quick for her, he had his hand in hers and his other arm firmly around her waist.

'Let's get you back to the bungalow. Lie down. I'll get you something to eat and drink. We never had any lunch. Do you think that's what's wrong?'

She tried not to smile. If she counted the days in life she'd missed a meal she'd be here all day. But she'd never done that when she was pregnant. And she'd never done it in a different climate.

'Do you want me to carry you?'

'Don't you dare,' she shot back. 'I'll be fine walking.'

Caleb was still talking. 'I'm still going to ask a doctor to come and see you.'

'No. I don't need a doctor. You're probably right. I probably just need something to eat. I'll be fine.' She glanced at her watch. 'Look at the time. We have to pick up Tristan from the kids' club.'

'Forget the kids' club. He's safe there. Let's get you settled down, then I'll pick up Tristan and take him to play on the beach. That way you get a chance to rest.'

He was steering her along the path, practically doing the walking for her. It only took five minutes to reach the bungalow. He kicked open the beach doors and took her straight inside. The air conditioning was an instant relief. She went to sit down on one of the sofas, then changed her mind.

Caleb was over at the fridge, pulling out a bottle of chilled water. She walked through to the bedroom and pulled off her dress and swimming suit. She wanted room for her body to breathe and the swimming suit felt oddly restrictive.

Even though it was the middle of the day she picked up her short satin nightdress. She was going to lie down for an hour.

'Here you go.' She jumped out of her skin. She was facing the other way and was just dropping the nightdress over her bare behind. She hadn't even thought.

Caleb looked at her as he set the water down next to her bed. 'What's wrong?'

She shook her head. 'Nothing. It's fine. Or I will be once I've had a lie down.'

Her head was spinning. What if she'd been facing the other way? What if he'd noticed her changing figure and actually asked her about it? Could she really have lied to him?

'What about a piece of that chocolate cake you spotted? I could walk over and get you a slice. You could probably do with the sugar boost.'

She sat down on the bed. 'No, maybe tomorrow. I think I'd feel sick if I ate that right now. I'll just have an apple.'

'Nope. Try again. You just keeled over. An apple isn't going to cut it. You need more than that.'

She wrinkled her nose. 'I don't really want anything big.'

He nodded. 'Leave it with me. I'll find something.'

She took a drink of the water and lay back in the comfortable bed. If she could sleep for just an hour she'd be fine. She rested her hand on her stomach. Could she have hurt the baby when she fell? No. Caleb had caught her. There was only a hint of a stomach. But it felt a little firmer.

Maybe her blood pressure had dipped a bit. Or, it was

just what she'd thought, she'd skipped a meal and her blood sugar had dipped. That could make anyone woozy.

She closed her eyes for just a second. Only for Caleb to return and shake her shoulder.

'Here, sit up and eat this, then I'll leave you alone.' It was a huge bowl of sliced fruits. Apple, strawberry, melon, grapes, peach and pineapple with some kind of sauce drizzled over it.

'Where did you get this?'

'I spoke nicely to the kitchen. Said you needed something refreshing.' He handed her a fork and sat at the end of the bed.

Now she couldn't hide her amusement. 'What are you doing?'

He folded his arms. 'I'm making sure you eat something.'

'You don't have to watch.'

'Call me a stickler.'

She tasted one of the strawberries. 'Hmm, that's lovely. What's the sauce?'

'I have no idea. Chef's secret.'

She smiled. 'Well, I don't know what it is. But I like it.' She kept eating. He was actually serious. He was going to watch her eat. 'I'm fine. But I'm tired. Once I've eaten this, I'm going to sleep for a while. Why don't you go and get Tristan? We were due to pick him up. I don't want him to think we've forgotten about him.'

Caleb was watching her with those intense brown eyes. He glanced at his watch and sighed. 'You'll eat everything and go for a sleep?'

It was like being told off by the head teacher. But she could actually see the concern on his face. It kind of gave her a warm rush in her stomach. He was actually interested in her. He was actually paying her some attention.

How ironic because she needed him to be distracted. She needed him to be thinking about something else.

She gave him a smile. 'Honestly, I'm fine. Thank you. I'll see you and Tristan later.'

She could see him still hesitate. It was hard. Not long ago they'd been shouting at each other in the bandstand. He'd been angry with her, and she'd been angry with him too.

But as soon as she'd been unwell everything had been forgotten. Caleb had been the model husband. And he still was.

He finally stood up. 'Okay, then.' He picked up the bucket and spade. 'I'll go and get Tristan and take him to the beach.'

He took one step to the door. Then, before she could even think, he crossed the room and dropped a kiss on the top of her head.

'See you later.' He walked out of the door and Addison looked down at the bowl of fruit and held her breath. Once she was sure he was gone she put the bowl down and curled up on the bed.

She pressed her hand to her stomach. 'Stay safe, baby,' she whispered.

Tristan was full of energy. He'd loved playing with the other kids but was even more excited about playing with his dad on the beach.

'Can I bury you again, Daddy?'

Caleb shook his head. 'I don't think you could dig a big enough hole. Let's have a sandcastle competition.'

Tristan agreed and rushed back to the bungalow to find some wrestlers for his castle. He came back thirty seconds later with one for Caleb too.

They played for over an hour. Eventually Tristan

flagged. Caleb had set some towels under a few of the palm trees and carried him over to go to sleep.

He could have gone back in the bungalow but didn't want to disturb Addison.

He was horrified by what had happened. A white flash had shot across Addison's face just before her legs had crumpled underneath her. He'd jumped across the bandstand to catch her and lower her to the ground.

Terror. That was what he'd felt. Addison had never had health problems before. She'd always been really healthy. And she'd never talked about fainting before. If he had his way she would have been taken to see the doctor. But she'd insisted she was fine and just needed to lie down.

A horrible feeling of dread crept through him. Some of the things she'd said started to circle around in his mind. Twice. Twice, she'd used the expression 'what if I was hit by a bus?' She'd issued him that ultimatum. Telling him to come on holiday or her and Tristan wouldn't be back.

It didn't matter that the sun was currently splitting the sky, Caleb felt a chill. She was pale, and she'd fainted. She hadn't been eating too much and she hadn't drunk much either—only that strawberry daiquiri the other night.

Was Addison ill? Was something wrong with his wife?

He stood up and started pacing. The more he paced, the more his brain spun around and around. She wanted him to reconnect with her, and reconnect with Tristan. He hadn't even realised they'd disconnected in the first place but he was beginning to realise just how switched off he'd been.

She was definitely acting strangely. And that thing that he couldn't put his finger on was an innate sadness. An aura that had been coming from her since they'd left on holiday.

He could feel himself start to panic—something Caleb definitely wasn't used to. Could Addison really be ill?

But she'd tell him—wouldn't she? His breath caught in his throat. That was what she'd been telling him. That was what she'd been spelling out. He was never there to tell. How could she tell him if there was actually something wrong with her if he was never there to have that conversation?

He couldn't bear it. He couldn't bear it if his beautiful wife was ill. He looked around him. His heart skipped a beat. Paradise. She'd booked them a month in paradise.

Was there more to this? Was Addison more than ill? His hand reached out to the nearest palm tree. He squeezed his eyes closed. Her sister had died of cancer. She'd spoken before about being worried it was in her genes.

Was that why she kept giving him a scenario where she wasn't around?

He knelt to the ground and put his hands on his head. Tristan was sleeping peacefully at his feet. Was there a chance his son might not have a mother in the future?

He felt sick. He felt physically sick.

Was she trying to give them this time to create some more memories together? Was she hoping he might form a better connection to Tristan in case she wasn't there in the future?

This was all crazy. It was all in his head. But what if there were a tiny possibility any of it could be true?

He groaned. He'd shouted at her. For the first time in his life he'd actually shouted at her.

When he'd kissed her, he'd thought things might start to get back on track for them. He'd always loved kissing Addison and today had been no different. He loved the smell of her hair, the touch of her skin. He loved the shade of lipstick she liked to wear, and how she had to fold her clothes a certain way.

He loved the fact when she was reading a book she always put it down with the back facing upwards, like a warning not to touch. He loved the fact she would happily buy a box of chocolates, eat the orange and strawberry creams and leave the rest.

He loved the fact that when they had guests around to dinner, she'd frequently run along the street to the local Belgian patisserie and buy a giant pavlova, decorate it with fruit and pretend she'd made it.

He let out a long, slow breath. All these little things. All these little things that they'd both forgotten about over the last few years. He hadn't really had time to think about.

She was right. She was right about everything.

They'd been drifting apart from each other and he hadn't even noticed.

He hadn't paid her and Tristan the attention that they deserved. He hadn't been around them enough.

And when she'd actually tried to talk to him—or he'd tried to talk to her—both had made some kind of excuse not to have that conversation. It was almost as if they'd forgotten how to communicate with each other.

He hadn't wanted to listen. He didn't want to acknowledge his part in all this. He just wanted to pretend that everything was fine. That nothing had gone wrong between them.

Was he actually in danger of losing so much more than he could even imagine?

Addison had to be here. She had to be in his life. He couldn't function without her. She was the glue that held him together.

When she'd fainted today he'd been shocked. She looked so pale and so fragile. Was she afraid if he called a doctor to see her, he might find out something she didn't want him to know?

He had to try and temper his feelings and emotions. He had to respect Addison's wishes. She'd said no and if he went over her head and asked Reception to call a doctor it would cause yet another fight between them that they didn't need.

He picked up the sleeping Tristan and walked as silently as possible into the bungalow, putting Tristan in his own bed. Then, he walked quickly back over to the reception area and into the resort shop. It only took him a few minutes to find what he was looking for.

He was determined to make things right. He was determined to make things better.

He was doing his best to push all the other stuff out of his mind. The fact that there might actually be something wrong with his wife.

He had to concentrate on the here and now. And that was him and Addison. Him, Addison and Tristan.

Hopefully, by the time she woke, he would have started to build bridges between them. He needed his wife to have faith in him. He needed his wife to trust him enough to tell him what was on her mind.

And he had to start somewhere.

CHAPTER FIVE

WHEN SHE FINALLY woke someone had drawn the shutters on the beach bungalow's windows. Even though they blocked out the sun, the wind was still able to get through them and, as the window was open, the full-length white curtain was fluttering in the wind. Just how long had she been asleep?

She stretched and sat up, taking a little drink of the now lukewarm water. She glanced at the clock. Nearly two hours. That was how long she'd slept. But the surprising thing was, she really did feel better for it.

Something caught her eye. A flickering. She stood up and took a few steps forward, stopping at the entrance to the large en suite bathroom and catching her breath.

The lights were out in the bathroom and it was lit only by an array of candles around the edges of the white bath. The bath was full with bubbles reaching right to the top, the aroma of vanilla, frangipani and orange pulling her in.

She couldn't help but smile. Caleb. Caleb had done this for her. There was even a little dish with some dark chocolates in it and a glass of white wine sitting next to the bath. She walked over and touched the side of the glass. Condensation wet her finger; it must have only been poured recently.

Where did he get all this? Had he gone shopping while she'd been sleeping?

She heard some shouts outside and walked through to the main room. The doors were wide open to the beach. Caleb and Tristan were running in and out of the surf and from the variety of characters spread at the entrance it was obvious she'd just missed a wrestling match.

This was the kind of thing she'd dreamt of. When she'd sat in the travel agency and made the booking, this was the kind of thing she'd wished for their family holiday. Caleb and Tristan were happy. At first he'd looked a little awkward—as if he were having trouble actually relaxing—but now they were playing just the way a father and son should.

She walked back through to the bathroom and pulled her nightdress over her head. What about the wine? She couldn't drink it, so she poured a little of it down the toilet. He would never know.

The bath was perfect. She tied her hair up in a knot and sank down into the bubbles. Part of her was grateful and part of her felt a little guilty—because she knew that was how Caleb was feeling.

That was why he'd done this. He'd obviously got a fright this afternoon and so had she.

It was clear their fight was never going to be mentioned again. But how did they move on from here?

She wanted to hope that things were going to change. She wanted to hope things were going to be better. But she didn't want that to be because she was pregnant. It had to be because Caleb had realised that things had reached breaking point and had to turn around.

When they'd been fighting earlier he couldn't even acknowledge what was wrong. Had her being unwell been his wake-up call?

The little seeds of thought that had planted in her brain earlier started to sprout tiny shoots and grow. Maybe this wasn't all Caleb's fault? Maybe she should shoulder some of the responsibility too?

They'd argued about having more kids. She'd just assumed he would agree. Instead, he'd drawn further away and she'd felt more and more isolated.

The atmosphere in the house had changed. And part of that was her. She definitely felt a little hostile towards him. Why didn't he want to expand their family?

She closed her eyes and rested her hand on her stomach. She was praying for so much right now. She was praying for this baby, praying for her marriage and praying for herself. She hadn't just struggled when Tristan had been born.

She'd felt numb. It had been as if everything was happening around her. Even now she struggled to put it into words. She hadn't felt that initial wave of love that others talked about. She'd felt relief that labour was finally over. Then, when everyone else had left, she'd stared at the little baby in the crib and wondered how on earth she would love him as she was supposed to.

Now, she knew that love was something that grew and embedded itself into you every single day. For a while she'd felt disjointed. And the numbness had spread to her relationship with Caleb. Was she failing everybody?

But gradually things had changed. The terrifying screaming bundle had become manageable. Tristan eventually learned to sleep for more than ten minutes at a time. The ache and constant mastitis in her breasts—the thing that made breastfeeding excruciating—finally quietened down. Her health visitor persuaded her to let Caleb bottle feed Tristan with expressed breastmilk for a few hours every night. At first the guilt had crippled her. She was failing at feeding her child too. But gradually she learned to relax about it. He was gaining weight. He was thriving. The mastitis was settling. She felt more rested. Now, she could feed him during the day and early evening without associating it with pain and discomfort. And Tristan started to react to her. He smiled. He watched her. He giggled. And the connection between them grew, just like the connection between her and Caleb.

This was why she was determined to be prepared this time around. Maybe this was why she was reluctant to tell him? Was there a chance that Caleb might not be happy about her being pregnant again? This baby hadn't been planned. And now, there could be other difficulties.

But it was the oddest feeling. Her hand pressed against her stomach. Even with all the issues, she was happy that their baby was in place. She could feel a surge of love. There was no numbness. This baby was loved already.

The warm water was relaxing her muscles and letting all the tension dissolve away. Wine would have been perfect. Chocolate would just have to do.

It was the little things. The little things that showed he was considering her again. She just had to see where that would take them.

Addison finally appeared at the doorway a few hours later. Caleb had just thrown Tristan over his shoulder for the last time.

'Hey, how are you feeling?' The empty wine glass was in her hands.

'Good. Thank you. The bath was great.' She did look better. There was a little more colour in her cheeks and she'd changed into a bright green short dress scattered with tiny sequins.

'How about we take it easy tonight too? Do you want to order room service?'

Tristan wriggled around in his dad's arms. 'We're going in the shower. And then I'm getting some sausages.' He pointed over at the bungalow on the water. 'Can we all sleep in there tonight? We haven't yet and I want to watch the fishes.'

Caleb shrugged. He didn't want to do anything that would tax her, but room service and crossing the walkway to the water bungalow should be fine. 'What do you think? We could all just sleep in the big bed?'

She hesitated. 'What if Tristan wakes up in the night and wanders out? I'd hate for anything to happen.'

Caleb nodded. 'Let me check. Although we haven't been using our locks much around here, I'm sure there is a lock on the bungalow door. We could lock it for through the night and that way we know he's safe with us.'

She gave a little smile. 'Yeah, that sounds good. It might be nice to listen to the sea while we're in bed.'

'Right, then, I'm going to throw us in the shower and we'll be back to order dinner soon.'

Half an hour later they were sitting at the table in the over-water bungalow eating dinner. They'd both gone for the speciality fish of the day—red tuna—and Tristan was happy with his sausages, potatoes and peas. There were a few other families on the beach and the staff came out and set up the screen for the film.

'What is it tonight?' asked Addison. 'Do you know?'

He gave a little laugh. 'I think it's *Jaws*.'

Her mouth fell open. 'It is not. No way. They can't show that on an island where sharks are around every day.'

He smiled. 'Okay, maybe it's not. I think it's a comedy about weddings.'

She flung her napkin at him. 'Rat fink.' She shook her

head. 'I love those kinds of films, but I'm just too tired. Do you mind missing it?'

'Of course not. Anyway, I've moved things around a little inside. We won't need to watch a film.'

Tristan was looking very pleased with himself. 'I helped Daddy.' He looked over his shoulder. 'But don't tell anyone we've done it.'

Now, she was definitely curious. She hadn't been back inside the over-water bungalow lately. 'What on earth have you two done?'

Caleb and Tristan bumped elbows and gave each other conspiratorial glances. 'Let's wait until after dinner,' said Caleb. 'We'll keep it as a surprise.'

Addison gave a nod. It was so nice seeing them like this. There was no getting away from the fact that, like a lot of little boys, Tristan hero-worshipped his dad. Had she got in the way of that? She'd stopped trying to organise time for them both together. She'd used to attend a yoga class once a week and they'd always had some time alone then. But after missing a few classes she'd stopped making the effort and the time for the two of them had been lost.

Now, Tristan was in his element as he had his father's full attention. Which was exactly how it should be.

Caleb stretched his hand across the table and gave her hand a squeeze. 'You feeling okay?'

'I'm good. I don't know what happened earlier. Maybe it was the heat? Or maybe it was something I ate.'

His face was shaded from the sun lowering in the sky, but it couldn't hide his intense brown eyes that were fixed on her. She was trying to deflect—and he wasn't buying it for a second.

He hadn't moved his hand. It stayed exactly where it was. 'You won't let me get you checked over by a doctor?'

She shook her head. That was the last thing she wanted.

She knew exactly what was wrong with her—she just wasn't ready to share. But the fact that she could see on his face that he was truly worried about her gave her a warm little glow.

At first she'd been so mixed up, so confused. She'd needed time to process what Dr Mackay had told her. And none of her initial decisions had changed but she was gradually becoming calmer.

If her baby had Down's syndrome she would cope. She'd been given an early warning. She would have time to prepare. Time to speak to Dr Mackay at length and have her other scans carried out. If there were heart issues, hearing or vision problems, then she'd have to prepare herself for what lay ahead.

One thing was for certain. She already loved this child. It was part of Caleb and it was part of her.

She put her best smile on her face. 'I don't need to be checked over. I'm fine.'

He slowly pulled his hand away. 'I've changed our booking for the snorkelling. It was supposed to be tomorrow but I thought we could delay it for a few days. Just until you're sure everything's fine.'

He was being cautious. He was being careful with her.

'We'll just have a day on the beach tomorrow, or around the pool. Tristan can jump around in the kids' club for a while and I'll entertain him for the rest of the day. You could go to the resort spa if you wanted to.'

What a nice thought. On a regular day she'd love a massage or manicure. But after the day she'd had she wasn't ready for anything like that. And she wasn't entirely sure if some of the massage oils were suitable for use in pregnancy. This was a small place. If she asked the question word could get out.

She shook her head. 'Not tomorrow. But maybe next

week. A day at the pool sounds good. You know what? I might even make you buy me a piece of that chocolate cake.'

He gave her a careful nod. It was obvious he was prepared to give her a little leeway right now. And she'd take it.

She was beginning to see flashes of the Caleb that she'd fallen in love with again. It was reminding her of exactly what could lie ahead.

He was attentive again. He was talking to her, *really* talking to her, without having a hundred business deals in his head. He was looking at her again as if she actually existed, instead of just being part of the furniture.

Things were moving in the right direction.

But was this a permanent change or just a temporary holiday arrangement?

Addison's face was a picture. 'How on earth did you do this?'

He and Tristan exchanged proud looks. They'd rearranged the whole over-water bungalow. The key feature in the bungalow was the glass panel, normally housed beneath the coffee table, which showed the underwater activity in the coral beneath the bungalow. Tristan loved it. And Caleb loved it too. He'd never seen fish like it. Every colour under the rainbow, some darting past, some spending hours around the coral.

So, he'd managed to upend the giant bed onto its side and push it through from the bedroom into the living room. Then he'd dragged the sofa back through to the other room. Now, they could lie in bed tonight and watch the fish swim right in front of them.

Addison raised her eyebrows. 'Do you think we'll get in trouble?'

He winked. 'I won't tell if you won't.'

She held out her hand to Tristan. 'Want to go and get ready for bed, buster?'

He jumped up and down. 'I'm going to watch the fishes all night!'

It didn't take long for them to get ready. They changed for bed, closed up the beach bungalow and took along a few snacks. Caleb held up the bottle of wine he'd grabbed from the fridge. 'Want a glass of wine?'

Addison glanced at Tristan. 'No, not tonight. I'll just have some water.' She walked over and plucked the giant bag of crisps from his hand. 'But I might take charge of these. I don't want crumbs in the bed.'

It didn't take them long to be tucked up in the giant bed. They locked the main door but left the curtains open so they could watch the spectacular sunset, shooting reds and oranges across the darkening sky.

Tristan shouted every time he saw a new fish. By the time his eyelids were starting to droop he'd given them all names. He crawled back up into the middle of the bed and zonked out.

Addison was lying facing Caleb, Tristan's head between them.

'What do we do now?' she teased. Her blonde hair had fallen over her face and her bare shoulder was revealed with only the tiny spaghetti strap of her satin nightie showing.

He groaned. 'Don't even go there. We're stuck—locked in our water bungalow—with a sleeping four-year-old between us.' He lifted up his hands and laughed. 'I couldn't make this up if I tried.'

The last rays of the sun were illuminating the dark sky behind her. For once the shadows were gone from her eyes. She didn't look tired. She just looked relaxed.

'I'm sorry I haven't been around,' he whispered.

She licked her lips. 'Sorry can be easy to say, Caleb. What happens when we get home?'

There was a little flutter inside his chest. 'I wasn't sure you were coming home.'

'Neither was I.' She gave her head the slightest shake. 'I need to be sure.'

'Sure about what? Sure that I love you? Of course I do. I always have. I always will.'

Her eyes filled up.

'Addison, tell me what's going on.' He kept the frustration out of his voice. He kept his tone neutral.

Her jaw tightened. Seconds before she'd been happy. Seconds before she'd been relaxed. Why had he even started this? He should have left her alone. He should have been happy that they'd all ended up in bed together as a family. After the day she'd had, it should have been enough.

She lifted her hands. '*This* is what's going on. Us.'

He felt every muscle in his body tighten. He wasn't going to get angry. He wasn't. No matter how frustrated he felt.

Instead he stroked his finger down her arm. Lightly. Gently. None of the things that he felt right now, but everything he had to show his wife.

When he reached her hand, he slid his palm over her hand and intertwined their fingers. 'This is us,' he whispered. 'This is exactly us.'

A tear escaped down her cheek. 'I hope so,' she whispered before she closed her eyes and went to sleep.

CHAPTER SIX

CALEB HAD BEEN tiptoeing around her for the last three days. They'd virtually done nothing apart from eat food, take Tristan to kids' club for a few hours, walk around the resort and relax in the shade.

She'd finished three books. If she kept going like this she'd have to wander around the pool and steal someone else's book while they were in swimming.

They'd slept in the over-water bungalow for two nights and then eventually gone back to the beach bungalow after Tristan had tried sleeping like a starfish. Tristan had slept in his own room and Caleb had cuddled in behind her with his arms around her.

When they walked around the resort he held her hand or had his arm around her shoulder.

The waiter arrived with breakfast as usual. Because she felt so rested she'd been up early this morning and was ravenous. Caleb had gone for a run along the beach and came back with the sweat dripping from him.

He emerged from the shower towelling his hair and grinned at her heaped plate of scrambled eggs with toast. Tristan was lining up all his sausages in a row to match his toast soldiers. 'Is there anything left?'

She shook her head. 'We decided to put you on a diet. Coffee only.'

He laughed and poured himself a cup before finding his breakfast hidden under a silver dome. 'Better eat up quickly, Tristan, we're going snorkelling this morning.'

Tristan's eyes lit up. 'Snorkelling? Yeah! Will we find Nemo?'

Caleb gave her a little wink. 'I have it on good authority that there definitely should be a whole school of Nemos where we're going.'

Tristan opened the picture book they'd bought him of all the different fish around the island. He pointed to the bright orange and white clown fish. 'That's Nemo,' he said seriously to Addison. 'That's the one I'm looking for.'

'Doesn't he sometimes hide in the sea anemones?'

Tristan looked over his shoulder. 'Only if a barracuda is about. They can be very bad.'

Addison nodded. He was so serious. He was going to love today.

She flung some things together into a bag.

Caleb appeared behind her. 'Are you sure you're okay with this? You don't need to come if you don't want to.'

She grabbed her floppy hat. 'It's only two hours and it's quite close by. I think it'll be fine. If I don't feel well, I'll let you know.'

There were eight other people waiting to board the white boat to the nearby coral reef. They were a happy bunch, all clutching onto small snorkels and goggles. The journey across the lagoon to one of the small atolls only took five minutes. Once they arrived they had the option of joining the snorkelling or staying on the nearby beach.

Addison had dressed carefully. She was wearing a swimming costume, black with white panels at the side, which gave the illusion that her waist hadn't thickened quite as much as it had. She wouldn't slip her dress off until the last minute, and hopefully, since she'd be in waist-high water, nothing would be noticed.

Tristan was jumping around. He was wearing an all-in-one, which meant she didn't need to put quite so much sunscreen on as before.

As soon as they arrived, Caleb jumped into the water with the rest of the adults and held his hands out for Tristan. Perfect. It gave her time to get into the water unobserved.

The coral was beautiful. Jaggy in places, but the boat crew gave them some plastic shoes for their feet.

All the tourists spread out amongst the coral reef, keeping relatively still so as not to scare any marine life away. But there was no need to worry—the marine life was abundant.

It took Tristan a few goes to get the hang of using the snorkel. Once he'd figured out he could breathe with his head under the water he loved it.

Addison had lowered herself into the water as Caleb taught Tristan how to use his snorkel. By the time she reached them they were in slightly deeper water with it almost reaching their shoulders.

'Hey, guys, this is great.'

Caleb reached out and hugged her with his spare arm. He was holding onto Tristan with the other.

Tristan's head bobbed back up. 'I think I've just seen Nemo!' he exclaimed.

They all put their heads back under just in time to see a cluster of orange and white clown fish dart around the coral reef. Addison had her camera and took a quick snap.

It seemed that Tristan had memorised the whole book of tropical reef fish. He could name just about all of them. By the time they'd finished he'd spotted blue and yellow scribbled angel fish, orange spiny squirrel fish, blue and orange majestic angelfish and yellow trumpet fish. Addison snapped as many pictures as she could.

It was easy. It was relaxing. At one point Caleb grabbed her around the waist and planted a kiss on her lips, then laughed at her shocked expression. 'Last time I kissed you, you fainted. I thought at least if I kissed you in water it might break your fall.' He leaned forward and pressed his forehead against hers. 'It seems I make women weak at the knees.'

She thudded her hand off his chest. 'And I was just trying to improve your reflexes. It's said they get slower with age. What age are you next birthday?'

This was what they used to be like. Teasing each other constantly. And she'd missed that. More than she'd even realised.

The guide shouted everyone back to the boat. Addison had a mild moment of panic that she'd be right next to Caleb and he might notice her changing figure. She needed to tell him. And she needed to tell him soon.

But as they moved towards the boat the other tourists separated them. She was able to climb back on board and slip her dress over her head before reaching down to grab Tristan.

The journey back was quick and after a shower they dropped Tristan off at kids' club for a few hours.

'What do you want to do today?' asked Caleb.

He looked totally chilled, totally relaxed. He was strolling along in a pair of knee-length khaki shorts and a short-sleeved white shirt, with his hair still damp from the shower. His skin was starting to turn a golden brown colour—the shade that her paler skin would never reach. It made him suit his white shirt all the more and she could see the admiring glances from some other passers-by. She couldn't resist teasing him some more.

She turned towards him. 'I think I want to be bad.'

He almost tripped over his own feet. His hands shot out from his pockets. 'What?'

She stepped right up in front of him, momentarily sucking her stomach in, and pressing her body against his. As soon as she moved the telltale gleam appeared in his eyes.

She ran one finger up from his waist to his chest. 'I think I want some chocolate cake.' She stepped back and laughed.

He shook his head and started laughing too. He stuck his hands back in his pockets and walked past her. 'Just for that,' he growled playfully over his shoulder, 'there'll be no chocolate cake for you.'

She kept laughing and ran to catch up with him, tucking her arm in his as they walked to the patisserie.

'Coffee?' he asked as he grabbed a tray.

She shook her head. 'No, decaf tea for me.'

He bent down and glanced behind her.

'What are you doing?'

He stood back up. 'Who are you and what have you done with my coffee-addicted wife?'

She shrugged. 'I fancied a change.'

'Just as long as that's all you're changing,' he shot back as he placed their order.

Her stomach gave a little flip-flop. He was joking. She knew he was. But she also realised how her actions were affecting him. He might look relaxed and chilled, but things were obviously still preying on his mind as much as they were hers.

She'd seen the change in him. She'd seen the improvement. She finally felt as if she was recapturing a little of what they'd lost. She just needed to know it would continue when they got back home. It was amazing how different he could be when he wasn't permanently attached to his work.

They sat down at a shaded table next to the lagoon. One of the resort staff was putting leaflets on all the tables.

Addison picked one up.

'What is it?' asked Caleb as he set down the cakes and drinks.

She turned it around to face him. 'It's a ball at the resort next door. Apparently they do it every year to support breast cancer.'

He gave her a smile. 'Did they know you were coming? You won't be able to resist something like that.'

He reached over to read the leaflet. 'What do you think?'

He was right. She couldn't usually resist a chance to support a fellow cancer charity. 'I didn't exactly bring any clothes suitable for a ball. And I'm quite sure you didn't either.'

He gave a nod. 'You could be right. I think I'm going to run out of socks before we get home.'

'And I'm quite sure they won't allow kids at a ball. Isn't the resort next door for adults only?'

He nodded. 'Yeah. I hadn't thought about that. But they do have a babysitting service here. If it was someone we trusted—like the girls from the kids' club—maybe we could arrange that?'

Addison took her first bite of the chocolate cake. Wow. She sagged back into her seat.

Caleb raised his eyebrows. 'That good?'

She nodded and his fork was over in an instant, swiping a piece of her cake. 'Hey!'

He put it in his mouth quickly and she watched his face. When the taste hit he sagged back in his chair too. 'Oh,' was all he said.

'Yip, oh.'

He gave her a cheeky wink and lifted up his lemon tart. 'How about a swap?'

She picked up her plate and held it close to her chest. 'Not a chance. Get your own.'

He put down his own fork and pushed his plate away. 'Nope. Can't eat that now. It's a poor second place. I'll make do with the coffee.'

She grinned at him. 'I hope you aren't trying to guilt me into sharing.'

He shook his head. 'I know you too well for that.'

One of the staff walked past and paused when she saw his plate. 'You didn't like the lemon tart?'

He hesitated. Obviously a bit embarrassed. He hadn't even had a chance to reply before the ever-efficient member of staff picked up the plate. 'Shall I swap it for something else?'

She was facing Caleb and had her back to Addison.

She scowled at him and mouthed *don't you dare*. But he shot the woman a beaming smile and nodded, pointing at Addison's plate. 'Could I have a piece of the chocolate cake the same as my wife, please?'

She gave a nod and hurried off.

Addison leaned across the table towards him. 'I can't believe you got away with that.'

He laughed. 'Neither can I.'

The staff member brought the cake back and nodded to the leaflet on their table. 'Oh, the ball. It's fabulous. We wouldn't normally publicise an event at another resort, but this one is special and it is for charity. Are you going to go?'

Addison smiled. 'We'd love to, but we didn't exactly bring any clothes suitable to wear to a ball—' she pointed towards Caleb's shorts and her sundress '—and we'd need to find a babysitter for our son.'

Caleb gave her a quick wink and pulled the chocolate cake towards him, taking his first forkful.

The staff member waved her hand. 'Oh, don't worry about clothes. Most people don't bring anything special. We have somewhere you can hire clothes. There are dresses suitable for a ball—' she turned towards Caleb, whose mouth was currently full of chocolate cake '—and suits for the gentlemen. And we have a babysitter service at the resort. It comes highly recommended. You can even request which sitter you get.'

Caleb swallowed quickly and leaned forward. 'Do either of the staff from the kids' club do the sitter service?'

She gave a nod. 'Yes. Both Kohia and Desere work for the sitter service. You could request either one of them.' She took a final glance over to Caleb. 'Ah, you prefer the chocolate cake?'

He gave her a big smile and Addison tried not to laugh.

'Thank you so much. The chocolate cake is delicious.'

He kept the smile on his face as the woman walked away and then the two of them dissolved into laughter.

'Shh,' hissed Addison. 'You'll get us banned from the best cake shop on the island.'

Caleb sat straight up in his chair. 'Don't say that. I don't think I could stand it.'

Other people were looking at them now, wondering what they were laughing about.

Addison shook her head and picked up her fork and waved it at him. 'If I had to choose between you and this cake it could be a hard pick.' She took another quick bite. She was nearly done.

Caleb took another bite too, then stood up and grabbed her hand, pulling her straight up against him. 'Mrs Connor, that's a terrible thing to say to your husband.' He had that twinkle in his eye. The one that did crazy things to her.

She wrapped her hands around his neck. 'Mr Connor, people are watching.'

He gave her a squeeze. 'So they are. What are we going to do about it?' He was nuzzling in at her neck now. The electricity could light up a whole resort.

They were practically making out in front of the rest of the customers. 'Run,' she whispered.

And they did.

Straight back to their over-water bungalow.

CHAPTER SEVEN

HE WAS STILL nuzzling at her neck an hour later. 'What time is it?'

'Time we picked up our son.'

They'd just about made it back inside. She dreaded to think what items of clothing might have fluttered past others on an ocean breeze.

If he'd noticed any change in her figure he hadn't mentioned it but, the truth was, she might have distracted him.

'Please tell me tonight's film is suitable viewing for a kid,' he mumbled.

They were lucky. It was. They sat on the beach with Tristan sitting at their feet. He watched part of the old Hollywood musical that was showing, then proceeded to play with his wrestlers.

She was lucky too. It was the same waiter that served them and as he bent to ask her what she wanted, he gave her an unobtrusive wink and asked, 'No mint?'

She gave a nod and when the drink arrived she could tell it was alcohol free. Perfect.

Except it wasn't perfect. She wanted to be honest with her husband. She wanted to tell him the truth. But he'd been trying so hard these last few days. They were recapturing everything she wanted to and there was no mistaking that the little part inside that she'd thought had died or gone numb was very much alive. Every day she fell a little in love with her husband again.

She was afraid that when she told him the truth they'd be plummeted back to reality. Back to the fact that this baby could be at risk. Back to getting their heads around the real world, the plans they might need to make and consider.

Before, she'd just been angry. Angry that this had happened to her and angry that she couldn't share with her husband because he was never around.

Leaving and doing this on her own had actually seemed like the simplest option.

But that was because she wasn't allowing her heart to enter the equation. Practicalities could be so much simpler. But practicalities came without the emotional support that every person needed.

What she needed was the husband she had beside her right now. The husband that was caring, attentive and obviously loved his family. Could they just stay here for ever, trapped in this little bubble?

She sighed and put her head down onto her knees. Even her daydreams were stupid. A place with no phone or Internet wouldn't be any use. She didn't even know what kind of medical facilities they had on the island.

His work wasn't here and her charity wasn't here. No. Her brain wasn't even going to allow her to have that daydream for a few seconds.

She put her head up just in time to see the hero and heroine of the musical dancing in each other's arms. They were quietly singing to each other.

Her heart gave a little squeeze. It was clear from the heroine's expression on her face she was wishing for something she couldn't have. Was that what she was doing too?

She picked up her drink and took a quick sip to ease her

dry throat. She didn't really want that to happen to her. She wanted to have this baby. She wanted her husband by her side, loving this baby just as much as she did. She wanted Tristan to love his baby brother or sister.

Caleb chose that moment to slide his hand up her back. 'Hey, what's wrong?'

He glanced at the screen and smiled. 'Wanna dance? Want me to sing to you?'

She laughed. 'Please no. No one deserves that.' She shifted position and let her head fall on his shoulder.

Soon. She'd tell him soon.

CHAPTER EIGHT

'HOW ARE YOU FEELING?'

He'd made plans for them today but wanted to make sure Addison was fit enough.

She leaned up in the bed and rested her head on her hand. The smallest action and it gave him a little pang. When they'd first married Addison's still-sleepy face had been his favourite sight first thing in the morning. These days he always left before her alarm had even sounded. He missed that look.

'I'm fine. What's up?'

He moved over and sat at the side of the bed. 'I'd made plans for us to take a tour of the island today.'

'On a boat again?'

'No. On that single track they call a road,' he joked. 'Apparently they take us in a four-by-four. It takes us part way up the mountain, around the lagoon and, if you want, we can take a little walk into the jungle. But if you don't feel up to it, it's fine. I can cancel.'

She shook her head and sat up in the bed. 'I told you, I'm fine. Too much sun and too little food—that's all it was. What time do we go?'

He smiled. She wanted to go. She even seemed pleased. Little by little it felt as if they were reconnecting again. She didn't seem quite so angry any more. Every day she was a little more relaxed. A little more open to his touches and gestures.

'In around an hour. We have plenty of time for breakfast.'

She drank tea again. It was becoming a habit. He could hardly believe she'd stopped drinking coffee. But at least she ate some breakfast: some eggs and a croissant with butter and jam.

An hour later they were ready to go. Addison had her floppy hat with light baggy trousers and a green strappy top. Her sunglasses were already on her face and she'd covered them all in suncream. Tristan had insisted on bringing a wrestler with him and they all bought bottles of water before they left the resort.

As they waited outside Reception an older-style four-by-four screeched up next to them and their exuberant guide jumped out. 'Connor family? Welcome to the land tour of Bora Bora!'

Addison raised her eyebrow at Caleb and grabbed hold of Tristan's hand. 'Yes, that's us.'

'I'm Hiro, your guide. Jump on, folks, you're going to have the time of your lives!'

Caleb helped Tristan and Addison up into the four-by-four and gave Hiro a nod as he climbed on board. He'd barely sat down before the Jeep took off again. They picked up another couple at the next resort then Hiro gave them some maps for their tour.

'We have lots in store today. We'll meet another two cars on the way. We'll head up the mountain first to catch some spectacular views, then we'll take a tour of some World War II relics left on the island and some ancient religious sites. We also plan a little tour into the jungle to show off some of the island's natural fauna. If anyone has anywhere particular they want to go, let us know. We're flexible.'

Addison smiled and sat back in her seat. Caleb double-checked Tristan's seat belt and held onto the handle on the door. 'Watch out for the bumpy roads,' shouted Hiro as they took off again.

'They're not kidding,' said Addison under her breath as they bumped along. The resort staff had already told them that the road around the lagoon and the few inland roads had been cut out by the US military during World War II to allow the transportation of cannons and ammunition.

The journey part way up Mount Otemanu was entertaining. Hiro pointed up above them. 'Our beautiful lady is believed to have been formed from two volcanoes that rose from the ocean floor seven million years ago. She is mainly unspoilt.' They stopped part way up the mountain and Hiro turned his attention to Tristan.

'I have a little story for you, young man.'

Tristan's eyes widened. It was clear he was mesmerised by their cheerful guide. Hiro reached over and picked Tristan up, turning him around to look up at the green-covered peak. 'Look closely. Do you see that cave, half-way up the mountain?'

They all followed his gaze. Sure enough, a gap in the greenery revealed a cave in the side of the mountain. 'It's a very special cave,' he said proudly. 'It's called Te Ana Opea. Some people call it the clinging cave.' He moved his face closer to Tristan's. 'I'll tell you a secret,' he said in a pretend whisper.

'What?' Tristan's eyes were still wide.

Hiro was delighted with his audience. The man was a true performer. 'There's a legend in Bora Bora that a couple who stayed in the cave had a child with the body of a human and a head…' he paused, building excitement '…of a centipede!'

Tristan gasped and put his hand over his mouth. 'Can I see it? Can I see it?'

Hiro, the storyteller, lowered his voice again. 'No one has ever seen it. But the centipede's name was Veri and legend has it that every night the terrifying screams of a child can be heard coming from the cave.'

Caleb shot a look at Addison. Would she be annoyed that Hiro was going to give their child nightmares? But she was taking it in the humour it was given. She was shaking her head and smiling. Tristan started to smile too.

He pushed Hiro's shoulder. 'You're kidding.'

Hiro shrugged. 'Just listen tonight. See if you can hear anything.'

They stopped a little further down the mountain where there was a gap and Hiro pointed out the panoramic view of several privately owned *motu*s. Several belonged to long-standing island families but others were owned by billionaires and rock stars.

Addison turned to Caleb and gave him a nudge. 'Buy me a *motu*, Caleb. I want my own little island, palm trees, white beach and clear blue water all around.'

Hiro laughed. 'For the smallest *motu*, it costs around a million dollars. Good luck, my friend.'

Caleb slung his arm around Addison's shoulders. 'Sorry, honey, I guess you're going to have to make do with a rock—or maybe even a boulder.'

Hiro winked at him. 'We can help you out with something else a little later.'

The Jeep started again and Addison frowned. 'What on earth is he talking about?'

Caleb shook his head. 'I have no idea. Maybe I should get worried.'

Next stop was at the edge of the jungle. Hiro handed out hats to the guests who didn't have one. 'You need one to keep the bugs off,' he said.

Caleb dug into his pocket and pulled out Tristan's base-ball cap with the flap at the back for his neck. Addison already had her hat and he smiled at the one Hiro handed to him. 'Think I look like Indiana Jones in this?'

She almost snorted. 'Let me tell you, if we get into this jungle and get chased by a giant ball or strange people shoot poison darts at us, you're in trouble.'

He shrugged. 'You forget. I know what your weakness is now. I can get out of just about anything with a piece of that chocolate cake.'

Hiro led them slowly on a well-worn path through the jungle. Caleb had been afraid that Tristan might be a little bored on the tour but Hiro went out of his way to enter-tain their son. As they wound their way through the dark green trees he slid his hand into Addison's. She didn't object; in fact, she seemed to start chatting even more.

The jungle was full of things they would never have found on their own. Hiro pointed out ginger, ylang-ylang, vanilla, wild hibiscus, mango and coconut trees. 'Once we get back to the road, we'll find the stall with the real frozen coconuts and you can taste how delicious they re-ally are.'

'Where does he get his energy from?' whispered Ad-dison. 'He's like a supercharged battery.'

Caleb nodded. 'I know he whispered to Tristan earlier, but I kind of wish I could turn down the volume a little. I'm exhausted just listening to him.' He looked down to Addison. They'd been in the jungle for about twenty min-utes now and the heat was slowly building around them. 'Hey, are you feeling okay?'

She slapped her hand gently against his chest. 'Quit fussing. I'm fine.'

He pretended to stagger. 'Hey, I just want to check that you'll be able to carry me out of here.'

She laughed. 'Not a chance. And anyway—' she glanced over her shoulder to see if anyone else was listening '—if I manage to shake you off in here I get to eat all the chocolate cake myself.'

He stopped dead and pressed his hand against his heart. 'Oh, no. That's brutal.'

She raised her eyebrows. 'You married a mercenary. Live with it.'

Tristan had walked on with Hiro and they'd stopped just ahead. 'Welcome,' shouted Hiro, 'to one of my favourite archaeological sites on the islands. The turtle petroglyphs.'

They all stepped forward. Giant boulders were sitting next to a little rock pool. The ancient carvings of turtles were faint but clearly visible. Some of the boulders were grey and some were clearly coral.

'How on earth did they get them up here?' asked Addison.

Hiro tapped his nose. 'No one actually knows. It's a mystery. They think they've been here for over a thousand years.' He threw up his hands. 'Imagine, a thousand years ago someone sitting in the jungle, carving this turtle with such care and attention to detail. A thousand years later it is still here. What do we have today that we think will survive a thousand years?'

'This place is amazing,' whispered Addison. 'I can almost picture someone doing it.'

Caleb smiled. She was enjoying this. He'd been a little nervous that it wouldn't have lived up to expectations and they should actually just have spent the day on the beach, but Hiro was an entertaining guide and no part of the tour had been too taxing yet. He dropped a kiss on her head but then she surprised him. She tilted her chin up to him and kissed him on the mouth.

It was the briefest kiss—only a second. But it sent a jolt straight through him. A buzz. A connection. Something he'd been longing for since she'd looked him in eye and given him that ultimatum. Since he'd realised he was in danger of losing his wife, losing his family.

And the buzz had been initiated by her. It was almost a relief. She still felt something. There was something still there.

He'd been worried. Addison seemed to have put up invisible barriers. Ones that he had no idea how to penetrate or break down. Maybe they weren't quite so impenetrable as he feared.

He needed to talk to her. He needed to tell her why he'd been avoiding her. Why he'd been avoiding the conversation about more kids. Nothing would make him happier than to have another Tristan running around. He just didn't want to lose his wife in the process. If it was the choice between Addison or more kids, she would win every time.

Their walk back through the jungle to the road was at a leisurely pace. Hiro piled them all back into the Jeep and drove just a little further down to one of the roadside stalls. There, they all sampled the half-coconuts, filled with frozen and iced coconut. It was delicious. But after a few sips through a straw Addison handed hers back over and made a face.

'You don't like it?'

Hiro pulled a flask from his back pocket. 'Would you like to add some rum?'

The other guests held out their coconuts straight away.

'What do you think?' Caleb smiled at Addison. 'Might make it more appealing.'

She shook her head. 'No, no, thanks. Not for me.'

He shrugged and finished his drink quickly. The rest of the tour moved along at a pleasant pace. Hiro showed them a huge variety of guns and cannons left from World War II. They were dotted all over the island. Then he drove them down a narrow winding road that ran along the edge of the island.

'Any idea where we're going?' Addison put her head on Caleb's shoulder.

Caleb shook his head. 'I'm guessing that this is the magical-mystery part of the tour.'

It didn't take long for a sign to come into view. 'Here we are,' shouted Hiro. 'Welcome to my family pearl farm.'

He ushered them out of the Jeep and into the nearby shop sitting right on the edge of the lagoon. It was a perfect setting and as they watched some other tourists with snorkels and masks appeared at the wooden jetty in the water. All were clutching something in their hands.

'What are they doing, Daddy?' asked Tristan.

It didn't take long to realise. He knelt down next to his son. 'I think they've been diving in the lagoon for oysters.'

'What do you need an oyster for?' Tristan looked confused.

Addison gave a knowing smile. 'This place is called a pearl farm, honey. Some of those oysters will contain black pearls, like the ones on that sign—' she pointed next to her '—or like the ones in the cabinet over there.'

Even though it was afternoon and the sun was high in the sky, Hiro's energy hadn't diminished at all. 'Who would like to dive for their own pearl? I have equipment here that you can all use. Come on over, folks.'

Addison had moved across to the glass-fronted cabinets showing all the black-pearl jewellery. It was beautiful and there was a jeweller working in full view, mounting pearls in silver or gold to make a variety of items.

Tristan watched in wonder as one of the latest batch of divers came in and opened his oyster revealing a tiny black pearl.

'Can we get one, Daddy? Let's get one for Mummy.'

He bent down again. 'I'm not sure that every oyster has a pearl.'

Tristan glanced at Addison, then leaned forward and whispered, 'But let's try anyway.'

Caleb rolled his eyes. 'What do you think?' he asked Addison.

She gave a little shrug. 'Well, we're here now. I'm all for supporting local businesses.' Then she winked. 'Plus, I'm not the one that will get wet.'

Caleb grimaced as he changed into a pair of swim shorts that Hiro handed him, wondering who'd worn them before. Addison walked Tristan down the jetty and sat with her feet dangling in the water. She had a change of clothes for Tristan in her bag so just took off his socks, shoes and T-shirt and covered him in suncream. Caleb jumped into the lagoon, holding onto the jetty edge, and waited until the rest of the guests were ready too.

Hiro swam up alongside. 'I'll keep the little guy on the surface—' he handed her a kid's life jacket '—while your husband dives for the oyster.' He pulled a pair of goggles over Tristan's head. 'We'll watch your daddy go down to the bottom.'

Tristan clapped his hands with excitement. He was beginning to turn into a water baby. Not that Caleb minded. He'd never leave his four-year-old near water but both he and Addison had noticed how confident Tristan was getting. As long as one of his parents was near he would happily try and swim in the lagoon or the pool and he was doing really well. The swimming pool wasn't a place that Caleb had frequently taken his son back in London. But it was definitely something to reconsider. Addison was sitting directly above him as he bobbed in the water. 'How about we get a family membership to that new gym back home? It's got a swimming pool and I'm sure it does kids' swimming lessons.'

She tilted her head to the side and lifted her sunglasses to look at him. 'Swimming lessons would be good for him. It would be even better if we could go in the pool with him afterwards.'

'We'll both take him. Or I'll take him if you want a break.' It would be good to spend some time with Tristan alone. When he'd found out they were expecting a little boy he'd had all these great ideas about things he could do with his son. Because of work, most of them hadn't got off the ground.

Addison licked her lips and put her sunglasses back in place. 'That sounds good.'

He almost sighed with relief. She hadn't been accusatory. She hadn't mentioned all the times he'd let them down before. The tension between them definitely seemed to be lessening.

'Come on over, folks. Let's find us some pearls.'

Hiro came and put his arms around Tristan and guided the rest of the party a little way from the jetty. They treaded water for a few minutes as Hiro gave them some instructions as to where to dive to find the pearls. He made it sound relatively easy. 'These are the finest pearls in the world. The fragile black-lipped oyster, the *pinctada margaritifera*, produces our beautiful black pearls. Remember, that these pearls have taken two years to produce.' He was still holding onto Tristan. 'These pearls are one of the wonders of the world. When a tiny foreign substance gets inside an oyster it annoys it—like having an itch. Black lip oysters are very particular, they only react to one thing—a tiny round piece of oyster shell harvested from the Mississippi River. The oyster needs to scratch so it produces something called nacre. Over two years the layers of nacre build up—producing a pearl.'

He smiled widely at the people treading water around him. 'Choose carefully—' he wagged his finger '—because not every oyster will contain a pearl. And our pearls can be five different colours. Who will get a black one?'

Tristan was bobbing away happily in his life jacket, his little legs kicking beneath him. 'You have to pick the right one, Daddy,' he said seriously.

'No pressure, then?' Caleb smiled. He turned in the water towards Hiro. 'You'll take care of him while I dive? He can go back to the jetty with Addison.'

Hiro shook his head. 'He's fine with me. Go and pick the right oyster. Tristan and I will watch you. Won't we?'

Tristan nodded happily and Caleb took a few seconds to take some deep breaths. The lagoon was a little deeper here—but the oysters weren't on the bed of the lagoon; instead there were four farming sections spread out around the lagoon, each anchored by rope to a bottom. Each section had around twenty-two lines attached, with four to six oysters attached to each line. They were all invited to dive down under the supervision of Hiro, unhook one line, and then bring it to the surface to find out what was inside.

Caleb gave Addison a wave before he dived. She was leaning back on the jetty letting the sun's rays warm her face. She gave him a smile and waved back. It warmed him, spreading heat through his body in the cool water. If he didn't have a black pearl in this oyster he would keep diving until he got one. He didn't care what the cost was. It didn't matter that Addison probably didn't care either way. He wanted to do it for her. It was a tiny little thing. But for them, it would be a little piece of history. She'd have something from Bora Bora, something that he'd got for her. It was unique. Just as she was.

The guy next to him dived, quickly followed by his wife. He sucked in a deep breath and dived down through the clear water. All their other diving excursions had been in relatively shallow water. It was surprising—the light from above was almost like a spotlight inside the lagoon. He could see clearly all the way down. By the time he reached the section with lines his lungs had already started to burn a little. He unclipped the nearest line. He knew the size of the oysters had no bearing on the size of the pearl inside and he pushed back up quickly, gasping as he broke the surface.

'Daddy! What did you get?'

He let the water stream off his face and took a few breaths. Hiro gave him a nod. It only took a few moments for the rest of the participants to surface. 'Everyone back over to the jetty and we'll go inside to open the oysters.'

Caleb kept pace with Hiro as he swam Tristan back to the jetty. Addison lifted their son out of the water, towelling him dry and changing his clothes.

Caleb raised his eyebrows, gave a shudder and tugged at his swim shorts. 'Give me two minutes until I get into my own clothes.' He ducked into the changing room at the shop and quickly pulled his T-shirt and shorts back on. He was still wet but didn't really care. When he came out Tristan and Addison were standing next to one of the counters talking to a female assistant.

'Look, Daddy, this is yours.'

Tristan pointed proudly at one of the oysters and Addison folded her arms and teased, 'If it's empty, you're in trouble.'

The female assistant gave him a nod. 'I'm Meherio. I'm going to show you how we harvest the oysters.' She picked up the one that Caleb had brought ashore and gave them all a smile. 'This little beauty is yours and we have to treat it with care.'

She took a few minutes gently clamping the oyster into a vice. Then, she pried the bivalve open just enough to gently fish around to find the gem. She turned to them and whispered, 'We do this carefully because a good oyster can keep creating pearls for up to seven years. Our pearls actually come in five colours—blue, green, eggplant, peacock and gold. Only a few pearls are actually black. Most are a dark shade of green.'

Caleb realised he was holding his breath as she gently manoeuvred the pearl out from the oyster. He glanced towards Addison and Tristan, who were both holding their breaths and had their hands clasped in front of their chests. He couldn't resist; he pulled out his phone and snapped a picture.

'It's black!' shouted Tristan. 'It's black.'

'Not quite,' said Meherio as she held it between tweezers and inspected it in the light. 'But it's almost there.' She laid the pearl down on a piece of velvet in front of them.

It was odd. It was as if they were all mesmerised by the pearl he'd pulled from the lagoon. Meherio was obviously used to the effect the pearls had on people. She kept talking in a low voice. 'The lustre or reflective quality of the pearl's surface, along with its number of imperfections, are the key in determining its value.' She pulled out a ruler and measured the pearl. 'It's large.' Her smile was wide, revealing her perfect white teeth. 'Around fifteen millimetres.'

'Can I touch it?' Addison asked, her finger poised above it.

'Of course,' said Meherio. 'It's yours.' She glanced at Caleb. 'At least I expect it is.'

Caleb bent over to watch as she rolled the pearl gently on the velvet. It looked like an oil spill, with a rainbow of colours reflecting across its surface depending on the way she tilted it.

'Would you like to take it the way it is, or make it into a piece of jewellery? Our own jeweller can give you advice on what would work best for your pearl.'

'A necklace.'

They both said it at once.

Their gazes met, smiles on both of their faces. For a few seconds everything felt perfect between them. Everything felt the way it should. The way it was supposed to be.

This was the woman he loved with his whole heart. He could never imagine her not being in his life. He could never love anyone else the way he loved Addison.

It was simple.

They were meant to be.

He threaded his fingers through hers. 'Would your jeweller be able to mount the pearl for us?'

Meherio indicated the other side of the store. 'Come with me. You can choose silver or gold and our jeweller will mount the pearl for you while you watch.'

Caleb felt in his shorts pocket for his credit card. He didn't really care what the cost of all this was going to be. For him the experience was already priceless.

Addison stood watching as the jeweller worked, leaning back against Caleb. His hand snaked around her middle. He liked this. He liked the fact that she felt comfortable enough to not think about what she was doing, but after a few seconds she closed her hand over his and moved his hand a little upwards.

He had a quick glance around the shop. He could hardly touch his wife's breast in public. So he just laughed and nuzzled in at her neck. 'Are you sure you didn't have any rum?'

She turned around towards him. 'Oh, I'm sure.' She paused for a second. 'Thank you.'

'What for?'

'For this. For today. It's felt…different.'

The jeweller gave him a nod and held up the pearl pendant on a long gold chain that Addison had chosen. 'Thank you,' said Caleb as he took it.

He moved behind her again and swept her hair away from the back of her neck. She looked up into the mirror in front of them, watching his actions with a hint of a smile. He opened the clasp on the chain and held the pendant in front of her, bringing it back slowly until it touched her skin. She didn't move. Didn't touch it. Just kept watching him in the mirror.

He lowered the pendant oh-so-slowly until it rested just above her cleavage, and fastened the clasp. Even from this position he could see the lustre and rainbow of reflections as her chest moved up and down with her breaths.

She was still watching him in the mirror. 'Thank you,' she said softly, in a voice that felt only for him. 'I love it.'

He bent to her ear and put his hands on her shoulders. 'You're worth it. You're worth a thousand of them.'

This was what was important.

This was the message he was trying to get through

to his wife. He could see in the mirror that she was staring off into the distance now—as if her mind was lost on something else.

Was she really listening?

CHAPTER NINE

'THIS WAY, MADAM. I'm sure we'll have something to suit you.'

As they opened the door to the room Addison was nearly blinded by sequins. Dozens of full-length dresses hung from hangers evenly spaced around the walls.

Addison held up her hands. 'Where did you get all these?'

Marisha, the resort employee, shrugged. 'Some people bring them on holiday, learn about the ball and decide to leave them behind. We had one holidaymaker who worked as a designer in New York. She sent us some dresses as a gift. Another woman worked in a designer boutique that was going to close. They shipped us all their remaining stock.'

Addison was smiling like a kid in a sweetie shop. 'This is fantastic. So, I just try a few, pick one and pay the hire fee?'

Marisha nodded. She pointed to a rack in the corner. 'Those dresses are already reserved.' Then she held out her hands. 'Everything else is yours to choose from.' She walked over to a rail. 'We arrange by size. So, find your size, pick a dress you like and feel free to try it on.'

Addison nodded and moved over to the rails quickly finding her size. These dresses were every bit as beautiful as anything she had at home. She picked up a floor-length red dress. Red wasn't usually a colour that she wore. 'Can I try this one?'

Marisha swished open a set of deep purple velvet curtains. The opposite wall was covered in long mirrors. 'You can try in here. Do you need a hand?'

Addison shook her head just as the pager at Marisha's belt sounded. She glanced at it. 'If you're fine, I'll go and check what this is and be back in five minutes.'

Addison smiled. 'No problem. I'm sure I'll still be here.'

She closed the curtain behind her and slipped off her clothes. The dress was heavier than it looked on the hanger—probably because of the amount of sequins on it. And it had tiny little straps—she'd need to rethink her underwear.

She stepped into the dress and pulled it up. The zip was at the side. And that was the problem.

As soon as she started to pull the zip up she realised she was in trouble. There was no way she wanted to force it and when she glanced in the mirror and realised how figure hugging it made the dress, her stomach was really obvious.

She needed to go up a size.

She slipped her own dress back over her head and padded out on bare feet to find something else. The red hadn't really suited. She needed something that suited her skin tone a little better.

There was plenty to choose from in the size up. She picked out a silver dress and decided to give it a go. The back was a little unusual—a low cowl back that caught the eye.

To her relief, this time the dress zipped easily. It was still figure hugging but because there was more room, it just made her look more curvy, enhancing her slightly larger breasts and widening hips without focusing on her stomach.

The thin straps and cowl back meant any bra would be out of the question, but the dress was supportive enough on its own.

'Oh, Mrs Connor, that's just beautiful.'

Addison jumped at the voice. Marisha had returned. She had her hand up at her face. 'Pick that one,' she urged.

She turned and looked back in the mirror. Once she'd got past the bling, the dress was actually really flattering. Marisha darted over to the corner and a pile of boxes. 'What shoe size are you? We'll have something that suits.'

Addison told her and a few seconds later Marisha pulled some high-heeled strappy silver sandals from a box. 'What about these?'

Addison smiled as she stepped over. They were just the perfect height to stop her full-length dress from dragging on the ground. 'Thank you. You better tell me what the charge will be for these items.'

Marisha gave her a nod and printed off a receipt. 'We actually ask that you pay over at the other resort. It all goes to their charity. You can pay for the hire at the same time you purchase your entry to the ball on the night.'

Addison glanced towards the other dresses on the reserved rail. 'So, do I just collect it on the night?'

'That's right. Someone will be here from six o'clock onwards. Just bring the receipt I printed for you, pick up the dress and have a great time.'

Addison touched the strap on her shoulder. 'I almost don't want to take it off.' She gave her head a shake. 'But I must. Give me five minutes.'

She ducked back behind the curtain and slid the dress

off. Let them go to the ball. Let them dance as they used
to and have fun as they used to.

Reality could wait another few days.

Caleb was pacing around and giving the occasional tug at
the unfamiliar dress shirt. The suit was fine. It was made
to measure—for someone that wasn't him. He wasn't
sure he liked the whole 'hire a suit' business but since
he couldn't go to a ball wearing a polo shirt, shorts and
baseball boots he didn't really have any other options.

The sitter had arrived an hour ago. Tristan had been
ecstatic. Should he be worried that his kid was so happy to
see someone else? Kohia was a natural. She'd been playing with the wrestlers within a few minutes and Tristan
couldn't be happier.

Addison was being a little secretive. She hadn't shown
him what was in the dress bag she'd brought in the bungalow a little earlier and had disappeared into the bedroom to get ready.

Most of the other couples they'd met in the resort
were going to the ball too. He glanced at his watch again.
They'd all agreed to meet in the reception area—if Addison didn't hurry up they would be late.

A few seconds later the door to the bedroom swung
open. Caleb caught his breath. She was stunning.

Her blonde hair hung in loose curls over her shoulders
and the silver floor-length dress highlighted what a great
figure his wife had. Every time she moved it glistened
and shimmered and when she turned around to pick up
her bag and he saw the back view he knew exactly where
every set of eyes would be tonight.

She shot him a beaming smile and walked straight over
to him. 'Who knew my husband could scrub up so well?'
she teased as her perfume drifted around him.

Her green eyes were outlined with a little black and she had some pink lipstick on. He bent down and whispered in her ear. 'I've changed my mind about the ball. Let's just split to the over-water bungalow.'

She threw back her head and laughed, giving him a glimpse of her killer cleavage. It must be the dress—or some weird kind of bra—Addison's boobs didn't usually look so big. He felt like a teenager. He just wanted to touch them.

She crooked her arm towards him. 'Are we ready?'

'You're stunning.' The words just came straight out.

Her smile spread from ear to ear and he could see genuine happiness shining from her eyes.

Wow. When was the last time he'd stopped to notice just how gorgeous his wife was? And it wasn't that Addison didn't take care of herself at home—she did. But, by the time he left for work or got back in the evenings Addison was generally in bed. To make it worse, his mind was usually still full of work and the things he had to do—emails to send, a conference call to Japan at some time in the middle of the night, or share prices to check.

He sucked in a breath. *This* was what he should be paying attention to.

Maybe it was time to look at the business again? Harry had already dropped a few hints. They'd gone through three assistants in the last seven months. The amount and pressure of work seemed to wear people down in record time. At least his secretary was still there. She didn't seem to have any problem telling him exactly what her hours were and that she would stick to them.

He needed to pull that pile of CVs out of the drawer. A few had been personal recommendations from colleagues—people he trusted.

They could do with another partner and an assistant

for each partner. They were lucky. Their office space was ample. They could do that. Making those kinds of changes wouldn't even have a detrimental effect on their income. They needed help more than they needed extra income.

They needed their lives back.

He'd sound out Harry when they got home—see if he agreed.

He slipped his arm into Addison's and they both said goodnight to Tristan. The sun had already started setting, sending orange and red streaks lighting up the sky behind the lagoon. By the time they reached the other resort it would be dark.

They walked quickly through the winding paths to the resort reception. Most of the other couples were waiting, with a few others joining a couple of minutes later. There must have been around a hundred people ready to go and join the ball. One of the resort staff met them all and, instead of taking them along the main path, he showed them another route that led to a gate between the two resorts that was usually hidden. It made the walk much shorter. 'Thank goodness,' breathed Addison. 'I wasn't quite sure how it would feel in these heels.'

Caleb nudged her. 'I could have always given you a piggyback.' Then his eyes ran up and down the length of her dress and he broke into a smile. 'But somehow I don't think in that dress it would quite work.'

Even though the evening was warm she gave a little shudder. It was almost as if she could read every single illicit thought he currently had in his mind. Their eyes fixed together for a few seconds. She raised her eyebrows. 'We're going to the ball,' she reminded him.

'Darn it.'

As they walked through to the next-door resort there

was a collective gasp around them. The whole place was lit up like a Mardi Gras.

Music floated through the air towards them. First, the sounds of an outdoor Hawaiian band, greeting guests as they arrived with multicoloured leis, then, as they neared the main complex, the sounds of an elegant concert band lured them inside.

Smartly dressed waiters were holding silver trays packed with drinks. Caleb automatically picked up two glasses of champagne and handed one to Addison. She was looking around in wonder.

In some ways it was like being back in London. The room was full of gentlemen in tuxedos and women in glittering floor-length dresses. They certainly knew how to throw a ball.

There were information stands in the hallways, telling the guests about breast cancer, along with posters of different people with their stories underneath. Caleb tightened his grasp on Addison's hand while his stomach threatened to land on his shoes. He was watching her carefully. Looking for any sign that would hint that she was affected by something similar. But how on earth would he know? Addison's sister had died of ovarian cancer. Any one of these posters telling each person's story could bring a tear to her eye. That was why she was so good at all this.

Sure enough, she started to read all the stories. Twelve women and two men. Every single one was touching. Some had an early diagnosis and some had a late diagnosis. Some had ignored signs as they were too busy with life.

That struck a horrible chord. One of the men affected was just a few years older than him. He'd noticed a tiny lump as he showered but as he was a regular at the gym had put it down to a muscle strain or injury. He couldn't afford to take time off work as he was so busy. It had taken him months to attend his doctor.

Most of the stories were of survivors, a few, sadly, were not. As they walked along the row he slid his arm around Addison's waist and pulled her closer to him.

She didn't appear to be sad. In fact, she engaged with every one of the people manning the stands and spoke passionately about raising awareness of the different types of cancer. The ball was raising funds for a mammogram for island residents. Although the local hospital was well-equipped and could deal with emergencies, it didn't have a mammogram for screening. Residents had to attend Tahiti if they wished to have breast screening and the ball was to aid funds to start the screening service on the island.

Caleb took a few minutes to pay for their tickets, clothing hire and leave a generous donation. They were lucky. They were in a position to be able to do that—as were most of the people attending the ball tonight.

Addison was still chatting. She was swapping emails with someone and agreeing to send them some materials from her charity. She'd hardly touched her champagne, her fingers just stroking up then down the chilled glass.

He put his empty glass on a waiter's tray and picked up another as he waited for her. She joined him a few minutes later, bright-eyed and breathless. 'Sorry, I couldn't stop talking. Everything they are doing here is wonderful.'

Animated. That was how she was right now because she was involved in an area she was passionate about.

'Do you want something different to drink? A cocktail?'

She glanced down at her glass and shook her head. 'This is fine.'

They moved inside the main ballroom. The band were sitting on the stage all dressed in black and white, with the conductor in front of them. The sound reverberated around the room. It was loud but elegant. They were playing Hollywood show tunes and some people were already singing along.

White linen tablecloths covered the round tables around the dance floor, decorated with a bright array of tropical flowers. On either side of the ballroom, doors opened out into the resort gardens to allow the air to circulate freely.

A huge buffet was spread out on long tables. This wasn't a formal sit-down dinner. People were free to choose what and when they wanted to eat. Several of the couples from their own resort were already eating and gave them a wave.

'Want to sit down?' Caleb asked.

She put her hand on his arm. 'Not really. Not yet.' She glanced towards the dance floor. A few couples were dancing already.

Caleb shook his head. 'Oh, no. You want to dance already? We just got here.'

Dancing wasn't his forte—never had been. It had been one of the things that his friend Reuben always teased him about. He usually only danced when Addison pulled him up on the dance floor. The rest of the time he was happy just to spectate.

Addison turned towards him. As she did the coloured strobe lights in the room caught her dress, turning her into a shimmering rainbow of colour. She looked down and laughed. She held out her hands. 'Ever get the impression that someone is trying to tell you something?'

He must have hesitated too long because she looked around the room, tossing her hair over one shoulder and then the other. 'I'm sure I can find someone in here who will dance with me.'

That was all he needed. He set down his champagne

glass and grabbed her hand, pulling her towards the dance floor and praying that nothing remotely fast would come on.

He was lucky. Cole Porter's 'I've Got You Under My Skin' started playing. This, he could manage. This meant that he got to hold the woman he loved and just sway.

Addison was in his arms instantly, his hands on her hips and her hands on his shoulders. She sang along as they swayed. An older man and woman near them started gliding around the dance floor as if they were on ice.

He leaned forward and mumbled in Addison's ear. 'There's always one.'

'Maybe I should send you to dance lessons?'

'How about if I promise to do it for our tenth anniversary?'

He moved a little faster and spun her around, catching her off balance and using the opportunity to pull her even closer to him.

Her eyes widened. She looked surprised and gave a little bite to her bottom lip.

What did that mean? It was like an icy wind rippling over his skin. Did Addison not intend to be around for their ten-year anniversary? Or was it something out of her control? His brain was playing tricks on him again. Pulling ridiculous thoughts out of places that usually didn't exist. He was normally so rational. But it seemed that somewhere along the line a tiny element of fear had embedded itself within him.

Fear of losing Addison.

It was unthinkable and chilled him to the bone.

He plastered a smile on his face. It was a simple bite of the lip. It meant nothing. His wild imagination needed to be put back into its box. He'd done exactly what Addison had asked—he'd come on this holiday. He was spending as much time with them both as possible. And he was enjoying it.

Once he got home he'd speak to Harry. He'd try and reduce his hours at work. He'd make sure he spent more time with Addison and with Tristan. Maybe they could even think about adding to the family? If they were both thinking of reducing their hours it could be a possibility.

Addison was still staring at him. 'You'll learn to dance for our anniversary?'

He spun her around again. 'Of course I will. Wait and see. I'll be the next Johnny and you can be the next Baby.' He laughed and spun her around again. 'I won't leave you sitting in a corner.'

She put her hand up to her forehead. 'The thought of you in tight black trousers trying to jive is making me feel faint.'

She smiled as the music came to a close. 'Feed me, Caleb. Give me time to recover.'

He slid his arm back around her waist and walked over to the buffet. There was a huge variety of food. Chefs were waiting behind the serving area, with fish sizzling in the pans in front of them, restocking the buffet constantly. Off to the side was a large table of desserts. Addison picked up a plate and started working her way along. She wasn't a huge eater, only putting some spiced chicken and a little fish on her plate. Caleb had filled his plate completely by the time he reached the end of the buffet table and could happily have gone back for more.

They wandered over to one of the large tables and sat down. The band was still playing and the ballroom seemed to be getting busier by the second. A waiter appeared beside them. 'Would you like some champagne, or something else?'

Caleb wasn't a huge champagne drinker. 'Can we change to something else?'

Addison gave a nod just as another waiter passed carrying a tray with blue cocktails.

'They look interesting. We'll have two of those, thanks,' he said quickly.

Addison proceeded to choke on her mouthful of food. 'Hey.' He patted her back. 'What's up?'

She frowned and grabbed the waiter just before he left. 'Can I have some water too, please?' She turned back to Caleb. 'I'm not sure about the blue things. I've a sneaky suspicion it might be gin—and you know I hate that.'

He shook his head. 'No. I bet they're rum. All the cocktails around here are rum—and you love those.'

He gave a little nod to another couple who came and sat down beside them. Their plates were overloaded.

The guy reached over with his hand and spoke in a strong American accent. 'Hi, I'm Steven Shankland, this is my wife, Mindy.' He quirked his head. 'Haven't seen you two around here. Are you just visiting for the ball?'

Caleb stood up to shake the guy's hand. 'Yes, I'm Caleb Connor and this is my wife, Addison. You'll guess from the accent we're from the UK. We're staying at the resort next door with our son.'

Mindy looked up from her monster plate as Caleb hid a smile. She was stick thin. Was she really going to eat all that? 'What's the resort like? We considered it, but finally decided on this one.'

Addison smiled. 'It's exactly what I wanted—very peaceful. Our son is having a great time. We have a beach bungalow and an over-water bungalow with a glass panel in the floor. He's loving every second.'

Steven looked at her curiously. 'What do you guys do in the UK?'

Again, Caleb tried not to smile. He admired the directness of Americans. But he wasn't going to give too much away. Addison shot him a slightly anxious glance. He could tell she didn't want this to turn into a business conversation.

'I have my own business in London, dealing mainly in finance. Addison runs a charity for ovarian cancer. What about you—what part of America are you from?'

Although Steven was curious, Caleb had met lots of men like him before. They always preferred it when a conversation came back around to them.

The waiter appeared with the two blue cocktails and a glass of water for Addison, taking Steven's order before he left.

Steven had launched into a great story, all about living in Boston and being a surgeon. Mindy barely lifted her head as she continued to plough through the plateful of food.

Caleb slid his hand underneath the table to give Addison's leg a squeeze. Her hand disappeared under the table too and she interlocked her fingers with his. For some reason he didn't want to share his wife tonight. In the past, they'd both been pretty sociable and been happy to be in anyone's company.

But time now felt special. Selfish or not, he only wanted to spend it with Addison.

The waiter came back with Steven and Mindy's drinks and Caleb pulled Addison up, grabbing their plates. 'Excuse us a second, we're off to restock.'

'Thank goodness,' breathed Addison as they wove their way through the crowd.

Caleb dumped the plates and pulled her towards the dessert table. It was piled high with puddings, cakes, tarts, profiteroles, ice cream and fresh fruit.

'What would you like?' He selected a fork and speared a tiny piece of chocolate cake, holding it out towards her. She smiled and leaned forward, eating it quickly.

'Delicious,' she declared. 'But that's actually enough.' She moved a little closer. 'What I'd actually like to do is dance with my husband again.'

The noise level around them had increased and the band seemed to have got louder too. The dance floor was busier. More and more people were up there—some of them looked professional.

Caleb took a deep breath. 'Okay, then, if that's what you want to do...'

Addison nodded her head. 'Absolutely. That's what I want to do.'

Nothing could compare to the way she felt in her husband's arms and she was the complete focus of his attention. She knew Caleb didn't like to dance but he could manage a slow shuffle around the floor and that was good enough for her.

It was so easy to slip her arms around his neck, press her body up against his and let his lips come into contact with hers. His hands traced little circles on her bare back, sending a million little pulses in every direction. The music, the surroundings, the people around them all blurred out of focus. The only person she was paying attention to was her husband.

It finally felt as if she had got him back. It finally felt as if this was the man she'd fallen in love with. And everything should be perfect now.

Except it wasn't.

Twice tonight she'd made an excuse about alcohol. She hadn't touched her first glass of champagne, putting it down on another table the first time that they'd danced.

The blue cocktail was still sitting at their old table untouched.

She hated that. She hated that she hadn't been honest with her husband. But she hadn't been ready to. And now she was.

His lips met hers again and she closed her eyes. This was what she had missed. This was what she remembered. Every inch of Caleb's body, the breadth of his shoulders, the way he held her in his arms and the feel of his lips against hers.

She moved her hands from around his neck and slid them under his jacket and along the thin material of his shirt. One hand moved from her back, catching the back of her head and tangling in her hair. The other was still tracing little circles on her back. It was hypnotic; it was mesmerising. If she could capture this moment and just keep it here, she would.

The song finished and she took a step back, conscious that people could be watching them. She hated that she might spoil things—spoil what they'd just recaptured. But real life was knocking persistently at the door. She needed her husband's support right now—she needed to tell him what they might be facing.

Caleb's brown eyes were fixed directly on hers. 'Wanna get out of here?' he mumbled.

'Sure.' It sounded so definite, but her heart was racing. Her guilt complex wasn't going to let her keep this secret any longer. Now she had back the man she wanted she had no excuse.

His hand closed over hers and he walked with big strides towards the open doors to the gardens. She almost had to run to keep up.

The cooler night air hit them as soon as they walked outside. Caleb shrugged off his jacket and put it around her shoulders. The gardens at this resort were just as beautiful as those next door.

The smell was intensely fragrant, enticing her to lose herself further in the gardens. They were surrounded by delicate flowers like the white Tahitian *tiare*, along with colourful splashes of gardenia, jasmine, flowering vines of many species, and vibrant hibiscus in stunning shades.

'Listen to the birds,' she said as she looked around in wonder. It was almost like being at a private party.

'Look.' Caleb pointed as the birds darted first one way amongst the greenery, and then the other. Blue lorikeets, fruit doves, kingfishers and cuckoos were all around them.

'It's like being stuck in paradise,' she murmured.

'So it is,' he echoed, but when she turned back Caleb's eyes were on her and not the birds.

She held her breath. She had to tell him.

Then he laughed, put his hands on her hips and pulled her closer to him. He started to sway and sing at the same time. Caleb *never* sang.

They weren't in public now. No one could see them in amongst the green of the gardens. He kept his voice low, singing quietly, only to her. It seemed that Caleb had his own version of 'I've Got You Under My Skin'. His dancing was a bit freer too. He spun her around as he sang, lifting her up and letting her see the twinkle in his eyes.

'Caleb,' she squealed. 'What are you doing?'

It squeezed at her heart. It was like a whole new side of Caleb. One that had been revealed on a holiday where he'd finally managed to shake off the pressures of work. One that had given him the chance and space to be with his family again.

He was holding her under the arms, facing him, but up above the ground, up above his head. She was looking down and laughing because he was still singing to her.

Their bodies were close together as he lowered her oh-so-slowly to the ground and she could feel every part of him.

Just when she thought he was finished, he spun her around again then put her in a backward dip. Their faces were only inches from each other. She lifted her hands to his shoulders again. He was breathing heavily. She was guessing she wasn't as light as he remembered. His after-shave drifted towards her on a little gust of wind. It was the honeymoon one again. And it was definitely stirring up memories.

She reached up and touched his jaw, feeling the tiniest hint of stubble underneath her fingertips. He dropped a kiss on her lips and spun her upwards again at lightning speed until she was facing him.

Her head gave a momentary judder. She was feeling a tiny bit dizzy.

He noticed and smiled. 'Too much alcohol?'

Her heart stilled. She knew he was joking but she couldn't let the night end without being honest with him.

She took a deep breath and went ahead before she changed her mind again. 'Caleb, we need to talk. There's something I need to tell you.'

The evening had almost been perfect. Almost. Right up until that point he'd thought he was waltzing his gorgeous wife home and into bed again.

Then he'd seen her take a deep breath and fix her clear green eyes on his.

If this were a science-fiction movie time would have stopped at this point.

But it wasn't. It was here and now.

For so many days he'd wanted to know what was wrong with Addison. But for the first time in his life he felt afraid to actually hear the words.

There were too many possibilities. Too many outcomes that he might not like. She was sick. She didn't love him any more. She wanted to leave. She'd met someone else. All of them had crept into his head at some point and he'd pushed all of them away.

He kept his voice as steady as possible. 'What is it, Addison?'

But her voice wasn't steady. Her voice was shaking. 'I'm pregnant.'

What? *What?* 'What?' It was probably the last thing he'd expected to hear. Relief swept through him in an instant. She wasn't dying. She wasn't leaving. She did still love him. 'You're pregnant?' There was the briefest second of hesitation as all the fears he'd had about her being unwell again tried to clamour to the surface. But he pushed them away. Relief was still flooding through him. His wife wasn't ill. Anything else they could deal with. 'That's wonderful!'

He picked her up again and swung her around. Another Tristan. Or maybe even a little girl. It didn't matter. He would take either. Just as long as his family was in one piece.

He sat her down and touched her stomach, dropping to his knees and kissing it. 'Hello, baby, how are you?' He couldn't stop grinning. It was important that he didn't say anything to upset her. At some point, he'd sit down with her and talk—talk about why he had worries. They could plan ahead. But just not now. 'When are we due? How far along are you?'

His hand was still resting on her stomach. There was a definite slight bump. Why hadn't he noticed? Didn't women show a bit quicker with their second babies?

'Fifteen weeks tomorrow.' His head shot up; there was a definite waver in her voice. He stood up and caught her head in his hand.

'Hey? What's wrong? Fifteen weeks, that's nearly four months. Didn't you know—did you only just realise?'

It made sense to him. That could be the only possible reason she could be upset. His brain did the rapid calculations. 'So baby is due in November?'

He gave her a giant hug. 'That's brilliant, another Connor for Christmas.'

It was almost as if his brain had gone into overdrive. This was why she was pressing him not to work so hard. This was why she was going to employ someone else at the charity. Pieces of the puzzle were starting to fall into place.

He put both his hands up to her cheeks. 'Don't worry. Everything will be fine. I promise. I'll speak to Harry when I get home. We'll see about hiring another partner and some more associates. It's about time we expanded. I'll make sure everything is in place before this baby arrives.'

He was so buzzed he could hardly think straight, so when tears pooled in Addison's eyes and one slid down her cheek he was astonished.

'I did know,' she whispered.

It was the expression on her face, the pain in her eyes. None of this fitted with what she'd just told him.

'What?' He pulled back. 'Then why didn't you tell me?'

Addison's breathing was stilted. She couldn't look him in the eye.

He put his hands on her shoulders. 'Why didn't you tell me? Why didn't you tell me about the baby?'

She brushed him off and took a few steps away.

'Didn't you think I would be happy?'

She spun back around. 'That's just it, Caleb. I didn't know. I don't know you any more. We hardly see each other. Up until now, I don't remember when we last spent any time together.' She shook her head. 'You'd already told me you didn't want to have more kids.' She pressed her hand on her stomach. 'Then, this happened. I didn't know what to do.'

'What's that supposed to mean?' His raised voice sent a bird shooting from a nearby bush into the sky above. Adrenaline was surging through him. 'Don't you want to have our baby?'

Her face crumpled. 'Of course I do. That's not what I said.'

'So, what do you mean—*I didn't know what to do*?'

The tears were flooding down her face now. He hated to see Addison cry—always had—but he couldn't stop the rage that was racing through him.

She'd kept this from him. Something that should be happy news they could share with the world—she'd deliberately not told him.

Words couldn't even begin to describe how much that hurt. Were they really so far apart that his wife couldn't tell him she was pregnant?

Addison lifted her hand and wiped her eyes, smearing mascara across her face. She straightened her back and looked at him. 'I didn't know if I wanted to stay. I didn't how you'd feel about another child when you'd said no before. I didn't know if it was good to bring another child into a marriage that is already so strained we can barely talk to each other. I want to be able to talk to my husband the way we used to. Not like we are now.'

He could tell she was trying her best to be strong but her voice was still shaking.

'You want to leave?' This night just got better and better.

She closed her eyes for a second. 'I thought I did. I thought you didn't have time for us any more.'

He ran his hands through his hair and took a few steps, trying to stifle his frustration. 'So, my crime is that I'm busy. I work too hard. I support my family. That's why you wanted to leave?'

He was struggling. He was really struggling with this. Part of him felt relief that she hadn't told him she'd met someone else. But the reality that she'd actually considered leaving him was devastating.

The thought of not seeing Addison and Tristan every day made part of him want to curl up and die.

Addison was shaking her head. 'You know how things have been, Caleb. Don't pretend that you don't.' She pointed down with her hand. 'This is the first time in about two years that you've actually been with us.' She pressed her hand over her heart. 'Been with me. Do you know how lonely I've been?'

'Do you know how lonely I've been? Do you know what it feels like to make another excuse to stay at work rather than come home, because you never know the reception you'll get?

'And have I passed the test? Have you changed your mind now you're actually telling me about our baby?'

She hesitated. She actually hesitated. She cleared her throat. 'We've talked about this. You said that you would stop working so hard. That you would make adjustments. I want us to be a family. I want us to be together. I love you, Caleb, but I'm not afraid to do this on my own. You've been taking us for granted. I need you to *want* me to be there. You've just told me you don't want to come home.'

'Of course I want you to be there. But I don't think this is about me wanting you. I think this is about you wanting me. Do you actually want me to be in your life?'

It was a horrible question to ask. A horrible thing to say out loud. His heart felt like putty in her hand.

Addison looked pale, or maybe it was the moonlight and the silver dress. She reached down and pulled her shoes from her feet. 'I can't do this. I can't do this any more. I'm too tired. I'm going back to the bungalow to sleep.'

He stepped forward. 'You can't go away now. You've kept one of the most important things in our life from me. It was as good as lying to me.'

This time Addison raised her voice. 'Do you know what? I tried to tell you. I tried, Caleb. I phoned you at work. I asked you if you'd be home for dinner that night. I dressed up—I put on the pink dress that you'd bought me and cooked you your favourite dinner. Then, I did what I did the first time. I put the pregnancy test under a silver dome, sat it at your plate setting and waited for you to come home.' She shook her head. 'Do you know what that feels like? To be so happy, so excited and dying to share the news?' She put her hands on her hips. 'Well, I waited, Caleb. I waited and I waited. I sat there for three hours waiting for you to come home. No phone call. No message. Nothing. And it made me realise just how you prioritised your life. Because even when your wife phones you, even when she asks you specially when you'll be home, as soon as you put down that phone it just vanishes from your mind.' She clicked her fingers. 'Poof! Just like that. How do you think that feels? So don't dare tell me that I lied to you by omission because you weren't there, Caleb, you just weren't there!'

He'd never heard Addison shout like this before. He'd never seen her so worked up. She was furious—and she wasn't finished yet.

'So don't you dare tell me I can't go away. I can. And I will.'

Her dress swished as she turned and disappeared along the path.

He should go after her. He knew he should.

But he just couldn't. They needed time apart. They needed space.

He heard muffled voices a little bit away. No doubt other guests had heard the shouting in the garden.

He tugged at the neck of the tuxedo shirt. It was driving him crazy.

He couldn't pretend he wasn't hurt. He couldn't pretend he wasn't angry. Those first few seconds of finding out Addison was pregnant again had been truly magical. But those few seconds had been snatched away with the realisation of everything else.

Something crept over him, like an icy cold hand sliding down his spine.

She hadn't answered. She hadn't answered that final question.

Do you actually want me to be in your life?

Had he left things too late to actually resolve?

The champagne from earlier roiled in his stomach. He loved his wife. He loved his son. And he loved this baby too.

But was it all too late?

'Sir, are you all right?' It was one of the resort staff. Someone must have told them about the shouting.

'I'm fine,' he replied as he tugged off the bow tie and turned in the other direction.

The beach. That was where he'd go. It would be quiet. It would be empty. It would give him some time to think things through.

Because the last thing he was right now was fine.

CHAPTER TEN

THE DRESS MADE it difficult to walk as quickly as she could. Parts of the path had tiny stones that jagged the soles of her feet but she didn't want to stop to put her shoes back on.

Things couldn't have gone worse. She'd turned a perfect evening into a nightmare. All because she'd felt overloaded with guilt.

She'd hurt him. She'd cut him to the bone and she realised that.

His reaction when she'd told him she was pregnant had made her realise what she'd done. He'd been happy. On a normal day it was the perfect reaction.

Sure, there had been a tiny second of hesitation. But he wasn't angry about the baby.

But when he'd asked when the baby was due her tongue had stuck to the top of her mouth. She'd had to admit the truth.

It would have been easy to say she'd just found out. It would have been easy and simpler to make up some feeble excuse as to why she hadn't noticed her periods had stopped.

But it wouldn't have been true. It wouldn't have brought everything to a head.

Maybe she should have lied. Maybe she should have

said she'd just found out. But that would create more problems for her later.

Because no matter how hurtful it was, she had to let Caleb know that she'd thought about leaving.

It made her insides curl up. She knew exactly the effort he'd been making and she'd fallen a little bit more in love with him again every day.

She felt so guilty. Her husband had told her he didn't want to come home. He didn't want to come home to *her*. It hurt. It hurt because she knew why. She was distant with Caleb. She was cold. Their conversations were about Tristan's schedule. She'd been so fed up with him working that she never even asked him what kind of day he'd had any more. Just as he didn't ask her. She wanted things to change between them so badly. Being on Bora Bora made her feel as if they'd captured part of themselves again. The part that had been missing for the last year. They'd finally started to talk and communicate again. So, was she just about to ruin everything? Lying by omission. That was what he'd accused her of.

But she hadn't even told him the most important thing yet.

The fact that their baby was at high risk.

How would he react then?

She pressed her hands on her stomach.

He'd misunderstood her. When she'd said she didn't know what to do, he'd thought she was talking about the baby, not about them. And that horrified her.

Every bit as much as it had horrified him.

Trouble was it had made her angry and she'd started to vent all the pent-up frustrations of the last few years. She'd said things without thinking.

But she hadn't said the most important thing.

The bungalow was in sight. She took a deep breath and

gave her face a wipe. She didn't want to go inside when it was obvious she had been crying.

She hadn't been lying. She was exhausted and she needed to lie down. Tiny thoughts in her brain were pushing their way forward again. The ones that made her take part of the blame for this situation. She didn't even want to acknowledge them. To think about them at all. The sooner she got to bed, the better.

Kohia was sitting on the sofa watching the TV as she came in. 'Hi, Mrs Connor. Tristan was a dream. He went to bed a couple of hours ago.'

'Thank you so much, Kohia. I really appreciate it.'

Kohia picked up her bag and walked to the door. 'No problem. I'll see Tristan at kids' club tomorrow.' She gave a little smile, 'By the way, you might find some wrestlers in his bed.'

Addison forced a smile. 'No problem. See you tomorrow.'

She let out a sigh as Kohia left and she closed the door behind her.

She unzipped the dress then put it back on the hanger. It was beautiful and for a short time she'd felt wonderful in it. But for now, it only reminded her of one of the worst nights of her life.

She didn't even wash her face. Just pulled on her nightie and climbed into bed with Tristan. She snuggled her arms around the little warm body.

Comfort. That was what she needed right now.

But it didn't stop the tears from falling again.

Caleb watched the sun rise on the beach again. He'd eventually moved along the beach, nearer the bungalow. But he just couldn't bring himself to go in.

He still felt too raw and the last thing he needed to do right now was cause another fight.

Watching the sun rise on this beach was getting to be a dangerous habit.

A little after seven the waiter appeared with the breakfast tray. His stomach growled but he didn't think he could eat right now.

The door to the bungalow opened and Addison appeared.

She had one of his T-shirts and a pair of shorts on. Her hair was tied on top of her head and she looked deathly pale. It was obvious she'd had as restless a night as he had.

She walked over towards him and sat down on the beach next to him.

She held out her hand. 'Don't say anything. Let me speak. I need to get this out there.'

What now? She'd cancelled his flight home?

She wasn't looking at him. She was staring out across the lagoon, watching the egrets trying to swoop down and catch fish.

'I didn't tell you everything last night. I didn't tell you the most important thing.'

There was more? He was struggling with the not-talking part. He wanted to say so much right now. But, last night's lesson was to try and listen instead of just reacting. It was already proving hard to learn.

'I got a call just before we left the house.'

He nodded. He remembered. He'd been on a call himself and hadn't paid too much attention.

She started tracing circles in the sand with her finger. 'It was my doctor—my obstetrician. He needed to talk to me about some tests.'

'What tests?' He couldn't help himself. There was no

way he could keep quiet. His brain was starting to race again. There was something ominous about this.

'I'd had my baby scan. They do the nuchal screening test. The one where they measure the fluid at the back of the baby's neck. They take blood and use that, along with my age, to see if our baby is at high risk.'

He could remember parts of this. When she was pregnant with Tristan he'd held her hand through the scan. He could remember the sonographer fiddling to get the tiny measurement she'd needed for the scan. 'That's the test for Down's syndrome, isn't it?'

All the fine hairs on his arms stood on end. He turned to face her. His heart had started racing in his chest. 'Isn't it?'

She nodded. She opened her mouth to speak again and then stopped. Her hand was shaking as it traced the circles in the sand. He closed his hand over hers and tried to speak. 'What did the doctor tell you? Is our baby affected?'

She pulled her hand away, drawing her knees up to her chest and putting her hands over her face. 'I don't know. He told me our baby is at high risk.'

Panic seared through him. 'What does that mean? What's high risk?' He was trying to stay calm but it wasn't easy. He wanted to ask a hundred questions at once. He'd already been worried about how his wife would cope after delivering another baby. He hadn't even considered there could be extra complications. What if they were all just too much for Addison?

She turned to face him. This time she actually did look at him and it nearly broke his heart. The pain etched on her face was clear. She'd known this since just before they'd left. She'd had no chance to talk to anyone, to sit down and find out more. It seemed crazy. How had she managed to stay calm?

'For someone my age, normal risk would be around one in a thousand. Dr Mackay said my risk is one in one hundred and forty.'

Numbers. Caleb dealt with numbers at work every day. He was good with numbers. Numbers were what he based every business decision on.

But suddenly numbers didn't seem so secure.

The leap from one in a thousand to one in one hundred and forty seemed huge.

He felt stunned. It was as if someone had just taken the legs from under him—thank goodness he was sitting down.

Caleb gently stroked her cheek. 'What happens now?'

She pressed her lips together. 'Nothing. This is our baby. I love it already. I'm prepared to deal with whatever happens.'

He frowned. 'Addison? What did you think I meant? Are there other tests? Other things they need to do? Can we find out for sure?'

She shook her head. 'Dr Mackay asked me if I wanted an amniocentesis test. That would tell us for sure. But it carries a risk of miscarriage. I can't do it. I just can't.'

'Is there anything else they can do?'

She nodded. 'They can do a detailed scan at twenty weeks. It can look at the baby's facial features and all the vital organs. Some kids with Down's syndrome have cardiac problems—some babies require surgery straight away.'

'Oh, no.' He couldn't help it. The thought of their brand-new baby needing heart surgery straight away was terrifying.

He was silent for a moment, trying to process all the

thoughts in his head. 'Addison, I don't know enough about this. I don't know enough about Down's syndrome. If this is what the future holds, then we need to find out more. We need to prepare ourselves and prepare Tristan.'

They were side by side on the beach but he'd honestly never felt so alone. He wrapped his arm around her shoulders and pulled her closer to him. After a few seconds she put her head on his shoulder and started to sob.

Nothing else mattered. Nothing else mattered but this.

It was overwhelming. It was staggering. He was racking his brains—trying to remember anything he could. There had been a boy at his junior school—Alec someone—his brother had Down's syndrome. But he was embarrassed to admit that all he could remember was that the little guy had worn hearing aids and had had a really happy disposition. That was it. Alec had been fiercely protective of his little brother—and also fiercely proud. Why hadn't he paid more attention—why didn't he know more?

He rubbed his hand up and down Addison's arm. 'You should have told me,' he said softly. 'You shouldn't have kept this to yourself.'

Her head shot up and there was a momentary flash of anger. 'How could I? You were just about to tell me that you weren't coming on holiday with us.'

She was right. Of course she was right. That was exactly what he'd been about to do. Until she'd given him the ultimatum.

And now he understood why. She'd already been stressed about the pregnancy. She'd already been worried about their marriage. The news about being high risk must have tipped her off the cliff edge she'd been dangling from.

She hadn't even been able to talk to him about it. Because she hadn't decided if she wanted to stay.

He took a deep breath and tried to think rationally.

'Let's take a minute. Let's talk about this. One in one hundred and forty sounds scary initially, but that also means that one hundred and thirty-nine times out of one hundred and forty our baby won't be affected. Those odds are pretty good.'

She raised her head. 'I know that. But it doesn't really make me any less scared.'

He squeezed her. 'I'm scared too. I'm terrified. I hate not knowing things. And I don't know enough about all this. I want to run screaming somewhere and find a computer so I can scan the Internet.'

She gave a little laugh. 'For once in your life you don't want Internet for work.'

He shook his head. 'No. I don't. I want to know how to plan ahead. I want to know what else we should do.' He paused for a second. 'Are you sure you don't want to have the amniocentesis?'

She shook her head fiercely but he lifted his hand. 'Hear me out. There's still another twenty-five weeks to go in this pregnancy. That's a long time to worry. A long time to not know what's ahead. I understand about the risks of miscarriage. Do you remember what they are?'

She shook her head again.

The sun-kissed look she'd had on her face a few days ago seemed to have vanished. It had been replaced by a pale and strained look, tiny wrinkles around her eyes and deep creases in her forehead. She was now wringing her hands in her lap. All he could see was stress. It simply oozed from every pore.

He sat back a little, trying to appear more relaxed. 'Okay. I don't know the risks so it's difficult to know if it's something we should consider.' He gave her a weak smile. 'Before I say this, I want you to know that you're gorgeous as always.'

She gave a sigh. 'Sure I am.'

'You're stressed. I'm not surprised. But I need to know if it's been the stress of keeping this secret that's made it worse, or if it's just the worry in general. I'm thinking about the next twenty-five weeks. I'm thinking of keeping our baby safe. If you're going to spend the next few weeks not sleeping and with your blood pressure through the roof then maybe we should think about the test. Is the not knowing actually going to make things worse?'

It felt like a reasonable question. It felt like the kind of discussions they should be having. Her voice wasn't quite so shaky this time. 'I think I've just been angry,' she said quietly. Her green eyes met his. 'Angry at everything. Angry at me. Angry at you. Angry at my blood test.'

She put her head in her hands again. 'And I've felt panicky.'

'Why?' He needed to coax her. He needed to get everything out there.

She bit her lip. 'It's not easy to say out loud, but we both know I struggled when Tristan was a baby. You were better at the night-time stuff than I was. You had more patience. I reached a point where I had to walk into another room because I couldn't stop him crying.' She stared off into the distance. 'And the rest.' Her fingers toyed with a little bit of hair at the side of her head. 'I felt numb then. It took me time to connect with Tristan. I felt useless. I felt as if I was failing as a mother and...' she met his gaze '...as a wife.'

He reached out and touched her. 'Addison, I've been scared too. When you mentioned having another baby I panicked. And I never panic.' He sucked in a deep breath. 'Last time around I felt as if you were slipping through my fingers and I couldn't do a damn thing to stop it. I might have worked regular hours then, but I was still at work all day. I could see you disconnecting. I could see you struggling. You were home all day with Tristan and I spent all day worrying about how I could try and help you get back to normal.' He shook his head. 'I phoned that health visitor so many times I'm sure she could have got me done for stalking.'

Her eyes were filling with tears again. 'That's why you didn't want to have more kids? Because of me?'

He nodded. 'Of course I want more kids. But what I also want is my wife. It was me who got you pregnant. It was me who did this to you. I was terrified you might feel like that again.'

'I'm sorry, Caleb. I'm sorry I didn't sit down and tell you straight away that I was pregnant. I'm sorry that the second I got that phone call from Dr Mackay I didn't call you over to listen too.'

He tilted up her chin towards him. 'Addison Connor, you are a great mum. Don't ever doubt that—not for a second. Tristan is lucky to have you and this baby will be too. I am going to be with you every step of the way. We're in this together. For ever.'

She wrapped her arms around herself and looked back to the horizon for a second. 'I was worried. Worried you wouldn't be around—not like the last time. And if I struggled with Tristan and he didn't have any health conditions…what if I'm not good enough now?'

'Addison, don't. Don't think like that. You are good enough. You're perfect. And you won't be on your own. I'll be there. I promise I'll be there. And Lara will be too. You'll have help. You don't need to panic. Health problems or not, this baby will be the most loved, most cared for on the planet.'

He gave her a nudge. 'And who said Tristan didn't have problems? He had killer colic. I compared notes with the guys at work. Our boy could have won the screaming contest every day of the week. Our little guy was hard work.'

Addison's lips tilted upwards a little. 'Is that where you got all the crazy cure-colic ideas from?'

He nodded. 'Yip, and we tried them all. To be honest all the guys really said it wouldn't go away until he started being weaned. But I couldn't tell you that at the time. It's just one of these things that you have to grin and bear.'

She looked surprised. 'You compared notes on our baby?'

'Of course, that's what we guys do.'

The smile disappeared from her face and she put her hand to her stomach. 'And will you do that with this baby?'

She still looked so unsure about everything. Now he knew what was wrong, he could recognise the look in her eyes. It was fear. And he felt it too.

'Of course I will. I will brag about first smiles, first waves, first tooth and first time they bite me with that tooth.'

He shook his head. 'You've no idea the things that went through my head.'

She wrinkled her nose. 'What are you talking about?'

He ran his fingers through his hair. 'I knew something was wrong. I was worried. Worried that you'd met someone else, worried that you might be sick—'

'You thought I might be sick?'

'I just didn't know. I kept thinking about your sister and…'

She touched his jaw. 'Oh, Caleb.'

'But I totally missed the *she might be pregnant* thing.'

She glanced down at her boobs. 'I was worried you might guess.'

He raised his eyebrows. 'I should have. My observations skills are obviously out of practice.' He frowned for a second as something else crossed his mind. 'What about the alcohol—the cocktails?'

Addison smiled wearily. 'Yeah, that's not been easy. I had to ask that waiter for a non-alcoholic strawberry daiquiri and I've just managed to not drink any of the champagne or wine.'

He opened his mouth in surprise. 'That's what you were doing at the film? I thought the mint thing was strange but never questioned it. I really am slow on the uptake these days, aren't I?'

Addison didn't speak for a few seconds. Then she let out a visible sigh. It was as if all the tension around her neck and shoulders seemed to dissolve. Her whole body just crumpled a little.

For a few moments things had been a bit easier between them. They'd actually been talking. The fault-finding and recriminations had been put aside.

'It was easier when I didn't tell you,' she said.

'What?'

He could see her swallow. 'When I didn't tell you, then all I had to focus on was us—and if we could make it. My head was full of everything. Would I have to move? Where would Tristan go to school? Would you want to see the new baby? How I would cope with the baby. What the impact on Tristan would be if we split.'

He hated hearing those things. He hated that she'd even thought them and he hadn't known. But he could see the bigger picture here. He could see just how truly scared his wife had been.

He closed his hand over hers again. 'And if you're thinking about all that—then you're not thinking about how our baby will be? If there might be health problems, surgeries. You're not worrying about the future and how they might cope in life. You're not thinking that far ahead and wondering what happens when you and I aren't here any more.'

She briefly closed her eyes. 'Exactly. All the things I'm just terrified to consider.'

Caleb looked out over the bright blue lagoon. He moved his hand back around her shoulders. 'You know, everyone wants their baby to be perfect. Over the years treatment and care for babies and mothers has improved and now they have all these tests. But the thing is, you can't predict everything. Look at the amount of times you hear about things after a kid arrives. Babies can be born with disabilities that aren't picked up on scans. Some babies are perfect right up until delivery—we've all seen the stories in the news about babies getting stuck and having a lack of oxygen. They can have something hidden—like cystic fibrosis. They can develop things. Harry's goddaughter has diabetes. His friends spend their whole life plotting around insulin pumps and eating. The teenage boy at the end of our street had meningitis a few years ago when he started university. What I'm trying to say is there are no guarantees in life. Is it good, or bad, to know what's ahead?'

She clasped her hands in front of her. 'I just don't know.'

His brown eyes were fixed on hers. 'I want you to know something. I want you to know that I'm happy about this baby. I want you to know that hasn't changed. The possibility of having a child that requires surgeries still terrifies me, but this baby? It's ours. It's on its way and I love it already.'

Her lips turned upwards in a grateful smile. 'I do too,' she whispered. 'You've been so good about this. You've been so good to me. I should have told you straight away. I should have spoken to you more. I couldn't even see that I'd started to shut you out. I'm so sorry, honey. I was unfair. I couldn't see beyond my own feelings to think about yours.'

He brushed some loose strands of hair back from her face. 'Thank you for saying that. But we're past that now. We're both past that. We need to look to the future. The future for our family. We need to move forward. We can't keep living in the past.'

The breeze had started to pick up around them and a few more strands of her hair had escaped from her bobble. He stood up and held his hand out towards her. 'Let's get some breakfast. It's probably cold but at least it's something.'

She nodded and put her hand in his. When he pulled her up he pulled her straight into his arms against his chest.

They stood there for a few seconds taking comfort in each other's arms.

Right now, she was the only person that could comfort him, and he was the only person to comfort her. Exactly the way it should be.

It was only morning and she was exhausted again. Probably because she hadn't slept all night.

She had been so determined to just get the words out there the next time she saw him. Keeping it to herself had been too much of a burden. She'd needed to share. She'd needed to be able to talk things through with someone.

Last night he'd been angry with her and she'd felt terrible. She'd reacted badly and then just left because she hadn't been able to deal with the consequences.

This whole time she'd really only been thinking about

herself. She hadn't considered Caleb's feelings in any of this. Probably because of how she was feeling.

Now, she realised how unfair she'd been. How well he'd coped with the news she'd just given him. She'd had two weeks to think about things—even though she'd tried not to. But that instant decision—the one she'd made in a heartbeat while on the phone to Dr Mackay—she knew he was right there with her. She should have had faith. She should have believed in her husband.

Now she knew why he'd said he didn't want to expand their family. It wasn't because he didn't care about her. It was exactly the opposite. It was because he did care about her.

He'd had the same worries that she had. Part of it hurt that he hadn't spoken to her—just as she hadn't spoken to him. But in a way, now she understood. She'd struggled to put those thoughts into words just as much as he had. She'd shut him out—even though she hadn't realised she was doing it.

Now, they were ready to face the future together. The weight that had nestled on her shoulders for the last few months had finally came unstuck.

They walked into the kitchen and stopped dead. Tristan was up. He hadn't slept as late as normal and it seemed that he'd helped himself to breakfast.

Tomato ketchup was everywhere. On his face, in his hair and on the table.

Caleb started to laugh and stepped forward. Tristan's plate was cleared. 'Did you eat all your sausages already?'

He grinned and nodded.

Then Addison noticed something else. She cleared her throat and pointed to the plate where Caleb's breakfast should be. It seemed to have been moved around the plate with one key ingredient missing. 'Did you eat Daddy's sausages too?'

Tristan nodded again, obviously pleased with himself.

'Oh, no,' said Caleb. 'He's over-sausaged. What's the betting he's sick in half an hour?'

She held out her hand to Tristan. 'Let's get you cleaned up while Dad makes me tea.'

A quick shower and change of clothes later Tristan was colouring at the other side of the table.

Caleb set her decaf tea down in front of her along with some toast. He smiled. 'It must be killing you not to drink coffee.'

She shook her head. 'Don't even go there. We're not going to discuss coffee at any point.'

It was odd, watching her husband work about the kitchen in his tuxedo. She was wearing his old clothes with her hair tied up on her head and he still had his suit for the ball on. They must have looked like the oddest couple on the beach.

'Don't you want to get changed?'

'I will. Let's have breakfast first.'

He sat down opposite her. He took a drink of the decaf tea he'd made for himself and grimaced. He was watching her carefully. 'Now I know what's going on, I'd like you to get checked out.'

She put her tea down. 'Why?'

'Because you fainted the other day. You wouldn't let me call a doctor. I should have. I'd like you to get checked out.'

She took a bite of her toast. She had a feeling already that she wasn't going to win this argument. 'I've not had any bleeding, any cramping. It's kind of late for that. I'm past the stage that a miscarriage would normally happen.'

'So what made you faint? Was it your blood pressure?'

He shrugged his shoulders. 'I don't know enough about these things. But I'd really like to know there's nothing else to worry about.'

She looked around. 'I'm not sure what kind of maternity services they have around here. I know there's a hospital but I don't know if they have midwives or nurses.'

'We can ask at Reception.' He nodded towards Tristan and mouthed, 'Shall we tell him?'

She was surprised. She hadn't even considered telling Tristan yet, not when she hadn't told her husband. But now there was no reason not to.

She gave a little nod. Caleb turned towards Tristan and picked up a crayon. He started colouring in part of his drawing. 'Hey, Tristan, Mummy and Daddy have got something to tell you.'

Tristan barely acknowledged he'd spoken. His little tongue was poking out and he was concentrating hard on keeping his blue crayon in the lines. He looked up for a second to see what Caleb was doing. 'Make that bit purple, Daddy.'

Caleb gave a nod and picked up a purple crayon. 'How do you feel about babies?'

His eyes widened. 'Jacob at nursery has a baby. So does Lucas and Lily.' He screwed up his nose. 'Lily's baby is a girl.'

Caleb kept going. 'Do they like having little brothers and sisters?'

But Tristan didn't answer the question. Like a typical four-year-old he went off at a tangent. 'My nursery teacher is having a baby. It's hiding in her tummy.'

Caleb glanced at Addison. 'I know someone else who has a baby hiding in their tummy.'

'Is it Mrs Foster? She looks like she has a baby in her tummy.'

Addison let out a giggle. Mrs Foster was their next-door neighbour and was around eighty years old. She certainly did have a large tummy.

She could tell Caleb was trying not to laugh. 'No. No, it's not Mrs Foster. I don't think she'll have any more babies.' He touched Tristan's arm. 'What about if I told you that Mummy was going to have another baby? Would you like a little brother or sister?'

His head shot up and he stared at Addison open-mouthed. 'We're getting a baby?'

She gave a little nod. 'We are.'

'Can it share my room?'

She could see Caleb trying to be tactful. 'Not right away, but maybe later. When you came home from hospital you had a crib in Mummy and Daddy's room for a few months, then you moved into your own room.'

'The baby will get my room?'

Caleb shook his head. 'No, no. The baby might get the room that's next to yours. Or the one across the hall.'

'Will he be there when we get back home?'

Addison started to laugh. 'What have you done? I think we'll get these questions for the next six months.' She leaned forward and grasped Tristan's hand. 'Do you want to come and feel my tummy? The baby is in there right now but it's still quite small.' She tried to think in kids' terms. 'It will come after Halloween and before Christmas.'

Tristan jumped down from the chair and ran around the table, putting his hand on her stomach. 'My nursery teacher's tummy is much bigger than that. Can we visit the fish again today?'

And that was that.

He was four. His attention span had moved on to the next thing. She was relieved that he seemed happy. There was no need to tell him anything else. There was plenty of time for that.

Caleb swept him up into his arms. 'How about we go and have a look at some of the fishes under the water bungalow?'

'Yeah, Daddy!'

They came back fifteen minutes later when she'd finally showered and changed out of Caleb's T-shirt and into a pale blue dress. Caleb stripped off his tuxedo and jumped in the shower straight after her. He was ready ten minutes later and picked up Tristan with one hand and held out his other towards her. 'Ready?'

Was she? She put her bag over her shoulder. 'Yes. Let's go.'

The staff at Reception were well trained. It only took one phone call to arrange for her to see one of the local doctors at the hospital. They even arranged transport for them.

Her stomach churned nervously. She was sure she was fine. She was sure. So why was she so nervous?

Caleb reached forward and took her hand again. Tristan was playing with his wrestlers. He hadn't even asked any questions about where they were.

'Addison, before you go in, I want you to know something.'

'What?' She couldn't stop the anxiety in her voice.

His brown eyes met hers. 'I want you to know that I love you. I want you to know that I'm with you every step of the way. No matter what news we get today, or in the future, I'm going to be right by your side. I'm sorry it's taken me this long to get my priorities in order. I'm sorry that I didn't tell you the truth about being worried.' He pressed his hand to his heart. 'I'm happy about this baby. I really am. Yes, I'm still worried and I'll probably ask

Dr Mackay a hundred questions when we get back. But whatever happens was meant to be. I believe that. Ten years ago I met the woman of my dreams. And she still blows me away every single day.'

A tear slid down her cheek.

'I only want a life with you. I can't begin to imagine life without you. If our next baby is a night-time screamer then I'm on duty. I'm on duty to do whatever you want.' He reached into his pocket and pulled out a crumpled piece of paper. 'I wrote this last night when I was sitting on the beach. I have to tell you it was the easiest thing I've ever done.'

She took the paper with a trembling hand and unfolded it. There, in Caleb's characteristic scrawling writing— with a few words scored out here and there—was the finest thing she'd ever seen.

Connor and Shaw Associates are looking for a dynamic and motivated individual to become the third partner within their firm...

'I'll get the advert posted as soon as we get home.' He pulled a receipt out of his other pocket. 'I've also written an advert for the three assistants. It's time for me to prioritise. And that's you, Addison. It's always been you. I guess I just got lost a little along the way.'

She gave a nod. 'I'll phone your secretary and put all our appointments in your schedule. I love you, Caleb. I've always loved you, even when I tried to convince myself that I didn't. I don't want to do this alone. I want to do this with you. I want to know that if we get told something scary that we can cope and be strong. I promise I'll listen to whatever you have to say.'

Caleb lifted her hand and placed it on his chest. 'I

need you, Addison. I need you every single day. I can't be *me*, without *you*. Don't doubt for a second how much I love you.'

They were the words she'd wanted to hear for so long. It was the reassurance that he would make time for her, Tristan and this new baby. It was relief that if she needed to talk, if she needed to cry, she could do it with the person who was the most important to her. If she was scared, she could tell him. If she needed help, she could tell him. If she just wanted him to hold her hand, he would be there.

He reached up with a thumb and brushed her tear away. 'Don't cry, honey. Let's celebrate our baby,' he whispered.

'Mrs Connor?' The voice startled them. A doctor in a white coat was standing in the corridor. He held out his hand when she nodded. 'I'm Dr Akana. Please come this way.'

Caleb squeezed her hand before she stood. 'You're the strongest woman I know. Whatever happens, it happens to us.'

He was sincere. He meant every word and even though she was terrified it made her heart sing.

The doctor led them along to a consulting room. Tristan immediately sat in a corner playing with his wrestlers.

The doctor invited her to sit down and checked her file. 'Mrs Connor, I understand that you're pregnant and had a fall a few days ago?'

She gave a nod.

He moved around the desk and sat next to her. 'If you don't mind, I'll ask some questions and examine you.'

'That's fine.'

He was thorough, checking her obstetric history, the story of her fall, asking about any pain, cramping or bleeding, then checking her blood pressure and urine.

She paused for a second. 'I had some…news.'

He looked up from his notes. She could almost see him choosing his words carefully. 'Okay, then, what kind of news?'

She bit her lip. 'My nuchal screening test put me at high risk.'

He glanced at the dates on her chart. 'I take it you found out just before you came on holiday?'

She nodded.

'And you didn't decide on any more testing?'

She shook her head firmly.

He gave her a reassuring smile. 'I want to be clear. Everything is looking fine. The purpose of today is to just check you and the baby are okay—I won't be able to tell you any more about your nuchal screening. I'll leave that for your obstetrician back home. Are you okay with that?'

She glanced at Caleb and gave a nod.

'Would you like to hop up on the trolley and I'll have a feel of your tummy and check for a heartbeat?'

She felt a little surge of panic. Instinct wanted her to run from the room but that was just silly. Caleb appeared beside her, putting his arm around her and almost carrying her along and over to the trolley.

She sat down and swung her legs around, lifting her dress to reveal her slightly swollen tummy. The doctor washed and warmed his hands before touching her. He was quick. 'Everything feels right for your dates. No pain anywhere that I'm touching?'

She shook her head. He pulled the ultrasound machine over. 'Just a little gel on your tummy,' he said as he opened the tube and turned the machine on.

She couldn't breathe. Caleb must have seen the panic on her face as he moved around to the other side of the trolley and held her hand.

Dr Akana positioned the probe and swept it over her

abdomen. He took a quick look at the screen. 'I won't be able to tell you anything else about being high risk. This scan is just to check baby is thriving. Have you booked in for a detailed scan at twenty weeks?'

'The appointment should be waiting when I go back.'

He nodded. 'That's good.' He pointed at the screen. 'Here we are, baby is looking good. Here's the skull, the spine, this is the femur—the thigh bone and this little flicker is the heartbeat.'

She let out her breath as Caleb squeezed her hand again. His eyes were fixed on the screen and he had a wide smile on his face. 'Hey, Tristan,' he said. 'Come over here and have a look at your little brother or sister.'

Tristan's head shot up and he walked over, staring at the screen.

Dr Akana pointed out the parts of the baby to him just as baby started kicking. Tristan let out a squeal. 'Look at that! He wants to play football.'

'*He* might be a she,' said Addison quickly. 'We don't know yet.'

Caleb's eyes hadn't moved from the screen. 'Would it be possible to get a printout?' He seemed transfixed.

Instantly she felt guilty. Last time around he'd come to every appointment with her. He'd been more nervous than her when it had come to the first scan. This time she'd gone alone—and cheated him out of his first chance to see their child.

Dr Akana nodded and pressed a button before lifting the probe and wiping her stomach clean. He tore the picture from the machine and handed it to Caleb before helping Addison down from the trolley.

'Everything looks fine, Mrs Connor. I think your earlier thoughts about not eating and drinking enough could be true. Your urine is clear, your blood pressure fine and I can't see anything else to worry about for now.'

The relief was instant. 'Thank you,' she said quickly.

He stood up to shake her hand. 'If you have any other concerns, or you feel unwell, you can come back and see me any time.'

Five minutes later they were outside and in the car heading back to the resort.

Addison leaned against her husband as he wrapped his arms around her. It was the first time in the last few years she'd felt happy and secure. The worries were still there, but this time they were shared. This time, they weren't just hers.

They were in this together. They wouldn't repeat their past mistakes. They'd learned and they'd grown together as a couple—as a family. If she was scared, or unsure, or felt the slightest bit numb, this time she would talk to her husband. She wouldn't think there was something wrong with her. She wouldn't think she was failing. She'd realise that it was probably hormonal—probably outside her control—and just try to work through it with the support of the man that loved her.

'What do you want to do tonight?' he asked.

She smiled and glanced at Tristan, who looked up at her with his big eyes. She knew exactly how to answer this question.

She turned her head to plant a kiss on Caleb's lips. 'We're in Bora Bora. What else? I want to lie in our big bed in the water bungalow and watch the fish with my two favourite men in the world.'

He nodded. 'Your wish is my command.'

And it was.

EPILOGUE

'PUSH, HONEY, PUSH.'

It was official. Caleb felt one hundred per cent useless.

'Almost there,' said the midwife reassuringly as she looked up from her position at the bottom of the bed.

He was at the top end, Addison leaning back against him, exhausted and panting.

The twenty-week scan hadn't shown any clear abnormalities. The nuchal measurement was still slightly enlarged and they'd accepted it was a wait-and-see situation.

This morning Addison had felt tired and Caleb had volunteered to take Tristan out to the park for a while.

One hour later she'd been in hard labour. Caleb's mobile had rung merrily in the kitchen when she'd tried to phone him and Reuben had practically broken every rule of the road getting her to the hospital before screeching back to the park to find Caleb.

'Don't tell me to push. You push.'

He took a deep breath. He needed to be strong for his beautiful wife, even though he was terrified for her. She gripped his hand again as another contraction hit and he watched the colour drain out of his fingers, then they changed to an attractive shade of blue.

Reuben and Lara were sitting outside with Tristan. All

waiting for baby news. When they'd got back from Bora Bora his best friend was engaged to his nanny. Reuben had wanted to get married as soon as possible, but since Lara wanted Addison to be her witness they'd decided to wait until after the baby was here.

Now, they were all waiting.

'Here comes the head,' shouted the midwife with a big smile on her face.

Addison let out a scream. 'Aargh…'

Caleb held his breath. This was it. This was the moment they'd both been waiting for.

'Head's out, pant now, Addison,' said the midwife.

Caleb's throat was bone dry. He wanted to be down at the bottom of the bed, he wanted to watch his child come into the world but Addison needed him here.

The midwife changed her position. 'Okay, folks, get ready for the next contraction and baby will be here.'

He'd be lucky if he could ever use his hands again. But he didn't really care. Anything was worth it. His family was worth it.

Addison gritted her teeth. 'Come on,' she shouted as her face turned redder and redder.

Ten seconds later baby was out and flipped up onto her chest.

The paediatrician was here and waiting. The neonatal unit had a bed ready if needed.

Addison's hand reached up, touching her baby's back and cradling baby towards her. Caleb bent forward for a better look. He hadn't heard any noise yet.

Baby was looking right at him, unblinking with a scowl on its face. As he watched there was a little shudder as air was sucked in and baby's colour started to pink up.

He'd never seen anything so beautiful.

He glanced downwards. They'd decided not to find out

what they were having this time. 'Hey.' He touched Addison's cheek. 'Tristan will be mad. We've got a daughter.'

'A daughter?' She was still catching her breath. Her eyes filled up with tears. 'A daughter. We've got a daughter.'

Caleb was still looking at his daughter's scowling face and watching her little chest rise and fall when the paediatrician tapped his shoulders. The little girl that would probably break his heart a million times over and give him a nervous breakdown. He couldn't wait.

'Breathing seems fine. But do you mind if I check her over?'

The midwife looked up. 'Dad? Do you want to cut the cord?'

He nodded and walked to the bottom of the bed, taking the scissors with slightly shaking hands. He cut between the clamps and watched as the paediatrician carried his daughter over to the crib with the heat lamp for a few minutes.

Addison started to shake a little. So he walked back and put his arm around her shoulders. 'I hate to break it to you,' he said, 'but even though her eyes are blue, they're on the dark side. I think she's going to take after her dad.'

'Just as long as she doesn't inherit your talent for snoring.' Addison was smiling. She looked exhausted. The labour had been quick and two weeks early, catching them all a little by surprise.

The paediatrician was listening to their daughter's chest. 'Sophie?' Caleb asked.

She nodded, her smile getting broader by the second. 'Yes, definitely Sophie.'

The second midwife was over next to the paediatrician, writing down a few notes, then wiping baby's face and body.

The paediatrician wrapped her blanket loosely around her and carried her back. 'Well, she might be two weeks early but at seven pounds fifteen ounces you might be glad of that.' He gave them a reassuring nod as he handed her back. 'Breathing and observations are fine, heart and lungs clear and—' he met both their gazes '—no sign of anything else.'

'Really?' Addison's question was almost a whisper.

The paediatrician gave a clear reply. 'Really.'

Her breath came out in a whoosh.

'Do you want five minutes?' asked the midwife. She understood. She understood completely.

'Please,' said Caleb.

The midwife handed over the buzzer. 'I'm right outside.'

The two midwives and paediatrician filed out.

Caleb moved behind Addison again, letting her lean back against him with their daughter back on her chest.

'Welcome to the world, Sophie.' He moved his hand over Addison's and intertwined his fingers with hers.

'Thank you, Caleb,' Addison whispered.

'What are you thanking me for? You're the one that's done all the hard work.'

She shook her head. 'Thank you for the last six months. Thank you for keeping your promises.'

He reached up and touched her cheek. 'Love you, Addison Connor. Nothing else is more important than you and our family.'

He planted a kiss on her lips. 'I've never been happier.'

'Me either.'

And together they watched their little daughter give a little squirm, then a little cry. Addison smiled. 'There could be trouble ahead.'

'Can't wait.'

Then he kissed her again and went outside to introduce their son and friends to the latest member of the Connor family.

* * * * *

MEET THE FORTUNES!

Fortune of the Month: Graham Fortune Robinson

Age: 32

Vital statistics: Broad shoulders, rugged build and a heart as big as Texas.

Claim to fame: Graham has shunned the family's multimillion-dollar business in favor of a rancher's life on the Galloping G. His father would say he has "untapped potential." Graham believes he is already living the dream.

Romantic prospects: Impossible. He's crushing on his childhood buddy Sasha-Marie Smith. She has a seven-year-old daughter and is expecting a second one. Did we mention that she is technically still married? Her soon-to-be ex walked out on her and she's seven months pregnant. He's sure romance is the very last thing on her mind.

"I've never done what anyone has expected of me. I'm a cowboy in a family of computer geeks. I'd rather punch a cow than a time clock. And I'd rather live alone than settle.

So now I've finally found my Miss Right. But the timing is absolutely wrong. Sasha has a baby on the way. Maybe she's still stuck on her ex. And for sure she doesn't think of me as anything other than a friend. What kind of guy pursues a woman who's got so much weighing on her slender shoulders?

On the other hand, what self-respecting cowboy can ignore a beautiful damsel in distress?"

The Fortunes of Texas:
All Fortune's Children—
Money. Family. Cowboys.
Meet the Austin Fortunes!

WED BY FORTUNE

BY
JUDY DUARTE

First Published in Great Britain 2016
By Mills & Boon, an imprint of HarperCollins*Publishers*
1 London Bridge Street, London, SE1 9GF

© 2016 Harlequin Books S.A.

Special thanks and acknowledgement to Judy Duarte for her contribution to the Fortunes of Texas: All Fortune's Children continuity.

ISBN: 978-0-263-91991-2

23-0616

Our policy is to use papers that are natural, renewable and recyclable products and made from wood grown in sustainable forests. The logging and manufacturing processes conform to the legal environmental regulations of the country of origin.

Printed and bound in Spain
by CPI, Barcelona

Since 2002, *USA TODAY* bestselling author **Judy Duarte** has written over forty books for Mills & Boon, earned two RITA® Award nominations, won two MAGGIE® Awards and received a National Reader's Choice Award. When she's not cooped up in her writing cave, she enjoys traveling with her husband and spending quality time with her grandchildren. You can learn more about Judy and her books at her website, www.judyduarte.com, or at Facebook.com/judyduartenovelist.

To Allison Leigh, Stella Bagwell, Karen Rose Smith,
Michelle Major and Nancy Robards Thompson.
And to the fabulous Marcia Book Adirim,
who has those amazing stories of
the Fortunes dancing in her head.

Thanks for working with me on the
2016 Fortunes of Texas Anniversary series
and for making this book a pleasure to write!

Chapter One

Graham Robinson had spent the morning working up a good sweat, thanks to a drunken teenager who'd gotten behind the wheel of a Cadillac Escalade after a rowdy, unsupervised party last night.

The kid had apparently lost control of the expensive, late-model SUV and plowed through a large section of the fence at the Galloping G Ranch, where Graham lived. Then he left the vehicle behind and ran off.

Both Graham and the sheriff who'd been here earlier knew it had been a teenager because on the passenger seat a frayed backpack, as well as a catcher's mitt, sat next to an invitation with directions to a ranch six miles down the road.

Sadly, the same thing could easily have happened to him, when he'd been seventeen. That's why he and

Roger Gibault, his friend and the owner of the ranch, were determined to turn the Galloping G into a place where troubled teenage boys could turn their lives around.

Back in the day, both Graham and Roger's late son had what Roger called rebellious streaks. Graham's dad, the patriarch of the famous Austin Robinsons—and an alleged member of the Fortune family—wasn't so open-minded.

But after Peter's tragic death, things had changed. Graham had changed. Now, instead of creating problems for others to clean up, Graham was digging out several damaged posts and replacing broken railings.

After he hammered one last nail into the rail he'd been fixing, he blew out a sigh and glanced at the well-trained Appaloosa gelding that was grazing nearby on an expanse of green grass. He'd driven out here earlier in the twelve-year-old Gator ATV, but the engine had been skipping. So after unloading his tools and supplies, he'd taken it back to the barn, where Roger could work on the engine. Then he'd ridden back on the gelding. Hopefully, Roger had the vehicle fixed by now. If not, they'd probably have to replace it with a newer model.

When the familiar John Deere engine sounded, Graham looked over his shoulder. Sure enough, Roger had worked his mechanical magic and was approaching at a fairly good clip.

Moments later, the aging rancher pulled to a stop, the engine idling smoothly.

Glad to have a break, Graham winked at his elderly

friend. "Did you come out here to check up on me and make sure I wasn't loafing?"

"I knew better than that. I'd be more apt to make sure you hadn't worked yourself to death." Roger lifted his battered black Stetson, then raked a hand through his thinning gray hair.

The fact that he hadn't returned Graham's smile was cause for concern. "What's up?"

Roger paused for a beat, then said, "Sasha-Marie just called. She's on her way here."

Graham nearly dropped the hammer he was holding. Roger and his niece had once been close, but they'd drifted apart after her marriage. "Is she still living in California?"

"I don't think so. But I'm not sure."

When Sasha-Marie had been in kindergarten, she lost her parents in a small plane crash. Her maternal grandparents, who lived in Austin, were granted custody, but she spent many of her school vacations with Roger, her paternal uncle.

Since Roger and his late wife had only one child, a son who'd been born to them late in life, Sasha-Marie became the daughter they'd never had and the apple of her doting uncle's eye.

Roger had been proud when she went off to college, but he hadn't approved of the man she'd met there and started dating. After she married the guy and moved out of state, Roger rarely mentioned her.

Graham hadn't met her husband. He'd been invited to the wedding, although he hadn't attended. He'd come down with a nasty stomach flu and had stayed on the ranch.

According to Roger, it had been a "big wingding," and most likely the sort of elegant affair that Graham's family usually put on, the kind of function he still did his best to avoid whenever possible.

On the morning of the wedding, as Graham had gone to replenish a glass of water, he'd met Roger in the Galloping G kitchen. Roger had been dressed in a rented tuxedo, his hair slicked back, his lips pursed in a scowl. His job was to give away the bride, but he hadn't been happy about it.

"This ain't right," he'd said.

Graham thought he might be talking about the monkey suit he'd been asked to wear. "You mean all the wedding formalities?"

Roger shook his head and clucked his tongue. "I tried to talk her out of it, but she won't hear it. Just because she's gone off to college, she thinks she's bright. But she's been so blinded by all the glitz and glamour she can't see what a louse her future husband really is."

Having grown up in tech mogul Gerald Robinson's household, Graham had experienced plenty of glitz and glamour himself. He knew a lot of phony people who flashed their wealth, which was one reason he was content to be a cowboy and manage the Galloping G for Roger.

The other reason was that he wanted to look out for the old rancher and his best interests. That's why the news of Sasha's return today was a big deal.

"Is Sasha's husband coming with her?" Graham asked.

"Nope." Roger placed his hat back on his head, adjusting it properly and shading his eyes from the afternoon sun.

Graham wondered if the older man would offer up another comment, but he kept his thoughts to himself. That really wasn't surprising. He'd been pretty close-lipped about Sasha since the wedding, which must have been eight or more years ago. Graham had tried to get him to talk about his anger and disappointment, thinking that might help. But he respected the man's silence. He also sympathized with him.

After Sasha gave birth to a baby—a girl, if Graham remembered correctly—Roger had gone to visit her in California. He'd not only wanted to see his great-niece, but he'd also hoped to mend fences. Two days later he'd returned to the ranch, just as quiet as he'd been before. Graham's only clue to what had transpired was the response to his single question about how things went.

"Not well," Roger had said. And that had pretty much been the end of it.

Graham stole a glance at the man who'd become more of a father to him than his own dad. But then again, they'd weathered Peter's death together, leaning on each other so they could get through the gut-wrenching, heartbreaking grief.

Bonds like that were strong. And they lasted a lifetime.

Roger stared out in the distance at the two-lane highway that led to the big ranch house in which he now lived alone. Was he looking for Sasha's car?

Or was he just pondering the blowup that he'd had with her husband? Graham wasn't privy to all that had happened on Sasha's wedding day, but he did know that Gabe had, in so many words, told Roger to butt out of Sasha's life.

So the rift had always weighed heavily on his mind— and it probably still did.

"It's a good sign that she felt like she could call and talk to you," Graham said.

"I agree." Roger heaved a heavy sigh. "She didn't tell me what brought about the sudden change of heart, but that doesn't matter."

"Either way, for your sake, I'm glad she's coming without her husband."

Roger snorted. "I always figured Gabe for a fast-talking womanizer who'd end up breaking her heart down the road. But that didn't mean I didn't want to be proven wrong."

"You won't hold any of that against Sasha, will you?"

"Hell no. I'd never do that. But I'll tell you, Graham, it hurt like a son of a gun when she left Texas. And while I'm glad she reached out to me just now, I'm leery about pushing myself on her too quickly."

Whatever had gone down between Roger and the groom at the church had nearly destroyed the relationship Roger once had with his niece.

"How long is she going to be here?" Graham asked. He assumed it'd be for a few days to a week.

"I don't have the foggiest idea, but I told her she could stay as long as she wanted."

Sasha had been a cute kid. She'd tagged along after Graham and Peter when they were teenagers, wanting to be included—and being a pest more times than not. She was probably close to thirty now, but Graham would always remember her as a skinny young girl with braces and a scatter of freckles across her nose.

Roger glanced out to the road again, squinting as he scanned the empty stretch of blacktop.

"Do you know what kind of car she drives?" Graham asked.

"Nope." The older man turned, sporting a wry grin. "I guess it's pretty obvious that I'm watching for her to arrive."

"Just a bit."

When a car engine sounded in the distance and grew louder, both men turned and spotted a white Honda Civic heading down the road. A blonde woman was driving, although the car was too far away to get a glimpse of her face.

"That might be Sasha-Marie now," Roger said.

It was hard to know for sure, although Roger was clearly eager to have her back on the Galloping G, no matter how short her stay.

"I'll finish up here," Graham said. "Why don't you go back to the house so you can greet her?"

"Nope. I want you to come with me. You can get those tools later. Mount up."

Graham scanned the fence he'd been working on, realizing it wasn't going anywhere. And apparently, neither was that Escalade if he enclosed it in the pasture before the owner came to claim it.

"All right," he said, "but why do you want me to be there?"

Roger scowled and rolled his eyes. "Because I never have been able to keep my opinions to myself. And if I slip up and say 'I told you so' or something negative about that jerk she's married to, I'll probably make things worse than they already are. So if you think I'm about to blurt out something like that, I want you to give me a wallop upside the head."

Roger had a point. He was a good man, hardworking and honest to a fault. But he'd never been one to hold back an opinion, no matter how rough it was around the edges. So Graham left his tools near the post he'd just cemented back into place, grabbed the Appaloosa's reins and swung into the saddle. "Okay, then. Let's go."

Neither of them knew for sure if the blonde driver had been Sasha, but on the outside chance that it was, they'd both be welcoming her home.

Sasha Gibault Smith parked near Uncle Roger's big white barn, but she didn't get out of the car right away. Instead, even though she needed to stretch her legs, she remained seated, gripping the steering wheel and studying the ranch she used to love to visit.

She'd started out from Los Angeles yesterday morning and had spent the night in El Paso, but it had still been a difficult trip, one she'd made with her tail tucked between her legs.

She adored Uncle Roger, but whenever she'd gone

against his advice, he'd had a habit of saying, "I told you so" or "Dang it, girl. Why don't you ever listen to me?" And this time, he'd been especially right in his assessment of Gabe Smith.

Needless to say, she wasn't looking forward to adding any additional guilt to what she already carried, especially now. That was one reason she'd been reluctant to call her uncle until she was only thirty minutes away.

She hadn't gone into detail about why she was coming back to Texas. Nor had she apologized for anything she or her now-estranged husband had done to hurt him. She'd merely asked if she could stay with him on the Galloping G for a while.

Before answering her question, he'd had one of his own. "Is Gabe coming with you?"

She'd said no, that it was just her and Maddie, and left it at that. She hadn't been ready to tell him any more over the phone.

"Stay as long as you want," Uncle Roger had said. "The city isn't a good place to raise a child." At that point, he'd paused, maybe rethinking his response. "I mean, city life is okay. Lots of cultural stuff and shopping, I suppose. But the fresh air and sunshine will be good for Maddie."

Bless his heart, Roger was the gruffest yet kindest man she'd ever known. And she was looking forward to mending their relationship, something she should have done a long time ago. But Gabe had made it so difficult. He'd made *everything* difficult.

She glanced into the rearview mirror to the backseat, where Maddie dozed. Her seven-year-old daughter was the only good thing that had come of her relationship with Gabe, so how could she regret marrying him?

But still, why hadn't she listened to Uncle Roger when he warned her about him?

Because she'd been dazzled by Gabe's charm and enamored with the very idea of love, that's why. She'd lost her parents when she was young, and all she'd ever wanted was to create a family of her own. But that dream had certainly backfired on her.

She'd been a fool not to see the truth. Gabe hadn't been capable of loving anyone but himself. And the fact that she'd signed the prenuptial agreement he'd said would appease his wealthy father only made it worse. What would Roger have said to *that*?

She could only imagine. She placed a hand on her growing baby bump, which had made it more difficult to reach the gas pedal, as well as the steering wheel, since she was merely five foot two, anyway.

The second pregnancy not only had led to her and Gabe's split, but had also complicated things. Gabe, who hadn't really wanted to have kids, would have to provide financially for both of them. His family came from money, so that hadn't bothered him nearly as much as the idea of coming home day after day to Sasha and the kids.

In fact, once Maddie was born, he began spending more and more time at the office. Sasha tried not to resent his time away from home since he'd said he was doing it for them, that he was only trying to be a good provider for his family. And maybe that was true. But she'd soon realized that Gabe was a quitter. Whenever something didn't go the way he liked it, he'd move on to another job.

The poor baby she was carrying, another little girl, hadn't asked to be brought into the world. But Gabe had barely gotten used to having Maddie. So when he found out Sasha was expecting again, he packed his bags and moved out.

It's not like she had intended to get pregnant this time. In fact, she still marveled at how it had even happened, since she and Gabe were so rarely together.

But none of that mattered. Her only priority now was her children. Come hell or high water, Sasha would do everything in her power to provide her daughters with love and security. And what better place to do that than at the Galloping G?

She just hoped Uncle Roger would agree. Her heart told her he would, but she'd never know until she broached the subject.

Again, she glanced in the rearview mirror. She didn't want to wake Maddie from her nap quite yet. The little girl hadn't felt comfortable in that motel room last night and had taken a long time to fall asleep. So to provide Maddie a few extra minutes to snooze in comfort, Sasha lowered the power windows to allow the afternoon breeze to blow through the car. Then she pulled the key from the ignition and placed it in her purse.

Before she could open the driver's door, a John Deere Gator drove into the yard, followed by a cowboy on horseback.

The man driving the Gator was Uncle Roger. And the cowboy…?

A Stetson shielded his face, but not his broad shoulders and rugged build. When he tilted the brim, she recognized Graham Robinson, and her breath caught.

His saddle creaked when he placed his hands on the pommel and leaned forward, checking her out without the hint of a smile. But she wasn't smiling, either. Talking to Uncle Roger would be hard enough without an audience.

What was Graham doing here? Hadn't he kicked his cowboy stage by now? Shouldn't he be working at Robinson Tech, raking in the dough and living the fast-paced urban life he'd been born into?

Not that he hadn't practically lived on the Galloping G during the summers when she used to come and visit. Graham and her cousin Peter had been best friends— and almost inseparable. Then, after Peter died, Graham had practically moved in.

She'd had a huge crush on the older teenage boy back then, but he'd only considered her a kid and a nuisance. In retrospect, she could understand why. He'd had his choice of high school girls. Why would he take a second look at her?

Besides, he and Peter were always talking about parties and all the places local teenagers hung out. Once she'd even heard them mention something about skinny-dipping with a couple of cheerleaders. So, no, Graham had never looked at her as anything other than a pesky little kid.

Uncle Roger approached first, which didn't surprise her. He was, after all, the one she'd come to see.

She tore her gaze from Graham, a wealthy man by all

rights who appeared to be more comfortable on horse-back than in a snazzy BMW, something he could well afford to buy. At least, he'd never been without a wad of cash in the past. His dad owned a big tech company and had been loaded. He probably still was.

When Roger reached her car, Sasha was reluctant to get out. She hadn't told him about her pregnancy, although he was about to find out.

He took off his hat, revealing more silver in his hair than the last time she'd seen him. His face had weathered, too.

Her heart cramped at the thought that she and Gabe might have contributed to the signs of age.

"How was the drive?" he asked.

She lifted her hand to her eyes, blocking the glare from the afternoon sun. "It was long. But not too bad."

Uncle Roger took a peek into the backseat. "Looks like Maddie dozed off. You gonna wake her up?"

"I hadn't wanted to. She didn't sleep well last night. We stayed in a roadside motel, which had a truck stop next door, so it was pretty loud outside. But she's been eager to get here. And to meet you. It's all she could talk about."

As Uncle Roger studied her sweet, dozing daughter, Sasha stole another glance at Graham. He was dismounting now.

The years had been good to him, and as he swung a muscular leg over the saddle, all those girlish feelings returned tenfold. For one crazy, thoughtless moment, that silly crush she'd once harbored came rushing back full force and nearly stole her breath away.

She'd never met a man who could hold a candle to Graham in looks. In fact, if she weren't seven months pregnant and still—at least, *legally*—married, she'd be a goner.

Well, that wasn't true. She was older and wiser these days. And she'd learned the hard way that no man was perfect. Besides, she'd be swearing off romance and concentrating on her children for the next couple of years.

"You gonna sit in that car all day?" her uncle asked.

No, she wasn't about to do that. And while she wasn't eager to reveal her condition to either Roger or to Graham, she opened the door, grabbed her purse and slid out of her trusty Honda Civic.

The moment she did, Uncle Roger let out a slow whistle. But it wasn't Roger's reaction that concerned her now. For some dumb reason, she looked straight at Graham and waited for his response.

The first thing Graham noticed when Sasha got out of the car and stepped into the afternoon sunlight was that she was no longer the cute little tomboy he remembered. She was a stunning blonde and absolutely beautiful.

But damn. She was also *pregnant*. And while he was no expert, from the looks of it, she was about ready to deliver.

Were women in her condition supposed to travel, especially on long road trips?

Roger stepped away from Sasha's car, then strode toward Graham and reached out his hand. "Gimme those reins. I'll take care of your horse."

What the hell? And leave Graham to make small talk?

He would have objected and insisted on putting the horse away himself, but Roger was probably afraid to stick around any longer for fear he'd say something to screw things up before he got a chance to take Sasha's luggage inside. Speaking of which…

"Let me get your bags," Graham said.

"They're back here." Sasha, with the strap of her purse over her shoulder and her hand perched on her belly, rounded the car and opened her trunk.

She hadn't brought much, just two suitcases, so maybe she didn't plan to stay long.

"Is this it?" he asked.

"I…uh…" She gave a shrug. "I shipped everything else."

Everything? What all had she thought she'd need? Was she going to move in?

He lifted both bags from the car, and she shut the trunk. As he carried the suitcases to the front porch, he stole a peek at the lovely blonde.

Somewhere along the way, she'd shed the braces. And in spite of her obvious pregnancy, she'd blossomed into a shapely woman, one he found incredibly attractive. His heart rate had escalated to the point he felt what could almost be classified a sexual thrill just looking at her.

What did that say about *him*? What kind of man found a pregnant married woman so appealing?

He wasn't going to stew about it. Instead he shook off the question, as well as any answer he might be able to come up with. He was just surprised to see her and how much she'd changed, that's all.

"Is your daughter going to be okay in the car?" he asked.

"I'm only going to leave her in there for a minute. I thought I'd put my bags into the room where I used to sleep. But maybe I'd better leave them in the living room until Uncle Roger tells me where he'd like us to stay. I didn't mean to be presumptive."

"I'm sure it's fine to put everything in your old bedroom," Graham said, leading the way.

As far as he knew, Roger hadn't changed a thing since Sasha was last here, the summer of her junior year. He'd wanted things to stay the way she'd left them. But after her high school graduation, she'd stayed in Austin to prepare for college.

So she could easily see that the room with lavender walls, dotted with posters, still bore evidence of the teenager she'd once been.

Graham placed the bags on the bed, which boasted a white goose-down comforter.

Sasha set her purse on the antique oak dresser, then thanked him for his help.

"No problem."

They merely stood there, caught up in some kind of weird time warp. Then she nodded toward the doorway. "I'd better go wake up Maddie."

Graham followed her outside, watching her walk, the hem of her yellow sundress swishing against her shapely calves. From behind, he'd never have known she was expecting a baby.

When they reached the front porch, she paused near the railing, took a deep breath of country air and scanned the yard. "I've really missed this place."

Roger would be glad to know that. It would make it easier for them to put the past behind them.

"It's been a long time," Graham said, finally addressing the elephant in the room. "How've you been?"

"All right." She turned to face him and bit down on her bottom lip, as though things might not be "all right." But if that was the case, she didn't mention it. "How about you? I see you're still hanging out on the Galloping G."

"I live here now. In the foreman's quarters. I guess you could say I'm your uncle's right-hand man."

She pondered that bit of news for a moment. "I guess some things haven't changed."

Actually, she was wrong. A lot had changed, and there were more big changes coming down the pike.

"So, how's your family?" she asked.

"Same old, same old." It was a stock response to keep from going into any real detail. Sasha didn't know that he'd never been close to his father—and even less so now that he'd chosen not to work at Robinson Tech, like most of his other siblings.

When she nodded, he offered a more interesting response and something she might soon hear from the neighbors. "My brother Ben and my sisters Rachel and Zoe have gotten married recently. And my brother Wes is engaged."

"That's nice," she said, providing her own stock response. "How recently?"

"All within the last six months." Then, for some damn reason, he added, "We might also be taking on a new last name."

Her brow furrowed. "What do you mean?"

Since it was too late to backpedal now, he continued with the unsettling truth. "Apparently, my dad was once a long-lost black sheep in the Fortune clan. His name was Jerome, not Gerald."

Graham decided not to mention that Ben and some of his other siblings had taken on the Fortune name. But he wasn't about to do that, especially when his father refused to admit the connection.

"Wow," Sasha said. "And you never knew?"

"No, Dad kept that a secret from us, along with other things." Graham wasn't about to go into all that. Not now, anyway. Maybe not ever. He wasn't particularly proud of the fact that his old man, a guy most people considered a quirky tech mogul, had eight legitimate kids, as well as who-knew-how-many illegitimate ones.

"How do you feel about that?" she asked, easing close enough for him to catch the faint hint of her orange-blossom scent.

He blew out a sigh, hoping to eliminate the taunting smell, as well as his lingering concerns of being a shirttail relative to such a famous family. It didn't work in either case.

"It's been a lot for me to take in," he admitted. "So now my life on the Galloping G holds an even bigger appeal than it did before."

"I can imagine. News like that would be…stunning. How do your brothers and sisters feel about it?"

"Actually, some of them hope it's true. But the others aren't too keen on it." Graham, of course, was on the not-exactly-pleased side of it.

He paused for a beat, realizing Sasha didn't have siblings—or even a cousin any longer. So he didn't want to sound as though he resented having a big family. "I suppose you can never have too many relatives. It's a cold world out there, so the more people who have your back, the better."

Instead of smiling or commenting, Sasha just stood there as tears welled in her eyes.

Uh-oh. He hadn't meant to trigger her sadness. Was she missing Peter? Her parents?

She swiped below her eyes with the backs of her hands. "I'm sorry. Just the result of my pregnancy hormones at work."

That made sense. And it made him feel a lot better about setting off her tears. "How far along are you?"

"Seven months."

"Your husband must be thrilled."

Sasha glanced down at her sandals and didn't speak or look up for several beats.

He must have put his foot in his mouth again, although he had no idea why. Was she unhappy about the baby?

"I'm sorry if I was out of line," Graham said.

Sasha shook her head. When she looked up and caught his gaze, her eyes were glossy. "Gabe and I…

split up." Her hand again went to her belly, caressing the mound where her baby grew. "Actually, he left me."

Graham couldn't imagine what would cause a man to walk away from his family when his wife was pregnant. He'd never met Gabe Smith himself, but Roger had. And the old rancher's opinion of the guy was enough for Graham to believe the worst about him.

He'd never reveal that to Sasha, though. So he said, "That must be rough."

"We're doing okay. And on the upside, I'm now able to come visit Uncle Roger. Maddie is excited to see a real ranch—and horses."

Before Graham could respond, a little girl sidled up between them. She stuck out her hand to Graham and smiled, revealing a missing front tooth. "Howdy. Put 'er there, cowboy!"

He was captivated by her happy expression, by the long blond hair and bright blue eyes, so like her mama's.

What kind of man would leave such an adorable duo? Not that Graham had ever had any reason to admire Gabe Smith. But surely he'd come to his senses and chase after them.

For some strange reason, that thought caused his gut to clench, and he found it nearly impossible to speak. He did, however, reach out and take the child's little hand in his.

"You must be Maddie," he said.

"Yep." The girl stood tall, a big ol' grin stretching across her face. "And *you* must be Uncle Roger."

Chapter Two

Apparently, Maddie had awakened from her nap and gotten out of the car on her own. And while the little girl had no way of knowing who Graham or even Uncle Roger were, the idea that anyone could possibly confuse the two men brought a smile to Sasha's lips.

She placed her hand on the top of her daughter's head, her fingers trailing along the silky, pale strands. "This isn't Uncle Roger, Maddie. It's his friend Graham."

As the child cocked her head and scanned the handsome man from his dusty boots to his black hat, a grin dimpled her cheeks and lit her eyes. "So you're a real cowboy, just like my uncle?"

Graham smiled. "I reckon you could say that, Miss Maddie."

The girl laughed. "Can you say something else cowboy-like?"

"Honey, Mr. Graham isn't here to entertain you." Sasha straightened and turned to the handsome man. "She's a big fan of horses and all things Western."

"Then this visit to the Galloping G should be good for her," Graham said.

Yes, it would definitely do her daughter good. Sasha hoped it would do the same for her. She had some healing to do. She also had a relationship to mend. So why couldn't she seem to turn and walk away from the sexy cowboy who was so good with her daughter?

She glanced toward the barn, where Uncle Roger had disappeared.

"I love horses," Maddie said. "Especially real ones."

Graham chuckled. "A girl after my own heart. Have you ever ridden a *real* one, Maddie?"

"No, not yet. But I have a pretend saddle I put over the back of our sofa at home. And I play like I'm riding that."

Graham glanced at Sasha as if questioning the truth of Maddie's statement.

So she smiled and nodded. "Maddie would ride that towel-draped leather sofa all day if I'd let her."

The little girl lived and breathed horses. And, apparently, she admired the men who worked with them. So, if Sasha wasn't careful, her daughter would pester poor Graham and Uncle Roger to death.

Hoping to defuse what could be an awkward situation, she addressed her daughter. "Mr. Graham has a lot of work to do, honey. And the sooner we let him get back to it, the better."

"That's not a problem," Graham said. "I really don't mind taking a break. In fact, if Maddie wants, I can take her around the Galloping G and show her what a 'real cowboy' does all day, including a broken fence I need to repair."

"That's nice of you," Sasha said, "but it isn't necessary. We just got here and should probably settle in. Besides, Maddie needs to learn a little patience."

"I'll tell you what," Graham said. "While you two unpack, I'll go pick up my mess in that south pasture. When I get back, I can give you that tour." Then he winked at Maddie. "Your mom can come, too."

Sasha probably ought to tell him no. She had a lot to talk over with Uncle Roger. But she couldn't very well have that kind of a heart-to-heart until later this evening, after Maddie went to bed.

For the third time since arriving—or maybe it was the thirty-third—she turned her gaze on Graham, who'd grown an inch or two taller and filled out nicely. He wore a gray T-shirt that didn't mask the muscles in his broad chest. His biceps, which had never been small, now bulged, straining the hem on his short sleeves without any effort on his part.

He still bore the scar on his arm from a riding accident he'd had years ago, a jagged mark left from a barbed-wire fence. But like everything else about him— his hat, his jeans, his smile—he wore the cowboy image well.

She'd always admired Graham and found him attractive in more ways than one. He was—or at least used to be—a straight-up guy. And in spite of the money his family had, there were no pretenses about him, no games. He said what he meant and meant what he said.

Graham was nothing like Gabe, which made him even more appealing now. And that was a good reason for her to steer clear of him. Besides, she was a pregnant single mother. And she'd arrived at the Galloping G with way more baggage than the suitcases she'd brought in the trunk of her car. Certainly way more than a man like Graham would want to deal with. He'd always had a way with the ladies—or at least the girls in high school. So she assumed that he was a free-wheeling bachelor with his pick of willing women.

Yet she found herself nodding in agreement. "Okay, a tour of the ranch sounds fun. While you're going to get your tools and whatnot, Maddie and I will unpack."

Graham lobbed her a crooked grin that nearly stole her breath away. But how could that be? She wasn't a love-struck kid anymore. And she'd experienced far too many of life's realities to even entertain thoughts of ever having a crush—childhood or otherwise—on anyone.

Yet as he turned to walk away, her heart fluttered and her pulse rate spiked, suggesting he still had the ability to send her sense reeling with a simple smile.

By the time Graham returned for his tools in the pasture, the sheriff had come back and stood next to a tow truck, pointing out the SUV that had caused all the damage.

The officer left the driver to his work, then approached Graham. "We'll have that vehicle out of here shortly. The owner has already been informed and has contacted his insurance company."

Graham nodded. "I'm assuming his son was driving?"

"Yep. But from what I understand, the boy lost his license and will be grounded for the rest of the summer."

"I can understand that." Graham could also understand the appeal of an unsupervised teenage party. He'd certainly attended more than his share of those.

But as an adult, he knew the dangers of drinking and driving, no matter what age one was.

After the sheriff left and the tow truck drove out with the SUV, Graham picked up the tools and supplies he'd left in the south pasture and took them to the barn. He hated to leave the repair work on that downed fence unfinished, but he'd do it for Roger. Fortunately, they didn't have any horses grazing out there now. But they would, once his friend Chase Parker delivered them on Friday.

His friend, huh? If that Robinson-Fortune family connection was true, Graham and Chase would be more than friends. They'd actually be related, since Chase was married to Lucie Fortune Chesterfield.

After putting away the tools and supplies, he went in search of Roger and found him leading Lady Jane from the pasture toward the barn.

"What are you doing?" Graham asked. "I thought you'd be inside, talking to Sasha-Marie and getting to know little Maddie."

"I *was* in there. For a while."

"How'd it go?"

"Okay, I guess. Maddie is a little chatterbox, which might prove helpful in piecing together what's going on. She mentioned that her daddy moved out of their house and into an apartment near his work."

"I'm sure that's true. Sasha told me that she and Gabe are separated."

Roger merely nodded as he continued toward the barn, the roan mare walking alongside him.

"What are you doing with Lady Jane?" Graham asked as he followed behind.

"That little girl loves horses, and I figure she'd like to ride a real one instead of her mother's sofa. So I'm going to stable Lady Jane so she'll be closer to the house."

"Good idea." Lady was a gentle mare and would be a good mount for a beginner.

Once they entered the barn, Graham opened the gate of an empty stall. "I assume you and Sasha had a chance to talk."

"Just enough to break the ice some, but not enough to get back on steady ground again."

"I got the feeling that she plans to stay for a while," Graham added.

"Yep." Roger removed the lead from Lady Jane's halter, then closed the gate. "I suspect she came here to lick her wounds, which is fine by me. The Galloping G is the perfect place for her to get back on her feet."

He was right about that. It was at this ranch where Graham and Roger had managed to heal from their terrible loss. And it was here that they hoped to help troubled teenage boys do the same thing.

"You have no idea how happy I am that Sasha-Marie and that jerk finally split up," Roger said. "I knew it was coming. But you'll be glad to know I managed to keep my mouth shut about it."

Graham placed a hand on his old friend's back and grinned. "I'll bet that was tough for a crusty ol' bird who's got a knack for speaking his mind, even when he's not asked."

"You bet it was. And not to toot my own horn, but you'll be glad to know that I didn't break into the 'Halle-lujah' chorus when Maddie announced that Gabe moved out of the house."

"Good thing you didn't, Roger. You never could carry a tune."

At that, the old man chuckled. "You're right. My singing would have chased her off for sure."

Graham didn't think so. Sasha had always enjoyed the time she'd spent on the Galloping G. So it didn't surprise him in the least that she would choose to come here to sort out things.

"I wonder what her plans are," Graham said. "Hope-fully, Gabe is paying her child support."

Roger blew out a raspberry. "I wouldn't be surprised if, once that guy hit the road, he never looked back. And if he didn't, it'd be okay by me. Gabe Smith was bad news, wrapped in a shiny wrapper. But Sasha doesn't need the likes of him. Not with me around, anyway. I'll look out for her. Besides, she has a college degree. I suspect she could put that to good use."

"There's time to ask her about that later," Graham

said. "For now, you ought to enjoy the time you have with her."

"Yep, I intend to. In the meantime, I'm going to go inside and fix dinner. I'd planned to make meat loaf and baked potatoes this evening. S'pose I still will. But if I'd known Sasha-Marie and Maddie were coming, I would have taken steaks out of the freezer. It seems like we have a lot to celebrate."

Maybe Roger did. But something told Graham that Sasha wasn't nearly as happy about the split as her uncle was.

"You might not want to make such a big deal out of it," Graham said. "She married the guy and undoubtedly loved him. She probably doesn't feel like celebrating."

"I wasn't talking about making a big whoopty-do that he was out of her life, although I'd sure as heck raise my glass to that. But I'm glad she's back at the ranch. I've missed her. And I've regretted not having a chance to get to know little Maddie. She's a cutie pie, isn't she?"

Yes, she was, at that. "She sure looks a lot like her mama."

"You got that right. And she's just as spunky, too."

Before Graham could agree, Sasha and Maddie stepped out on the big, wraparound porch.

"Looks like it's time for the tour to begin," Graham said quietly to Roger. "If she wasn't expecting, I'd suggest we take horses, which would no doubt please Maddie. But I think we should take the Gator."

"Good idea. I've delivered my share of foals and calves, but I don't know squat about bringing a human baby into the world."

Just the thought of Sasha delivering at the ranch and not in a state-of-the-art medical facility twisted Graham's gut into a double knot. He'd better suggest she find a doctor in Austin—and quickly. From the size of her baby bump, she'd need a good one soon.

Yet even the fact that she was expecting didn't take away from her beauty. How had he missed the corn-silk color of her hair before—or those expressive blue eyes?

"We're ready for that tour when you are," she said, as she and her pretty Mini-Me daughter stepped off the porch.

Sasha walked slowly, but Maddie marched right up to her uncle. "Are you going with us, Uncle Roger? Are you going to show us all your horses?"

Roger blessed the child with a smile and cupped her cheek with his liver-spotted, work-roughened hand. "Not this time, sweetie. I'm going to cook our dinner. But don't worry. Graham will give you a good tour— and probably a better one than I could."

The child looked at Graham with hope-filled eyes— their pretty color reminded him of a field of bluebonnets, blowing in the breeze. "Do you know where my uncle keeps his horses?"

"Actually, we only have a few right now. But come this weekend, you'll see five more of them grazing in the south forty."

Maddie's eyes widened. "A whole *herd*?"

Graham couldn't help appreciating her enthusiasm. "Well, it's not exactly a herd, at least, not a big one. We'll have our hands full with those five for now."

He'd thought his answer would appease her, but apparently, one of her questions merely led to another. "Where are you going to get them?" she asked. "Do you have to ride into the mountains and desert and wilderness to find them?"

Graham bit back a chuckle. "My friend Chase Parker has rescue horses already on his ranch. He's going to deliver them to us."

"I can't wait to see them," she said.

"Then I'll make sure you're around when they arrive. In the meantime, let's go check out the ranch." Graham glanced at Sasha and nodded toward the barn. "Come on. We'll take the Gator."

"You got *gators* in Texas?" Maddie asked, struggling to match his strides. "Do they bite?"

Graham smiled. "We don't have any alligators on the Galloping G. I was actually talking about our off-road utility vehicle."

He led them to the rear of the barn, where he'd left the Gator parked. Once he helped Maddie into the backseat and secured her with a seat belt, something the previous owner had installed, he and Sasha climbed into the front. Then he started the engine.

What a turn this day had taken. Graham's morning had started out in the usual way—a shower before downing coffee and the biscuits and gravy Roger had made for them. Then he'd ridden out to check on the pasture where they planned to keep the new horses.

When he'd spotted the damage to the fence, as well as the battered front end of the Cadillac Escalade that had been left in the pasture, wheel wells deep in the mud, he'd realized things weren't going to be as usual today.

But nothing had prepared him for Sasha and Maddie's arrival a few hours later, which ensured that, at least for the time being, things on the Galloping G would be far from ordinary.

He just hoped the changes would be good ones.

While Graham appeared to be doing his best to avoid any big potholes on the dirt road on which they'd been driving, the Gator made a quick swerve, causing Sasha to grab the dashboard and brace herself. She turned and looked over her shoulder. "Are you okay, Maddie?"

"Yep." The seven-year-old patted her seat belt and flashed a bright-eyed smile that revealed her missing tooth. "I'm all buckled in."

"Sorry about that," Graham said. "We had a heavy rain a couple days ago, and it left the road a mess."

"I remember the summer storms we used to have," Sasha said. "I actually thought they were cool."

The rumbles of thunder and the lightning that tore across the sky had been an amazing, celestial light show. Some people were frightened by the sights and sounds, especially when they struck at night. But Sasha hadn't been one of them. And she doubted Maddie would be, either.

Graham swung around a mud puddle. "Are the bumps and turns too jarring for you?" He nodded toward her belly.

Sasha cast a reassuring smile his way. "No, I'm doing

okay. And believe it or not, the baby seems to be enjoying it as much as Maddie is."

"Apparently, she takes after her mom in more than just her looks." Graham tossed her a boyish grin. "You always were a tomboy who tried to convince Peter and me that you were as tough and strong as horseshoes."

She responded with the title of a song. "Anything you can do…"

Graham laughed. "You used to sing that to us all the time."

That was true. She'd taunted them with the lively tune from *Annie Get Your Gun* every chance she got.

Sasha had never seen the actual musical on Broadway, or anywhere else for that matter. But one summer day, when she was visiting, Uncle Roger had taken them all to see a local talent show. She'd loved the performance by a high school girl and boy who'd sung that song.

"That's too funny," Graham said. "I'd nearly forgotten it."

Singing it to Graham had been one of her many ploys to get his attention, although it hadn't worked.

However, it did seem to catch his interest now.

Graham turned to the right, following a narrow road, and pointed to a grassy area. "This is the stretch of broken fence I've been fixing. I'll need to get it done soon because we plan to keep some of the rescue horses here."

Maddie let out a little gasp. "Can we come back again and see it? After the horses get here?"

"Sure." Graham shot a questioning look at Sasha. "That is, if your mom doesn't mind."

"No, of course not. Maddie would love to see them grazing in the field." Sasha's warm smile shot clean through Graham, setting off a spark in his chest.

He'd only meant to make Maddie happy, but the fact that Sasha realized he had a soft spot for her daughter and that she was so clearly pleased by it, caught him off guard. It also left him a little unbalanced, since he hadn't meant to earn her praise.

As a result, he decided to end the tour for today and head back. Several quiet minutes later, he parked the Gator on the side of the barn.

"What's that?" Sasha pointed to the concrete foundation they'd had poured last week. "Is Uncle Roger building something, maybe a new barn?"

"That's going to be the new bunkhouse. We were going to remodel the old one, but after we got started, we realized it was in bad shape and wouldn't meet code. So we decided to start from scratch. We also built a couple of cabins for the boys."

Her brow furrowed. "The *boys*?"

Apparently, Roger hadn't mentioned their plan to her.

"Horses aren't all we hope to rescue," Graham said. "We're going to take in some troubled teenagers and put them to work gentling the horses, something we hope will give them a new perspective on life."

Her eyes widened, and her lips parted. "Seriously? That's a great plan. And very admirable."

Graham probably should have let Roger tell her about it, since her uncle needed to score a few points. But what was done was done, so he shrugged. "The idea started out as a tribute to Peter, but then it sort of took on a spin of its own. We've already talked to the school board, as well as the juvenile probation department."

"Taking in those boys won't be easy," Sasha said. "And even though you guys should be able to relate well, there will be a ton of paperwork and regulations."

"Yes, we know." And Graham already had that covered. "As a side note," he added with a grin, "you weren't the only one who went to college."

"That's right." She returned his smile. "I forgot."

As much as he liked living on the Galloping G, and as much as he loved helping Roger, he had a bigger goal in life than just working on someone else's ranch.

"What was your major?" she asked.

"Business." He'd actually earned an MBA. "So I have it all worked out."

"I'd always assumed you'd eventually go to work for your dad."

"No, I'd never do that." He'd dreamed of having a business of his own someday, one that didn't have anything to do with Robinson Tech. In fact, even though everyone, especially his father and his siblings, had expected him to join them at the corporate offices after his graduation, Graham had refused.

There was no way he could ever work with his old man. He and Gerald Robinson might have buried the hatchet in some ways over the past couple of years, but Graham still resented his father's my-way-or-the-highway attitude.

Besides, he felt good about the nonprofit organization he and Roger were creating. And he planned to use his education and his connections to make it all happen just as they planned.

"Mommy," Maddie said. "Can I go in the kitchen and find Uncle Roger? He might want my help fixing dinner."

Sasha laughed. "Sure, honey. Go ahead. I'll be there in a minute."

When the little girl hurried toward the front porch, Sasha said, "Tell me more about this idea of yours. It's not that I'm trying to dissuade you. I think it's noble. But it's... Well, it just surprises me, that's all."

Graham had a feeling it wasn't just the idea that surprised her. It was the fact that he was still living here, eight years later. Some guys might be offended by that, but he liked being able to still pull her chain and tease her a bit. "I guess there's more to me than met your eye, huh?"

For a moment, their gazes met and locked. He expected her to comment, to tease him, to... He wasn't sure what was swirling around behind those pretty blue eyes.

Instead she let his comment go.

"Where did you come up with that plan?" she asked.

"Peter and I both had wild streaks. I'd like to think that we would have settled down in time, but I'm not sure that's true. I was pretty rebellious back in the day."

"I never understood why. The way I saw it, you had everything a kid could ever want."

Graham could neither agree nor disagree with her. It wasn't that he'd had an unhappy childhood. His father had supplied his family with everything they could possibly ask for, other than his time, of course. Gerald Robinson, or rather, Jerome Fortune—damn, would Graham ever get used to that name?—had always seemed to be at the office or away on a business trip. And while he supplied his children with plenty of material possessions, he'd held back on his affection. That in and of itself would cause plenty of kids to rebel. But Graham had other reasons for the issues between him and his dad. Things he'd never told anyone and certainly wouldn't share with Sasha.

"Maybe I was a born rebel," he said.

"Peter, too?" She slowly shook her head, not believing him. But her cousin had a wild side, too, even if she hadn't been aware of it.

Graham and Peter had met in middle school and become best friends. They were both energetic and creative, often getting in trouble in class—and partying on the weekends.

Roger had always taken their rowdy behavior with a grain of salt, saying boys would be boys. But Graham's dad considered it outright rebellion, especially when he knew Graham was probably his brightest child and had such unrealized potential.

"I guess you could say I sometimes led Peter astray," Graham said, although that really wasn't true. Still, he wasn't about to let the conversation continue on that same thread and open up any more than he'd already done.

Since Sasha remained seated in the Gator, apparently eager to hear more, he opted to change the subject.

"How long are you planning to be here?" he asked.

"I don't know. For the near future, I suppose. And until I can figure out my next step."

"Well, for however long it is, I'm glad you came back and that you brought Maddie. It'll be good for Roger."

He'd meant his comment to give her some peace, but her gaze nearly drilled a hole right through him. She seemed to be asking him something with her eyes, but he'd be damned if he knew what it was.

Chapter Three

Graham was right. Sasha's visit to the Galloping G might prove to be good for Roger. It would definitely be good for her and Maddie.

But what about you? she was tempted to ask Graham. *How do you feel about my return?*

A moment after the question rose in her mind, she shook the dust and cobwebs from it. Those days of carefree, youthful dreams were long gone, even if Graham was even more handsome, more appealing than ever.

Besides, even when life had been innocent and simple, that silly crush she'd had on him was hopeless. He'd never considered her anything other than a pesky kid. In fact, the last time she'd seen him on the Galloping G, when he'd come by to tell her uncle goodbye before he left for college, he'd called her "Sassy Pants" and had tugged on the ponytail she wore.

But then again, she'd only been fifteen at the time. She'd also been a late bloomer and had looked young for her age. Actually, she still did. Even though she was nearing the ripe old age of thirty, people often mistook her for Maddie's babysitter.

Trying to rein in her wild and inappropriate thoughts, Sasha thanked him for the tour. "Maddie really enjoyed it. And so did I."

"You're welcome. It was my pleasure. When Chase brings those horses on Friday, I'll give you a better explanation of our rescue operation."

She nodded but didn't make any attempt to get out of the Gator. She still had something weighing on her mind, a comment she'd made and the apology she owed him for it. "I'm sorry if I made it sound as though I didn't think you and Uncle Roger could handle running a home for wayward teenagers. Or that you didn't have legalities and logistics all planned out. I'm sure you do. I was just surprised to hear it, that's all."

Graham, his left wrist perched on top of the steering wheel, his right on the gearshift, studied her for a moment. As he did, their gazes held steady.

"No offense taken," he said. "You always have been one to speak your mind. And for the record, your uncle isn't the only one who's glad you're back."

Her heart warmed at his words. It had been a long time since she'd felt wanted or appreciated. Gabe certainly hadn't made her feel that way in the past few years. In fact, he never really had. "Thanks for saying that, Graham. Whether it's true or not, I appreciate hearing it."

"It wasn't just fluff to make you feel good, Sassy Pants."

She smiled at the nickname that had once driven her crazy. But today it flowed from his lips like an endearment.

Or maybe she was so starved for affection and validation that she would latch on to almost anything she could construe as a compliment. But whose fault was that? She only had herself to blame for remaining in a relationship that had fizzled out years ago.

In fact, in retrospect, her marriage had begun to unravel from the day she and Gabe returned from their honeymoon.

Sure, she'd thought that she'd loved him at the time and that he'd felt the same way about her. But the dream she'd once harbored, to finally have a home and family of her own, soon ended, and reality had set in as soon as the wedding-day sparkle was gone.

Tears welled in her eyes once again, and she blinked them back. But she wasn't doing a very good job of it.

"What's the matter?" Graham asked. "Are you okay?"

The last thing she wanted him to think was that she felt sorry for herself, when it was more her concern about raising her children without a father. The girls needed a loving, male influence in their lives. So she forced a smile to go along with the explanation she hoped he'd believe. "I'm fine. Just a few happy tears overflowing. It feels so good to be back on the Galloping G."

And it really did. But that didn't mean she wasn't grieving for the happy family she'd once thought she'd have.

She sniffled, then proceeded to climb from the Gator. "I'd better go inside and check on Maddie. She's probably driving poor Uncle Roger crazy."

"I'm sure he's fine."

She suspected that was true, but she couldn't stay outside with Graham forever, wishing things were different than they really were.

"Will we see you at dinner?" she asked.

"I usually eat most of my meals in the ranch house. Your uncle is one heck of a cook. So yeah. I'll be there."

She nodded, then turned away, leaving Graham seated in the Gator.

As she headed to the back door that led to the kitchen, she took a big breath, relishing the country air and the whinny of a horse in the pasture.

Yes, it was good to be back. While she was here, maybe she'd come up with a feasible game plan for the future. She had a degree in social work and might as well put it to good use.

But what about the cost of infant day care? Gabe had said he'd send additional money for that, but she wasn't sure she could depend upon him to carry through with it. But at least she'd get a decent amount of child support, which was one of the details they'd agreed upon when they filed for divorce. So she was right back to her most troubling dilemma.

She'd never intended to be a single mother, but life didn't always turn out the way a person expected it to.

Nevertheless, she would create a new family with her daughters—minus a daddy, of course.

She had no other choice. Her children's happiness depended upon it.

Uncle Roger, who'd been a cook in the navy years ago, outdid himself at dinner this evening. Or maybe Sasha felt that way because she'd missed sharing meals with him on the ranch.

After the first couple of bites, Sasha said, "I'd like to have your recipe for this meat loaf. Grandma Dixon used to make it, but she always covered hers with a weird mushroom sauce. I like your version much better. It doesn't need anything on top, other than some good, old-fashioned ketchup."

"I'll try to write something down for you," her uncle said. "But I'm not sure how to go about it. I just throw things together."

"Then you have a good sense about how something is supposed to taste. You're an awesome cook."

Uncle Roger beamed, his bright-eyed smile shaving years off his face. "Thanks, Sasha-Marie."

But it wasn't just the main dish that Sasha found remarkable. "I haven't had baked potatoes with all the fixings in ages." She pointed to the small bowls of toppings he'd set out on the table. "Butter, fresh chives, sour cream, grated cheddar, real bacon… You didn't skimp on anything."

When her uncle didn't respond, she looked up from

her plate to see him and Graham shooting glances at each other. She tried to read their expressions, to no avail.

Had they, over the years, created a silent language of their own? Then again, there was still a lot left to be said this evening, plus a hatchet to be buried. And they all knew it. Well, the adults did. Little Maddie was eating away, oblivious of the tension that still stretched between Sasha and Roger.

"Thanks for going to all this trouble for me," she said. "It's a perfect welcome-home meal."

At that, Uncle Roger broke into another grin. "I'm glad you're here, honey."

"Me, too," she admitted. And she was grateful that, in spite of the fact that he'd been hurt, he'd opened his arms and heart to her once again, just as he'd done after her parents died.

She speared her fork into a crunchy piece of romaine lettuce, as well as a plump chunk of tomato that had obviously come fresh from the vine. But she hadn't been prepared for the familiar taste of the vinaigrette. "Oh, my gosh. You even made Aunt Helen's salad dressing. Now I'm really impressed."

Roger's tired blue eyes lit up and he winked. "That was my way of having her here with us tonight."

"What a nice thought."

After they finished dinner, Roger brought out dessert: chocolate-chip ice cream and store-bought peanut butter cookies.

"I like ranch food," Maddie said. "It's really good."

Roger, whose smile stretched from ear to ear, said,

"You just wait for breakfast. I'll make silver-dollar pan-cakes for you."

The man had always been a whiz in the kitchen, going out of his way to make sure he pleased those shar-ing his table. And while Sasha should volunteer to do the dishes herself and give him a much-deserved break this evening, they still had things to discuss. And they needed to do that in private.

"I'll help you with the dishes," she told her uncle.

"That's not necessary. I clean up as I go."

"Yes, I know. But I'd like to talk to you."

As Roger nodded in agreement, Graham spoke up. "That sounds like a good plan to me." Then he turned his attention to Maddie. "Since you and I are off the hook for cleanup detail, let's go into the living room, kick back and watch the sports channel."

Maddie wrinkled her nose. "But I don't like sports. Don't you want to watch Disney or Nickelodeon or car-toons instead?"

Graham sat back in his chair, crossed his arms over his chest and scrunched his own face. "What do you mean, you don't like *sports*? Not even pro rodeo?"

Maddie sat up, her eyes brightening. "I thought sports meant football and basketball and dumb ol' golf. But I'd like to watch rodeo stuff."

"Something told me you would be okay with that." Graham glanced at Sasha and winked in camaraderie, setting off a warm flutter in her heart. She doubted he had any idea how that small, brief connection had affected her, just as he hadn't in the past, because he turned back to her daughter. "I'll make you a deal, Maddie. If we can't find any rodeo on TV, then I'll let you be in charge of the remote."

The child clapped her hands. "Deal!"

"Then what are we waiting for?" Graham pushed back his chair and stood. "Let's get out of here before they put you and me to work."

Maddie slid off her seat, then followed the handsome cowboy into the family room, leaving Sasha and Uncle Roger alone.

As her uncle began to clear the table, she said, "I owe you an apology."

He merely looked at her, waiting for her to explain.

"You tried to warn me about Gabe, and I should have listened. But I was young and headstrong back then. I was also in love with the idea of marriage."

"Yeah, well, I knew that no-good son of a…" Roger cleared his throat, pausing as if trying to temper his response. Then he blew out a heavy sigh. "Well, that's all muddy water under a rickety old bridge to nowhere."

"Yes, I know. But it needs to be said, just the same." She picked up the plates, bowls and silverware, while he grabbed the glasses.

"I s'pose you're right about that. But just so you know, when I was that age and had fallen for your aunt, I wouldn't have let anyone talk me out of marrying her. So I can't blame you for not listening to me."

"I'm glad you understand, but that isn't the only reason I need to apologize."

He arched a gray, bushy eyebrow.

"I'm sorry for not keeping in better contact with you. I should have done that." She stacked the dirty dishes on the counter near the sink, then took the glasses from him and set them down, too. "It wouldn't have hurt me to visit some and call you more often."

"Yeah, well…" Roger paused again, his craggy brow creased as if he was wading through his thoughts and feelings. Then he shrugged. "The phone line goes both ways. Besides, the fault is probably mine. I shouldn't have stirred things up at your wedding."

"I knew something happened that day, but I wasn't sure what. You were so quiet and grim." She reached into the cupboard under the sink for the bottle of dish soap. "And Gabe was… Well, he was as tense as a fence post and angry about something."

"Gabe and I had words," Roger said. "And I damn near beat the crap out of him. The best man and the groomsmen had to pull me off him. So I'm sorry about that." He chuckled. "Actually, I'm mostly sorry someone interfered before I had a chance to let him have it. I would have enjoyed giving him a black eye, a fat lip and a bloody nose. But it's just as well. If I had, it would have ruined your special day."

She laughed, imagining a battered groom standing at the altar. "You're right. I wouldn't have been happy about that."

"Either way, honey, I should have held my tongue. And my temper."

It wasn't like her uncle to get into brawls, especially at a church and dressed in a tuxedo. "What made you want to fight him?"

"The stuff he said to me. Things meant to rile me up, I 'spect." Again he shrugged as if it no longer mattered.

But it did matter, especially if they wanted to put it all behind them.

"What did he say to you?" she asked.

Roger pondered her question for the longest time. When she thought he might never answer, he said, "I wanted to have a talk with him before the ceremony. I figured, with your daddy and your grandpa gone, that job was up to me. So I found him and his friends waiting for the ceremony to start in one of the small rooms at the church. They were already dressed and throwing back shots of whiskey as if the bachelor party had never ended."

She'd smelled alcohol on Gabe's breath, tasted it, too. She'd assumed he'd been nervous and had wanted to take the edge off.

"Now, I'll admit," Roger said, "I ain't a teetotaler. But I didn't think the preacher or the Good Lord would have appreciated those boys tying one on at the church on a Saturday morning. And I told 'em so. But Gabe didn't take to being scolded. I should have taken the hint then, but I decided to try a different approach and asked if I could talk to him alone."

"When you spoke in private, what did he say?"

"Actually, he told me there wasn't anything I had to say that his buddies couldn't hear."

"Gabe could get pretty mouthy when he drank," Sasha admitted. "Especially when he was with his friends." One part of her didn't want to hear the details, but she needed to know. "So, then what happened?"

"I just told him to be good to you, to respect you. And then I said, if he didn't, he'd have to answer to me."

She wouldn't have expected any less from her uncle. Roger Gibault might be a bit gruff and rough around the edges, but he had a good heart. And he was respectful to women.

"Apparently, Gabe took offense at what I said and considered it a threat." Roger turned on the spigot, letting warm water flow into the sink. He squeezed a squirt of dish soap under the flow, then chuckled. "Hell, it *was* a threat. And he didn't like it."

When the water and bubbles reached the proper level, Sasha shut off the faucet. "Gabe never listened to his father, either. He didn't like being told what to do."

"That doesn't surprise me. It didn't take me but five minutes to realize he thought he was pretty damn special. And that he was a big-mouthed rabble-rouser. But I hadn't realized he was such an ass. If I had, I would have seen it coming."

"Seen what coming?"

"Gabe gave me a shove that sent me flying against the wall and damn near shook the church rafters. I hit it so hard I got an egg on the back of my head. Hell, the thud alone knocked a framed picture of the Good Shepherd onto the floor."

"Oh, my gosh. I hope he apologized."

"Nope. It didn't faze him. Instead he opened his yap and lit my fuse."

Sasha hadn't realized that their words had progressed to violence. "What did he say?"

"You want a direct quote?"

She nodded, bracing herself. "Yes, please tell me."

Roger's eyes narrowed to a glare, and his voice deepened, the tone chilly. "'Who do you think you are, old man? You aren't anything to me. And just so you know, I've got your little Sasha-Marie right where I want her— in my bed and under my thumb. So keep your mouth shut and don't even try interfering in our lives, or I'll make sure you never see her again.'"

Sasha cringed. Had she known this on her wedding day, she might have...done what? Told Gabe that the wedding was off?

No, sadly, she might not have wanted to believe the worst about him. She'd been so starry-eyed and hope-filled that day. But now, eight years later, she realized what Roger was telling her was true.

"I wanted to knock him down to size," Roger said. "So when I got my balance, I doubled up my fist and went after him. I landed a pretty good one on his chin, although I'd been aiming for his nose. He might have thought of me as just an old man, but I'm cowboy strong. And I would have beaten the crap out of him then and there, if his friends hadn't pulled me off him."

"I'm sorry, Uncle Roger. I had no idea what a mean, selfish jerk Gabe was."

"Well, what's done is done. After it was all over, I realized how embarrassed you would have been if I'd battered your groom until he was black and blue."

She smiled. "I almost wish you'd done it now."

He chuckled. "Me, too. But my mama and daddy taught me better than that. I just wish my temper didn't sometimes get the best of me."

She smiled and opened her arms. "Can I give you a hug?"

"You betcha." He stepped into the embrace, and they held each other close. That is, until the baby shifted and gave her a quick jab with either a little foot or fist.

"Well, I'll be damned." Roger dropped his arms, took a step back and looked down at her expanded belly. "I guess I'm not the only one in the family with a feisty side and a protective streak. That little one has a good kick."

"She's strong, that's for sure. And she's always making her presence known."

"Well, I'm looking forward to meeting her. I wish I could have seen more of Maddie when she was a baby. But…" He clamped his mouth shut and slowly shook his head.

"You came to see her when she was born. Then you left quickly. Did Gabe chase you off?"

"He didn't actually say anything too bad that time. Maybe because there hadn't been any alcohol involved and he didn't have an army of friends surrounding him. But each time I glanced at him, he glared at me, so I decided to end my visit and to stay away. I didn't want to avoid you, but I knew if I came around more often, things might eventually blow up again. Besides, I figured my presence alone would upset your husband and he might take it out on you."

"So you made that sacrifice for me?"

"That's what you do when you love someone, Sasha-Marie."

She placed a hand on his arm, fingering the softness of his worn flannel shirt. "I hope you know how much I love and appreciate you."

Roger's eyes glistened and his grin deepened. The hard feelings he'd once harbored had clearly softened.

He might have said that his anger had been directed at Gabe, but she suspected that he'd resented her for not listening to him in the first place, for not calling him regularly or visiting on occasion.

But he was right. That was all water under the bridge now.

"I'd better check on Maddie," she said. "She's liable to pester Graham more than I ever did."

Roger laughed. "You were a pistol when you were a youngster, that's a fact."

Sasha smiled at the truth. She might have been a little headstrong, but she'd also had a loving heart, just like Maddie, who shared the same vivacious energy. Thank goodness her daughter hadn't picked up any of Gabe's bad traits.

Instead Maddie resembled Sasha in so many ways, and not just because of their big blue eyes and fair hair.

As Sasha entered the living room, where she assumed Maddie and Graham were watching television, she expected the cowboy to jump up immediately, glad for her return and a chance to escape the precocious child.

But she hadn't been prepared for the sight that met her eyes. The two were seated on the floor, side by side. Maddie's crayons and coloring books were spread upon the coffee table. Seeing the two of them working—or rather, playing—together was enough to turn Sasha's heart inside out.

"Well, I'll be darned," Roger said. "I never would

have guessed it, son, but you make one heck of a baby-sitter."

Graham glanced up, a boyish grin stretched across his face. "I might be having a good time, but I'm not for hire. So don't get any ideas."

Unfortunately, Sasha was getting plenty of them. And they didn't have anything to do with hiring Graham to watch her children. But she couldn't afford to let that old childish crush get out of hand, especially when she knew her feelings would always be one-sided.

As a waning moon shone overhead that night, lighting the familiar path, Graham headed toward his cabin. He'd stayed at the big house long enough to see that Sasha and Roger had gotten things settled between them.

He was glad about that. He'd have to ask his old friend to share the details tomorrow during morning chores.

In return, Graham would have some things to tell Roger, too. While coloring with Maddie this evening, he'd gotten an earful. The girl was not only a cutie pie, but she was talkative to boot.

Sasha would probably flip out if she knew Maddie had filled him in on some of their family secrets. Not that she'd come right out and told him anything point blank, but Graham was pretty good at connecting dots and asking a few carefully constructed questions now and then.

From what he'd gathered, Gabe had traveled on business and was rarely home. But whenever he was around,

Maddie had to keep quiet and play in her room. *Shh!* her mama would tell her. *Daddy's tired, and you know how cranky he can get.*

"Was it hard to keep quiet?" Graham had asked the girl.

"No, because then Mama and I would leave. Sometimes we'd get groceries or go to the park. But we always got ice cream or a snack on the way home."

"Sounds like, in some ways, it was fun when he came home."

"Not always," she said. "Not when he yelled at me or Mama."

Graham had never met the man Sasha married, but he hadn't needed to. Roger was a good judge of character. And now little Maddie had added her own spin on what life with Gabe Smith was like.

As Graham reached the front stoop of his cabin, he stopped and turned, scanning the ranch that would soon be known as Peter's Place. He suspected Peter would have been proud of their plan.

As he turned back to reach for doorknob, his cell phone rang. He pulled it from his pocket and glanced at the lit screen. He didn't recognize the number, but he answered anyway.

"Mr. Gibault?" a man asked.

"No, this is Graham Robinson."

"Oh. Yeah. Sorry, I got my names and numbers confused. Anyway, this is Brad Taylor with the juvenile probation department. I have a young man I'd like to bring out to the Galloping G tomorrow. He's already passed the screening process. Are you ready for him?"

The bunkhouse wasn't finished, but they had a new two-bedroom cabin into which the boy could move. Graham also planned to hire a full-time counselor, as well as a teacher, since most of the boys would be lacking school credits. He and Roger had interviewed several applicants already, but they hadn't made any decisions yet. Of course, that was going to be a top priority now.

Still, he said, "Sure, we're ready for him."

"Good. Then we'll see you tomorrow. I'll email a copy of his file, as well as the psychological evaluation, so you can read them over before we arrive. Look for us after one o'clock."

"Thanks." Graham couldn't wait to tell Roger they would soon see their plan coming together.

After Mr. Taylor ended the call, Graham made one last scan of the ranch and noticed that Sasha had walked outside the main house and now stood on the wraparound porch. She didn't venture any farther than that. She just gripped the railing and looked out into the night, same as he'd done earlier.

Graham slipped the cell back into his jeans pocket. All the while, he watched Sasha, saw her wander over to the porch swing, then take a seat and set the thing in motion.

He wondered what she had on her mind. When she'd been a kid, she used to sit outside all the time, especially in the evenings. He asked her about it once, teasing her while he did. *What're you doing, Sassy Pants? Mooning over a boy?*

Maybe.

Does he know you like him?

At that, she'd let out a wobbly sigh. *I wish. But he doesn't even know I'm alive.*

The summer before Graham left for college, she'd sat out there night after night. He'd always assumed she was daydreaming about the boy she was sweet on.

Was that what she was doing now? Thinking about Gabe? Wondering if he'd come looking for her? Plotting some way to win him back?

As much as he hoped she was smarter than that, she was pregnant with Gabe's baby. So it made sense that she might want to hold things together.

Graham was sorely tempted to cross the yard and tell her she was better off without him. He could also assure her that he'd look out for her until she got back on her feet.

But what made him think she'd appreciate an offer like that? It wasn't as if she was mooning over *him*.

Too bad, he thought. For some totally illogical reason, a part of him wished that she were.

Chapter Four

Around one o'clock on Friday afternoon, Graham went to the barn to repair a broken hinge on one of the stalls. Chase had called earlier to say that he would be bringing the horses later today, but not all of them would be ready to be turned out to pasture or into one of the corrals. One might need to be stabled.

Graham had just tightened a loose bolt when he heard a car pull into the yard. He suspected it was the probation officer bringing their first teenage resident, but there was no way to know for sure unless he went outside. So he left his tools resting on a bale of straw and strode out of the barn and into the yard.

A white sedan with government license plates and a stoical teenager sitting in the passenger seat told Graham his assumption had been right.

The man behind the wheel had to be Brad Taylor, who'd asked if Graham and Roger were ready for their first kid to arrive. But ready or not, it was showtime.

When a red-haired man in his early forties climbed out of the sedan, Graham introduced himself and greeted him with a firm handshake.

"It's nice to meet you," Taylor said. "My supervisor said that you were highly recommended by the references you provided."

"I'm glad to hear that. I told you we were prepared to take in kids, and we are. But for the record, the teacher we just hired won't be able to start until next Monday."

"No problem." Taylor placed his hands in the pockets of his khaki slacks. "Jonah's behind on some of his credits, but he ought to catch up quickly if he's working one-on-one with an instructor."

"I hope so," Graham said. "In the meantime, he'll be able to settle in and get used to the way we do things around here."

"Thanks for providing a place for him," Taylor said. "He's not thrilled about coming here, but like I told you on the phone, his options were limited."

The email report had provided Graham with the kid's background, as well as the trouble he'd gotten into.

Jonah Wright came from a broken home. His dad had run off a couple of years ago, leaving the mother to raise Jonah and three younger children. The man didn't pay her any child support, so that forced her to work two jobs to make ends meet. She needed help and cooperation from all the kids, especially the oldest. But instead of taking on more family responsibility, Jonah started acting out and ditching school. His mother was at her wit's end. And when he was caught stealing a camera from the photography classroom at his high school, she feared he would lead her other children astray if he didn't straighten up.

Then, when a recent shoplifting violation at a department store resulted in Jonah's arrest and prosecution, she'd poured out her frustration to the court. At that point, Brad Taylor had stepped in and suggested the boy be placed on a working ranch to help him get his priorities in order. And that led to Jonah becoming the very first teenage resident of Peter's Place.

It wasn't until Brad opened the passenger door that Jonah slid out of the vehicle, wearing a black T-shirt with a white skull and crossbones on the front and a pair of pants that rode so low on his hips that, if he sneezed, they'd probably slip to his knees. His beat-up black sneakers were untied, the floppy laces frayed and dirty from being stepped on.

His very appearance screamed rebellion, and the scowl on his face suggested he wore a chip on his shoulder.

Graham reached out a hand, giving the teen a man's welcome. "I'm glad you're here. We have some rescue horses arriving in a couple of hours, and we'll need all the help we can get."

"I don't know squat about horses or cattle," Jonah said. "So if you're looking for a cowboy, you're out of luck."

Roger, who'd just come out of the house, approached just in time to hear the boy's comment. But like the loving, slow-to-react father he'd been to Peter, he glossed over the kid's attitude and appearance—something Graham had always liked and admired about him. Not that Roger hadn't given Peter and Graham hell at times, but he'd chosen his battles wisely.

"It ain't that hard to learn," the elderly rancher said. "You'll get the hang of it in no time at all, son."

The boy merely clicked his tongue, rolled his eyes and looked away.

Brad pulled the car keys from his pocket. "I'll be back in a few days to check up on you, Jonah."

The kid made another tongue click. "Whatever."

"Actually," Brad said, turning to Graham and Roger, "it might be sooner than that. I have another boy who's going to need placement. I'll know for sure after court next week, so I'll be in touch."

Graham shook his hand. "Like I said, we have room for six right now. And once the bunkhouse is finished next month and we've hired additional staff, we can add twenty more."

Brad nodded, then climbed back into his car. After he drove off, Sasha came outside and made her way to the new arrival.

Apparently, she wanted to meet Jonah, too. But Graham couldn't blame her for that. She was a mother and probably wanted to get a feel for the young stranger who was going to be living on the ranch.

"Hi there." She reached out a hand to greet Jonah. "I'm Sasha. My daughter and I are staying here, too."

The kid studied her outstretched hand for a beat,

then took it, albeit reluctantly. "You and your kid get in trouble?"

Sasha smiled. "I've made some bad choices in my life, but I plan to do things differently from here on out. And coming to Peter's Place is going to help me do that. I hope you feel the same way soon."

He shrugged. But his expression seemed to have softened a bit, just being around Sasha.

Hell, just being around her had caused Graham to rethink a few things, too. That glossy, white-blond hair that tumbled over her shoulders, those expressive blue eyes, the alluring scent of ripe peaches...

Don't forget, his better judgment countered, *she's also carrying another man's baby.*

"I hope you like spaghetti," Sasha said to Jonah. "My daughter and I are fixing dinner tonight."

"It's okay, but I like pizza a lot better."

Graham wanted to roll his eyes at the kid's attitude, but only when it was directed at Sasha. Instead he kept himself in check.

"Jonah," Roger said, "we'll show you where you'll be staying. Get your bag and come with us."

The boy grabbed the small canvas tote that held his belongings, then followed the men to the newly built two-bedroom cabin, which was only fifty yards from the older but similar structure in which Graham lived.

"Since you're the first one to move in," Roger said, "you have your choice of bedrooms and bunks."

Jonah scanned the small, ten-by-twelve living area, with its bookshelf, love seat and two chairs. "Where's the TV?"

"There isn't one," Roger said. "But you won't be spending much time in here, other than for sleep. If you need to entertain yourself, you'll find plenty of good books—like *Moby Dick*, which was always a favorite of mine."

There went another eye roll, followed by a tongue click. "How am I s'posed to play the video games I brought?"

"I'm afraid you won't be able to." Graham smiled. "But like Roger said, you won't miss playing them while you're in the cabin. You'll be too eager to get a good night's sleep."

The boy's jaw dropped.

"Breakfast is in the big house at six a.m.," Roger added. "If you're late, we don't eat lunch until noon. So I suggest you set the alarm."

Jonah, whose droopy britches revealed more than just the waistband of his red boxer shorts, shook his head. "Man, it's summer vacation. Didn't anyone tell you guys that it's okay to sleep in?"

"Not on the Galloping G, it ain't." Roger nodded to one of the two bedrooms. "Put your gear away, then come outside with us. We'll show you around and give you a list of chores."

Jonah let out an expletive, followed by a grumble.

Graham had told Brad Taylor that he and Roger were ready for that first kid. He just hoped that was true.

It was nearly four o'clock when Chase Parker arrived with the horses. At six foot two, the dark-haired rancher appeared to be a typical cowboy. But there was a lot more to Chase than met the eye. He didn't just run a horse rescue operation; he was also the heir to Parker Oil. And if you looked closely, you'd see he had on an expensive pair of boots, rather than the dusty, battered pair a ranch hand might wear.

Graham greeted his friend with a handshake, then introduced him to Jonah. The boy didn't give Chase much attention, but his dark, sour expression lightened when he spotted the first horse coming out of the trailer.

"Why is that one so skinny?" Jonah asked, pointing to a roan gelding.

"This is Barney," Chase said. "He was in an equine hospital before he came to my ranch. He's doing fairly well now, but you should have seen him two months ago."

"Was he sick?" the boy asked.

"No, he was abused and neglected. He was just skin and bones when I got him. But he was one of the lucky ones where he used to live. The other two horses were in such bad shape they had to be put down."

The boy grimaced. "That sucks. Someone should have knocked his owner's lights out. What happened to the guy?"

"He was charged with animal cruelty and neglect," Chase said.

The boy swore under his breath. "I hope he got life in prison."

"I'm afraid the penalties aren't that steep," Chase said. "But he's being punished."

"Here." Chase handed Barney's lead rope to the teen. "I'll get another horse."

"What am I supposed to do with him?" Jonah asked, but Chase was already back at the trailer.

"Give him a gentle stroke," Graham said. "Let him know that he can trust you, that you won't hurt him. Barney and the horses we're getting haven't seen much human kindness, if any. So they tend to get spooked easily. But he'll respond to a soothing voice and a soft touch."

For a moment, Graham thought the kid might balk at the suggestion. Instead he eased closer to the gelding and stroked his neck.

"You know," Jonah said, "when Brad told me you guys kept rescue horses, I figured they were wild mustangs."

"The Bureau of Land Management has strict fencing and corral rules for adoptive owners of the mustangs, but we could end up with some."

Chase returned with a chestnut mare. "This is Suzy Q."

"What happened to her?" Jonah asked. "Was she starved, too? She doesn't look as skinny as Barney."

"Suzy is a PMU mare from a farm in Canada. She was repeatedly impregnated for her urine, which was used in making drugs like Premarin, which are used to treat menopause. In her case, she was kept confined in a stall for six of the eleven months of her pregnancy. She couldn't turn around, groom herself or lie down. And her water intake was regulated to produce a maximum-estrogen urine."

"Dang," the boy said. "That's a crappy life."

"Yeah, it was pretty brutal." Chase gave the mare

a pat on the neck. "The United States has some strict laws about that these days, and Canada is starting to crack down on them. Unfortunately, the whole business is thriving in China now."

"What business?" the boy asked.

"Gathering urine from pregnant horses," Chase said. "They attach a type of catheter over a mare's urethra that's held in place by body straps that restrict her movement. Once she foals, she's only given a short time to recover, then impregnated again. When a mare is no longer able to 'produce,' most are sold for slaughter."

"How did you get her?" Jonah asked Chase.

"There was a raid on her farm in Canada, and I was able to take her and Ginger, who you'll meet in a minute."

"So you can see these horses are going to need gentle treatment and a lot of love," Graham said.

The boy, his brow furrowed, handed over Barney's halter to Graham, then strode toward the trailer, where Chase was unloading yet another gelding, that one an Appaloosa.

Jonah reached out to stroke the animal, but it threw back its head.

"Easy, boy," Jonah said. "I won't hurt you."

"He just needs a little time to get to know you better," Graham said.

When all five of the horses had been unloaded and placed in either the corral or one of the stalls in the barn, Graham thanked Chase.

"My pleasure. I'm just glad to know these horses found a good home and will get the care they need."

"Say," Graham said. "How's your wife?"

A grin stretched across Chase's face. "Lucie's great. We couldn't be happier."

"I'm glad to hear it."

Chase had married Lucie Fortune Chesterfield ten years ago in Scotland. They'd thought his parents had taken care of the paperwork to have it annulled, only to learn recently that the union was still in force. A couple of months ago, the couple struck up a romance once more and decided to stay wed.

Lucie worked for the Fortune Foundation, which had offered to sponsor Peter's Place as one of its charities. But Graham wasn't sure he wanted the funding, especially if there were strings attached. Lucie said there wouldn't be, so he was thinking it over.

Still, while he'd appreciate the additional financial support, he wasn't sure if things would get complicated, should the whole Robinson-Fortune connection prove to be true. His father might deny it, but there was reason to believe he was lying.

So what else was new?

"Well, I'd better get home," Chase said. "Lucie and I have dinner plans tonight."

The men shook hands again; then the neighboring rancher climbed behind the wheel of his truck.

"Have fun this evening," Graham said. "We'll talk soon."

Chase nodded, then started the engine and pulled away, his trailer now empty.

Graham checked his watch before turning to Jonah. "It's nearly dinnertime. You hungry?"

"Yeah, but what about the horses? Do they need hay or grain or something? Most of them are still pretty skinny."

"They already ate this morning, so we'll feed them again after dinner. I'll show you how it's done later tonight, since that'll be one of your jobs while you're here. Then, in the morning, before breakfast, you can take care of it on your own."

"So you weren't messing with me about breakfast starting at six?"

Graham chuckled. "Nope. But you won't be sorry. Roger puts out quite a spread in the morning."

"I have to," the old rancher said. "It's a long time before lunch, and you'll have to keep up your strength."

"Dang." But instead of an eye roll or a grumble, Jonah strode over to the corral and studied Suzy Q and Ginger, the two mares that were checking out their new surroundings.

Graham stole a peek at Roger, who smiled and nodded. So far, Peter's Place appeared to be working out the way they'd hoped it would.

After dinner, Graham waited for Jonah to help Sasha with the dishes. Then, as promised, he took the teenager outside and showed him how to feed the horses.

Jonah not only listened to the instructions, but also asked a few questions. Graham filled him in the best he could. Yet while the teenager seemed to be settling in at the Galloping G, Graham knew better than to believe a complete behavior and attitude change would be easy. But so far, he liked what he was seeing.

Once the evening chores were done and the barn was secured for the night, Graham walked Jonah to his cabin and watched him set the alarm clock for five-thirty in the morning.

"There's soap in the bathroom," Graham said, "as well as towels and washcloths in the linen closet. So you shouldn't need anything."

Jonah, who'd been pretty agreeable just minutes ago, shook his head and frowned. "I can't believe there isn't a TV in here. Or even Wi-Fi. I don't know what you expect me to do at night. Or how I'm s'posed to fall asleep."

"Why not try reading? It helps me." Graham crossed the small room to the bookshelf, which he'd purposely filled with a large selection of novels that a teenage boy might find appealing. "You might like *Lord of the Rings*."

"Nah, I don't want to read that. I saw the movie a jillion times. And before my mom took away the TV in my room, I played the video game. So I know that story backwards and forwards."

Graham could have insisted that books were usually ten times better than the movies, but he kept his opinion to himself. "How about one of the Harry Potter books? I'm sure you'll find something that interests you."

The boy gave a shrug, but held tight to his scowl. "I guess I'll check 'em out. Otherwise I'll die of boredom before morning."

That was all Graham could ask. Besides, it had been his plan all along to encourage the boys to read, although he wasn't sure if Jonah had figured that out.

"Just don't get so caught up in a story that you stay up too late. I guarantee that alarm clock will go off before you know it."

"I've never been a reader. Well, not since I was in middle school. That's when my old man ran off and my life went to hell."

"I'm sorry to hear that. But you're the only one who can turn things around for yourself now."

"You sound just like Mr. Taylor."

There was a reason for that. What they'd told Jonah was true. But Graham wasn't going to preach to the kid. He'd rather lead by example. "I'll see you in the morning."

"Yeah, whatever."

Jonah started toward the bookcase, and Graham left him on his own.

After closing the cabin door, Graham stepped out into the evening and headed toward his own place. As was his habit, he glanced at the big house and the window to Roger's bedroom. The light was off, indicating the rancher had gone to bed. But the porch light burned bright.

Under the yellow glow, he spotted Sasha sitting on the porch swing again. But this time, instead of leaving her alone, he changed course, crossed the yard and approached her.

"You want company?" he asked.

She slowed the swing to a stop and smiled. "Sure."

He scanned the porch, noting the chairs were about ten feet away from her.

"You can sit with me, if you want." She patted the spot next to her.

Did he want to get that cozy? For some reason, the answer was yes. So he took a seat beside her, the swing swaying and the metal hardware creaking as he did.

"What are you thinking about?" That was probably a better way of asking *who* was on her mind.

"My girls," she said.

Not Gabe? That was a relief. She might not realize it, but she and her daughters would be much better off without that guy in their lives.

"I'm trying to decide how I'm going to support them. I can get a job, of course. I have a degree in social work, so I'm sure I can find a position in Austin. But day care is expensive, especially for an infant. On top of that, it'll be hard for me to leave a newborn with someone else."

"What about child support?" he asked.

"I'm supposed to get it, but I'm not going to count on it. Gabe never was able to keep a job. And he's always refused to work for his father."

The fact that Graham had felt the same way about working for his old man at Robinson Tech didn't sit well. He hadn't expected to have anything in common with Sasha's ex.

They sat quietly awhile, lulled into a surreal sense of contentment by the slight motion of the swing they shared. Even the creaking of the chains, springs and bolts seemed to be mesmerizing.

Or was it just the presence of the lovely woman seated beside him?

He shrugged off the possibility, unwilling to ponder just what it all meant, and asked, "So, what did you think of Jonah?"

"He's angry at the world, but I suspect that has a lot to do with his father's abandonment. And the fact that he was expected to clean the house, cook the meals and babysit while his mother was at work."

"I got that idea, too. But he needs to accept the fact that his father is gone and his mom is doing the best she can."

"There might be more to it than that," Sasha said. "While he was helping me wash the dinner dishes, he mentioned that he used to be a star pitcher on his high school baseball team. He was only a sophomore at the time, and he played varsity. But he got cut from the team because he couldn't attend practice. And the reason he couldn't was that he had to look out for his younger brother and sisters. So I think his rebellion had a lot to do with resentment."

"That would have set me off," Graham said. Then again, anything Gerald Robinson had expected of him had set him off.

"I know you and Peter got into plenty of trouble when you were Jonah's age," Sasha said, "so you should be able to relate to some of the kids you'll be taking in."

"You're probably right. In fact, if Peter hadn't died, we might have ended up with probation officers, too."

"What do you mean? What kind of things were you guys doing back then?"

"Drag racing on Smoke Tree Lane, drinking and partying every weekend. The night Peter died, we'd taken the dune buggy Roger helped us build and went camping out at Vista Verde for Labor Day weekend. And we'd really tied one on." Graham rarely talked about that time in his life, but the memory flowed freely tonight, and sharing it with Sasha felt right.

"It sounds like Uncle Roger gave you guys a lot of freedom."

"Yeah, he did. My dad had told me he didn't want us leaving the Galloping G that weekend. I rarely ever listened to him and had no intention of doing it that night, so I just nodded in agreement. But my disobedience proved to be a devastating mistake."

"What happened?" she asked. "I knew there was an accident, that Peter crashed the dune buggy. But Uncle Roger never gave me any of the details."

"I didn't tell him too much about it, either," Graham said. "Just that Peter had been drinking and decided to go out for a moonlight drive."

"If you'd rather not talk about it, I understand." She reached across the seat and took his hand, a move that surprised him nearly as much as it comforted him.

"I try not to think about it, but it crops up on me sometimes." Like it did right now.

As Graham sat beside Sasha, remembering that horrible night as if it were yesterday. He held on to her as if she could keep him from falling back into that mire of guilt he'd trudged through for nearly a year after the accident.

"We made a number of bad decisions that day. The excessive drinking, the idea Peter had to drive in the dark, the fact that he didn't take time to buckle his seat belt… I wish I could go back in time and make better choices for both of us, but I can't."

"Drinking and driving that dune buggy without wearing a seat belt was Peter's fault, not yours."

She was right. And Roger had told Graham the same thing. But accidents happened in the blink of an eye, and you could never rewind the clock, even if you would have laid down your own life to have the opportunity to do so.

She stroked her thumb across the top of his hand, warming his skin and setting his senses reeling. Had she caressed his wrist instead, she would have felt his pulse pounding.

"I hope you don't blame yourself for his death," she said.

"I did for quite a while, but not anymore."

"I'm glad to hear that. Besides, my uncle said you were with him at the end. It comforted him to know that Peter hadn't died alone."

That was true, but sitting with Peter, holding him in his arms, trying desperately to stop the blood flow until he bled out… It had been the least Graham could do, but it hadn't been enough. And no matter what alternative scenarios had played through his mind over the years, nothing could change the reality of what had happened that night.

"Peter wanted me to ride with him, but I wasn't feeling too well. I'd had a lot to drink. But as soon as I heard the crash, which happened close to our campsite, I sobered up quickly and ran to him. He'd been thrown from the dune buggy and had hit his head on something. I used my cell phone to call nine-one-one, but the reception was bad up there. Somehow I managed to tell them where we were, but we were too far away for paramedics to get to us in time."

"Was Peter in pain?" she asked. "Did he suffer?"

"Fortunately, he was unconscious and didn't feel anything, as far as I know. Knowing that and the fact that I was with him at the end gave Roger a little comfort."

Roger, who'd been in his midsixties and a widower at the time, had been devastated when he lost his only child. And Graham had been crushed to lose his best friend, especially knowing the accident could have been avoided.

Sasha continued to run her thumb over his skin, singeing him until his thoughts shifted away from that awful night and back on the here and now.

"I was in California when I got word of the accident," she said. "I wanted to be here with you and Uncle Roger, but my grandfather wouldn't let me."

He gave her hand a squeeze. "It's probably just as well that you weren't. It was a difficult time. But Roger and I leaned on each other, which helped."

Sadly, he hadn't gotten any sympathy from his own father. Instead, he'd gotten the blame for it all, as well as scolding and patronizing sermons. *You brought this all on yourself,* his old man had said. *I hope you'll finally straighten up and become more responsible.*

Graham had straightened up his act, but he'd done it as a tribute to Peter and to Roger, not as a result of anything Gerald Robinson had said.

Over the next couple of years, he and Roger had grown especially close. In fact, Graham had been far more comfortable on the Galloping G than he'd been at home. And that was as true today as it had been years ago.

"It's nice that Roger has you," Sasha said. "I'd hate to think of him living all alone."

"I don't plan to live here forever, but I'm here now."

"Are you eventually going to work for your dad's company?"

"No. That life isn't for me."

At that point, the conversation stalled, leaving him to wrestle with his thoughts, with his disappointment in his father.

Moments later, he stole a glance at Sasha, saw her brow furrowed. He supposed they were both lost in their thoughts. In fact, so much so that they were still holding hands. He really ought to pull away, but he'd be damned if he knew why he didn't.

"The moon is pretty this evening." Sasha craned her neck to get a better glimpse of it. "That's one reason I like to sit out here. The scent of night-blooming jasmine is another."

"When you were a kid, you used to sit on the porch a lot."

She turned to him, her knee pressing into his, warming him to the bone, stirring his senses yet again. "Sometimes I'd see you watching me, but you never said anything."

"I was afraid you'd tell me all your boy troubles."

She smiled and slowly shook her head. "No, I would have kept those to myself."

For a moment he was tempted to tug on her hand, to get her to look him in the eye again, to... What? Kiss her? Now, that would be a dumb move to make. As far as Graham knew, she was still pining over her husband. Besides, Sasha and her children came as a package deal.

In spite of his efforts to talk himself out of the romantic thoughts that continued to bombard him, he wasn't having much luck. The lovers' moon overhead and the scent of jasmine wouldn't let him.

But instead of kissing her, which, admittedly, he was sorely tempted to do, he gave her hand that tug. And when she gazed at him, he used his free hand to cup her cheek. "Just for the record, Gabe was a fool."

Her lips parted, almost as if she was suddenly thinking about kissing him, too. But that was crazy. He knew better.

So he released her hand and got to his feet. "I'd better turn in. It'll be morning before we know it."

Then he stepped off the porch and headed for his cabin, wondering if he'd made the right decision by walking away.

Chapter Five

Last night, after Graham left Sasha on the porch, she'd stayed outside much longer than she would have had he not sat next to her and shared his painful memory.

She hadn't expected any of it—his company on the swing or his painful recollection of Peter's accident—but she was glad he'd opened up to her. As he did, her heart had gone out to him, and without a single thought of the consequences, she'd reached for his hand.

The moment she'd wrapped her fingers around his, she realized he might pull away from her, just as he'd always done when she tried to touch him in the past. But this time, he'd not only accepted her comfort, but also seemed to appreciate it.

As he'd held her hand, the warmth and gentle strength of his grip, as well as the intimacy of their conversation, stirred her once-tender heart back to life. And for the first time in years, Gabe Smith and his selfish ways had been the last things on her mind.

Then, when Graham cupped her cheek and gazed into her eyes, her heart wasn't the only thing that stirred. Her old crush rose from the ashes, resurrected and as strong as ever, and her thoughts took a romantic turn.

If the baby hadn't chosen to kick her at that very moment, reminding her that she was seven months pregnant, she might have thought...

No, the very idea had been too wild to ponder. Graham had only tried to be brotherly, to do and say what her cousin would have, if Peter had been alive and seated with her on the swing. He'd just wanted to make her feel better about her divorce and to validate what she already knew—that Gabe wasn't worth the grief.

Graham had been right about that, too. It was a conclusion Sasha had come to years before their split. She probably should have admitted that last night, but she'd been so stunned by Graham's touch, by the intensity of his gaze, that those old girlish dreams had gotten the better of her.

After he'd left her alone, she continued to relish the memory of what they'd just shared. When she'd finally decided to head indoors for the night, she'd glanced at Graham's cabin. The lights were off, which meant he'd probably gone to sleep. But why wouldn't he have dozed off? There hadn't been any romantic thoughts and yearnings to keep him lying awake.

Her gaze had drifted to the other cabin, the new one where Jonah was staying. On the other hand, the teenager's bedroom light still blazed bright. His rebellion might have gotten him into trouble, but he was in a good place now. If anyone could reach him, it would be Graham and Roger.

The more Sasha had thought about what the two men intended to do with the Galloping G, the more she wanted to be a part of it. Considering their character and what they'd been through, Roger and Graham would undoubtedly become solid mentors those teenagers could look up to.

She shut off the porch light and entered the house, ready to call it a night. When she checked the clock in her bedroom, it was nearly ten o'clock, so she undressed and climbed into bed, exhausted. But her thoughts remained on Peter's Place. She even dreamed about it.

By the time she woke the next morning, she had a plan of her own. She would stay on the Galloping G and work with Graham and her uncle to help those boys get a new perspective in life. She certainly had the right college degree for a job like that. Besides, she'd always had a heart for kids, especially the rebellious kind like Graham and Peter used to be.

As she showered, she realized that the burden she'd been carrying when she first arrived had lifted completely, and a smile stretched across her face. She continued to think about her newly hatched plan while she dressed for the day and couldn't wait to share it with Graham and Uncle Roger.

It was amazing. The ranch had been more than just a place to gather her thoughts and make a plan for the

future. The Galloping G—or rather, Peter's Place—
was her future!

And for the first time in ages, that future looked
brighter than it ever had.

Graham's stomach rumbled in complaint, reminding him that the coffee he'd drunk and the banana he'd
eaten wasn't going to keep him going until lunchtime.
But he hadn't wanted to be around Sasha this morning, so he was trying to avoid the kitchen in the main
house, where Roger was undoubtedly fixing breakfast.

Had she realized how close he'd come to kissing her
last night? Or how he'd lain awake for hours, stretched
out in the dark, just thinking about her? He'd also pondered just what his romantic interest in her might mean.

He'd tried to shake it off and talk himself out of
whatever he was thinking and feeling, but in spite of
his best effort, it wasn't working. He'd just have to avoid
her until he had it all sorted out and knew how to deal
with it.

As he made his way through the barn, he checked
the paddocks where Barney and King, the other gelding, were stabled. From the looks of things, Jonah had
listened last night and done as he'd been instructed.
Even the bucket of oats was sealed properly.

Graham had just stepped out of the barn and into the
yard when his cell phone rang. He glanced at the screen,
recognized his older brother's name and answered.

Ben Fortune Robinson was the chief operating officer at Robinson Tech, a job well suited to the competent

businessman who dressed impeccably and took a commanding lead in the family, as well as the corporation.

After greeting each other, they made the usual small talk.

"How's Peter's Place coming along?" Ben asked.

Graham told him about Jonah moving in, although he didn't go into detail about the boy's past or his struggles. "He's only been here a couple of days, but he seems to be settling in nicely. And he's good with the rescue horses."

"How many do you have?" his brother asked.

"Chase delivered the first five yesterday. I hope to have more by the end of the month."

"I'm glad to hear that."

Something told Graham his brother hadn't called to chat. It wasn't his style. "So, what's up, Ben?"

"Well, for one thing, Zoe asked me to set up another family meeting."

Ever since learning that their father might have once been known as Jerome Fortune, a black sheep in that wealthy family, the siblings had been struggling with the news. First of all, Jerome was reportedly dead. Or was he?

Ben had been pursuing leads and clues for months and was determined to prove that their father's real name wasn't actually Gerald Robinson, that he'd been born Jerome Fortune. Graham had to admit it seemed possible, considering all he knew about his father. In fact, Ben was so convinced that he'd taken on the Fortune name, something Graham would be reluctant to do, even if it did pan out.

To further complicate the Robinson family dynamics, several of their illegitimate half siblings had turned up over the past few months. As if a family of eight wasn't big enough.

Graham had been disappointed in his father's romantic antics ever since he'd been a kid and found him embracing their nanny in the dressing room near the pool. And in some ways, Graham was still as rebellious when it came to his old man as Jonah was with his.

Yet as much as he'd like to tell Ben they could all meet without him, that he didn't give a squat who Gerald might or might not have been, he couldn't bring himself to do it.

"When and where?" Graham asked.

"My place. It's not easy setting up something that works with everyone's schedule. But I'm shooting for a week from next Saturday, at two o'clock. Is that okay with you?"

They might have a few more boys by then, but they had hired a teacher now. And they were interviewing a couple of counselors to be on staff. So he wouldn't be leaving Roger in a pinch. "Sure, Ben, that's fine. I'll be there."

"Great. And, by the way, I have some news. *Good* news."

"What's that?"

"Ella and I are expecting a baby."

An unexpected emotion slammed into Graham, making it difficult to speak. His brother was having a baby with the woman he loved?

He was happy for Ben, of course. But at the same time, a niggle of jealousy wormed its way through his chest.

How could that be? Graham had rarely envied anyone, yet for some crazy reason, he suddenly felt as though he'd like to trade places with Ben.

"Congratulations," he managed to say. "That *is* good news."

And it was. So why the jealousy?

The back door squeaked open, and Sasha walked out onto the stoop, her hand resting on her baby bump. It was then that reality struck, taunting him with the truth.

Why couldn't it be Graham's child she was carrying?

Damn. Where had that thought come from? Graham wasn't the kind of guy who'd dreamed of being a husband and father. He sure as hell hadn't looked up to his old man. And the marriage between his parents had been strained more often than not. There hadn't actually been any outward hostility between them, but their marriage wasn't what he'd call warm or loving.

As far as Graham could figure, his mom put up with a lot from his dad—like the long absences and the shortness of affection—because she liked the perks, both financial and social, of being married to Gerald Robinson. And she hadn't wanted to do anything to rock the boat.

Still, his mother might have been good at faking a happy marriage in public, but not at home. Even as a child, Graham was pretty observant. And it seemed to him that the cooler his mother became toward his father, the more his dad withdrew and stayed away. And the more Gerald was gone from home, the chillier things got between the couple.

"Well, I'd better let you get back to work," Ben said. "I'd hate to read in the paper that one of those teenagers burned down the Galloping G while you were talking on the phone."

Graham smiled. "I won't be taking in any pyromaniacs—as far as I know. But I'd better get back to work."

"I'll see you next Saturday," Ben said, before ending the call.

Even after slipping his cell phone back into his pocket, Graham couldn't help pondering his brother's news. Ella was having Ben's baby. They'd be watching her womb grow big with child, knowing they'd created a son or daughter together.

Again, Graham glanced at the stoop. Sasha wasn't there anymore. A quick scan of the yard told him she'd gone out to the corral, where Jonah was helping Maddie offer Suzy Q an apple chunk.

The boy smiled at something the pretty mother said, and Graham wished he could overhear their conversation.

Hell, even though he had every right to join them, he turned around and headed for the barn.

There was something very wrong about having such intense feelings for someone he used to think of as a kid sister. Not to mention which, Sasha was still legally married and pregnant with another man's child. He'd have to keep his inappropriate emotions—and his sexual desire for her—under wraps. And right now the best way to do that was to steer clear of her.

But damn, he was hungry.

And not just for breakfast.

* * *

Sasha followed the sounds and aroma of brewing coffee and sizzling sausage to the kitchen, where Uncle Roger was busy fixing breakfast. A yellow mixing bowl sat on the counter, next to the old waffle iron that was plugged into an outlet and heating up. Roger glanced at the stove and into the cast-iron skillet, where the links of spicy meat were frying.

Maddie, her hair still sleep-tousled and in need of a mother's touch, was dressed for the day and wearing her boots. She stood on a chair she'd pulled up next to Roger so she could watch him work. At the round, old-style oak table, Jonah sat patiently waiting to eat, a large glass of orange juice in front of him.

"Where's Graham?" Sasha asked. She assumed he was still outside doing chores and that he would come inside shortly.

"He was here a while ago." Uncle Roger stepped to the right and lowered the flame under the links of sausage. "He poured coffee into a disposable foam cup, grabbed a banana from the fruit bowl and then went out again. He said he wasn't hungry."

That was odd. Breakfast was the biggest meal of the day. And hadn't Graham said he always looked forward to eating in the ranch house with Roger?

He wasn't avoiding her, was he?

Had he felt uneasy last night after telling her Gabe was a fool? Had he thought she'd been gaping at him like a lovesick puppy?

She probably had been, but she hadn't meant to. It

was just that the kindness in his eyes and his gentle touch had stirred something deep within her.

But Graham wasn't the only who felt uneasy or foolish. Sasha felt that way, too, because she still yearned for a man who'd never been interested in her before and surely wasn't now. How could he be when he was single and unencumbered, and she would soon be the divorced mother of two?

Graham had only meant to be kind and supportive. And after she'd connected nonexistent dots, she'd imagined that he might want to kiss her.

Gathering her dignity, she shook off the silly musing and studied her daughter, who was her top priority these days. Maddie had once loved party shoes and dresses as a preschooler, but she now favored jeans and cowgirl apparel. She loved being on the Galloping G and had already had her first riding lesson, and if Graham and Uncle Roger weren't so busy, she'd have another scheduled soon. So, if Sasha intended to stay here for the time being, she wasn't doing anyone any good by allowing herself to ponder fruitless dreams.

Rather than continue standing frozen in the doorway, wondering why Graham wasn't here, she crossed the kitchen, removed a teapot from the cupboard and filled it with water. Then, after placing it on one of the empty burners on the stove, she went to the pantry and removed a box of herbal teabags.

"What's for breakfast?" she asked, although she could see for herself what Roger was preparing.

Maddie, who still stood atop that chair, turned to Sasha and flashed a gap-toothed smile. "Waffles with bananas!" She reached for the can of whipped cream. "And I get to spray this on top!"

"Sounds yummy." Sasha glanced at the teenager, who'd just finished chugging down the entire glass of OJ. "Good morning, Jonah. Did you sleep well?"

The boy shrugged. "I guess so. But I'm not used to it being so quiet outside. Our apartment is on a busy street in Austin, and it's next to a rowdy bar. Plus, I used to sleep with the TV on."

Sasha's first thought was one of sympathy for the kid, but then she remembered Jonah's mother and how hard she was working to provide a home for her fatherless children—something Sasha could relate to.

She wondered if Graham had given any thought to the parents of the rebellious kids he hoped to help. The ones who had moms like Jonah's might need someone to talk to, someone who could help bridge the gap between parent and child. Someone like Sasha, who was also a single parent trying to raise her daughters on her own.

It was going to take that proverbial village to help the boys who came to live at Peter's Place and their families. And Sasha was eager to do her share.

She'd meant to talk to Graham about it after breakfast, when Jonah wasn't within earshot, but that plan wasn't going to work. So she might as well talk to Graham now, if she could find him. And since she had something important to say, she would just act as though nothing had happened last night.

Actually, nothing had.

"I'll be back," she announced to the kitchen crew.

Then she walked out the backdoor and went in search of Graham.

She found him at the side of the barn, loading up the Gator with wooden posts and tools. There was a determination in him today, an intensity she hadn't noticed before. His very movements and the crease in his brow only made him more attractive, more appealing.

Great. As if his sturdy, muscular build and gorgeous face weren't enough. But she pressed on.

Upon her approach, she said, "Good morning."

He glanced up, wearing only the hint of a smile, and gave a little nod. "Mornin'." Then he continued to stack fence posts into the back of the Gator, his biceps flexing and his black T-shirt stretching with the effort.

Ignoring the awkwardness that settled over her, she continued. "I'd like to talk to you."

He stopped what he was doing, yet his expression was one of apprehension.

Oh, good grief. He didn't fear that she'd ask him to go on a date or something, did he?

"Talk to me about what?" he asked.

"A couple ideas I had for Peter's Place."

At that, his masculine features softened and he gave her his full attention.

Again she wondered if she'd been right, if he'd been avoiding her because he'd sensed her attraction to him. But she cast the possibility aside and told him her idea about moving in with Uncle Roger and using her education to help out in some way.

"You mean," he said, tilting his head slightly to the side, "you want to be a counselor?"

"Yes. Or whatever else you might want me to do. I thought I might even develop a counseling program for the boys' parents."

He lifted his hat and raked his fingers through his short, light brown hair.

Was her question that difficult for him to answer? You'd think he'd… Well, he might not jump at the chance to have her help, but surely he wasn't opposed to it. Then again, maybe he wanted only male counselors for some reason.

She'd argue that the boys would need to learn how to relate to women, too.

Finally, he said, "That's a good idea. The families and parents will need to make a few adjustments, especially if the boys are going to ever return home. And Roger mentioned that you had a degree in social work."

"I've yet to use it," she admitted, "but I was an A student. At one time, I'd planned to get a job with the state or county. But you know how the old saying goes, 'Bloom where you're planted.' And it appears that I've been planted here." She tossed him a breezy smile, hoping he'd see the wisdom in her words, the truth of it, as well as the possibilities.

A slow grin tugged at his lips. "Yeah, I guess that's true. I know Roger would be thrilled to have you join the team."

"But what about you?" she asked. "I don't want to upset your plans."

He lifted a single shoulder and gave a halfhearted shrug. "Actually, it might be easier working with someone we know rather than a stranger."

Before she could rejoice in her victory, the screen door at the back of the house opened and slammed shut. They both turned to the sound and spotted Maddie making her way across the yard. She wore her cowboy hat now, covering the tangles Sasha had yet to help her comb out, and had something in her hand.

"Mr. Graham?" the child called out, drawing the adults' attention and diffusing the situation.

"Yes," he answered. "I'm over here, honey. By the Gator."

Whatever she held had been wrapped in a napkin, and she handed it to Graham. "Uncle Roger said to give this to you 'cause you're probably hungry."

"What is it?" he asked.

"A piece of waffle with butter and a smidge of syrup. I wanted to spray out a lot of whip cream on it, but Uncle Roger wouldn't let me. He said it would be too messy and sticky to carry."

"He was right about that." Graham took it from her and thanked her, but he didn't unwrap the napkin.

"Jonah told me he gets to work with the rescue horses," Maddie said. "He said you just pet them and talk soft and give them treats. Can I do that, too?"

Graham looked to Sasha for an answer. Either he didn't mind and wanted her opinion or he didn't want to hurt the little girl's feelings.

"I think it's best if you have a few more riding lessons with one of the other horses first," Sasha said.

Rather than accept Sasha's answer, Maddie turned to the handsome cowboy, her eyes squinting in the morning sun. "I can't wait to go riding again, but can I at least give Suzy and Ginger pieces of apple? Jonah said it's easy. You just hold your hand open, like this, so your fingers don't get in the way and get chomped on." She stretched out her palm to show the man.

Graham smiled. "Yep, that's how it's done. I'm sure the horses would like that."

"Good! And can I come to work with you on the fence, too—like Jonah gets to do today? I'm very strong." To prove her point, she flexed her biceps.

Graham reached out and gripped her little arm with his thumb and index finger as if gauging her strength. He released her and let out a slow whistle. "Well, what do you know, Maddie? You're pretty darn strong. But I don't think you're ready to tackle the fence yet."

"Then can I watch? I'll be good. And quiet."

Graham again glanced at Sasha. "That's up to your mom."

Surely he was just being kind and didn't want to disappoint her daughter by saying no.

"I'd rather you stayed near the house today," Sasha said. "I have some cooking to do and will need your help."

Maddie frowned, clearly preferring ranch work over the kitchen detail.

"I'll tell you what," Graham said. "I'll come up with some cowboy chores for you to do when your mom doesn't need you in the house."

"Okay. I can do that." The child brightened. "You can count on me, pardner."

Graham smiled. Apparently, he'd known that she'd prefer to do ranch chores. And the fact that he'd acted on that caused Sasha's heart to melt like a chocolate Kiss in the noonday sun. Maddie was clearly enamored with the man.

So was Sasha, for that matter.

But it wasn't about *her* feelings. It was about Maddie's. Graham seemed to like the little girl and didn't appear to be dismayed by either her presence or her offer to help. At least, not yet. But would he come to resent her, as Gabe had?

"Maddie," Sasha suggested, "would you go inside and tell Uncle Roger I'm about ready for that waffle now? And I'd love to have bananas and a little whipped cream on mine."

"Okay," Maddie said. "I'll fix the top just the way you like it." Then she turned away and hurried back to the house, providing Sasha with an opportunity to speak to Graham about the child's apparent hero worship.

When the screen door slammed shut, Sasha said, "I know you have plenty of work to do—and not just today. So I hope she doesn't become a pest."

"Like you used to be?" he asked, a grin slapped on his face.

"Yes, but you were stuck with me."

His gaze locked on hers, turning her heart inside out and shaking up everything she treasured. Those old childish feelings she'd tried so hard to tamp down rushed back front and center, only they were all grown up this time around.

But that wouldn't do. It wouldn't do at all.

She crossed her arms, hoping to put a lid on all she

held inside. "If you had been rude or taken a swat at me, my uncle would have had your hide."

He winked. "That's true."

"But don't worry. I'll find plenty of things to keep Maddie busy, chores and activities she can do in the house."

"She's a cute kid, and I actually enjoy talking to her. I never know what she's going to say next. But I'll tell you what. If she ever becomes a bother, I'll let you know."

"I'd appreciate that."

He studied her for a moment, and then his brow furrowed. "Are you really concerned about her becoming a nuisance?"

"Actually, I'm more concerned about her bothering *you*."

"Don't worry about me. I have seven brothers and sisters, remember?"

He didn't talk about them very much, so sometimes it was easy to forget that he hadn't been an only child.

"Yes, I know," Sasha said. "It's just that Maddie's father had very little patience with her."

"That surprises me. She's a sweet kid."

"It surprised me, too." Sasha could have gone on to list all of Gabe's shortcomings, but she didn't. After all, what would that say about her and her ability to choose a solid, dependable and loving mate?

"Did Gabe's impatience have anything to do with the reason you two split up?" Graham asked.

"That was part of it, I guess." Again, she hated to

reveal all the heartbreaking details, but she decided to share one. "Just for the record, it was Gabe who left."

"I'm sorry."

"Don't be. It was probably for the best."

When Graham didn't object or quiz her further, she added, "I'll be the first to admit that our life together was far from perfect, but I made a commitment to stick it out for the long haul."

"And he didn't."

"That's about the size of it." If Gabe had meant those vows, he wouldn't have found it so easy to leave her when she learned she was pregnant a second time.

"Anyway," she said, "enough of that. And back to Maddie. She's never felt especially close to her father, so I think that's one reason she's eager to strike up a relationship with Uncle Roger and with you. But I don't want her to get too clingy, so let me know if she does."

Graham cupped her jaw again. As his calloused thumb made circular strokes on her cheek, every nerve ending in her body sparked to life, and a bolt of heat zigzagged to her very core.

"Don't worry," he said. "Your daughter's a sweetheart. I can handle her."

Maybe so. Graham appeared to be a kindhearted and amazing man with the patience of Job when it came to kids and teenagers.

But what about Sasha herself? Could she handle being around Graham without revealing the feelings she still harbored for him, feelings she could no longer attribute to a childish crush?

She'd have to. Graham Robinson could have any

woman he set his sights on. And there was no way he'd ever choose a pregnant woman whose baby bump made her feel as big as Uncle Roger's barn—and just as sexy. And while her physical condition alone would surely hamper any chance of romance between them, that didn't bother her nearly as badly as the truth.

Graham had never considered her a viable love interest and probably never would.

Chapter Six

On Saturday evening, Brad Taylor called Graham's cell. This time he had the number and the name straight. "Hey, Graham. How's Jonah doing?"

"Actually, he's settling in better than I expected him to do at this point. He seems to enjoy working with the horses. He also has a good appetite. His only real complaint is the fact that he doesn't have a television or Wi-Fi in his cabin."

"So he's going through video-game withdrawal, huh?" Taylor chuckled.

"Yep, but he'll survive and be a better kid for it. In fact, I checked in on him a few minutes ago, and he was reading *Lord of the Flies*."

"Good. It sounds like Peter's Place was a smart move

for him." Taylor paused a beat, then cleared his throat. "Are you and Roger ready to take in another boy?"

Adding another teenager to the mix was sure to change the dynamics, but that wasn't necessarily a bad thing. "Sure. We'll take him."

"His name is Ryan Maxwell. He's sixteen and was caught vandalizing heavy equipment at a construction site near his home."

"What was his excuse? Boredom?"

"Yeah, pretty much. But I think it runs deeper than that. It usually does. From what I can see from his school records, he was in gifted and honors classes up until two years ago, about the time his parents were killed in a car accident."

"So you think he's rebelling because of his grief?"

"Yeah, maybe a little. But he's angry, too. His maternal uncle was granted custody of him, and that guy is a real tool. He hasn't been able to hold down a job and would rather go out drinking each night than stay home with the kid. This is Ryan's first brush with the law, and I'd like it to be the last."

"We'll see what we can do about that."

"I'll email you a full report on him this evening," Taylor said. "Then I'll bring him out to the ranch on Monday, around three o'clock."

The call had no more than ended when a knock sounded on Graham's cabin door. He assumed it might be Jonah, but when he answered, he found Sasha on his porch. She held a foil-covered plate in her hand.

"Hi," he said.

"I wasn't sure what you planned to eat tonight, but

Roger made carne asada tacos, rice and beans. There was plenty left over, so I brought you some."

Apparently, she had no idea he'd been trying his best to steer clear of her, even if it meant eating canned soup and a ham sandwich for dinner.

He took the plate and thanked her. "Actually, I already ate, but I have a little room left for a taco."

She blessed him with a pretty smile that turned him every which way but loose and made him wonder if avoiding her hadn't been such a good idea after all.

"Have you given any thought to letting me work with the boys or their parents?" she asked.

To be honest, he hadn't had a chance to run it by Roger, who'd undoubtedly love the idea. And while working closely with Sasha wasn't going to be easy for Graham, he couldn't very well tell her no.

"I'm okay with it, if you are. How soon do you want to start?"

"Actually, I've been trying to work with Jonah already. I think he likes me. At least, he's opened up some."

"Good, I'm glad to hear that. I'm sure you'll stay busy. Brad Taylor, Jonah's probation officer, is bringing a second boy Monday afternoon."

She brightened. "That's good. I'm sure Jonah will be glad to have another kid his age staying here."

"I'm sure he will."

"The Galloping G is a great place for a boy to become a man," she added.

It had certainly helped Graham to grow up and turn his life around. But as much as he wanted to see Peter's

Place come together, his business expertise could be best used to apply for state grants and to secure more donations for their nonprofit organization. So he didn't plan to remain working here forever.

"Just so you know," he said, "I'm behind Peter's Place a hundred percent. But I won't always be living in one of the cabins."

"Are you going to build a bigger house?" she asked. "I'm sure you'd be more comfortable."

She didn't get it.

"Once the foundation is up and running, I'm going to move to Austin," he explained. "But I won't just oversee it from afar. I'll visit regularly."

Her eyes widened, and her lips parted. "What do you plan to do in the city?"

"I grew up in a technologically astute household, so I have a certain savvy about that stuff, too. I also have an MBA. So while I enjoy working on the ranch, I won't be doing this the rest of my life."

"Are you going to start your own company?" She wrinkled her brow, then shook her head. "I'm sorry. I didn't mean to make that sound as if I didn't think you had any business sense. I just thought you loved…"

Her comment trailed off, but he knew what she'd been about to say. "I enjoy working the land, riding horses and spending time with Roger. But that doesn't mean I plan to play cowboy until I'm stooped and bent."

"I…" She paused and bit down on her bottom lip. "That's not what I meant."

No, but it was what she'd implied. Time and again, his father had accused him of all that and more.

"I'm not leaving tomorrow," Graham said.

She seemed to chew on that awhile, then began to nod. "Of course. But what plans do you have for financing Peter's Place? Before I tell Uncle Roger that I plan to stay here and help, I want to know the boys' home is secure."

"Don't worry about money. I'll make sure the ranch is solvent. And as a side note, the Fortune Foundation has offered to make it one of its charities. That hasn't been officially decided, but either way, there shouldn't be any financial concerns."

The wrinkle in her brow deepened, and her mind appeared to be going into overtime.

Something must be bothering her. But what?

Graham's announcement slammed into Sasha like a bull out of the shoot, although she shouldn't be surprised to hear that he planned to move on. After all, he was a Robinson, which meant he had a slew of options available to him, especially in the city. And while she hadn't expected him to stay on the Galloping G forever, he'd become as much a part of the ranch as her uncle was.

Was that a new decision? Was he leaving because she'd decided to stay? Did she make him that uncomfortable?

Graham studied her intently, as if he knew just how she felt about his pending departure.

"What's the matter?" he asked.

She couldn't very well admit that she'd been having romantic feelings for him, that she'd hoped... She slowly shook her head. "Nothing's wrong."

She was a big girl. She'd get over the loss. But what about Maddie? The little girl had so much love to give. And while Maddie had never been very close to her father, Sasha still worried about the effect Gabe's abandonment might have on her when it came to her future relationships with boys and men.

Even at seven, Maddie appeared to be looking for a male influence in her life. And once she'd met Graham, she seemed to have set her sights on him. Sasha didn't mind, since he was one of the white hats. Maybe that hadn't always been the case, but he certainly was nowadays. Yet Maddie's adoration was still a concern. The child seemed to be dead set on making friends with Graham, working with him on the ranch and getting more of those promised riding lessons. It was all she ever talked about.

In fact, if Sasha hadn't caught her running out the door on several occasions and redirected her, Maddie would be following her cowboy hero around from sunup until sundown.

So how would she feel when Graham moved on to greener pastures, something her father had done?

"I can tell something's bothering you, Sassy." Graham eased closer, so much so that Sasha caught a whiff of his musky scent.

She would never admit it, but she couldn't help feeling that her cowboy hero was about to abandon her, too.

But at least, for the time being, Graham wasn't going anywhere. Instead he moved closer still. "Are you concerned about me leaving you and your uncle on the ranch to deal with the boys on your own? If so, don't be. I've already sorted through potential job applicants and will line up competent people to work with you, experienced professionals who can guide you. And like I said, I'll return regularly—and often."

"No, it's not that. It's just…" No way could Sasha open up and reveal all the emotion she had bottled up inside. Instead she would only share a part of it. "I'm worried about Maddie. She seems to have really latched on to you. And I don't want her to wind up disappointed when you leave."

"I can understand that. She's a great kid, and I wouldn't want to see her hurt, either."

Tears welled in Sasha's eyes and she swiped them away. "I'm sorry. It's just that her father pretty much turned his back on her."

Gabe had walked out on Sasha, as well, but she really hadn't been bothered by his leaving. In a lot of ways, it had been a relief.

"Don't worry," Graham said. "I'll be considerate of Maddie's feelings and won't walk away without a backward glance." He placed his hand on her shoulder, and the heat of his touch spiraled deep inside her. The intensity in his gaze and the promise he made filled her with…warmth. And something more. They'd barely broached a friendship as adults, yet she hoped that they'd…that he'd…

Oh for Pete's sake. She didn't dare voice it, even to herself.

As they continued to study each other, she hoped her jumbled thoughts and emotions weren't evident in her expression.

"I'm not like Gabe," Graham said.

"Yes, I know." That was part of why Sasha was so drawn to him now.

Of course, she'd always thought the world of Graham. Sometimes late at night, while Gabe had been away on a business trip or at the office or at some meeting she'd suspected wasn't related to his work at all, Sasha had felt lonely and neglected. And when those blue evenings came, she would find herself thinking of the handsome teenage Graham and imagining him all grown up.

She knew that she'd been idealizing him at the time. She'd done the same thing with Gabe when they first started dating.

And while she'd come to the conclusion that marrying Gabe had been a mistake, she wouldn't regret it. Otherwise, she wouldn't have Maddie—or the baby she'd yet to meet.

"Don't get me wrong," Sasha said as she placed her hand on her baby bump and felt her little one shift position. "I cared for Gabe, but I found it difficult to respect him."

She hadn't planned to explain, but maybe it was best if he understood there were many reasons her marriage had failed.

"For one thing," she admitted, "Gabe was so determined to make it on his own and without the help of his dad that he refused to work for the family company."

"I'd be the last one to criticize a man for not wanting to work with his father," Graham said.

The fact that the two men had that one similarity crossed her mind. But that was different. Wasn't it?

She shook off the comparison. "I'm not saying he should have worked for his father. I understood why he wanted to do something on his own, which was understandable. But that wasn't the problem. Gabe couldn't seem to keep a job. Each time something didn't go his way, he'd quit. Believe it or not, during the eight years we were married, he probably had ten different employers."

"I can see why you'd be disappointed in him. Sometimes a man has to swallow his pride and learn to get along with others." Gabe reached out and stroked her shoulder and upper arm, offering her compassion and...

There she went again, imagining all sorts of motives behind the glimmer in his amazing blue eyes.

"Like I told you before," Graham said, "Gabe was a fool. He didn't have any idea how good he had it."

Sasha's heart rumbled in her chest, vibrating to the point she feared it might stifle the words before they left her mouth. "You have no idea how much I appreciate you saying that."

"It's true." He placed his hand along her jaw, then brushed a kiss on her forehead in what was surely meant to be a brotherly or friendly gesture.

But in spite of her better judgment, she gazed up at him. When their eyes met, he spoke to her in a way he never had—only without words.

The sweet kiss he'd given her brow had merely triggered something deeper, something stronger. Before she could contemplate just what that might be and what it might mean, he lowered his mouth to hers.

The moment their lips met, friendship and brotherly love flew by the wayside. And *ka-pow*! Her head swirled and the earth shook. But she'd barely tasted him and lifted her arms to slip them around his neck when he pulled away.

"I'm sorry," he said. "That was completely out of line. I have no idea why I did that. But it won't happen again."

Did he fear them getting any closer? Had he momentarily forgotten how complicated a romantic relationship with her would be? She certainly had. But reality struck hard.

"Listen," he said, nodding toward the Gator, "I've enjoyed talking to you, but I need to get back to work."

Then he did just that, leaving her alone in the middle of the yard, stunned by the strength of her desire and amazed at the feelings his brief kiss had evoked. Yet as he walked way, dashing the hope she'd dared to grasp, her heart cramped.

He'd called her ex a fool, but Sasha was the real fool. Graham could have any woman he wanted, especially when he moved to Austin. Why would he settle for a soon-to-be mother of two?

Either way, whatever special moment they'd shared was now over. And while her head told her why that was for the best, her heart refused to hear it and tears welled in her eyes.

She wasn't sure what she'd actually felt for Graham when she was younger, a crush or something much stronger than that. But she was grown up now and definitely falling head over heart in love.

Yet what good would that do her when she felt as big as a Brahma bull?

In any event, there was no way Graham had any interest in dating her. And even if he did, what man in his right mind would want to take on the fatherhood of a seven-year-old *and* a newborn in one fell swoop?

Graham was the epitome of a handsome and eligible bachelor. He was in his thirties, so he'd undoubtedly had plenty of admirers over the years.

No, if he was actually interested in having a family, he'd have one already.

The truth of that realization stole what little hope she'd harbored. Before returning to the house, she swiped the tears from her eyes and did her best to shake off the ache in her heart.

Her love for Graham would continue to be her secret for the rest of her life.

After walking away from Sasha, Graham thought about that kiss and swore under his breath. It might have lasted only a moment, but the effects had knocked him completely off stride. And in spite of his best intentions, he wasn't been able to keep his mind on anything else for the next couple of days.

He'd slipped up and let his hormones rule his brain. Damn. He still couldn't believe he'd actually let a brotherly kiss morph into something much more.

Thank God he'd finally come to his senses. He'd also made himself scarce, staying busy and away from the house and yard, something that should have been easy to do on a working ranch. Instead keeping his distance from Sasha—and even Maddie!—had been as tough as cutting into a serving of rawhide with a butter knife.

Even at night, after he locked himself away in his cabin, he still couldn't escape. He kept reliving that precious moment over and over. The kiss might have been brief, but it lasted long enough for him to know how good it had been, how good they could be together. And now that Graham realized the kind of passion he and Sasha could stir up, he feared that one kiss wasn't going to be enough to quench his thirst for her.

What had he been thinking?

That was the problem. He *hadn't* been thinking. At least, not clearly.

Even now, days later, it didn't seem to matter that Sasha was pregnant with another man's baby and that she had a seven-year-old in need of a father. For some reason, her motherhood seemed to only add to her appeal. So that was why Graham had chosen to stay away, to begin eating alone in his cabin. Maybe, if he were a better cook, he wouldn't mind.

But who was he kidding? It wasn't the meals he was missing.

Fortunately, he had a damn good reason to leave the ranch this afternoon. It was time for that family meeting at Ben's house. Only trouble was, he was pushing the speed limit so he wouldn't be late.

Early this morning, he'd taken Jonah out to finish working on the last stretch of broken fence, and the kid had gotten cut on a piece of buried barbed wire.

He was going to be fine, but taking him to the doctor and having his wound treated had eaten a big chunk of time out of the day.

But Graham was in Austin now. And right on schedule.

Once he reached the busy street on which Ben lived, he left his truck in a downtown parking structure, then walked a block to his older brother's place.

The four-story building Ben called home was flanked by skyscrapers and a small family-run deli that had been there for years. Graham still found it hard to believe that his oldest brother would prefer living here rather than a penthouse suite.

Maybe he'd consider moving now that he was married with a baby on the way.

When Graham arrived at Ben's and stood before the dark gray door, he glanced at his wristwatch, then rang the bell. As expected, Ben's housekeeper answered.

"You're late," the stern, gray-haired woman said. "Everyone else has already arrived."

Actually, Graham was right on time, give or take a minute or two. He could have given Mrs. Stone any number of excuses, if he were so inclined—the gash on Jonah's leg, the visit to Urgent Care, the traffic he'd fought, thanks to an accident on the interstate.

Instead he clamped his mouth shut and let the housekeeper lead him to the elevator, which he rode up to the floor where Ben's old-fashioned study was located.

Someone had brought in extra chairs, all but two of them taken. His sisters Sophia and Olivia had already arrived, and so had Rachel, who'd come from

Horseback Hollow. The girls, who'd been talking quietly among themselves, looked up when Graham entered.

Ben was seated behind his desk, while Wes, his twin, had chosen a chair by the door. The two men looked similar in build and had both dark hair and blue eyes, but they were different in style and temperament.

Kiernan, their youngest brother, sat next to Wes. The only one not seated was Zoe. She stood at the terraced window, studying the busy city outside.

"Good," Ben said. "Now that Graham's here, we can get started."

Graham took an empty chair, but Zoe remained at the window, her glossy, straight brown hair hanging down her back.

"Zoe?" Ben asked. "Did you hear me?"

"Sorry." She turned away from the downtown view, but she didn't take a seat. Instead she placed her hands on her hips and smoothed the fabric of her stylish yellow sundress.

"Why don't you start by telling us why you wanted me to call this meeting?" Ben asked Zoe.

"All right." She bit down on her bottom lip, as if what she had to say would take a great effort, but her struggle didn't last long. "I have a confession to make. I've been holding back information."

All eyes zeroed in on her, and she blew out a weary sigh before continuing. "I know for a fact that Dad *is* Jerome Fortune."

It took a moment for that bit of news to register, but once it did, all the siblings began to chatter.

Ben, who'd always been the take-charge type, told

everyone to quiet down. When the murmurs ceased, he asked Zoe, "How do you know that?"

"I recognized the Fortune ring that Charles Fortune Chesterfield gave his fiancée, Alice. Dad has one just like it. So I confronted him, and he finally admitted it."

Graham slowly shook his head. He hadn't wanted to believe it, but he wouldn't put anything past their old man. If this had all come down the pike a few years ago, when he still had a king-size chip on his shoulder, he might have stormed out of the house in disgust and anger. Yet even though he had a handle on his feelings now, that didn't mean he liked being betrayed and having to accept the fact that his father had been living a lie.

Damn. They were all living that lie.

"I'm sorry for not telling you sooner," Zoe added, "but Dad didn't want anyone to know."

"Why would it matter?" Wes asked. "We deserved to know. He shouldn't have kept it a secret from us."

"The story is actually pretty shocking," Zoe said. "When Dad left the Fortune fold, he'd wanted to get away so badly he actually faked his own death to sever ties with his family."

Their old man had gone to those extremes to run away? There wasn't much about his father's decisions, choices and antics that surprised Graham, but that bit of news certainly had.

The siblings started talking over each other, clearly stunned by Zoe's revelation.

Again, Ben asked them to be quiet. Then he said, "Okay, now we have the answer. But that leaves us with another question. Should we tell Kate Fortune?"

The conversation lulled, although why wouldn't it? Cosmetics mogul Kate Fortune had been meeting with various Fortune relatives, looking for someone to run her company.

At ninety years old, Kate looked a decade younger and was still as sharp as ever. She also had more money than she could possibly spend, thanks to the success of the Fortune Youth Serum she'd developed.

Kate would probably outlive them all, but she was determined to find someone in the family to take Fortune Cosmetics to the next generation. She had her own offspring already working for her, but she thought her company needed new blood and fresh ideas. So she'd been interviewing various Fortune family members, looking for someone to take under her wing.

If she knew the Robinsons were actually Fortunes, as had been suspected, she might want to talk to them, too. But then again, Gerald—or Jerome, as he'd once been known—had always been a black sheep.

"I doubt any of us would be seriously considered," Wes said. "And even if she were to choose one of us, Dad would have a fit if he thought one of his kids had gone to work for 'The Enemy.'"

Wes had that right.

"Unfortunately," Zoe said, "the decision about who to tell may have already been taken out of our hands."

"What makes you say that?" Graham asked.

"Because…" She took another deep breath and slowly let it out. "I told Keaton Whitfield."

"You did *what*?" Ben's face grew stern, and an angry flush settled on his cheeks. But Graham could understand why. His older brother had gone in search of their father's illegitimate children and found Keaton, a half sibling who lived in England and who favored Ben in looks.

Ben swore under his breath, but Zoe didn't back down. "Keaton and I talked after Joaquin and I got back from our honeymoon. He told me that he'd located two other possible offspring of Gerald Robinson. And one of them also remembered an emerald ring with the letter *F* on it."

Ben slowly shook his head, obviously pissed.

"I didn't tell Keaton *everything*," Zoe said, "just that the Fortune connection was a real one."

Ben clucked his tongue. "I can't believe Keaton came to you and not to me."

Graham could understand that. Ben was the one who'd first met Keaton. But Graham was more focused on the fact that there were more Robinsons—or rather *Fortunes*—out there.

The siblings talked among themselves about what this might mean. Some were pleased by the news, while others had been merely unsettled by it. Graham was neither. He'd never quite fit into the family, anyway. At least, his issues with his father hadn't helped that. And now...? Hell, he wasn't sure who his family was anymore. Obviously, they weren't Robinsons. But Fortunes?

When Ben used the intercom to call Mrs. Stone and ask her to bring in refreshments, Graham told his brother he couldn't stay. "I need to get back to the ranch, so you'll have to excuse me."

"I'm afraid I need to go, too," Zoe said.

Graham placed his hand on his kid sister's back. "I'll walk you out."

As the two of them left Ben's study, Graham glanced at the woman who was a newlywed and no longer a child.

Zoe had always been close to their father and had refused to think that the man had any faults. It really wasn't that she was naive. She just tended to see the good in people.

And now Zoe, like the rest of the Robinson-Fortune brood, was beginning to see just how flawed their father was.

Graham suspected that learning the truth must have been tough on her and that admitting she'd been wrong about him, when she'd been his biggest champion, had to be very humbling.

Once they left the house and stepped onto the sidewalk, Graham said, "It must have been tough for you to make that announcement."

"It wasn't easy. I feel pretty stupid for being the lone holdout, but once I learned the truth, I needed to speak up."

"Loyalty is a virtue, Zoe. And so is admitting when you were wrong. If I ever need someone in my corner, I hope you'll step up."

She smiled. "Thank you."

As they continued toward the parking garage, the soles of her high-heeled sandals and his boots crunched on the gritty concrete.

They'd only gone a few feet when Zoe's steps slowed,

and she turned to Graham. "I take it you've been skeptical about Dad for years."

He stopped along with her and nodded. "Remember Suzette, the au pair from France?"

"Yes, but just barely. She was very pretty, with long, dark hair and big blue eyes. She also had an intriguing accent. I thought of her as a princess. So what about her?"

"I caught Dad kissing her in the dressing room by the pool."

"How old were you?"

"Eleven or twelve."

Her brow furrowed as she thought about what he'd just revealed. "What did you say when you found them?"

"Nothing, really. Dad said I'd misread what I saw and that I'd be in big trouble if I told anyone."

"Did you?" she asked.

"Misinterpret what I saw?" Graham shook his head. "No, I wasn't stupid."

Zoe released a pent-up sigh. "When I was little, I caught him hugging our neighbor Mrs. Caldwell at one of their New Year's Eve parties. She was crying and talking about a baby."

"Whose?"

"She didn't say, but now I can only wonder."

The two exchanged a knowing look.

"I realize now that Dad lied to me about it," Zoe said. "He told me he was only comforting her because she was upset about something. He asked me not to tell anyone because Mrs. Caldwell was embarrassed that

I'd seen her crying. He also told me that he and I had a special bond."

"That's no secret," Graham said. "But what about the baby?"

"Dad told me that I'd misunderstood what I'd heard. Apparently, our father is a very misunderstood man."

"Um, yeah. You think?" Graham slowly shook his head, amazed at his father's growing number of scandals.

"Did you keep his secret?" Zoe asked.

"I tried to tell Mom—in my own way. But she didn't take the hint."

"I'm not surprised that she turned a blind eye. She had eight kids and probably wanted to hold her marriage together. It's what most mothers would do, I guess."

Graham didn't know about that, but it was what *their* mother had done over the years. In spite of the fact that she must have known about her husband's philandering, she hadn't confronted him. At least, not that Graham had been aware of.

"Anyway," he said, "I lost respect for Dad that day."

"Is that why you were so rebellious?"

A crooked grin tugged at his lips. "I was probably born with a rebel spirit. But after seeing Dad for what he really was, I decided to disappoint him, just the way he'd disappointed me."

His kid sister seemed to think about that for a moment, then she said, "If I'd caught Dad kissing another woman, if I'd suspected any of this, I might have been tempted to rebel, too."

Graham doubted it. Zoe had always been a good

girl. But then again, she was no longer the child he remembered.

"So, how's married life?" he asked.

At the question, Zoe brightened, reminding him of how sweet and fun-loving she'd always been. "It's amazing. I love Joaquin more and more each day. You really ought to consider settling down and getting married."

Should he? He hadn't given it any thought before, but now, as he pondered the idea, Sasha, Maddie and the baby came to mind. But Sasha wasn't ready for another relationship. Her marriage had ended just months ago. She needed more time, and Graham wouldn't push himself on her.

"I never thought I was cut out for married life," he told his little sis. "But your happiness is hard to hide. So maybe, if a special woman ever lands on my doorstep, I might consider it."

As they continued to their parked vehicles, Graham pondered the idea of love and marriage, of coming home each night to a wife and kids. Again Sasha came to mind.

Had he actually found that special woman already?

Chapter Seven

Sasha stood on the porch and watched as Graham talked to Brad Taylor. She wasn't sure what she'd been expecting when the probation officer arrived with the second teenager, but certainly not the kid who'd climbed out of the white sedan.

Graham had let her read the court paperwork he'd received so she'd be prepared to meet Ryan Maxwell. As a result, she'd made the usual assumption and figured he'd be a surly and destructive delinquent.

But unlike Jonah, Ryan didn't appear to be the least bit grumpy or hardened. Instead his shoulders slumped, as though he'd been beaten down by life.

He wasn't very tall for a fifteen-year-old boy, and he was much too thin. His glasses, which he continued to adjust on the bridge of his nose, were too big for his face. But his shy, frail appearance didn't erase the seriousness of the crime he'd committed. The damage he'd done to the equipment on the job site had cost the construction company nearly ten thousand dollars, and the owner wasn't taking that lightly.

Sasha wasn't sure what had been going on in the once-studious boy's mind or what had provoked him to put dirt in the fuel tanks of those tractors. But she meant to find out.

Taylor placed a hand on Ryan's thin shoulders and looked at Graham. "Where do you want him to put his things?"

"He'll bunk with Jonah." Graham turned toward the barn and called to the other teenager.

When Jonah walked out into the yard, he furrowed his brow, clearly checking out the new kid.

"This is Ryan," Graham said as he introduced the two teenagers. "Will you take him to your cabin and show him which bunk is his?"

Jonah, who'd just begun to shake his who-gives-a-rat's-ass attitude since arriving on the Galloping G, stiffened and slipped back into his tough-guy demeanor. "Yeah. Come on."

Ryan grabbed the canvas handle of his small bag and followed Jonah. They'd only taken a few steps when Graham called out to them, "As soon as Ryan puts his things away, bring him back here."

Jonah continued on his way, but he acknowledged the order with a wave of his hand and a "Got it, boss."

At that point, Sasha quit watching from a distance and made her way toward the men. When the teenagers were out of earshot, Graham turned to Mr. Taylor. "The report didn't mention it, but I take it Ryan doesn't have many friends."

"Before his parents died," Mr. Taylor said, "he was pretty active in a math and science club. So I assume he used to have friends who shared his same interests. But that changed when he moved in with his uncle and had to switch schools. He's a loner now."

"It would seem that way," Sasha said. "The report said he damaged that equipment on his own."

"I noticed that," Graham said. "Back in the day, when I was dead set on stirring up trouble, I was much braver when I had a buddy with me."

Buddies like Peter, Sasha realized.

About that time, Uncle Roger, who'd walked out of the house moments ago, stepped off the porch, crossed the yard and joined them. "That new boy is too skinny. I'll have to fatten him up."

Sasha smiled at the older man, who loved to cook. "If anyone has the culinary skill to do that, you do."

"Jonah's certainly been eating well enough to gain weight. So it sounds like you'll be fixing a lot more biscuits and gravy, as well as those homemade cinnamon rolls." Graham chuckled and placed a hand on his flat belly. "It's a good thing I've been eating on my own these days, or I'd be putting on pounds, too."

Sasha doubted that the extra calories had anything to do with Graham's decision to avoid Roger's meals, but she wouldn't stress over it.

Turning the focus of the conversation back on their newest teenage resident, she said, "From what I gathered, Ryan skipped a grade in school and was college-bound. I suspect having his dreams shattered first by the death of his parents, then by an alcoholic and unmotivated uncle, made him want to lash out on anyone or anything he could."

Mr. Taylor nodded in agreement.

"Well, he's at the Galloping G now," Roger said. "We'll just have to channel some of that energy and help him get back on track."

"That's the plan," Taylor said. "And since you seem to have it all under control, I'm going to take off. I'll give you a call to check on the boys in a few days."

Graham and Roger both shook hands with the probation officer. Then Roger walked him to his car.

"We'll be okay," her uncle said to Mr. Taylor. "Ryan needs a friend, and Jonah ain't as tough and unapproachable as he'd like us to believe."

"I think you're right," Taylor said as he climbed into his government-issued sedan. Moments later he drove away. His dust had barely settled when the boys returned.

"You want Ryan to help me finish up in the barn?" Jonah asked.

"It's probably a good idea if he had a tour of the ranch first," Graham said. "Think you can handle that?"

Jonah straightened his stance. "Sure, I can do it."

The screen door creaked open and slammed shut as Maddie came outside and approached the new boy with a grin. She took a moment to introduce herself; then she scanned him from head to toe, taking in his black cargo pants with a torn pocket and the black T-shirt with a picture of Chewbacca on the front.

She turned to Graham. "We're going to have to get him some real cowboy clothes, right?"

Sasha smiled. Leave it to Maddie to make sure everyone settled into ranch life—and quickly.

Graham reached for one of the girl's pigtails and gave it a gentle tug. "You're right, sweet pea. Looks like we'd better plan a shopping trip in Austin."

"I don't need anything," Ryan said.

"The minute one of those horses steps on your foot," Roger said, "you'll wish you were wearing boots."

The boy glanced down at his beat-up sneakers, which would be better off in a trash can than on a kid's feet.

He didn't need anything, huh?

Besides some new clothes and some meat on his bones, he was going to need plenty of kindness and understanding. He was also going to require a lot of guidance. Thank goodness he'd come to Peter's Place. He might have found himself in a lot more trouble if he hadn't.

"I gotta finish cleaning one more stall," Jonah said. "So I'll give him a tour as soon as I'm done."

"Good plan," Graham said. "I like the way you're taking your responsibilities seriously. And that you're determined to finish the job you started."

Jonah laughed. "Yeah, mucking stalls. Talk about *crappy* jobs."

Even the sad-faced Ryan smiled at the pun.

"But one reason I want to finish," Jonah added, "is

that it's Barney's stall. And he deserves to have it clean. So give me about five minutes."

After Jonah headed to the barn, Uncle Roger suggested that Maddie return to the kitchen to finish the chore he'd given her to do.

"Okeydoke," she said. "I like snappin' green beans." Then she dashed off.

Sasha took the opportunity to introduce herself to Ryan and to tell him she'd like to meet with him on a regular basis to talk about things.

"What kind of things?" he asked.

"Life—the past, the present, the future."

"I don't have much of a life or a future to think about, especially now. I made a really dumb mistake, and I'm sorry for messing with that equipment. But at least it got me out of my uncle's house."

"That might be true," she said. "But who were you punishing? Two years ago, you were thinking about college and could have been accepted by most of them. Now you've got time in juvie on your record."

Ryan frowned, then crossed his thin arms. "I was mad, okay? And I wanted everyone to know it."

"Mad or hurt?" she asked. "I lost my parents, too, so believe me, I know exactly how you feel."

"Do you?" The once-downcast kid straightened and stood as tall as his small stature would allow. "Did your parents leave a big insurance policy in trust for you so you could use it to go to college or buy a car or even a house someday? Did your uncle blow it all on drugs, hookers and booze?"

His words nearly knocked Sasha off-kilter, but she

rallied quickly. "I'd be as angry as hell, too, Ryan. But you're lashing out at the world, which isn't fair to anyone, especially you."

The teenager looked at her as if he was actually hearing and making sense of her words.

"You have an opportunity to turn everything around from this day forward," she added. "But changing the direction you're heading is a decision you have to make."

Ryan didn't say anything, but the cogs in his head appeared to be turning.

There was plenty of time to counsel him, but she suspected they'd taken a positive step forward already. Before any of them could comment, Jonah returned from the barn, brushing his dusty hands on his dirty, denim-clad thighs. "Okay, I'm done. I'll give you that tour now."

Ryan fell into step beside the bigger boy as they headed for the barn.

They were a sad pair, Sasha thought, although she had hope for both of them.

"I'd better check on Maddie," Roger said. "She might like snapping green beans, but she's probably already decided to quit on me."

As her uncle returned to the house, leaving Sasha and Graham standing in the yard, Sasha expected Graham to say he had to go back to work. Or maybe that he had to check on the teenagers. Either way, she figured he'd give her some reason he had to go. But he surprised her by remaining at her side.

He'd been avoiding her lately, so she was glad he hadn't made an excuse to skedaddle.

Before he opted to do just that, she decided to stretch out a little more time with him and asked, "So, what do you think?"

At the sound of Sasha's voice, Graham glanced up. He'd been so caught up in his musings about the boys and wondering how they'd do together that he'd probably missed something she'd said.

"What do I think about what?" he asked. "Ryan and the crime he committed?"

"Yes, that and whether you think he'll fit in here."

His biggest concern was how the boys would get along. Would they both be able to make some positive changes in their attitudes and their lives? Or would they hold each other back?

Graham lifted his Stetson, raked his fingers through his hair, then adjusted the hat back on his head. "Ryan's a smart kid. I think he'll do well here. And so will you."

She cocked her pretty head to the side. "Me? I'm not sure I'm following you."

The sunlight glistened on the white-blond strands of her hair, but he refused to let that distract him and explained what he'd meant. "I watched Ryan closely while you spoke to him. And I think he heard what you had to say. At least, he seemed to file away your comments."

"You really think so?"

Sasha had never lacked any confidence in the past, and the fact that she questioned herself now didn't sit well. He admired her manner, her way with the boys, although he didn't want to go overboard with his praise. It was too early to know how she'd do in the long run, although he suspected she'd be a natural.

"Yes, I liked what you told Ryan."

A smile claimed her renewed confidence. "Thank you. I thought it went over well, but you can never be sure, especially when talking to teenagers."

"That's true, but I think you nailed it. Ryan suffered one hell of a blow when his parents died, and I suspect he never had anyone to help him through it. Then, when his uncle damn near blew his plans for the future, he probably couldn't see any other way out of a bad situation."

Sasha nodded sagely. "You know, someone wise once told me that the essence of mental health is knowing that you have options. And Ryan has plenty of them, especially now that he's here."

She had a degree, but since she hadn't yet put it to use, Graham hadn't been entirely sure how she'd do working at Peter's Place. But after seeing her in action, first with Jonah and now with Ryan, he realized there wasn't any reason to hold any more interviews for an on-site counselor. Not when they already had Sasha.

"There's a home for delinquent teenagers in Austin," he said. "The setup isn't anything like this, but it might be a good idea if you took a look at it and maybe talked to the head counselor there. He might be able to help you develop your own program here."

"I'd like that." When she smiled, when her eyes lit up like that, it did something to him, something warm, something that skimmed his nerve endings and...

She folded her arms and rested them on her belly, reminding him of her condition and his inappropriate thoughts toward her. It also reminded him of her limitations. Maybe he ought to maintain that interview schedule after all.

"There's no hurry, though." He assumed she'd know what he meant. She wasn't going to be able to take on a full-time job for a while. He had no idea what restrictions her doctor had given her, although he had a sudden urge to find out and to make sure she took good care of herself and the baby. But did he have any right to pry?

They continued to stand in the yard in silence, but instead of thinking about the boys, as he'd done earlier, he studied Sasha and the way she bit down on her bottom lip, the way her brow furrowed. She was clearly pondering something serious.

Dang. Even concerned or worried, she was a lovely sight to behold. But he shook off his growing attraction.

"It might not be any of my business," he said, "but have you made an appointment with a local doctor yet?"

She looked up at him, those expressive blue eyes full of thoughts and emotions he had no idea how to read. "Are you worried about my pregnancy?"

As a matter of fact, yes. She appeared to be in good health, but he was still worried about her well-being— the baby's, too. And right this moment, everything about her concerned him. "When are you due?"

"August fifteenth."

That was about eight weeks away. His only experiences with labor and delivery involved broodmares. But this was different, *very* different.

"Just so you know," she said, "I have an appointment on Friday with an obstetrician in Austin."

"Good." That was a relief.

"I wouldn't let something that important lapse."

He didn't think she would. But he'd also heard that stress could bring on all sorts of physical ailments and complications for a pregnant woman. And Sasha must have suffered plenty of that over the past few months.

"I'd like to…" He paused, wishing he could recall what he'd been about to tell her. That he'd like to know what the new doctor had to say, he supposed. "I mean, I'm curious about that checkup, that's all."

"Do you want to go with me?" she asked.

Oh, hell no. He hadn't meant to be that forward or presumptuous. But then again, maybe that wasn't such a bad idea after all. But he was afraid to actually admit it.

"I could drive you there," he said. "I'd just hang out in the parking lot until you're finished. But that's up to you."

Damn. Now look at the can of worms he'd opened. That was another reason he needed to avoid her. It wasn't just the weird feelings she triggered in him whenever she was around; it was the crazy things he sometimes said.

"I must admit the drive from California was a bit difficult. My stomach is so big these days that I have to move the seat back so it doesn't rub against the steering wheel. And when I do that, my feet don't quite reach the gas or the brakes."

Graham had no idea how this conversation had actually unfolded, but he wasn't about to backpedal now. "I'd be happy to drive you to that appointment on Friday."

And for some wacky reason, he was even looking forward to it.

The next day, Graham showed up for breakfast in the ranch house, which not only surprised Sasha, but pleased her to no end.

"Good morning," she said. "You're just in time to have huevos rancheros."

"It tastes good, too," Jonah said. "So you better hurry up before me and Ryan eat it all."

Sasha glanced at the smaller boy, who'd just about cleaned his plate, which was a good sign, especially since Roger planned to "fatten him up" while he was here.

Jonah nudged Ryan with his elbow. "You like it, too. Don't you?"

Ryan stopped eating long enough to nod his agreement, the up-and-down motion causing his glasses to slip. He used his index finger to push them back on the bridge of his nose. She wondered who was in charge of taking him to an optometrist. The poor kid probably hadn't seen any doctors in a long while.

Roger, who stood at the stove filling a plate for Graham, chuckled. "I guess you finally got tired of fixing yourself a bowl of cold cereal every morning. I'm glad to hear it. Have a seat."

Graham didn't respond to the older man's comment. Instead he poured himself a cup of black coffee, took his plate and pulled out a chair next to Jonah.

"I like cold cereal sometimes," Maddie said. "Like today, when the food is hot and spicy and yucky."

Graham chuckled. "Your uncle is used to cooking for cowboys and sailors. I guess he forgot that little girls don't always like chilies and salsa."

Roger *hmph*ed. "I offer a variety of meals. We can't have silver-dollar hotcakes every morning. Besides, cereal isn't so bad, at least once in a while." He reached for the dishcloth and before wiping down the counter, added, "And just so all you ranch hands know, we're having my world-famous spaghetti for dinner tonight."

A slow grin stretched across Graham's face. "Now, that's what I call a treat. You can't believe how good Roger's meat sauce tastes. I'm tempted to join you guys."

And Sasha was tempted to steal Graham out of the kitchen, just so she could get him alone and tell him how she felt about him. But she knew better than that.

"By the way," Graham said, turning his attention to Maddie, "does your mom have any big plans for you today?"

The girl, who appeared delighted to be called on by the handsome cowboy, looked at Sasha. "Do you?"

"Not really." Sasha directed her question to Graham. "Why?"

"Because I think it's time to give Maddie another riding lesson."

At that, Maddie let out a squeal and clapped her hands. "I get to ride a horse again today?"

Graham took a sip of his coffee. When he lowered his mug, he grinned. "Sure. That is, if you're ready and it's okay with your mom."

"I'm ready right now." She pushed aside her plate and scooted her chair back.

Graham, his hero status in Maddie's eyes clearly growing by leaps and bounds, looked to Sasha for permission. But how could she possibly object? Maddie would ride every single day, from sunup to sundown if she could. But with as busy as the men had been, they hadn't had the time to supervise her. "Sure, it's fine with me."

"Good. Once I've finished eating breakfast and drinking my coffee, we'll go out and saddle Lady Jane."

Sasha's heart warmed at Graham's kindness toward her daughter. He'd already shown Maddie more attention in a couple of weeks than Gabe had in seven years. At least, when it came to quality time. That in itself was reason enough for Sasha to fall in love with him.

Well, maybe *love* wasn't the correct word. But it sure felt like the right one for what she was feeling.

Maddie carried her bowl of cereal, or rather the milk that remained, to the sink, where the boys would wash them after breakfast. Then she returned to her chair, placed her elbows on the table and plopped her chin upon her upturned hands as she proceeded to watch Graham eat, no doubt hoping he'd hurry.

Gabe would have found their daughter's behavior annoying and sent her away from the table. But it didn't seem to bother the rancher, who sported a big ol' grin stretched across his face.

A couple of minutes later, Graham finished his breakfast and carried his plate and empty coffee cup to the sink. "All right, sweet pea. I'm ready now. Does your mom want to watch?"

"You bet I do." Sasha wouldn't miss it for the world, and not just because she wanted to see her child taking part in an activity that made her so happy.

She followed Graham and Maddie outside, where the summer sun cast a glow on the ranch, mimicking the one that warmed her heart. When she spotted the bay mare that had been saddled and was waiting near the corral, she realized the lesson had been planned ahead of time.

"I love you," Maddie told the mare. "You're the best horse in the whole wide world."

Sasha smiled. If truth be told, Maddie had claimed to love the imaginary horse she'd made out of the sofa in the old house in which they'd once lived.

Graham lifted Maddie and placed her on the saddle. As the girl reached for the pommel, he adjusted the stirrups. Then he began to lead the mare around the yard. All the while, Maddie's bright-eyed smile couldn't get any larger.

Sasha wasn't sure how long her daughter's interest in horses and cowboys would last, but for now, you'd think Graham had offered her the moon.

As the back door creaked opened, she glanced over her shoulder to see Ryan and Jonah heading for the barn. The two chatted between themselves. Sasha might have been interested in what they had to say, but she was too intrigued by her daughter right now, by the pure joy on her face.

And she was far too caught up in all Graham had done for Maddie. Whatever she felt for him seemed to be growing stronger each day.

But where would that leave her and her family when he left?

Chapter Eight

Sasha had no more than locked the memory of Maddie's most recent riding lesson in her heart when her cell phone rang, putting a damper on what she'd thought of as a perfect day.

Before even looking at the lit display, she knew who was calling, and she'd been right. As much as she'd like to let the call go to voice mail, she answered, anyway. But that didn't ensure an upbeat tone when she said, "Hello, Gabe."

"Hey," her soon-to-be ex-husband said. "How're things going out there?"

It was nice that he cared enough to ask. She and Maddie had always been at the lower end of his priority list. But at least he'd followed up on his promise to call her after she'd had gotten settled at the ranch. "We're fine, Gabe. How about you?"

"Busy—as usual."

That was typical. Gabe had begun to build a life of his own way before the two of them separated. He'd blamed it on his adventurous spirit, something she'd found exciting and appealing when she met him during her freshman year in college. But over time, she'd realized that, in reality, he'd been a restless soul, a tumbleweed who rolled along from one interest or job to another.

"So, what's new?" she asked.

"For one thing, I was talking to my parents the other day."

Now, *that* was unusual. He'd never been especially close to his father. Or to his mother, for that matter. And for that reason alone, neither she nor Maddie had ever really bonded with his parents, not in the way she'd once hoped and imagined they would.

She wondered if they'd been upset by the divorce. If so, neither of them had taken the time to call her and ask how she was faring, how she was feeling. Was she wrong to think that was odd?

"How are they doing?" she asked.

"Actually, they're doing okay. Now, anyway. My mom found a breast lump a while back, something she hadn't wanted to bother me with. She's undergoing treatment but seems to be okay. And Dad had a minor heart attack last week."

"I'm sorry to hear that."

"Yeah. Me, too. So I figured it might be time for me to take my dad up on his offer to work for the family corporation."

Finally? It had taken two serious health issues for Gabe to see the wisdom in that? It was a good move for him and his father, but she wondered how long that would last. "I'm sure your dad will be happy to hear about your decision."

"I already told him, and he was. Anyway, my mom asked about our plans for the holidays."

"*Our* plans?"

"She wanted us—or rather me—to bring the girls for Christmas."

Sasha had assumed they'd be with her. In the eight years she and Gabe had been married, they'd only spent the holidays with his parents a couple of times.

"I know I've never been big on family celebrations or gatherings," he said. "But I'm turning over a new leaf."

She bit back a sarcastic response and tamped down her anger. Why hadn't he thought about doing that years ago when there'd still been hope for their marriage?

Instead she said, "I'm glad to hear that." And for Maddie's sake, she hoped it wasn't just another passing fancy.

"My mom wants to have an old-fashioned Christmas this year. She'd like to have Maddie help her to bake cookies and that sort of thing. I know it's early to be making plans this far in advance, but I thought we should start thinking about that, along with a visitation schedule."

"I suppose you can have Maddie on Christmas Eve," Sasha said. "But I want her on Christmas Day."

"Fair enough. I'll take her home to you in the morning."

She hadn't yet told him that she planned to stay in

Texas, but now wasn't the time. She'd prefer to wait until all the paperwork was signed and filed with the court. Besides, the holidays were still five or six months away.

Sasha's only response was to blow out a wobbly sigh.

"But what about…um…the baby?" he asked.

The "um…baby" had a name. She'd told him several times that she'd planned to call her Sydney, but apparently he'd forgotten.

"What about her?" Sasha asked.

"Mom wants her to come, too."

Sasha's heart dropped to the pit of her stomach. There was no way she'd let Gabe take an infant for an overnight visit, and she was surprised he'd even suggested it.

Maddie had been a fussy, challenging baby who'd required much of Sasha's time. And Gabe had avoided being around her every chance he got. If Sasha wanted to stir up a fight, she'd remind Gabe how resentful he'd been—and not just because of the noise. He hadn't liked taking second place, even to his daughter. So it was difficult to believe that their girls were becoming more important to him.

"I'm sorry," Sasha said. "I don't feel right about letting you take the baby for more than an hour. She'll only be a few months old, and I plan to breast-feed."

"I understand that. And believe me, I know how tough it is when babies get fussy. But my mom will help out. Won't you agree for her?"

Sasha had never held anything against Gabe's mother, although Claire Smith been so caught up with her bridge group, her golf friends and her charity work that she'd never made her family a huge priority, either. However, facing one's mortality would cause one to re-evaluate life and make changes.

Hopefully, Gabe was actually planning to make a few changes himself. And wouldn't that be good for the kids?

Yes, it would. And she actually appreciated that.

But how would a visit to California impact her first holiday season on the Galloping G? She hadn't shared a Christmas dinner with Uncle Roger in... Well, she couldn't remember when. And she'd planned to make a big deal out of decorating the tree, hanging stockings and baking with Maddie.

And then there was Graham...

Oh, for Pete's sake. Who knew where he'd be by then? Hadn't he told her he'd be moving to Austin in the near future?

"I don't know," she said. "I need some time to think about it. In the meantime, would you consider celebrating with your family the weekend before or after the holiday?"

"If that's the only way you'll agree, then maybe we'd better do it earlier. I think my mom is going to kick the cancer, but...well, you never know."

As much as Sasha would like to hold on to her resentment and to prohibit Gabe from seeing the children at all, especially overnight, she couldn't do that legally. And even if she could, she wouldn't. Neither would she prevent his parents from seeing their grandchildren.

"We'll work something out," she said.

"Good. I'd appreciate that. It might be nice if you

and the girls joined us for Thanksgiving, too. It would make my mom really happy."

Well, it wouldn't make Sasha happy. She'd had enough of those awkward family dinners, when Gabe and his father would often have words, then lapse into silence. And the fact that their divorce would be final by then would only make things more nerve-racking, more strained.

"Let's talk about this later," she said. "By the way, is Mr. Stanley back in town?" She and her attorney had suggested a change in their agreement, but Ron Stanley, Gabe's lawyer, had been on vacation when she left town.

"I have no idea. Like I said, I've been swamped with one thing or another. I guess I'd better call his office and ask."

She wished she could believe him. He'd always been one to downplay the seriousness of a situation, especially if it mattered to her. "Please call today. I don't want to prolong this thing. And you're a born procrastinator."

"Is there some reason you need the divorce to be finalized immediately?"

Graham came to mind. But she was dreaming again.

"Yes," she said. "I'd like to put it behind me for good."

"Sheesh, Sasha. It's pretty obvious you've been talking to your uncle. That crusty old man has a mean streak and hasn't ever liked me."

She had the urge to sling her cell phone across the room. How dare Gabe blame any of their problems on Uncle Roger?

"I don't want to fight with you," she said. "Just follow through on your part of the agreement in a timely manner, and I'll do the same."

"Don't worry. I'll take care of things on my end. And after I do, maybe I'll come out there to visit."

Seriously? He'd never wanted to before, and she'd asked several times. The thought of him showing up on the Galloping G unsettled her.

When the call ended, she still felt compelled to wind up and let the phone fly. Instead she swore under her breath and turned away, only to see Uncle Roger in the doorway.

Did he realize who she'd been talking to? A scowl on his face suggested he did. And if that was the case, he'd probably stood in the doorway long enough to have heard plenty.

He closed the gap between them and crossed his arms. "What did that…guy have to say?"

"Not much. He just wanted to ask how Maddie was doing." Sasha offered up a smile, hoping her uncle hadn't sensed her frustration and worries.

He let out a *hmph*, but his expression mellowed, which indicated he'd accepted her explanation.

Thank goodness for that. No matter how badly she'd like to share her mounting fears with someone, Roger didn't need any more reasons to dislike Gabe.

Besides, if Gabe showed up on the Galloping G as he'd said he might, she didn't want her ex-husband and her uncle coming to blows.

The afternoon sun slipped down in the western sky as Graham and the boys continued to work on the downed fence. It would have been fixed already if Roger would have used the insurance money to hire professionals to do it. But he and Graham had decided it would be a good project for the boys. They'd actually made a surprising amount of progress so far, especially since each of the teenagers seemed determined to outwork the other.

If truth be told, they were both doing a fine job, even Ryan, who'd yet to bulk up or put on that much-needed weight.

A hammer pounded on wood, followed by a boy's voice crying out a string of obscenities. Graham turned away from the post he'd been centering to see Jonah gripping his left hand while jumping up and down.

He didn't need to ask what happened, although he probably ought to assess the injury.

"He got his thumb instead of the nail," Ryan said.

Graham nodded, then made his way to the bigger boy. "Let me see."

"I think…I busted it." He grimaced and swore again. "Thank goodness this isn't my pitching arm. But damn, it hurts like hell."

As soon as Jonah was willing to unlock his grip, Graham checked out his thumb. He'd caught the tip of it. The nail was already turning black and blue, and he would eventually lose it.

"I think it's just a bad bruise," Graham said. "But if you want me to take you to the Urgent Care for an X-ray, I can. Either way, let's call it a day. We've already gotten more work done than I expected us to."

Jonah glanced at Ryan, then back at Graham. "I don't need to see a doctor."

"The offer stands. In the meantime, let's go to the house and put some ice on it."

The boy swore again for good measure, then muttered, "Whatever."

Once back at the house, they found Sasha in the kitchen. She'd just brewed a gallon jar of sun tea. When she turned around and offered them a glass, she noticed Jonah holding his wrist.

"Uh-oh." Sasha was by the boy's side instantly, gauging the seriousness of the injury. "What happened?"

Graham folded his arms across his chest. "He had a run-in with a hammer."

"That's a nasty bruise," she said. "And it's swelling. I'll get some ice."

Ryan, who stood to the side, observing Sasha's efforts to render first aid, made his way to Graham. "There's still a couple hours of daylight left. You want me to do anything?"

"No, you can go back to your room, shower and rest up for dinner."

"Maybe I should go see about the horses," Ryan said. "I could give them carrots or an apple or something."

"Good idea." Graham reached into the fruit bowl on the counter and removed two red apples. "There's a paring knife in the cupboard next to the left of the sink. Take it with you."

As Ryan proceeded to do as he was told, Graham added, "Just don't cut yourself. I only allow one accident per day."

Ryan smiled, a rare reaction but a good one. "Got it, boss."

Sasha set a bowl of ice water on the table in front of Jonah, then took a seat beside him and watched as he soaked his sore thumb.

She was wearing a white T-shirt and a pair of snug-fitting blue jeans, nothing fancy. But she looked especially pretty today. She'd pulled her hair up into a messy topknot, revealing a pair of diamond studs in her delicate earlobes.

Graham wondered if Gabe had given the dazzling earrings to her. He wouldn't be surprised. Sasha was the kind of woman Graham would shower with gifts. And expensive ones, at that.

"I hope this doesn't screw up my mobility," Jonah said.

Graham knew he wasn't just referring to dexterity. The kid loved baseball, and according to that report Brad Taylor had shared, he was a good player.

Before Graham could bring up the subject, Sasha did it for him. "That reminds me, Jonah. I asked around and found out the name of our local high school baseball coach. I know the season is over, but there's always next year. I know Mr. Atwater would like to meet you. What would you say if I invited him out to the ranch someday?"

Jonah's jaw dropped, his once-surly attitude nowhere in sight. "No kidding? You'd invite the coach here?"

"Sure," Sasha said. "I've heard you've got one heck of a pitching arm."

The boy shrugged. "I'm pretty good. At least, I used to be when there was someone to play with. But are you saying there's actually a chance I could attend the high school instead of taking classes here with Mrs. McCrea? And that I might even get to play ball again?"

"I can't see why not. If you continue to work hard and promise not to get into any trouble, I think we could work that out." Sasha glanced at Graham. "Don't you agree?"

"We'll talk to Mrs. McCrea and see what she thinks about a transfer."

"You won't be sorry," Jonah said. "I'll work my ass off this summer. And I'll keep out of trouble. I promise."

He studied his hand—not the one with the bum thumb, but the one he used for pitching fastballs and curves. He turned it one way, then the other, opening and flexing his fingers.

It was a shame he'd had to give up baseball before, but it was an even bigger shame that he'd acted out and gotten into trouble.

Sasha placed her forearms on the table and leaned forward. "You know, if you really want to punish someone by your rebellion, you might try channeling it in a way that it won't hurt you."

"What do you mean?" Jonah asked.

"I might be wrong, but I have a feeling you blame your father for bailing out on you and your family."

"Damn straight. It's all his fault."

"But the only ones you hurt when you got into trouble were your mom and yourself."

The boy lowered his head and scrunched his forehead, but he neither agreed nor offered up a defense.

"Unfortunately, your dad left your mom in dire

straits financially. So she was forced to work two jobs to feed you and your younger brothers and sisters. She needed someone's help, and that someone was you."

Jonah looked up and caught Sasha's gaze. "I let her down. I know. But dang, she let me down, too."

"How?" Sasha asked.

"I don't know. Maybe she shouldn't have spent all her time at work and then paid more attention to the younger kids than she did to me."

"Whoa," Graham said. "I think it's admirable that your mom did everything she could to hold the family together. And she probably wasn't able to give anyone the time they deserved, so she focused on the ones who needed her most."

"Yeah. I know. But…" The boy pursed his lips and held back his thoughts, something he wouldn't have done the first day he arrived.

"I know it feels as if your mom set out to hurt or punish you," Sasha said, "but I doubt that's the case."

His shoulders drooped. "Yeah, I know. But it wasn't fair."

"Maybe not. And I'm sure that she's now wishing that she'd done things differently when you were at home. I know that's the way I feel when I mess up. But for the record, life *isn't* always fair. Sometimes a person you thought you could lean on or depend upon will wimp out and not follow through on his or her obligations. And that means someone else has to become the responsible one."

The boy didn't respond, but he seemed to be pondering her words. Graham was pondering them, too.

She had to be speaking from personal experience, but Jonah had no way of knowing that.

Sasha fell silent. When she glanced at Graham, a smile flickered across her lips. He winked at her, letting her know that he'd not only agreed with her, but had caught on to what she'd implied.

As their gazes locked, silently binding them together once again, all those weird, inexplicable feelings he'd been having tumbled around in his chest, threatening to trip him up—if he'd let them. But he couldn't think about that now.

Instead he thought about the kind of social worker and counselor Sasha was going to make. The boys who stayed on the ranch were going to be lucky to have her here.

Graham ought to be comforted by the fact that things would run smoothly at Peter's Place, even when he was gone. And in a way, he did feel better.

Only trouble was, the plans he had to start his own business in the city no longer seemed quite so pressing. And he wasn't in any big rush to leave.

On Friday morning, as promised, Graham drove Sasha into Austin for her doctor's appointment. They didn't talk much on the way. For one thing, he wasn't quite sure what to say to her. Other than friendship, there wasn't much he could offer. At least, that was all until her divorce was finalized.

He hadn't planned to ask, but the question rolled off his tongue without a thought to whether it was appropriate or not. "Are you and Gabe just separated? Or have you actually filed for divorce?"

"The paperwork has been filed, although there's an amendment that needs to be made. Why?"

Because he wondered just how invested she was in her marriage. Would she be open to a reconciliation if the opportunity arose? And if not, when would she be free so he could… Do what? Pursue her himself?

"I was just wondering," he said.

A mile down the road, he looked across the seat where she sat, staring out the window at the passing scenery.

Curiosity prompted him to question her again. "When will it be final?"

"I don't know. Soon, I think."

He hoped so—for her sake. Okay, and maybe for his own sake, too. He stole another glance at her, watched her place her hand over her ever-expanding baby bump.

Was she worried about her upcoming doctor's appointment? Did she wish she still had a husband to go through pregnancy and childbirth with her?

Graham knew a couple of guys who'd actually gone to obstetrical appointments with their pregnant wives, but he wasn't the father of Sasha's baby. So it still surprised him that he'd not only volunteered to go with her, but that he'd also considered asking if he could go in the exam room with her.

It was weird, though. He would've thought that he'd feel uncomfortable to even consider something like that, but for some reason, he didn't.

Truth be told, if she asked him to, he'd probably agree. But why would she ask? She'd never given him any reason to think she'd want him there.

After parking his pickup, he remained behind the wheel and turned in his seat. "Do you want me to wait for you out here? Or should I go inside?"

She tucked a strand of hair behind her ear. "I have no idea how long I'll be, and it could get warm out here. Why don't you come in with me?"

He figured she meant he should come as far as the waiting room, which was probably best. So he opened the driver's door and got out. Once she slid out of the passenger seat and he locked the vehicle, he walked with her to the entrance. He pushed open the glass door for her, then they proceeded to the elevator.

"It's on the third floor," she said, pushing the proper button to take them up.

When the elevator doors opened, they stepped out and walked along the hallway until they found 302. Again, he opened the door and followed her inside. While she signed in at the front desk, he removed his Stetson and scanned the waiting area. He spotted a couple of empty chairs and pointed them out to her when she returned.

Sasha took a seat, leaving the one next to her for him. She'd no more than settled into the chair when she whispered, "I've heard great things about this doctor."

"I'm glad. It's nice to know you'll in good hands."

Moments later, a tall, dark-complexioned man in his late thirties or early forties entered the room. He checked out the empty chairs before taking the seat next to Graham. Moments later, he snatched a *Parents* magazine from the table beside him and began to thumb through it.

Graham wondered where the guy's wife was. Had she been called back to see the doctor already? Was she going to meet him here?

Not that it mattered. He looked at the magazine offerings: *Good Housekeeping*, *Baby Talk*... Nothing he found especially appealing.

He wasn't sure how long they'd have to wait. After all, a lot of doctors didn't run on time. But he was here for the long haul.

Several minutes later, a woman wearing pink scrubs called Sasha's name.

"Oh, good," she said, getting to her feet. "I shouldn't be too long, but who knows?"

Apparently, she didn't want him to go in with her, which was her call. "No problem. I'll be here."

Sasha nodded, then grabbed her purse and headed toward the smiling nurse in the doorway.

Once she'd disappeared behind the door that led to the exam rooms, the man next to him leaned toward him. "First baby?"

"Uh, no. I'm just a friend of the mother's. How about you?"

"Yep. First-time dad here." A smile stretched across his face, lighting his brown eyes. "My wife and I tried for years to have a baby on our own, but we didn't have any luck. So we're adopting a baby that will be born around Thanksgiving, and now we're going to really be parents."

"Congratulations."

"Thanks." The man set his magazine aside. "You have no idea how happy we are—or how excited I am to be able to attend the OB appointments. In fact, I'm supposed to meet my wife and the birth mom here in about forty-five minutes."

Graham smiled. "You're early."

"Yep. That's how eager I am for this appointment. We're supposed to have an ultrasound today, and we're hoping to find out if we're going to have a boy or girl."

"That's cool," Graham said, surprisingly happy for the guy.

"Yep. It's not every day that you get to meet your own son or daughter. And I couldn't care less that we don't have the same DNA. Anyone can be a sperm donor, right? But it takes a special man to be a dad."

Graham knew exactly what the guy meant. His own father had kids all over the world, but he hadn't actually raised some of them.

A sperm donor, huh? That about sized it up, he supposed.

He thought about Sasha, about her daughters. Gabe Smith had supplied those girls with his DNA and was their legal father, but was he going to actually step up and take a loving, parental role with them, especially now that they lived out of state?

From what Roger had said and Graham had gathered, it wasn't likely. Gabe Smith might not be "special" enough to be a real dad. So who would man up and be there for those girls—and for their pretty mom?

Graham?

The idea of assuming that kind of responsibility ought to scare the hell out of him. But for some reason, he thought he might be up to the task.

Chapter Nine

After her exam, Sasha stopped by the reception desk and scheduled her next appointment to see the obstetrician for two weeks from today. Then she returned to the waiting room, where she'd left Graham.

When he spotted her, he took his hat from the table in front of him, got to his feet and ambled toward her. "So, how did it go? Is everything okay?"

"It went very well. They already have my medical records, so that made for an easy transition."

"Good. Do you like the new doctor?"

"Yes, I do. She has a nice way about her and really seems to know her stuff."

"That's got to be a relief." Graham opened the door for her, and they stepped into the corridor that led to the elevator.

Sasha had worried about changing doctors in mid-stream, but once she'd made up her mind to start a new life without Gabe, she hadn't wanted to wait until after she'd recovered from childbirth to move to Texas.

When they reached the elevator, Graham hit the down button.

"So the baby's doing all right?" He glanced at her belly, and a crooked grin tickled his lips. "From the looks of it, she certainly seems to be growing."

Sasha rested her hands over her expanding baby bump, glad to know little Sydney was healthy. Yet, as a result, she herself had become bigger and more cumbersome. But there wasn't much she could do about that.

"Everything is right on track," she said. "I should deliver in a little over six weeks."

The elevator doors opened, and Graham let Sasha enter first. Considering how happy she was to have him by her side, she ought to glide into the car, her feet on little clouds. Instead she waddled like a plump, well-fed Christmas goose.

Once Graham had joined her, they descended to the lobby.

"If there's anything I can do…" He paused, then shrugged. "I mean, if there's anything you need, just say the word."

A friendly face and a hand to hold during labor would be nice, but she'd gotten by without either last time. She'd told herself that Gabe would have been there if he hadn't come down with the flu. Since Maddie had decided to make her entrance two weeks early and Gabe's parents had been on a golf vacation in Hawaii at the time, Sasha hadn't had anyone to coach or support her through it all.

That was all behind her now, but still, it would be comforting to know someone would sit by her side when baby Sydney entered the world. As much as Sasha loved Uncle Roger, he'd probably be more helpful if he drank coffee in the hospital cafeteria and waited until he got word that it was all over.

She shot a glance at Graham. Could she...?

No, if she broached a question like that with him, he'd probably balk at her audacity, which would ruin their budding friendship. So she kept that thought to herself as they left the medical building and crossed the parking lot.

When they reached the spot where Graham had left his pickup, he asked, "So, now what? Do you have any shopping you need to do?"

"I'd rather do that next time I'm in Austin. I want to check on Maddie. Plus, I have a couple of calls I need to make."

"All right." Graham circled to the passenger side of the pickup, pushed the unlock button on the remote and opened the door for her.

How sweet—and gallant. Just like a knight in shining armor. Again she was struck by how handsome he was, how kind. And how very different he was from Gabe.

But she couldn't very well pursue anything romantic with him at this point. So she slid into her seat, blowing out a soft sigh of resignation as she did.

After Graham started the engine and backed out of the parking lot, they headed to the ranch.

"Thanks for driving me," she said.

"You're welcome. I'd be happy to do it again for your next appointment."

"I'd appreciate that." And she would. In fact, she'd better start focusing on the future and the positive changes that had occurred since she'd left California.

As difficult as it was going to be to go through labor and delivery, and then raise two daughters on her own, she had a lot to be grateful for and should count her blessings. After all, she had Maddie, Uncle Roger... and now Graham, who was proving to be a good friend.

She just wished that someday he'd become more than that.

That night, after the boys ate dinner and returned to their cabin to do the homework assignments their teacher had given them, Uncle Roger volunteered to read a bedtime story to Maddie.

"Only one?" Maddie cocked her head to the side. "I brought some really, really good books from home. Maybe you could read all of them to me."

Roger chuckled. "Sure. Why not?"

As Maddie took her great-uncle by the hand to lead him to her bedroom and the books she'd stacked next to her closet door, Sasha told them she'd be back shortly. Then she stepped out the front door, crossed the yard and went to Graham's cabin.

Ever since she first arrived on the Galloping G, she'd been tempted to visit him so they could talk privately. But other than delivering a meal now and then, she hadn't been able to come up with an excuse that was good enough. But she had one now.

After she'd arrived home from her doctor's appointment, she called the local high school, which was open to kids needing to take remedial courses during the summer. She hoped to connect with someone who could relate to the boys and their interests.

Chuck Atwater, the baseball coach, wasn't at work, but Caroline Stewart, the head of the science department, was. So Sasha had told her about Peter's Place and the boys who had recently come to live here.

Mrs. Stewart seemed genuinely interested in Ryan, especially when Sasha mentioned his interest in science and math, his tragic past and the trouble he'd gotten into.

"I'd be more than happy to talk to him," the teacher had said.

When Sasha had told her about Jonah and his interest in baseball, she said she'd get in contact with Coach Atwater. So things were coming together nicely.

She hadn't set a date for the teachers from the high school to visit the ranch, since she'd wanted to talk it over with Graham first. So that was what she planned to do now.

After climbing the steps to his cabin, she lifted her hand and knocked.

Graham answered the door wearing only a pair of worn jeans. The sight of him bare-chested almost knocked her to her knees.

Sure, she'd noted his broad shoulders, muscular chest

and bulging biceps before, but she hadn't been prepared for those taut abs.

Under normal circumstances, it would have been easy to focus on his sparkling blue eyes and gorgeous face. But that was when he was fully dressed in all his cowboy glory—and not when he was obviously ready for bed and sexier than ever.

"I…uh…" She couldn't seem to form a single word, let alone a greeting. But that didn't matter. He appeared to be just as surprised to see her.

"Hey!" A crooked grin tugged at his lips. "I thought you might be one of the boys."

"I'm sorry. I didn't realize it was so late." She glanced over her shoulder, at the path she'd taken, wishing she hadn't come. "You know, what I had to say really wasn't that important. I can talk to you tomorrow, maybe at breakfast."

"It's not late, and I wasn't asleep. Come on in." He swung open the door and stepped aside so she could enter the small quarters he called home. It was a modest abode for a man related to the Robinson and Fortune clans.

Sasha hadn't been in one of the Galloping G cabins for years, and certainly not this one, with its small stone fireplace and open-beamed ceiling. The wooden floor was dotted with several colorful throw rugs that looked fairly new.

Graham didn't have much furniture, just a leather sofa, a rustic lamp with a cowhide shade and a television mounted on a wall bracket. He'd been watching a sports channel, the volume on low.

A dark oak coffee table held a TV remote and a long-neck beer bottle, resting on a folded napkin he'd used as a makeshift coaster.

Graham picked up the remote and shut off the TV and the ball game he'd been watching.

"Have a seat," he said, indicating the sofa, which was her only option. That meant they'd be sitting side by side.

She brushed her palms, which suddenly seemed a bit clammy, along the fabric of her sundress and bit down on her bottom lip. Dang, what on earth had she been thinking when she came to talk to him this evening? Her mind was swirling with all kinds of inappropriate thoughts and scenarios that couldn't possibly play themselves out. She ought to make an excuse to leave before things got any more awkward, but she did her best to shake off her insecurity and sat down.

"So, what's up?" he asked.

Right. Her actual reason for coming to talk to him. "I placed a call to the high school today and spoke to one of the teachers about Peter's Place and the boys."

"Good idea. What did they say? Were they concerned about having a 'bad' element infiltrate their campus?"

"Well, I'm sure that crossed their minds, although it's a public school and I think they have to take them." She tucked a strand of hair behind her ear. "I told her we already had a teacher working here and that we'd only send the boys to the high school if they were ready to mainstream into a regular classroom situation."

"How did that explanation go over with them?"

"Actually, very well. I spoke to Caroline Stewart,

the head of the science department and the one who teaches a couple of AP classes. I told her about Ryan's potential, and she'd like to meet him."

"That's great." Graham stretched out his bare arm along the back of the sofa.

"I thought I'd invite her out to see the ranch and to meet the boys next weekend. Hopefully, she can bring Chuck Atwater, the baseball coach. He's not working at the school this summer, but Caroline said he's looking for new talent for next season."

"Wow, you've been busy—and productive. I'm impressed." A broad smile and a glimmer in his eyes convinced her that he wasn't just blowing smoke. He truly valued her efforts.

Just knowing that he admired her touched something deep inside, something that yearned to be appreciated, to be needed.

Graham, whose arm still stretched along the sofa's backrest, shifted in his seat, his fingers moving closer to her shoulder.

Focus on his eyes, Sasha.

"Was Mrs. Stewart apprehensive about the trouble the boys got into?" he asked.

"Somewhat, I think. But I explained that Ryan's primary purpose in damaging that equipment was to get himself removed from his uncle's home."

"Did Ryan actually come out and admit that?" Graham asked.

"Not in so many words, but I'm sure of it."

Graham's finger was dangling by her shoulder. She

tried not to think about how easily he could touch her—if he were so inclined.

"What made you decide to be a social worker?" he asked.

Good question. She needed to keep the conversation on track. "When I was in the Girl Scouts, our troop would sometimes work along with a sorority that took on service projects. A couple of times we served meals to the homeless. We were also included in other projects to help people who were struggling to make ends meet. And that's when I decided I'd like to do that kind of work when I grew up."

"You have a big heart."

"I guess so, especially for those who aren't as fortunate as I am." She turned in her seat, facing him. "You know, losing my mom and dad was tough, but I had loving grandparents and, of course, Uncle Roger to help me through it. I never had to worry about where I'd sleep at night or when I'd get my next meal. A lot of people—and sadly, way too many children—aren't that lucky."

"That's why I'm glad we can help some of those kids here."

We? She smiled at the thought of being Graham's teammate. She liked it—a lot.

"It's amazing what love, kindness and understanding can do," she said.

"You've got a real gift, Sasha. I heard you talk to both Ryan and Jonah. You're able to relate to them. So becoming a counselor is a good career move for you."

"I've wanted to work with kids for a long time. After Peter died, I was devastated. So my grandparents sent me to counseling. The experience was a good one, and I took courses in psychology and social work when I was in college. The rest is history."

"I'm so proud of the woman you've become." He trailed his fingers along her upper arm, radiating heat to her shoulder and setting off a rush of tingles that nearly unraveled her at the seams.

What was going on? Why had he touched her like that? Did she dare read something into it?

The emotion glowing in his eyes warmed her heart in such an unexpected way that she forgot her momentary concern and pretended, just for a moment, that something romantic was brewing between them.

She tossed him a playful grin. "I'm glad to hear you say that, especially when you once thought of me as a pest."

"Yeah, well, I wish I'd known then who the woman that little girl was going to grow up to be. Things might have been…"

His words drifted off, but her heart soared at the implication. Might he have given her the time of day? Might he have developed feelings for her?

As she searched his expression, looking for an answer, their gazes locked. A bolt of something powerful snapped and crackled in the silence, until he pulled his hand away and muttered, "Dammit."

"What's the matter?" she asked, although she feared what he might say.

"This is a real struggle for me, Sasha."

She had a wild thought that he actually might be attracted to her, but she was crazy to even consider it for a moment. Yet she waited to hear him out, bracing herself for disappointment.

He merely studied her as if she ought to know just what he was talking about. But she couldn't be sure. And she'd be darned if she'd read something nonexistent into it.

He raked his fingers through his hair, mussing it in a way she found appealing.

"I'm feeling things for you that I have no right to feel," he admitted.

The revelation stunned her, pleased her. Thrilled her. And she found it difficult to think, to respond.

"Seriously?"

He slowly shook his head. "I'm afraid so. And I'm sorry, especially since you still belong to another man."

Sasha hadn't "belonged" to anyone in a long time, and if truth be told, the only man she wanted to belong to was Graham. But she was still afraid to make any assumptions about what he was saying.

"For what it's worth," she said, "I might still be legally married, but I won't be for long. The divorce will be final soon."

"I'll have to wait to ask you out until then."

Graham wanted to date her? Her surprise must have been splashed all over her face, because he asked, "Does that shock you?"

"Yes, it does. To be honest, I had a humongous crush on you when I was younger."

"Really?" A slow grin stretched across his face. "You never told me."

"I knew you weren't interested back then. So it's kind

of nice to know you…like me now." Could she have downplayed her feelings for him any more than that?

"So you're not opposed to going out with me?" he asked.

If she weren't still legally married and seven months pregnant, she might have insisted that they go out right now. But she was afraid to jinx things, to lose Graham before she'd actually won him.

Sure, he'd kissed her before. But he'd apologized afterward. What was she supposed to think?

"I can't believe you actually want to date me," she said.

"You can believe it. I'd actually like to do more than just that."

As if his words hadn't thoroughly jerked the rug out from under her, he slid across the seat and slipped his arms around her in a move that was more than persuading.

As their lips met, hers parted, allowing him full access to her mouth. His tongue sought hers, and the kiss intensified until she had no doubt about what he meant, what he felt.

Could this really be happening? Should she risk telling him how badly she'd wanted this, wanted him?

Not when she was afraid to blink—or to pinch herself. Dang, if she was dreaming, she didn't want to wake up.

Savoring his taste, his musky scent, she lifted her hand and placed it on his bare chest, felt his body heat, the whisper of hair on his skin, the steady beat of his heart.

She probably should put a stop to this. Shouldn't she? Yet she really wasn't legally or emotionally bound to Gabe any longer. Besides, their marriage had been a sham for years.

Whether it was right or wrong, Sasha continued to kiss Graham for all she was worth. But just as she felt herself weaken, as she felt compelled to spill out all her romantic thoughts, he drew back.

"I'm sorry," he said. "I don't want to hurt you or the baby."

She doubted he'd hurt either of them. After all, the doctor hadn't said anything about abstaining from sex. But she was so caught up in his admission, in his unselfish concern for her and her child, that she didn't press the issue or encourage him to throw caution to the wind.

So she said, "All right."

She feared he might get up at that point, ending the tender romantic moment, but he drew her closer. As she leaned into him and settled into his embrace, she felt truly loved and cared for in the first time since…well, forever, it seemed.

Yet the idea of trusting Graham with her heart scared her to death.

What would she do if he tired of her, a fussy infant and a precocious little girl? What if this dream come true ended before it even got started?

Not that she thought Graham lacked commitment. Look at all he'd done to help Uncle Roger with the ranch, with Peter's Place. He'd also been mentoring Jonah and Ryan.

But there was something else that caused her concern—

his refusal to work at Robinson Tech. After all, families were important. And while she admired all he'd done on the Galloping G, she worried he might walk away from her if the going got tough.

Just as Gabe had.

As Graham rested his head against Sasha's, he relished the feel of her in his arms and the light scent of her peach-blossom fragrance. The heated kiss they'd shared, as well as the memory of the first one, convinced him that what he'd been feeling for her was the real deal.

There was no longer any doubt in his mind that he wanted her, and he was determined to make the three of them—rather, the *four* of them—a real family.

He had to admit that becoming an overnight father would be a big change for him, but he adored Maddie. And he was already feeling something for the little one Sasha carried, the baby who was due to be born in six short weeks.

He could open his heart and tell that to Sasha now. In fact, he probably should, but she might not be ready to hear something that heavy, especially when she was still reeling emotionally from her split with Gabe.

Still, she'd agreed to date him, which was a big step in the right direction.

He'd like to ask her to stay the night with him, to just lie next to him and cuddle. But she couldn't do that. He supposed he'd have to be content to hold her like this for as long as she'd let him.

A moment later, she said, "I probably ought to go back to the house. It's past Maddie's bedtime."

He understood why she had to go. "Tell her good-night for me."

"I will." Yet she didn't make a move toward leaving. And he didn't remove his arm from her shoulders.

He sensed that she had something on her mind, words she wanted to say, yet didn't.

If so, what was she holding back?

And why?

Did she still have feelings for her ex? Graham sure hoped that wasn't the case. And for more reasons than the obvious. Gabe Smith didn't deserve her or their daughters.

"I don't want you to keep Maddie waiting," he said. "But for the record, I could sit like this all night."

"Me, too."

Truthfully? Did she still harbor any remnants of the crush she'd once had on him, the one he hadn't been aware of? He hoped so, because he'd meant what he'd said about liking the woman she'd grown into. Of course, that wasn't exactly right. He *loved* the woman she'd become.

Either way, he didn't want to scare her off. So he was determined to keep his feelings under wraps, to be patient and take it slow and easy.

It seemed like the best plan to him. And one he didn't think would backfire.

On Sunday morning, when Mrs. Stewart and Coach Atwater came to visit the ranch, Graham and Sasha met them outside before introducing them to the boys. If Graham ever had a reason to respect the teaching profession, it was after seeing these two in action.

Chuck Atwater, a tall, lanky man in his late forties or early fifties, wore a pair of jeans and a black T-shirt with a brightly colored superhero logo. Graham had to do a double take because the laid-back guy with a receding hairline didn't look like a coach. At least, he didn't resemble any of those Graham used to have.

And Caroline Stewart, who was much younger and more stylish than he'd thought the head of the high school science department would be, surprised him, too. He'd been expecting to see a female geek. But apparently, he'd been watching too many episodes of *The Big Bang Theory*.

Nevertheless, he and Sasha gave them a tour of Peter's Place, starting in the barn, where they met Roger. Next, they walked over to look at the older cabin that served as a classroom, then on to the new one that housed the boys. When they returned to the front yard, Graham left them to talk to each other and made his way over to the corral, where Ryan and Jonah were working with the mares.

"Would you guys come with me?" he asked. "I have some people I'd like you to meet."

Both boys appeared reluctant to leave the horses and join the adults, but they followed Graham to where the teachers stood with Sasha, and the introductions were made.

Jonah, who always had an opinion and a comment to

make, was both solemn and respectful when he shook hands with Coach Atwater.

"I hear you play baseball and that you have a pretty good arm," the coach said. "I'd like to see you pitch."

"I don't have a mitt. All my stuff is still at my mom's house." Jonah shrugged a single shoulder. "I didn't think I'd have much use for it on a horse ranch."

"Not to worry," Atwater said. "I have a bat, balls and a couple of mitts in the trunk of my car."

"I haven't done any pitching in a while," Jonah said, "so I'm probably a little rusty."

"No problem. We can play catch until you loosen up." Atwater placed a hand on the boy's shoulder. "Come on."

Graham watched the coach and the hopeful pitcher stride toward the silver Chevy Malibu. Hopefully, Jonah was as talented as he said he was. Either way, Graham suspected that just knowing he had a chance to play baseball again might keep him on the straight and narrow.

At the sound of Sasha's voice, he turned to see her talking to Mrs. Stewart. Her arm was draped around Ryan's thin shoulders.

"It's nice to meet you," the teacher said. "From what I hear, you're a math and science whiz."

"He'd also like to attend a four-year university after graduation," Sasha added.

Ryan didn't appear to be nearly as enthusiastic about the topic as the adults talking to him, but he seemed to listen respectfully.

"You know," Mrs. Stewart said, "it's never too early

to check into grants and scholarships. In fact, if you join our math and science club, you'll get a lot of information to help you in selecting which university you'd like to attend, as well as everything you need to know about financial aid."

Ryan used his index finger to adjust his glasses. "I might be interested in joining that club."

For the first time since arriving at the Galloping G, the boy stood tall, his shoulders not the least bit hunched.

Graham would like to have seen a whopping big smile on his face, but he'd settle for the fact that Ryan no longer looked so beaten down.

He glanced at the side of the barn, where Coach Atwater knelt, a catcher's mask on his face, a glove in his hand. Jonah took a pitcher's stance, then wound up and threw a fast ball.

Hey. That wasn't bad. Things appeared to be working out nicely today—thanks to Sasha, who'd made it all happen. She was a natural-born social worker and would do a fine job counseling the kids at Peter's Place.

If things continued to develop between her and Graham, he wondered how she'd feel about him leaving. Not that he was in a huge rush to go now, but he did have plans of his own and wanted to utilize the MBA he'd earned.

He wouldn't abandon her, Roger and the boys, though. So, for the time being, he was committed to remaining on-site.

Thump!

At the sound of a baseball striking dead center in

a catcher's mitt, Graham turned to watch Jonah's try-out. Atwater returned the ball, and Jonah wound up for another pitch, this one a curve that again landed dead center.

"Whoo!" Atwater said. "That was a nice one."

Graham was impressed, too. He folded his arms across his chest and burst into a grin. He hadn't expected things to go this well. When he glanced at Ryan, he spotted the hint of a smile, something he'd wondered if he'd ever see.

Sasha had scored a big success today. Both boys seemed to realize they now had an opportunity to create a better future than the one they had been facing when they arrived.

Of course, they weren't out of the woods yet. In spite of the strides the boys had made so far, there was still a lot of work to be done. Graham also knew that some of the boys who came to stay at Peter's Place wouldn't settle in and transition this easily. There were bound to be struggles and possibly complete failure.

Brad Taylor had, however, said he'd be sending the teenagers who'd be more likely to benefit from living and working in a rural ranch setting. Still, there were no guarantees.

Graham glanced at Sasha, at the way the sun glistened off the white-gold strands of her hair, at the way her eyes twinkled when she studied her first two troublemakers and watched as they seemed to come around.

If truth be told, he was beginning to see an unexpected future for himself, too. He just hoped Sasha would be a part of it.

Chapter Ten

Graham, who was leaning against the corral and watching Jonah brush Ginger's coat, was about to tell the boy it was time to finish and clean up for dinner when a sleek black Town Car drove into the yard and parked near the barn.

The driver, who wore a dark sports jacket and slacks, got out of the late-model luxury vehicle and opened the door for the passenger in the backseat. He reached out his hand to an elegant older woman dressed in an expensive, cream-colored pantsuit and helped her exit.

The pair had either made a wrong turn and was lost, or Kate Fortune had decided to pay Graham a visit.

Who else could it be?

He pushed away from the corral and went to meet her. From what he'd heard, she'd celebrated her ninetieth birthday at the beginning of the year, although he'd never know it by looking at her. If he had to guess, he'd think she was in her late sixties or early seventies. No doubt that was due to her daily use of the Fortune Youth Serum, which she'd developed. Now she was a living advertisement for the product that had made her a billionaire.

She reached out a bejeweled hand to shake his. "I'm Kate Fortune. You must be Graham Robinson."

"Yes, ma'am. It's nice to meet you."

She smiled, her crow's-feet deepening a wee bit. "I'd heard you were much more than a cowboy, but you certainly look the part."

He didn't see any point in responding. Or in arguing.

She wore only the hint of a smile as she gave him another once-over. "I've heard a lot of nice things about you."

He'd heard plenty about her, too. She was an astute businesswoman, successful and well respected.

"Do you know why I'm here?" she asked.

"I have a good idea. Word's out that you've been making the rounds, visiting all the Fortune relatives. Apparently, you're giving the Robinsons the same courtesy."

"Yes, but just so you know, I'm not convinced that your father is really Jerome Fortune."

"I can understand your skepticism. But I'm convinced. Either way, it really doesn't matter."

"Why do you say that?"

He gave a single shoulder shrug, much like the way Jonah might have done. "I have my own life, my own dreams. And they don't revolve around the Robinsons or the Fortunes."

She studied him a moment, then said, "You'll find that I'm fiercely devoted to my company and equally committed to my family."

"I don't doubt it." In fact, he admired that about her.

Kate glanced at the corral, where Jonah stroked the mare's neck. At the same time, he batted at a fly with his free hand. As he did, the waistband of his new pants slipped low on his hips. The kid was going to need a belt or to have his britches altered.

"Anyway," Kate said, dragging Graham's attention back to her visit. "I believe you're bright, honest and fair. You also seem to be less invested in being a Fortune than the others."

That was true, but he refused to address any of her assumptions. Instead he said, "Thank you for the courtesy of an interview, which I'm sure is just a formality." It had to be obvious to her that, dressed like a cowboy, he wasn't boardroom material.

"I hear that you're developing a home for troubled teenagers," she said. "And it intrigues me. Would you mind showing me around?"

"Not at all." Maybe she'd like to make a tax-deductible donation. "We can start with a tour of the barn. But if you want to see the property, I'll get the Gator and drive you around."

"I'd like to see *everything*. Just let me slip on a pair of walking shoes."

Then a full tour it was.

Once she'd changed from her high heels, Graham took her into the barn and showed her the two horses stabled in the stalls, explaining the horse rescue part of their program. He also told her his and Roger's reason for creating Peter's Place.

"Two of the boys have already moved in," he added.

"I take it the young man who was brushing the mare in the corral is one of them."

"Yes, that's Jonah."

A grin tickled her lips, which bore a perfect application of red lipstick. "Perhaps you should take him aside and suggest that he'd do a better job if he pulled up his jeans and didn't show off his underwear."

Graham chuckled. "Actually, that's one of the new pairs we purchased for him recently. You should have seen how low he wore his old pants and just how much of his boxers showed."

"I can only imagine."

Graham took Kate out to the side of the barn and helped her into the Gator. While he drove her around the property, she seemed genuinely interested and asked a lot of questions, the kind a new buyer or another rancher might ask.

Apparently—and not surprisingly—Kate had done her homework before coming out here.

"Tell me," she said, "why haven't you purchased your own spread?"

"I might do that someday, but right now Roger needs me." The boys needed him, too, although he didn't mention it.

"You're very close to Roger Gibault." It was a statement, an assessment, it seemed.

Graham wasn't sure how deeply she'd researched his background, but she probably knew plenty already. So he merely said, "Roger is a good man. And he's been a second father to me."

He expected her to jump on his implication that Gerald Robinson, aka Jerome Fortune, had been lacking in the daddy department. But if she did, he'd keep his mouth shut. His old man didn't need any more bad press.

"Have you ever wanted to be a father yourself?" Kate asked.

Graham's foot nearly slipped from the gas pedal. How much did she know? And better yet, how much about himself did he want to disclose?

In spite of his usual preference to keep things close to the vest, he said, "Actually, I'd love to be a dad someday. I also think it would be cool to have a legacy to pass down to my children."

"But you don't work for Robinson Tech." Again, it wasn't a question, just a statement. And an accurate one at that.

Was she naturally so astute? Or had she been talking to someone? Either way, it was a fact, so he supposed it really didn't matter.

"I plan to make my own mark on the world," he said.

"With Peter's Place?"

"That's just a part of it. Creating a home for troubled kids, where they can work with rescued horses, is my way of honoring a friend—and his father. But I do plan to start my own business one day."

"What kind of business?"

"I have a few ideas, but nothing set in stone yet."

"Do those ideas have anything to do with ranching?"

"Not really." But he would like to have his own

spread someday. Maddie would like growing up on a ranch and having her own horse.

They continued the tour in relative silence, and Graham's thoughts remained on Sasha and her daughters, on his dream to make them a part of his life. In fact, he hadn't realized just how much he'd hoped that would all come to be until he found himself saying, "There's a little girl who lives here. I've been teaching her how to rope and ride, and it's been a lot of fun."

Mentoring that little cowgirl had given him an immense feeling of pride, and he felt like her stepfather already.

Actually, talking to Kate and showing her the ranch had helped him sort through a lot of things, like his feelings for Sasha and wanting to create a family with her and her daughters. For that reason, he was going to have to lay it on the line and tell her how he felt about her.

Once he did, maybe he could start building that legacy he wanted to share and start planning for the future.

"You know," he said, another thought coming to him, "I was never close to my father, so I never understood why he was so insistent that I work at Robinson Tech and why he was so upset when I refused. But I think I understand now."

"Does that mean you're having second thoughts about joining the firm?" Kate asked.

"No, not about that. But I do have a new appreciation for what my father was offering me."

As he drove the Gator back to the house, he stole a glance at the elegant older woman seated across from him, her hands clasped in her lap, a two- or three-carat diamond glistening in the sunlight. Her brow was furrowed, and she appeared to be deep in thought.

Had the situation been reversed, he suspected she might have quizzed him about his thoughts. But he wasn't about to ask her.

When they reached the yard, he pulled alongside the Town Car so she wouldn't have very far to walk. He would have helped her from her seat in the Gator, but her driver beat him to it.

Before getting out, she reached across the seat and shook his hand. "Thank you for your time, Graham."

"It was my pleasure."

"I just might like to make Peter's Place one of my charities. I'll be in touch." Then she climbed into the backseat of her car. Moments later, the vehicle had turned around and was heading down the drive.

What an interesting woman. And what a surprising visit. He hoped she would choose to fund Peter's Place. There was so much Roger could do with the ranch and boys' home if he had another wealthy benefactor besides the Fortune Foundation.

He needed to tell Sasha about the possibility of a donation from Kate. And yes, while he was at it, he also needed to share his feelings for her and his dreams for the future, for *their* future.

He glanced at the corral, where Jonah had been working with the mares. Neither of the boys were within sight, so he figured he'd better check on them first.

That heart-to-heart with Sasha would have to wait. But not for long.

* * *

When Graham came out of the barn after checking on Ryan and Jonah, he spotted another unfamiliar car parked in the front yard. He'd no more than started for the house when Roger walked out onto the front porch, the screen door slamming behind him. He shook his head, clearly miffed about something, then plopped his hat on his head and proceeded down the steps and into the yard.

Before Graham had a chance to ask his old friend what was bothering him, Roger said, "You better do what I'm doing."

Graham furrowed his brow. "What's that?"

"Keeping my distance for a while." He turned and headed toward the barn.

Before the man could stomp off, Graham grabbed him by the arm and stopped him. "What are you talking about?"

Roger grimaced, then nodded toward the house. "Gabe Smith is inside."

The news nearly knocked the wind out of Graham, and he found it difficult to breathe, let alone wrap his mind around what that might mean. "What's he want?"

"Apparently, he and Sasha have something to work out," Roger grumbled, then swore under his breath. "I hope she's not falling for a line of bull. She'd be a fool if she did."

Graham was the fool. He'd waited too long to tell her how he was really feeling.

But would that have mattered?

"As luck would have it," Roger said, "Maddie invited

the guy to stay for dinner. And since I'll be damned if I'll risk ruining the relationship Sasha and I just patched up, I knew better than to object."

"I take it he agreed to stay."

"Yep." Roger let out a *hmph*. "And wouldn't you know? I made a pot roast, and plenty of it. Too bad he showed up and screwed up everything. I wish I'd fixed Hamburger Helper or some other inexpensive, effortless meal."

"Well, what's done is done," Graham said. Yet a cloak of apprehension settled over him.

"Dang it," Roger said. "I just hope he doesn't plan to spend the night."

At that thought, Graham's gut twisted into a knot. He tried to shake it off but didn't have any luck. He glanced at the car parked in front of the house, then at the front door. There could only be one reason for Gabe's visit. He'd come to his senses and wanted Sasha back.

Graham felt compelled to bust right in on the two of them and tell Gabe he was the one who was too late. Graham and Sasha hadn't just been tiptoeing around an attraction; they were actually feeling something strong and lasting. They had chemistry. And they also had a history.

But Sasha and Gabe had two children, which was pretty damn binding.

Just for the record, Sasha had once told him, *it was Gabe who left.*

That meant their split hadn't been her idea. And that she would have stayed married to him otherwise.

I'll be the first to admit that our life together was

far from perfect, but I made a commitment to stick it out for the long haul.

No, Sasha had meant to hold on. She'd made her vows before God and everyone in attendance at their wedding. That had to mean something to her, too. And on top of that, she was a mother and had her children to consider.

Hadn't Graham's own mother done the same thing, even when faced with his father's numerous affairs?

His thoughts drifted to the conversation he'd had with his sister Zoe after the last Robinson family meeting, after he'd mentioned that he'd seen his father kissing the au pair.

Graham had told Zoe that he'd tried to tell their mom about his father's cheating, but she hadn't taken the hint.

Zoe hadn't been surprised and had come up with a reason for it. *She had eight kids and probably wanted to hold her marriage together. It's what most mothers would do, I guess.*

Would they? Given the chance to save her marriage, would Sasha decide to take Gabe back and try to make a go of it?

Hell, she was also pregnant and no doubt feeling an urge to nest. Besides, she might not want to go through labor and delivery on her own.

Either way, Graham wasn't going to hang around and watch it all unfold. Talk about pain and misery…

The sudden urge to escape from Sasha, the ranch, the painful emotion threatening to choke the life out of him was nearly overwhelming, so he turned to leave, although he didn't have any actual destination in mind.

"Where are you going?" Roger asked.

"I've got things to do," Graham responded as he continued to walk toward the barn. He might be able to find something to keep him busy in there.

Still, none of those chores were the least bit pressing. But that didn't matter. Nothing good would come of him meeting Gabe Smith face-to-face.

Instead of enjoying a big helping of Roger's pot roast, Graham remained in his cabin during the dinner hour and warmed up a can of chili beans. He served himself a bowl, then opened a box of saltines and a bottle of beer and ate in front of the television.

He tried not to think about what was going on back at the big house, while everyone sat around Roger's kitchen table and enjoyed a family-style meal. But it was impossible not to. What made things worse was that Graham couldn't do a damn thing about anything that was happening.

It was easy to imagine, though. Gabe was telling Sasha that he'd missed her and Maddie, that he'd come to realize his mistake in letting them go. He was undoubtedly promising to be the kind of husband and father he should have been.

If he meant what he said, and if he was able to pull it off, Sasha, Maddie and the baby deserved Gabe's best.

Graham's thoughts drifted to his own father, a man who'd reached out to mend fences on several occasions. His dad had even offered him a position at Robinson Tech, which Graham had refused.

During the talk with Kate Fortune earlier today, he'd

had an epiphany about fatherhood. And while he'd been thinking about Maddie and her baby sister at the time, he'd reevaluated a few things in his own life.

Should he reconsider his dad's offer?

Moving to Austin would certainly get him away from Sasha and his memories of her.

In spite of his reluctance to forgive his father and to accept any personal responsibility for the lousy relationship they'd had in the past, he reached for his cell phone and placed a call.

His dad answered on the third ring, apparently after looking at the lit display and recognizing Graham's number. "Well, I'll be damned. It's the prodigal son."

Graham had half a notion to make some kind of snide retort, but he had to admit that his father's tone hadn't been snappish or surly. And he really couldn't blame him for calling him that, especially since he felt like one most of the time.

"Yeah, it's me. I thought I'd call and...say hello."

His old man didn't respond. But then, Graham didn't approach him often, especially to chat. Still, it was probably time to change that habit.

"I also wanted to suggest we end the cold war," Graham added. "For what it's worth, I admire what you've built in Robinson Tech."

Again, silence stretched across the line. Gerald Fortune Robinson had never been one to keep his thoughts or opinions to himself, so it seemed safe to assume he was a bit taken aback by Graham's admission.

But then again, there were a lot of things Graham *didn't* admire, like his dad's philandering. But that wasn't something he wanted to address today. He knew the kind of work it had taken his father to succeed—especially if he'd walked away from his Fortune ties and made a success on his own.

"Are you having second thoughts about working with me?" Gerald asked.

Was he? "Let's say that I may have been stubborn in refusing to talk it over with you."

"Well, for the record, the job offer still stands."

"Thanks, I appreciate that." But did Graham dare to take it? Was he that desperate to escape Sasha and everything that reminded him of her?

"I really like what I've been doing here at the Galloping G. Things seem to be working out well. So I'd have to figure out a way to work with Roger from a distance. I'll have to give it some thought."

"Good. I'm glad to hear it. And I'm glad that MBA I paid for might actually benefit me and the company."

Graham had only said he'd consider it. "We'll have to talk it over the next time I'm in town."

"When do you think that'll be?"

"Soon." Graham didn't want to give him a date, which would lock him in before he was actually ready for a conversation like that.

Besides, each time he thought about what was going on inside the ranch house, he realized that even a move to Austin wasn't going to be a sufficient balm for his battered heart.

Sasha had missed Graham at dinner, but she knew he sometimes ate at home. And with her soon-to-be-ex-husband's unexpected arrival, that was probably for the best.

She couldn't believe Maddie had actually suggested he spend the night with them, but fortunately, when she'd suggested he'd be more comfortable at a hotel in Austin, he'd opted to get a room before flying home tomorrow morning.

She and Gabe still had a lot to iron out when it came to coparenting, but if he was truly trying to be a better family man, she was willing to work with him. They'd worked out a reasonable holiday visitation schedule and had agreed on the last legal issue, assuming both attorneys concurred. But she still wanted to run her thoughts by someone she trusted to offer her sound advice. Since Uncle Roger would be biased, she decided to speak to Graham.

She could have walked to the cabin, but her back had started to bother her about the time Gabe arrived, and after standing at the sink and doing the dinner dishes, she really didn't feel up to the effort. So she called Graham instead.

The phone rang four times. She was just about to leave a message on his voice mail when he answered.

"Hey," she said. "Are you hungry? We have plenty of leftovers here."

"Thanks, but I already had dinner."

She paused a moment, thinking he might expound on his answer, but he didn't.

"I'd like to talk to you," she said.

"That's not necessary. I understand completely. It was probably the best decision for you to make."

Huh? She bit down on her bottom lip and furrowed her brow. What decision was he talking about?

"Don't worry, Sassy. I don't want to stand between a man and his family, so I'll bow out gracefully. Have a good evening." He hung up before she could get a word in edgewise.

What in the heck had just happened?

Chapter Eleven

Sasha continued to hold the telephone receiver long after Graham ended their call.

She was stunned and still trying to make sense of what he'd told her, as well as his haste to end the conversation before it had even gotten started. Apparently, he'd assumed that she and Gabe had patched things up. He hadn't even taken the time to ask or to let her explain.

Had he just jumped on an easy out and used it as an excuse to cut bait while he had the opportunity?

Sasha was still standing in the center of the living room, befuddled and rubbing an ache in the small of her back, when her daughter sidled up to her.

Maddie wore her pink jammies and held her stuffed bunny. But her expression was splashed with concern. "What's the matter, Mommy?"

Sasha cupped a hand on her little girl's head, felt the silky strands of her hair. "Nothing."

"Are you sure?"

No, she wasn't. Everything appeared to be falling apart. But she didn't want Maddie to worry about anything, so she forced a smile and stretched the truth to the limit. "Yes, I'm fine. Now go to bed. I'll come in there in a few minutes to read you a story."

As Maddie padded down the hall, Sasha's thoughts returned to Graham and the conversation they'd just had. Or rather, the words he'd said, since he hadn't let her respond.

She'd called to tell him that her divorce would be final within the next two weeks. Gabe had only flown to Texas to visit, as he'd told her he would. He'd wanted to iron out those visitation issues and the one last detail.

Hadn't she explained as much to Graham? She'd thought so. At least, she'd tried to, but he'd jumped to the wrong conclusion.

Had he been looking for a way out? Had he gotten scared and realized that he didn't want to take on the responsibility of a husband and father? Not that he'd actually said as much, but...

Unable to focus on anything other than Graham's distant tone and brief response, she picked up the phone and called him again. But this time, it only rang once and went right to voice mail.

He'd shut off his phone?

Maybe he was on the line with someone else. Or his battery had run down. He might have turned in for the night.

She supposed there could be any number of reasons she hadn't been able to get through to him, but she wasn't buying any of them. In fact, she was tempted to march across the yard and talk to him in person. But in reality, she wasn't up for a confrontation tonight. Not after the stress she'd had while working out a fair and feasible holiday visitation with Gabe, a schedule that would require her to fly to California with the girls in November and then again in December.

Besides, her back ached something awful, and she wasn't about to do anything to make it worse.

What she really needed was a warm, relaxing shower. But first, she went through Maddie's bedtime ritual, taking time to read *Sleeping Ugly* and *The Paper Bag Princess*, her own favorite stories. Then she kissed her daughter good-night.

When Maddie tucked her bunny under her arm and rolled to the side, Sasha headed to the bathroom and took a relaxing shower. She remained under the spray of warm water until her backache eased. By the time she'd slipped into her cotton nightgown, she felt much better.

She climbed into bed and closed her eyes. But she didn't fall asleep for the longest time. She continued to think about Graham and the way he'd shut her out. As a result, she tossed and turned so much during the night that she woke with another ache in her back. She'd nearly forgotten the discomfort of those last six weeks before Maddie's delivery.

As much as she loved baby Sydney, and as eager as she was to see her and hold her in her arms, she couldn't help thinking that her pregnancy might have contributed to Graham having second thoughts. She could actually understand that, but he should have been honest with her.

By breakfast, she'd worked herself into a real stew and was spitting mad at Graham for withdrawing so abruptly and not allowing her a chance to speak or to explain.

Apparently, he chose to walk away from emotional conflict. He'd certainly done that with his own family.

And now he was doing it with *hers*!

She'd had so much hope for him, for *them*. She'd planned to talk to him about it privately after breakfast, but he didn't even show up for a cup of coffee.

Well, if he thought he could avoid her and ignore those blood-stirring kisses they'd shared, he was mistaken. There was no way she would roll over and let him get away with it. So she went in search of him and found him in the barn.

He was giving Jonah and Ryan a list of chores to do that day, so she waited for him to finish. Once the boys headed out, she caught his gaze.

"What's up?" he asked.

"We need to talk."

He lifted his hat, then readjusted it on his head. Had she unbalanced him by asking him to address his thoughts and feelings honestly? If so, good.

"About what?" he asked.

Seriously? He didn't have a clue?

She crossed her arms, resting them on the shelf her expanding womb provided. "You've been running from things all your life. And if you don't start facing your fears and conflicts, you'll never reach your full potential. On top of that, you'll also fall short when it comes to advising and mentoring the boys."

His brow creased, yet he continued to hold back his words, as well as his thoughts.

So she pushed on. "Graham, you have a master's degree in business administration and aren't really using it. Sure, Peter's Place is a noble project. And you've done wonders with it. But what about *you*? What will make you happy in the long run?"

His eye twitched, which was the first indication that her words hadn't just dissipated in the air.

"Don't worry about me," he said. "I'll be fine."

He couldn't have dismissed her any more thoroughly than if he'd told her to get out of his life. So she turned and walked away.

She doubted he realized it, but when push came to shove, she had her daughters to think about and a new family to create. And if that meant Graham wouldn't be a part of it, so be it. She just wished that it wouldn't hurt so badly to move on without him.

Graham remained in the barn long after Sasha left, trying to make sense of what she'd said. And why she'd said it.

What did Robinson Tech have to do with anything? His biggest problem right this moment had to do with Gabe Smith, who'd apparently driven off sometime after nine o'clock last night and before breakfast this morning. No telling where he'd gone or when he planned to return.

Graham might have asked Sasha where the guy had gone and when he'd be back—if he'd had the chance. But he'd been completely stunned by the accusations she'd launched at him. He'd never run from anything in his life, other than the current heartbreak over Sasha and her ex. And he wasn't afraid of his feelings. He just didn't wear them on his sleeve.

Besides, he'd talked to his dad yesterday and said he'd consider the job offer. Not that he actually planned to take it. But he'd given it some thought.

Graham swore under his breath, then headed out of the barn to check on the boys, who'd taken the mares out to graze in the pasture for a while. He'd been giving them more and more responsibility each day, and they were handling it just fine.

Rather than walk to where Jonah, Ryan and the horses were, he took the Gator. When he got within twenty yards of them, he shut off the engine and watched for a while. As he did, he felt a surge of pride. They'd clearly listened to his instructions and were doing a good job of gentling the mares.

Peter's Place is a noble project, Sasha had said.

Damn right it was. Yet it wasn't the only thing he wanted to do with his life. Sure, he'd serve on the board of directors and offer financial support. He'd also visit often. But he wanted to have more than just a "project."

If things had been different between him and Sasha, he might have put up an argument when she'd accused him of running from his feelings and responsibilities. But why should he have to defend himself? He might have been a rebel once, but he was proud of the man he'd become. And he was proud of his dreams.

Couldn't she see that?

Apparently not. Thank goodness he'd decided to let her go before he got any more involved.

"Hey, boss!" Ryan called out.

Graham, who'd been gazing in the distance, looked at the boy.

"Isn't that Maddie?" Ryan pointed across the field, where the little blonde pixie in a cowboy hat was following the dirt road he'd just driven.

"Yeah, that's her," Graham said.

But what was she doing out here all by herself?

He turned the Gator around and went to meet her. When he pulled alongside her and parked, she slapped her hands on her hips and shot him child-size daggers from her eyes.

She was usually happy to see him. So what was that all about?

"What are you doing?" he asked.

"Looking for you." Her expression softened a bit, but she was clearly on a mission. And he doubted anyone else had sent her on it.

"What can I do for you?" he asked.

"You made my mommy sad, and that wasn't very nice."

Graham didn't think Maddie had pegged her mom's feelings accurately. Sasha was clearly angry, although he wasn't sure what kind of burr had gotten under her saddle.

But whatever it was, it had affected Maddie enough

to send her out to find him and give him a piece of her mind. Or so it seemed.

Graham patted the seat next to him. "Climb up here and tell me why she's sad. And why you think it's my fault."

"Because she misses you. And so do I."

Graham let out a weary sigh. What was he supposed to tell the child? That he'd hoped to maybe be her step-dad someday? That he'd been crushed when he realized that wasn't going to happen?

"Did I do something to make you mad?" Maddie asked as she climbed into the seat next to him. "Is it my fault you don't want to eat with us or be with us?"

"No, of course not. What makes you think that it could possibly be your fault?"

"Because my daddy used to be cranky whenever he came home. And now that he doesn't live with us, he's nicer to us."

Graham wasn't about to defend Gabe Smith, but he didn't want the poor kid to think that she was responsible for the mess he'd fallen head over heels into. "None of this has anything to do with you, sweet pea. When you're a little older, you'll understand."

"I don't have to wait until then. I get it *now*." She hung her head. "You're going to leave us, just like Daddy did."

"But your father came back."

She shook her head, her pigtails swishing back and forth. "Not forever. Just for last night. He went away again because Mommy told him to go."

Sasha asked Gabe to leave?

Was that what she'd meant to talk over with him? Had he connected the wrong dots and made a false assumption?

He'd been so caught up in his disappointment and sorrow that he'd thought…

Damn. He'd been wrong. No wonder she'd accused him of running from his feelings.

"Does your mom know you're here?" Graham asked.

Maddie shook her head, sending those pigtails waving again. "When I saw you leaving, I was afraid if I went into the house and asked for permission first, I wouldn't be able to find you."

"You shouldn't have wandered off without telling anyone." Graham reached for his cell to call the house, only to get a busy signal. Maybe the phone was off the hook. He tried Sasha's number next, but it rolled over to voice mail.

"Your mom is probably looking all over for you," he said. "I'll drive you back to the house."

"Will you please talk to her?" Maddie asked. "Will you tell her you're sorry?"

"You bet I will." He had several apologies to make, one of which was for keeping his feelings to himself, something he was determined not to ever do again. Especially with her.

As Graham pulled the Gator into the yard, he spotted Sasha on the porch, one hand on her baby bump, the other over her heart. She wore a pair of shorts, a pink maternity top and an expression that was a hodgepodge of emotions like fear, concern, apprehension.

"I have her," Graham said as he climbed from the Gator. "She's fine."

"Thank God." Yet Sasha remained on the porch. She removed the hand she'd had on her chest and reached for the railing as if she needed it for support and to hold her upright.

Graham made his way toward the woman he loved, prepared to go down on bended knee if he had to. "Now that Maddie's home safe and sound, I need to talk to you."

"I'm afraid that'll have to wait," she said.

It was then that he realized Maddie hadn't been the only thing that had her worried and apprehensive. "What's the matter?"

"My water just broke."

Graham had known that apologizing for being a stupid jerk and sharing how he felt about Sasha wouldn't be easy, but he hadn't expected to do it at the hospital between her contractions.

When she told him she was in labor, he'd practically stumbled up the steps to get to her, to offer her a hand to hold and a shoulder to lean on. And while she had to have been worried about having a premature baby, she'd already called the doctor and had packed an overnight bag.

Roger had agreed to stay at the ranch and watch Maddie while Graham had helped Sasha into his pickup and rushed her to the ER.

He'd apologized several times, but for the most part,

she merely nodded and made funny breathing sounds, which he assumed was some sort of Lamaze technique.

Oh, God. This couldn't be happening.

But it was.

Fortunately, the doctor had already prepared the hospital staff for Sasha's arrival. So once they entered the automatic doors to the ER, she was immediately whisked away and taken to the obstetrical ward.

Graham hadn't been about to let her go through labor alone, so he'd followed along at a steady clip.

"Thank you for being with me," she'd said during a break in contractions.

He reached for her hand and gave it a gentle squeeze. "I wouldn't be anywhere else, Sassy."

She blessed him with an appreciative smile, but it didn't last long. As another contraction struck, Graham continued to hold her hand, although her grip on his fingers tightened like a vise.

Fortunately, several minutes later, the doctor, a woman in her late forties, came in.

"I'm scared, Dr. Singh," Sasha admitted. "It's too early for her to be born."

"Five weeks isn't all that early," the doctor said.

As she began to slip on a pair of gloves, Graham removed his hand and stood. "I'll step out of the room."

"You won't leave me, though," Sasha said. "Will you?"

"No. I'm in this for the duration." And he didn't just mean labor and delivery. "I'll be standing outside the door."

Graham stepped into the corridor, but he didn't have

to wait very long. The doctor came out soon afterward, so he took a moment to ask his own questions. "Is everything okay?"

"Yes, Sasha's doing fine. I'm going to order an epidural, which will make her a lot more comfortable."

"Good. That's a relief. I hate seeing her in pain."

The doctor smiled. "This probably won't take very long. I suspect we'll have a baby in a couple of hours."

Graham was glad to hear that, especially if little Sydney was going to be okay. He thanked the doctor and returned to Sasha's bedside, where he remained until the anesthesiologist arrived to give her the epidural. But this time, he didn't leave the room.

Within a minute or two, Sasha settled back into bed, her pain all but forgotten.

"Now we just have to wait," she said.

"Actually, we also have to talk. I'm not sure if you heard what I was telling you in the pickup, honey, but I'm sorry for reacting the way I did when Gabe arrived. I know I acted like a complete jerk, but I thought for sure that he'd realized what an amazing woman you are. I assumed that he'd come to the ranch to tell you he was willing to do anything to hold his family together."

A wry smile stretched across her face. "You obviously don't know Gabe very well. He was somewhat apologetic, but he really doesn't want to be a full-time husband and father."

"The guy's crazy. I'd give anything to have a wife like you."

She shot him a look of surprise. But then, why

wouldn't she? He'd kept that secret locked up inside for way too long.

"I love you, Sassy. More than I ever thought possible. I should have told you before, but I was afraid to. Do you think you could give me a chance to prove that I deserve you, Maddie and the new baby?"

She smiled, and her eyes brightened. "Believe it or not, the only man I've ever really loved is you."

"Me?"

"I've loved you for years, Graham. Back when you didn't even know I existed."

He was glad to hear that, but… "What about Gabe?"

"I thought I loved him when I married him, but he wasn't the man I thought he was." She glanced at the monitor, watched as another contraction seized her, this one not causing any pain or discomfort. Once it started to subside, she continued. "I wish I could say I was heartbroken over our split, but that couldn't be any further from the truth. And the fact that Maddie didn't appear to be all that upset by the breakup certainly helped me come to the conclusion that a divorce was for the best."

"You have no idea how relieved I am to know that. When he arrived, I thought it meant that he was having second thoughts."

"Only about visitation. He'd like the girls to spend both holidays with him and his parents. So that means I'll have to go, too. And while I'm not happy about it, I agreed."

"If it will make things easier for you, I'll go along, too."

"Seriously?" Her expression morphed from disbelief to delight. "You'd do that for me?"

"I'd do it for all of us. I want us to be a family, Sassy."

She reached for his hand and gave it a squeeze. "I want that, too."

An hour later, the nurse returned to examine Sasha. And this time, she said, "It's time. I'll call the doctor and prepare the room for delivery."

Things happened quickly at that point. Graham had intended to step out of the room as the time got close, but Sasha asked him to stay. And in truth, he'd hoped she would.

He'd held her hand while she pushed her—no, *their*—new daughter into the world, a tiny, squalling little girl, with a red face, blond hair and a voice that was loud and strong.

"Is she okay?" Sasha asked the doctor.

"She looks great to me. She may have to stay in the NICU for a while, but I don't anticipate any problems."

Graham whispered a prayer of thanksgiving, then blew out a wobbly sigh. Being a new dad was a little scary, but it also felt good.

Sasha was able to hold baby Sydney for a moment, but the nurse soon took her to the NICU.

When they were finally alone, Graham placed a kiss on Sasha's forehead. "I'm so proud of you. Do you have any idea how much I love you?"

She smiled. "No, but I can't wait for you to show me."

He laughed. "Well, I realize some things will have to wait until you're fully recovered. But just know that I plan to propose as soon as your divorce is final."

"There's nothing I'd like more."

Graham's heart filled to the brim. Things were certainly working out a lot better than he'd once thought.

"By the way," he said, "I'm going to spend the night with you tonight."

"Here? At the hospital?"

"If they'll let me."

"They will. I'm just surprised that you…" She bit down on her bottom lip, then slowly shook her head and grinned. "Well, darn, Graham. You've sure turned out to be a real trouper."

"Yeah, well, unlike Gabe, when I make a commitment, I stick by it. And that means I'm going to stay with you and the girls for the rest of my life."

Then he placed his lips on hers, sealing that vow with a kiss.

After Sasha called Roger and spoke to both him and Maddie, Graham decided he had a call of his own to make.

For some reason, becoming a father made him want to reach out to his own dad.

Gerald Robinson picked up on the third ring. "Well, I'll be. Two calls within a short period of time."

"Yeah, well, I wanted to let you in on my good news," Graham said. "I'm getting married. And you'll get not only a daughter-in-law but two instant grandchildren."

"Who is she?"

"Sasha-Marie Gibault, Roger's niece. I've known her for years, but we recently reconnected and fell in love."

"Well, if you're happy, then I'm happy for you," he

said. "But I have some news of my own. I've decided not to hide anymore. I met with Kate Fortune earlier today and told her the whole story about my past."

Graham would've loved to be a fly on the wall when that happened! His father had been hiding the truth for years, but at least he was finally admitting it.

"Kate had already suspected it," his dad admitted, "but she wanted to see how the story would play out."

"She's one sharp woman," Graham said.

"I agree. She also told me that she selected the person she wanted to run Fortune Cosmetics."

Graham assumed it would be one of the closer Fortune cousins, although now that his dad had come clean, he supposed he would add Fortune to the Robinson name, just as Ben and some of the others had done. Prior to that, he hadn't wanted to get caught up in the family drama.

"So, who did Kate choose?" Graham asked.

"You."

Graham nearly choked on the news. "That makes no sense. You must have heard wrong."

"I'm never wrong about anything," Gerald said, true to form. "Kate saw something in you and wants you to run her business. And for the record, I think she made a good choice."

His father's admission stunned him even further. He couldn't remember the last time his dad had acknowledged that he had any talent or admirable qualities. As much as he'd tried to convince himself over the years that it really didn't matter, that wasn't true.

"That's why I tried so hard to get you to come and work with me," Gerald added.

Now, that was a pleasant surprise. Graham had always suspected his father had only wanted to have some control over him.

"For the record," Gerald said, "I'm proud of you and what you've helped Roger do with the Galloping G. In fact, I'm going to make a sizable donation to the project."

"Thanks, I appreciate that." Graham glanced at Sasha, who'd dozed off. There'd be time to share his news with her later, although he wasn't sure he'd want to commute to Minnesota, where Fortune Cosmetics was located. Would she agree to move there with him?

"You might be happy to hear that Kate has enjoyed her time in Texas, away from the miserable winters. So she's going to move the corporate headquarters to Austin. She also said that her company is the kind that allows for job sharing and working from home. So that means you can remain close to Roger and the ranch."

Wow. Graham didn't know what to say. He didn't know anything about cosmetics, but he wasn't afraid to learn. Not when Kate was offering him the chance to work alongside her in a billion-dollar company and utilize his MBA. So there was no reason not to accept her offer.

"That's good news," he said to his dad. And he wasn't just talking about the job. The fact that Gerald had admitted his relationship to the Fortunes meant that Graham could do so, too. He'd also use his ties with the Fortunes and the Fortune Foundation to build

Peter's Place into the kind of ranch he and Roger had envisioned it to be.

"Listen," Gerald said, "I have a meeting I have to attend. But I'll stop by the ranch to meet your fiancée and my new grandchildren soon."

They said their goodbyes, then ended the call.

As Graham slid his phone back into his pocket, he turned to Sasha and watched her sleep.

How strange life could be. And how wonderful. Before long, he'd marry the woman he loved with all his heart.

The future had never looked brighter.

Chapter Twelve

Four months later, as fall settled over Austin, turning leaves to crimson and gold, Graham and Sasha turned into the long driveway that led to the Silver Spur. Kate Fortune and her husband, Sterling Foster, had recently purchased the exclusive ranch where Kate had celebrated her ninetieth birthday at the beginning of the year.

According to Graham's sisters, the house was amazing and the grounds pristine. Yet Kate and Sterling planned a big remodel, after which, they would rename it Sterling's Fortune.

Sasha glanced out the window and spotted several Thoroughbreds grazing in a lush, green pasture framed by a white fence. The Silver Spur certainly didn't resemble any of the ranches she'd ever visited. In fact, it was impressive by anyone's standards, and she could scarcely take it all in.

Neither could she believe that Kate was hosting a wedding reception for her and Graham here. They'd married quietly this afternoon, with only Uncle Roger and a few close friends and family members in attendance. But Kate had insisted they needed a "real" celebration, and from what Sasha had gathered, no one argued with Kate.

"We're here," Graham said as he pulled into the circular drive, where a valet service had been set up to handle the parking.

Maddie, who sat in the backseat next to baby Sydney, said, "Wow. Is this where the queen lives?"

She certainly does, Sasha was tempted to say, since Kate Fortune clearly lived like one. Instead she smiled at her daughter and said, "No, honey. But it does look like a palace, doesn't it?"

As the valet opened the door first for Sasha, then for Maddie, Graham unlatched the baby carrier from the bottom part of the car seat and carried it with him. They could have found a sitter, but Graham thought this should be a family affair. And Sasha agreed. Even Uncle Roger was coming today, although he'd insisted upon driving himself.

The new family climbed the steps, which were flanked by stone pillars, to the front door. Graham rang the bell, and a butler wearing a black suit and a polite smile answered and welcomed them into the marble-floored entry.

"Sterling," Kate's voice rang out as she swept down a

circular stairway. "Hurry up, dear. Our guests of honor are here."

She greeted them warmly, then turned to Maddie and smiled. "Look at you in that gorgeous dress. You look as pretty as a princess."

"Thank you." Maddie, who did indeed look the part in her pink vintage flower-girl dress and the party shoes she'd also worn to the wedding, gave a little curtsy. "And you look like a *queen*, Miss Kate."

They all laughed, but there was a lot of truth to her statement. Kate looked elegant, as well as lovely.

She'd also been incredibly kind to Graham, taking him under her wing and sharing her business acumen. She'd told him that Fortune Cosmetics needed someone of his caliber on board. And when he'd mentioned that Sasha planned to stay on at Peter's Place, she agreed with Graham that he needed to continue at the Galloping G for the indefinite future.

In the meantime, he would be her consultant at Fortune Cosmetics until he felt comfortable taking over as CEO.

"I know this party is to celebrate your marriage," Kate said, "but I plan to announce your new position in the company. I hope that's okay with you, Graham."

"Of course," he said. "And again, I want to thank you for the opportunity."

"You're welcome. Now come with me and see how we've decorated for the reception." She led them into a large room cleared of the typical furniture. Instead round banquet tables draped in white linen and topped with bouquets of red roses and fine china and crystal had been set up.

She hadn't spared any expense, or so it seemed. But from what Sasha had heard, she could well afford it.

The doorbell rang, and Kate said, "It looks like the guests have begun to arrive. Please excuse me while I greet them."

When she left the room, Sasha turned to Graham. "I can't believe she even offered us the use of her private jet and had planned to spring for a honeymoon."

"I told her we couldn't leave the kids," Graham said. "But don't worry, Sassy. We'll have plenty of opportunities to fly anywhere you want to go in the next few years."

"I know." She lifted her mouth to his, giving him a kiss before the guests, many of them Fortunes, began to trickle in.

And that was exactly how they began to arrive, in a steady stream. First came Graham's brother Ben and his lovely pregnant wife, Ella, along with Ben's twin, Wes, and his fiancée, Vivian. Both couples welcomed Sasha into the family, taking time to compliment Maddie and to coo at Sydney.

Sasha was glad to see Graham's siblings and their significant others becoming closer than ever before. Once Gerald had come clean and admitted who he really was, the meetings the Robinson siblings had begun to have earlier this year had gone from stressful to friendly, and she hoped they would continue to gather on a regular basis. Family was important, and she was glad she'd been so warmly accepted as a Robinson and a Fortune.

Chase Parker and his wife, Lucie, arrived next, followed by Lucie's brother, Charles Chesterfield Fortune, who held his son, Flynn, in one arm and clasped his fiancée Alice's hand with the other. Joaquin and Zoe Robinson Mendoza soon joined them.

The room stilled momentarily when Graham's parents entered the room. Gerald Fortune Robinson, also known as Jerome Fortune, was in his midseventies and still a dashing and handsome man. With salt-and-pepper hair, dark eyes and prominent eyebrows, he reminded Sasha of Sean Connery. He had his hand on Charlotte's back when they entered, but immediately removed it. He nodded at Graham and Sasha, but headed for one of several bars that had been set up along the perimeter.

Charlotte, also in her midseventies, had short, platinum blond hair and green eyes. While she bore a regal appearance and had a penchant for pearls and designer pantsuits befitting a Texas millionaire's wife, she seemed to be even more in vogue today. Yet she didn't immediately seek out Graham or Sasha. Neither did she join her husband at the bar. Instead she snatched a glass of red wine from a silver tray one of the waiters carried.

Before long, the house was abuzz with family, not only those who'd once thought they were just Robinsons, but also the ones who'd recently learned of their Fortune connection, like the Hayses, Chesterfields and Joneses. Then, of course, there were those who'd always known they were Fortunes.

Twenty minutes later, Kate rang a sterling silver bell, and everyone hushed.

"I have an announcement to make," she said. "I've chosen Graham Fortune Robinson to run my company."

Murmurs and a few "congratulations" followed. Apparently, she'd kept that news to herself. And Gerald, who'd been the one to tell Graham, had been sworn to secrecy.

"You might wonder how I made my decision," Kate said. "I realize Graham isn't a typical corporate man, but I observed the way he ran Peter's Place and the way he worked with the boys. I admire his even temper and his openness to new ideas. Most of all, I believe he has an appreciation of family that even goes above and beyond what I've seen in everyone else, which, of course, is more than admirable."

A spontaneous round of applause sounded, after which Graham spoke up. "I want to thank Kate publicly for the faith she has in me. I won't let her or Fortune Cosmetics down."

"I'm sure you won't," Kate said. "I also want to take this time to announce that another member of the family, Lucie Parker, will be overseeing a new branch of the Fortune Foundation, which will open in Austin within the next few months."

As Lucie smiled and nodded, Chase grinned proudly, slipped his arm around his wife and drew her close.

Kate cleared her throat, commanding everyone's attention once more. "I also want to apologize to Gerald on behalf of the entire Fortune family for the mistreatment he experienced when he was younger. Family may not always get along or see eye to eye, but I can't imagine how badly things must have been for him to turn his back on them entirely. And I promise that, going forward, the Fortunes will be there for Gerald and the generations of Fortune Robinsons to come."

That last announcement was greeted with applause by almost everyone in the room.

Was Sasha the only one who'd glanced at Graham's parents and caught the scowl on Charlotte's face? But then again, the woman had been through a lot during her thirty-five-year marriage, some of which couldn't have been pleasant. Sasha didn't think many women could adjust to changes like that easily.

"You know," Kate continued, "over the course of my life, I've seen and experienced quite a bit. Twenty years ago, I was kidnapped and left for dead. I never thought I'd live to be ninety or to see so many of my relatives find love, marry and start new generations of Fortunes." She smiled as she scanned the room. "My experiences since coming to Texas six months ago have far exceeded my expectations. There are so many family members here with diverse personalities and talents, I now feel even more confident that the Fortunes will prosper long after I'm gone.

"Although," she added with a wink, "thanks to Fortune's Youth Serum, that might not be for quite some time!"

As laughter erupted in the room, she nodded at several waiters, and they began to pass out flutes of champagne.

When everyone had a glass, including Maddie, who'd

been given sparkling apple cider, Kate asked them to lift their drinks in a toast.

"To the Fortunes!" Kate said. "I can't wait to see what you all do next."

Crystal clicked upon crystal, ringing out in celebration, as everyone chimed in, "To the Fortunes!"

"Now let the wedding reception begin," Kate said as she made her way to Graham and Sasha.

"I realize you didn't feel comfortable about leaving town while the baby was so young," she said. "But I've set up a honeymoon suite for you two here. I also took the liberty of talking to Graham's sisters, Zoe, Rachel, Sophie and Olivia. And they're more than happy to watch over the girls for the next day or so. I believe they had to draw straws for the opportunity, and Zoe won."

Graham turned to Sasha. "Kate mentioned the idea to me earlier, so I packed a bag for us, as well as one for the girls."

"Zoe has a fun and entertaining evening planned," Kate added. "She told me that she purchased *The Gingerbread Man*, which she plans to read to Maddie. Then they'll make and decorate gingerbread cookies. I believe there's also a Cinderella movie involved."

"So, what do you say?" Graham asked Sasha. "It's up to you."

"I'm stunned. First by Kate's wonderful offer, then by Zoe's enthusiasm." She reached out and embraced Kate. "Thank you for all the kindness you've shown us."

Then she turned to Graham, her husband, the love of her life. "I can't believe you were involved in the planning and that you were able to help pull off such an amazing surprise."

A smile stretched across his handsome face. "I take it that's a yes."

She rose on tiptoe and pressed a kiss on his lips. "It most certainly is! I'd love to have a honeymoon with you here."

And thanks to Kate Fortune, tonight would be a night to remember.

Several hours later, as the guests began to file out of the Silver Spur and head home, the newlyweds looked forward to their wedding night.

Sasha had felt a little uneasy about leaving the girls at first. But Maddie had been so excited about her first sleepover with Aunt Zoe and Uncle Joaquin. And baby Sydney was already on a good schedule and sleeping through the night. Besides, Zoe assured her they'd be just a short walk away in one of several guest quarters on the property.

So how could she possibly give it another worrisome thought? Once she'd agreed, her heart soared in anticipation.

When Graham asked where they were to go, Kate had pointed to the back door and beyond.

"You can't miss it," she said. And she'd been right.

The "honeymoon suite" had been set up in one of the smaller cottages. White twinkly lights adorned the trees in the front yard, while flickering votive candles lined the walkway. The forest-green railing that surrounded the small porch also sported festive little lights that blinked and winked at Sasha and Graham as they made the walk from the main house.

On the porch, two ceramic pots filled with bright red geraniums flanked the green door. Graham had no more than used the key to unlock it when he turned, swept Sasha off her feet and carried her inside.

"I declare, Mr. Fortune Robinson, you're even more gallant and chivalrous than I thought."

He laughed. "Just wait and see how romantic and loving I can be."

Once inside the small, cozy living room, where a fire blazed in the hearth and candles flickered on the mantel, he set Sasha's feet back on the hardwood floor.

She scanned the cozy room, amazed at what Kate had prepared for them. A bouquet of red roses sat atop the glass-topped coffee table, along with a sterling-silver ice bucket holding a bottle of Cristal champagne and two flutes. A tray of chocolate-dipped straw-berries, as well as an array of crackers and cheese, rounded out the display.

Kate had thought of everything, including an MP3 player. Something told Sasha that the kitchen would be stocked as well, with coffee, orange juice and a variety of sweet rolls and breakfast foods.

After Graham carried in their bag and placed it in the bedroom, he called out, "Honey, if you think the living area is nice, you ought to see this."

Sasha joined him, noting the king-size canopy bed that was draped with a white goose-down comforter that had been sprinkled with rose petals.

The backside of the fireplace they'd seen in the living room opened up in the bedroom, allowing both rooms to enjoy the roaring blaze. To round it out, there was a whirlpool tub, with a stack of white fluffy towels and two robes awaiting them.

"I can't believe this," she said. "It's awesome."

"And tonight, it's ours." Graham crossed the room to the MP3 player. Soon a love song filled the room with soft music, setting a romantic tone.

"I don't even know where to start," she said, thinking of the champagne and strawberries, along with the whirlpool and the bed.

"I know where to start." Graham swept her into his arms and kissed her, lightly at first, and then deeper, hungrier.

As she drew him close, as his tongue delved deeply into her mouth, mating with hers, she had to admit he'd made a perfect choice.

Their bodies pressed together, setting off a heady rush of heat through her blood. Their hands stroked each other, caressing and stimulating a ragged ache in her core.

The times she'd imagined how special their lovemaking would be, how amazing and heart-stirring, paled next to what they were sharing this evening. Their honeymoon would finally unite the two of them as one. And the bond would last not just tonight, but forever.

Graham led her to the bed, where he kissed her again, long and deep. His hands slid along the curve of her back and down the slope of her hips. Then he pulled her forward against his erection, letting her know how much he enjoyed claiming her as his wife, his lover and his lifetime partner.

* * *

When Graham thought he was going to die from the strength of his desire for Sasha, she ended the kiss, then slowly turned her back to him and lifted her hair out of the way so he could unzip the classic black dress she wore.

As he helped her peel the fabric from her shoulders, he kissed her neck, his tongue making small circles in the tender spot behind her ear.

She removed the dress completely and let it drop into a pool on the floor, then stepped out of it.

Beautiful Sasha was his, now and forever.

He unbuttoned his shirt and withdrew his arms from the sleeves. Then he tossed the garment aside. Next he unbuckled his belt and unzipped his slacks.

When he'd removed all but his boxer briefs, he eased toward her. She skimmed her nails across his chest, sending a shiver through his veins and a rush of heat through his blood.

But he wasn't the only one fully aroused and ready. She swayed at his touch and had to hold on to him to remain steady. But he took mercy on her, and on them both, lifted her into his arms and placed her on top of the bed.

Surrounded by rose petals, and with her hair splayed upon the pillow, she looked like a dream come true. *His* dream.

His wife. His Sasha.

Graham wanted nothing more than to slip out of his boxers and feel her skin against his, but he paused for a beat, drinking in the angelic sight. "You're the best thing that's ever happened to me, Sassy. And I love you more than you'll ever know." Then he bent over her and brushed another kiss on her lips.

She pulled him close. All he could think to do was to climb into bed with her, to trail kisses from her neck to her belly and lower.

Torn between driving her wild with need and needing to be inside her, he climbed next to her and continued to prove just how much he loved her. And how much they needed each other.

"I can't believe how special this is," she said. "Or how amazing this night will be."

"I plan to make every night special for you, starting now." Unwilling to prolong their foreplay any longer, he hovered over her.

She reached for his erection and guided him right where he belonged. He entered her slowly at first, relishing the slick, warm feel of her. As her body responded to his, as she arched up to meet each of his thrusts, their honeymoon began in earnest.

Time stood still, and nothing mattered but the two of them and what they were doing to and for each other.

As Sasha reached a peak, she cried out, arched her back and let go, taking him with her. Their climax exploded into a swirl of stars, bright lights and colors. He thrust one last time, shuddered and released along with her.

Making love had never been like this before, two hearts, two lives, two dreams, all melded into one.

As Graham held his new wife close, they celebrated their newfound fortune: each other.

Forever.

For always.

From this night forward.

* * * * *

MILLS & BOON®

Cherish™

EXPERIENCE THE ULTIMATE RUSH OF FALLING IN LOVE

A sneak peek at next month's titles...

In stores from 2nd June 2016:

- **His Cinderella Heiress** – Marion Lennox *and* **Marriage, Maverick Style!** – Christine Rimmer
- **The Bridesmaid's Baby Bump** – Kandy Shepherd *and* **Third Time's the Bride!** – Merline Lovelace

In stores from 16th June 2016:

- **Bound by the Unborn Baby** – Bella Bucannon *and* **His Surprise Son** – Wendy Warren
- **Wedded for His Royal Duty** – Susan Meier *and* **The BFF Bride** – Allison Leigh

---

Lynne Graham has sold 35 million books!

To settle a debt, she'll have to become his mistress...

Nikolai Drakos is determined to have his revenge against the man who destroyed his sister. So stealing his enemy's intended fiancé seems like the perfect solution! Until Nikolai discovers that woman is Ella Davies...

Read on for a tantalising excerpt from Lynne Graham's 100th book,

BOUGHT FOR THE GREEK'S REVENGE

'Mistress,' Nikolai slotted in cool as ice.

Shock had welded Ella's tongue to the roof of her mouth because he was sexually propositioning her and nothing could have prepared her for that. She wasn't drop-dead gorgeous... *he* was! Male heads didn't swivel when Ella walked down the street because she had neither the length of leg nor the curves usually deemed necessary to attract such attention. Why on earth could he be making *her* such an offer?

'But we don't even know each other,' she framed dazedly. 'You're a stranger...'

'If you live with me I won't be a stranger for long,' Nikolai pointed out with monumental calm. And the very sound of that inhuman calm and cool forced her to flip round and settle distraught eyes on his lean darkly handsome face.

'You can't be serious about this!'

'I assure you that I am deadly serious. Move in and I'll forget your family's debts.'

'But it's a *crazy* idea!' she gasped.

'It's not crazy to me,' Nikolai asserted. 'When I want anything, I go after it hard and fast.'

Her lashes dipped. Did he want her like that? Enough to track her down, buy up her father's debts, and try and buy rights to her and her body along with those debts? The very idea of that made her dizzy and plunged her brain into even greater turmoil. 'It's immoral… it's blackmail.'

'It's definitely *not* blackmail. I'm giving you the benefit of a choice you didn't have before I came through that door,' Nikolai Drakos fielded with a glittering cool. 'That choice is yours to make.'

'Like hell it is!' Ella fired back. 'It's a complete cheat of a supposed offer!'

Nikolai sent her a gleaming sideways glance. 'No the real cheat was you kissing me the way you did last year and then saying no and acting as if I had grossly insulted you,' he murmured with lethal quietness.

'You *did* insult me!' Ella flung back, her cheeks hot as fire while she wondered if her refusal that night had started off his whole chain reaction. What else could possibly be driving him?

Nikolai straightened lazily as he opened the door. 'If you take offence that easily, maybe it's just as well that the answer is no.'

_MB523_OSA

MILLS & BOON®

Mills & Boon have been at the heart of romance since 1908… and while the fashions may have changed, one thing remains the same: from pulse-pounding passion to the gentlest caress, we're always known how to bring romance alive.

Now, we're delighted to present you with these irresistible illustrations, inspired by the vintage glamour of our covers. So indulge your wildest dreams and unleash your imagination as we present the most iconic Mills & Boon moments of the last century.

Visit **www.millsandboon.co.uk/ArtofRomance** to order yours!